The Dragon Isles.

He felt himself swept over the glorious landscape, the towering mountains, the lush glades, the verdant forests. Past the main isles and out to sea again, to a temple wreathed in fire and light. Within the temple, at the crest of land, sea, and sky shone a brilliant blue-white diamond— twice as large as a man's skull.

Mikal Vardan's heart beat faster as he beheld it.

Then he blinked, and the images faded from him eyes.

"They're real," Mik whispered.

CROSSROADS

The Dragon Isles

STEPHEN D. SULLIVAN

THE DRAGON ISLES

©2002 Wizards of the Coast, Inc.

Distributed in the United States by Holtzbrinck Publishing. Distributed in Canada by Fenn Ltd.

Distributed to the hobby, toy, and comic trade in the United States and Canada by regional distributors.

Distributed worldwide by Wizards of the Coast, Inc. and regional distributors.

First Printing:
Library of Congress Catalog Card Number: 2001097184

9 8 7 6 5 4 3 2 1

US ISBN: 0-7869-2827-1
UK ISBN: 0-7869-2828-X
620-88626-001-EN

U.S., CANADA,
ASIA, PACIFIC, & LATIN AMERICA
Wizards of the Coast, Inc.
P.O. Box 707
Renton, WA 98057-0707
+ 1-800-324-6496

EUROPEAN HEADQUARTERS
Wizards of the Coast, Belgium
P.B. 2031
2600 Berchem
Belgium
+ 32-70-23-32-77

Visit our web site at **www.wizards.com**

DEDICATION

To my children, Julie & Kendall—
May your lives be filled with wonders beyond measure and
treasures beyond price.

ACKNOWLEDGEMENTS
Thanks to Tracy Hickman and Margaret Weis
for many reasons: Firstly, for creating this world,
secondly for allowing me to play in it as an author
(after spending years as a "mere" cartographer),
thirdly for your many years of support and
encouragement, and finally—and most importantly—
for your many, many years of friendship.

Special thanks to my readers & advisors, Kiff Scott &
Ed Henderson, for getting me through the rough spots.

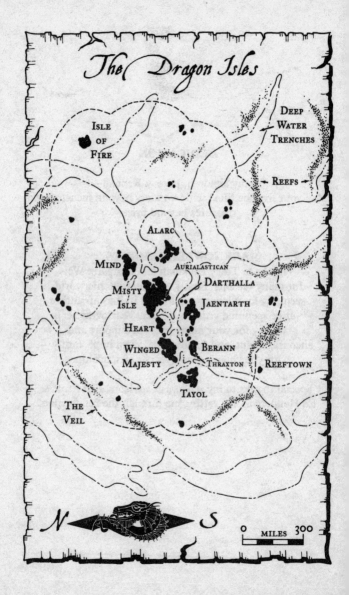

The Dragon Isles

DEEP
WATER
TRENCHES

← REEFS →

ISLE
OF
FIRE

ALARC

MIND

AURIALASTICAN

DARTHALLA

MISTY
ISLE

JAENTARTH

HEART

WINGED
MAJESTY

BERANN

THRAXTON

REEFTOWN

TAYOL

THE
VEIL

N   S

0   MILES   300

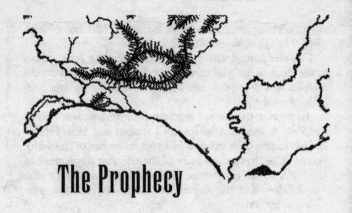

The Prophecy

Sunlight streamed over the aquamarine ocean, reflecting from the whitecaps and filling the air with dazzling color, as the Dragon Isles rose majestically from the sea.

Wreathed in fire, they came, but quickly cooled. In an instant, green life took root and covered them to all but the highest, cloudcapped peaks. Fish surrounded them and animals swarmed to their fertile shores. Soon the isles teemed with life.

The azure sky flashed like lightning. A thousand brilliant stars hung in the heavens—silver, orange, yellow, red, golden. No, not stars . . . metallic dragons.

They swarmed over the isles, changing the shape and nature of the land. They pushed up mountains, felled forests, and altered the course of rivers. They built mighty edifices and founded settlements. The good peoples of the world swarmed to their shores.

The people shaped the land now as well. With the help of the dragons, settlements became towns, and towns became

1

cities. Metallic dragons soared the skies, and noble ships plied the crystal blue ocean.

Temples sprang up—some dedicated to lost gods, others to the glory of the isles themselves. Treasure flowed into the temples and the towns and the cities, and the Dragon Isles became wealthy.

To protect the isles, a mighty enchantment was raised: the Veil. A special treasure-filled temple was built for the spell at the top of a volcano in a remote corner of the archipelago. The fires in the belly of the isle and the plumes of ash rising to the heavens connected the enchantment to the world below and the sky above: earth, air, and fire, surrounded by water.

At the sacred mountain's base, a second, devotionary temple rose up beneath the waves of the placid sea. The dragons and the free peoples of the isles gave their sweat, money, and magic to the effort. A great, bejeweled key in four pieces was made to seal the pact—one piece for each element: diamond for earth, emerald for water, opal for air, and ruby for fire. The dragons set a monstrous blue-white diamond at the upper temple's summit—above a hoard of treasure—to commemorate the deed.

Stone guardians, each in the shape of dragons with glittering diamond eyes, rose from the sea bedrock. The Veil arced up between them, suffusing earth, sky, and sea. The spell set the isles apart from the world—only those who knew its secret, dragons and favored mortals, could pass its defenses.

The heart beats at the source
Of bastions unveiled
Portends the final course
And stands alone unfailed
Who seeks to find the isles,
Amid the turbid seas
Sail north beyond known lands
To dragon gods appease

'Neath gaze of Palatine
On late midsummer eve
Then trace the chart divine
The pathway to receive
Beyond the palace walls
Where heavens meet the deep
Lie gleaming dragon halls
Your destiny to keep
To seven cities' light
By silver water course
Before the second night
Discover then the source

PART I

DREAMS & PROPHECIES

Chapter One

A Fateful Voyage

aptain Mikal Vardan sprinted to the rail of *Kingfisher* and dived over the side into the pounding surf. The storm lashed his body, trying to tear away his dagger, as he plunged into the water. Mik gripped the knife tightly between his teeth; if he lost the weapon, his friend would surely die.

The magic from his enchanted fish necklace suffused Mik's body. The gale-tossed water cleared before his sight, and warm, sweet air filled his lungs. One day, Mik knew, the necklace's erratic magic would fail him; thankfully, today was not that day.

He spotted the struggling form of Tripleknot Shellcracker in the azure darkness before him. The kender kicked his small feet and briefly poked his head above the surface before the sea monster pulled him under once more.

The creature circled the kender tightly with its green-scaled tentacles, trying to drag Trip farther into the deep. The creature was like nothing Mik had ever seen before—a hideous cross between a serpent and an octopus. Whiplike tendrils surrounded its serpentine head, while a dozen fat tentacles sprang from its slender body. The thing had surged out of the storm onto *Kingfisher*'s deck and killed three sailors before retreating over the side with the kender in its grasp.

Fire had driven it off the ship, but Mik could not fight it with fire here. All he had was an enchanted necklace that let him breathe under water, a diver's stout dagger, and his wits. He prayed they would be enough to save his friend.

Trip had weapons of his own, but the creature held the kender's arms pinned against his sides. Though he struggled mightily, Trip couldn't reach his slender pearl-handled knives.

Mik swam toward his friend as rapidly as he could, fighting against the heaving waters. The storm's fury slowed the monster as well. Gigantic waves surged up from the deep and thrust the beast back toward the surface.

A tentacle flashed by the sea captain's head. Mik grabbed it and pulled himself hand-over-hand, like a sailor scaling the rigging, toward the creature's bloated body.

The monster spewed smaller tendrils at the sailor. Mik pulled his dagger from between his teeth and slashed, severing the limbs before they could grab him. Purplish blood clouded the ocean, swirling before Mik's eyes.

"Hang on, Trip!" he called. "I'm coming!" The sea garbled his words, and he couldn't tell whether the kender heard him. He could barely make out his friend through the turbulent waters.

A tentacle clouted Mik on the back of the head, and lights danced before his eyes. He felt a snake-like appendage wrap around his mid-section, trying to squeeze the life out of him. Even with his necklace turning the water to air, he still needed to breathe. Black unconsciousness closed in around him.

Fighting back the darkness, he plunged his knife into the tentacle at his waist and tore sideways. The tentacle ripped nearly in half and lost its grip. Mik swam free and shot across the gap separating him from his friend.

Trip could hold his breath for longer than almost anyone Mik knew, but he was looking pale and blue as the ship captain reached him. Mik thrust his dagger into the tentacles holding the kender and quickly cut them away.

The sea monster shrieked, its piercing wail audible even above the crashing surf and the raging storm.

Mik pushed Trip upward, and the kender kicked weakly toward the surface.

The beast thrashed in the surging water, stirring up whirlpools of bubbles and staining the water with its purplish blood. Tendrils whipped against the sea captain, biting into his skin as he clawed for the surface.

Two thick tentacles wrapped around Mik's ankles and dragged him down as the monster lurched back into the deep. Mik stabbed at them with his dagger, but as he did, another tentacle wrapped around his arm. He tried to wriggle out of the thing's grip, but the creature's strength was too great.

He grappled with the ensnaring limb, trying to free his knife as they sank ever deeper into the brine.

Another tentacle came to seize him, and another, and another. He twisted from side to side, trying to deny their deadly grip. One brushed across his throat, threatening to rip away his enchanted necklace. Mik imagined himself drowning even as the creature crushed him to death.

He refused to give up.

Using both hands, he twisted his dagger sideways and slashed it across the ensnaring arm. The tentacle's flesh tore, but it did not let go.

Something flashed by him in the storm-tossed gloom—a shark, perhaps, or sharp-toothed razorfish. A grim smile crossed the sailor's bearded face. So many ways to die in the deep.

A bright shape flitted out of the bubbling, blood-stained darkness. It slashed down and across the monster's tentacle, near Mik's ensnared hand. The tentacle fell away and Mik found himself free.

"Thanks, Trip!" Mik burbled, recognizing the pale shape in the water nearby.

The kender, his cheeks puffed out with fresh air, nodded and slashed swiftly again with his twin pearl-handled daggers. In moments, they severed all the rubbery arms holding the ship captain.

Trip darted aside and headed for the surface again as the enraged creature reached out to grab them once more. Instead of following the kender, though, Mik dived straight for the center of the flailing mass.

The creature's pale green eyes, large as dinner plates, swiveled toward the sailor. The arms turned inward in a futile attempt to stop his descent.

Mik seized the creature's flabby, scale-covered skin with one hand to anchor himself. With his other hand he plunged his dagger as far as it would go into the monster's center.

The creature's distressed cries rang in his ears as he twisted the knife sideways, cutting across the bony ridge between the thing's eyes. The monster flailed at him.

He ripped out the dagger, bursting one of the greenish eyes as the weapon pulled free. The creature's tendrils waved frantically around him like a mass of angry snakes. He kicked away from it and burst free. Mortally wounded, the monster sank slowly into the depths.

Just before Mik reached the storm-tossed surface, he saw Trip diving down once more.

The kender spotted him, grinned, and then turned back toward the waves above.

They broke through the surf an arm's-length apart.

"Hey, thanks for saving my life!" Trip gasped, spitting salt water from his lips.

"Don't mention it," Mik replied.

They gazed through the storm and spotted *Kingfisher*'s three tawny sails bobbing over the waves a short distance away.

"Can you make it?" Mik asked.

The kender nodded, and they both fought across the breakers toward the caravel. *Kingfisher* rolled nimbly on the ocean, her raised bow and high stern deck staying well above the surging seas. The ship's red sides glistened in the rain as though they'd been freshly painted. The great blue eye painted on the bow for good luck seemed to stare at the castaway mariners as they returned.

The crew dropped a boarding net over *Kingfisher*'s side, and the kender and the captain grabbed hold when a wave swept them near. They clung as the storm alternately tried to pound them into the gunwales or rip them back into the sea.

Crewmen aboard the aging caravel pulled on the net as Mik and Trip climbed up, and the castaways soon tumbled to the sodden deck, exhausted. They lay on the well-worn planking, panting to regain their strength. Driving rain and sea spray washed over their faces.

A shudder ran through Mik's body and he felt suddenly cold. He glanced down and saw one of the jeweled scales of his enchanted necklace crumble into dust. The price of the magic seemed higher every time he used it. Magic was fading from Ansalon and soon even artifacts like the necklace would be nothing more than fancy jewelry.

A shadow fell over Mik's face and he gazed up at Karista Meinor. Lightning flashed. The pale brilliance reflected from the aristocrat's steely eyes and illuminated her well-rounded form. She looked beautiful, even amid the storm, even with her billowing silks soaked and clinging to her tanned skin.

She eyed the drenched sailor angrily. "That was a foolish thing to do, captain," Karista said. "You could have been killed. I didn't hire you to get sacrifice yourself for a kender. I hired you to do a job."

"I didn't sign on to watch my friends die," Mik replied. His brown eyes narrowed. "Or even my enemies."

Bok, Karista's huge bodyguard and paramour, stepped forward and helped Mik to his feet. "The kender's a stowaway," he said, "of no value to milady's expedition. We should have tossed him overboard when we first discovered him."

Trip, still sputtering on the rain-soaked deck, glared at Bok, uncharacteristically holding his tongue.

"I'm still the captain here," Mik replied. "It's my decision who stays aboard and who takes up company with the razorfish. Unless, of course, you'd care to hire someone else to complete this little errand of yours."

Karista waved one bejeweled hand at him dismissively. "You know that's impossible," she said.

"We'd never find another captain before the typhoon season hits," Bok added.

Mik smiled. "How unfortunate."

Karista's ruby red lips pulled tight across her straight white teeth. "Your experience makes you uniquely valuable to this expedition, captain," she said. "As you well know."

Mik nodded.

"Nevertheless," she continued, "I hired this crew, and supplied this ship, and . . . *forgave* the considerable debts you owed my family."

"That's not the only reason I agreed to do this," Mik countered.

"Be that as it may," she said, "our agreement is not fulfilled until this mission arrives at a satisfactory conclusion."

"I signed to sail you where you want to go," Mik said. "Whether you find what you're looking for when we get there . . . ? That's your gamble."

Karista nodded slowly. "Indeed," the aristocrat said. "But if the legends are true, you stand to gain nearly as much as I."

"That's the other reason I came."

"So we're in agreement, then?" Karista asked, arching one thin eyebrow.

"Just so long as I make the decisions aboard this ship," Mik replied.

Karista bowed slightly and rain ran in long rivulets from her wavy brown hair. She cast an indifferent glance at the kender, still fuming silently. "Insofar as running the ship," she said, "I accede to your superior knowledge."

Thunder crashed.

"Well, *we* ain't so sure about that," boomed a loud voice.

A tall man with a scar pushed through the group of sailors surrounding the rescued mariners. He was nearly as large as Bok and looked even meaner. A lanky woman with short blond hair stepped up beside him.

"Some of us think," she said, "that it might be time for a *new* captain."

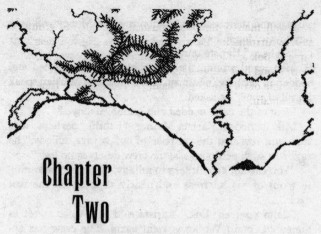

Chapter
Two

Into Unknown Seas

Though the storm was abating, the wind still howled around *Kingfisher* and rain washed the decks. Tall waves caused the caravel to lurch precariously. *Kingfisher*'s crew, though, stood ominously still as the tall crewman and the lanky female sailor stared into Mik Vardan's brown eyes.

"We don't intend to follow this witch to our deaths," the man said, pointing to Karista Meinor, "no matter how good she pays."

"Five have died already," the woman put in. "And your little friend was almost the sixth." She glanced at the kender.

"Little . . . !" Trip said, rising to his feet.

"None of us plans to be next," the man growled. "We've already sailed beyond the charts—beyond all good sense. None of us is sailing any farther."

"We want to know our destination," the woman added. "The Meinors' money and your reputation as a salvage captain may have lured us this far, Vardan—but we've done no salvage and there's no destination in sight. Money will only buy loyalty for so long."

"So I see," Karista muttered.

Mik gazed around the assembled crew, grim-faced and sodden in the howling storm. "Do Pamak and Marlian speak for all of you?" he asked.

Most of the crew nodded and grumbled, "Aye."

Mik turned to Karista Meinor. "I think, perhaps, it is time you revealed the purpose of our voyage, milady," he said. "In such perilous seas, the crew deserves no less."

"You cannot give orders to milady," Bok said, stepping in front of his mistress and nearly slipping on the wet deck.

"Calm yourself, Bok," Karista said, her voice sweet as honey. "Captain Vardan is right again. The crew has endured many perils just to reach this point. They deserve to know the goal for which we've risked so much."

As she spoke, the fierce winds died away as if on command. Karista nodded at the fortunate coincidence and mounted the short stairway to the ship's bridge. She stood above the crew, one hand gripping the rail, and raised her other hand high. Bok took up a protective position at the bottom of the stairs, shielding his mistress from the crew.

Sparks flashed from Karista's fingertips. She concentrated. Her steely eyes narrowed and sweat beaded on her brow. The sparks coalesced into a small ball of purplish light.

The crew regarded the unusual magical display with a mixture of skepticism and nervousness.

"What's she up to?" Trip whispered to Mik.

"I'm not sure," Mik replied, keeping a careful eye on the witch.

Trip nodded and whispered, "I'll figure out an escape route, just in case."

"Behold!" Karista said, and a flickering image of an archipelago with tall mountains appeared hovering above her hand. "This is our destination—the Dragon Isles."

A murmur of disbelief ran through the crew.

"The Dragon Isles are mere legend," the scar-faced man, Pamak, muttered.

"Not legend," Karista replied, "but a dream beyond the wealth of avarice." She blinked and the image flickered again, like a candle struggling in the breeze—though the storm's winds had died away. "This dream is within our grasp. This is why I have led you here—to the middle of the ocean."

"Even if the legend were true," the lanky woman, Marlian, said, "how are we to find the isles? Only good dragons are supposedly allowed there—and the good dragons have left Krynn, haven't they?"

"Oh yes, good dragons are there," Karista replied with a smile. She gasped, and the image of the island sputtered out. She leaned heavily against the rail and gazed over the assembled crew. "But in my cabin, under magical lock and key, is a scroll that I have obtained, which will lead us to the isles."

"Prove it!" Marlian called up to her.

Karista threw her head back and laughed. Gem-like rivulets splashed from her long, wavy hair. "Patience!" she cried exultantly. "You'll have your proof when I am good and ready."

"How do we know this isn't some witch's trick?" Pamak said.

A wizened sailor standing apart from the mutineers cleared his throat. His name was Poul and he was the oldest member of *Kingfisher*'s crew. His ancient bones could be seen clearly through his leathery skin. The rain had matted his thin white hair onto his head, and his face looked like a skull. His eyes, though, shown bright and green—like the eyes of a youth first put out to sea.

"I seen the Dragon Isles once," he said in a low voice, "when I was a young man. Beautiful, they was, like gems on the blue horizon. It was almost like you could stick out your hand and grab 'em—but they was always just out of reach. Back then, my captain said they was cursed."

"Aha!" Pamak said. "See? Cursed!"

Mik glared at the scar-faced sailor. "Let Poul speak, Pamak," he said.

Pamak scowled at the captain, but Mik neither blinked nor turned away. Slowly the scar-faced man nodded. "All right," he said. "I got respect for my elders. I'll hear the old man out."

Mik nodded to the leathery Poul.

"When you seen metallic dragons on the wing—even from ten leagues away—there ain't nothin' to compare to it," Poul continued. "It's somethin' you'll never forget—not in *two* lifetimes. I'd give anything to see those isles again. Anyone would be a fool to pass up the chance.

"The Dragon Isles are *real*, I'll vouch for that. I knows men that's seen them in the years since the gods and the good dragons left Krynn. They're as solid as you or me. A clever man—a clever ship—might find 'em—if one knew where to look." Poul settled back, away from the crowd once more.

"All of you respect Poul," Mik said. "The Dragon Isles *do* exist. I've seen the scroll in Lady Meinor's cabin. We're on course to find these isles even now."

"That's why I hired Captain Vardan," Karista said from the bridge. Her magic had temporarily depleted her energy, but now the momentary interruption had allowed her to regain her strength. "There are no sailors more experienced in the deep, uncharted waters of the Turbidus Ocean."

The assembled crew muttered their assent. Overhead, the clouds parted slightly, and the rain began to die away.

"You will all have a share in the profits of this voyage," Karista continued. *"Think* of the wealth of the Dragon Isles! Think of the rewards of opening a trade route to such a place!" Sparks danced in her steely eyes. A ray of sunlight broke through the clouds and caressed the beautiful aristocrat's form.

"My family is wealthy," she said to her rapt audience. "That wealth bought and provisioned this ship and hired all of you. We Meinors didn't get where we are by following wild rumors. You signed onto this trip because you believed it would be profitable for all of you—that your shares in the journey would outweigh the risks. Surely a few . . . *accidents* haven't changed that."

A mutter of agreement ran through the formerly disgruntled crew.

"All right," Marlian said, brushing the rain from her short, blond hair. "That makes sense to me."

"Yeah. We'll follow your plan for a while," Pamak added. Others added their assent.

Karista Meinor showed her straight, white teeth in a pleasing smile. "Then back to work, all of you," she said.

"Yes, back to work," Mik called. "We're lucky the storm didn't scuttle us while we stood around jabbering."

As the rest of the crew went about their business, Mik stopped Pamak and Marlian.

"Next time you two try to stir things up," Mik whispered to them both, "I'll deal with you one on one—or two on one, if those odds suit you better."

"Two on two!" Trip, close on his heels, interjected.

"I meant no disrespect, captain," Marlian said, sparing a frown for the kender.

A sly grin drew over Pamak's scarred face. "Any odds you like, any time . . . captain. It will be my pleasure." He gave a short, mocking bow before returning to his duties.

"I don't like them very much," Trip said after they'd gone.

"Marlian's just excitable and misguided," Mik replied. "Pamak, though, can be trouble. Nothing I can't handle."

"Nothing we can't handle," Trip repeated confidently.

The waves began to settle as the sky cleared. Mik took a few bearings from the sun and applied it to his knowledge of this area of ocean, then gave a corrected course to the helmsman. Then he went to his cabin below the bridge to put some salve on his wounds. Trip went with him and helped with the bandaging.

"Maybe Karista has some magical ointment we could use," Trip said as he wound a piece of fresh linen around a cut on Mik's right arm. "She seems to have lots of magic," he added enviously.

"I don't think I'd trust it if she did," Mik replied. "You remember how well her magical seaweed worked?"

Stephen D. Sullivan

"I'm sure she didn't mean for those two men to die," Trip said sincerely. "I saw her use the seaweed to breathe underwater herself, once. It worked fine, then. And it's worth a try in a pinch, I mean, if you're going to drown anyway."

Mik's brown eyes narrowed. "Trip . . . ?"

"I found a tiny piece that somehow got in my rucksack," Trip insisted. "Too bad I couldn't reach it when the monster had me."

The captain laughed and rubbed some salve on a thumb-sized welt on his calf, inflicted by one of the sea monster's suckers. "We had a narrow escape," he said. "Karista may have settled the crew for now, but we need to find those islands before a full-scale mutiny breaks out."

"This whole crew are mercenaries and cut-throats," Trip said frowning.

"Karista knew our usual crew wouldn't venture this far out beyond charted waters," Mik replied.

"Well, I have to admit, I'm really enjoying myself," Trip said, "but do you think she really knows where she's going?"

"That scroll is authentic," Mik said, "I'd bet my teeth on it. She's following an old prophecy, but most of it seems plain and simple to me. These waters are perilous, though." He grinned. "But the potential reward far outweighs the peril. I don't mind peril for a fat reward. Though stowing away wasn't the best idea *you've* ever had."

"After all we've been through?" Trip said. "I didn't want to miss out on the fun."

Mik cut a last bit of linen with his knife and finished bandaging Trip's shoulder.

"I think I'll climb the mast," the kender said. "It would be sleek to be the first to spot the Dragon Isles."

"It would at that," Mik said, adding, "Try to stay out of trouble."

"Always," Trip replied. He bowed curtly, then exited the cabin and walked through the map room onto the quarterdeck.

18

Mik crossed to the sea chest in one corner of the small room and unlocked it. Lifting the heavy lid, he reached in and pulled out a small, intricately carved silver box.

Kingfisher's captain took a piece of parchment from the box and carefully unfolded it. In the ragged vellum lay an artifact fashioned in curving golden arcs and exquisite lines. It was roughly square, with soft edges, though it was asymmetrical—or perhaps incomplete. Amid the shimmering golden loops of the setting lay a large black diamond. The parchment was covered with writing, but Mik ignored the words and gently lifted the artifact from its resting place.

The black diamond glittered in the cabin's semi-darkness, shining with a faint bluish light.

Mik gazed within the diamond's cloudy facets, and an image formed in his mind: jewel-like islands dotting an azure sea, snow-capped peaks reaching for the clouds. High overhead, metallic shapes arced through the clear air.

The Dragon Isles.

He felt himself swept over the glorious landscape, the towering mountains, the lush glades, the verdant forests. Past the main isles and out to sea again, to a temple wreathed in fire and light. Within the temple, at the crest of land, sea, and sky shone a brilliant blue-white diamond—twice as large as a man's skull.

Mikal Vardan's heart beat faster as he beheld it.

Then he blinked, and the images faded from his eyes.

"They're real," Mik whispered, unaware that he spoke at all. "The isles are real. The treasure is real. And I shall sail us to it." He clutched the artifact tightly in his hand, and its pale light danced across his brown eyes.

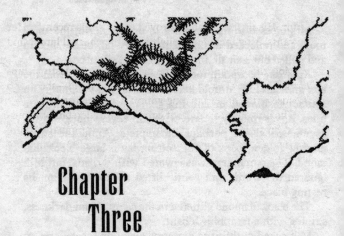

Chapter
Three

The Sea Dragon's Servant

og watched enviously as his mistress picked the remains of a ship from between her huge teeth. Mangler sharks, razorfish, and hideous kestel viperfins swarmed around the sea dragon, fighting over her leavings and attending her every whim. She paid them little heed. Only the Turbidus leeches, strange, twisted eel-like creatures fed on her own toxic blood, garnered any of the dragon's attention.

The leeches allowed Tempest to control her fishy minions. They connected the thralls to the immense sea dragon—sending her sights and sounds and smells from far distant places. To disobey Tempest was to court crippling, leech-inflicted pain. The lifespan of a bad servant was, naturally, very short.

Mog was a good servant. Not as servile, perhaps, as the swarms of leeches that ringed the dragon's neck like a living mane—but useful, and certainly powerful.

The dragonspawn flexed his hulking muscles and chewed the last bit of flesh from the bones of a drowned sailor. His mistress had destroyed many ships recently. Her servants, Mog included, delighted at the charnel larder laid before them.

Mog, though, knew that the mistress did not destroy ships in the Turbidus Ocean merely because she could—she did so because of the anger burning within her immense belly.

The dragonspawn did not completely understand his mistress' fury. He had seen the object of her desire many times, but he could not comprehend what fascinated her about those small bits of isolated rock. In the part of his reptilian brain that he shared with Tempest, Mog knew these islands as the Dragon Isles. He knew that she, Tempest the Great, somehow stood barred from entering the isles. He knew that the magic standing in her way was very ancient and that it was called The Veil.

Mog had difficulty comprehending that anything could thwart his mistress. Yet when she or her minions tried to approach the isles, they found themselves confused and disoriented. Always the Dragon Isles slipped away, out of their grasp.

Tempest lusted after the islands. Once, they had been home to many good dragons of Ansalon—gold, silver, brass, bronze, and copper. Now, however, many of the metallic dragons had fled, and the isles stood as mere shadows of their former selves.

Tempest lusted after the islands and the genuine treasures they contained—not the sanguine, meaty treasures that thrilled Mog, but wealth and power and magic. Such things were the hoard of dragons.

But The Veil kept her out. And so Tempest summoned storms and vented her rage upon ships passing through the Turbidus Ocean. Ships she feared might pierce the Veil and reach the Dragon Isles.

Her servants grew strong and fat on the blood of her victims. Yet Tempest remained no closer to her goal.

Her desire to reach the isles burned in her mind and, therefore, it burned in Mog as well.

All of Tempest's dragonspawn were strong, but Mog was the strongest. He was the first she had made, forming him out of the bodies of captured draconians as well as from her own blood and sinew and magic. He was, therefore, most closely connected to her, most clever, most powerful. He was the only one who could assume the shapes of both the sea's denizens and his mistress' two-legged enemies.

Mog was well-suited to the job of killing. Iron-like scales covered his humanoid body and limbs. The tips of his fingers and toes ended in sharp spikes. His webbed talons propelled him swiftly through the brine. His blood-red eyes easily pierced the gloom of the deep. Mog's rasp-like mouth could rip the flesh from any enemy he encountered.

Yet all this was still not enough to penetrate The Veil.

Tempest's unholy desire burned within him.

Mog groomed the blood from his scales and waited impatiently for the next ship.

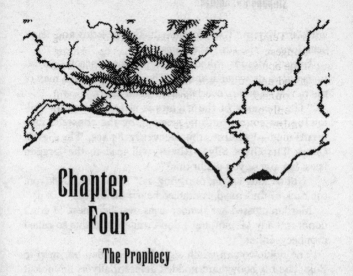

Chapter Four

The Prophecy

To seven cities' light
By silver water course
Before the second night
Discover then the source."

Karista Meinor looked around the assembled crew as she read the ancient parchment. A contagious fervor gleamed in her steely eyes. The sailors before her stood in rapt attention.

There was more to the prophecy, Mik knew, but Karista didn't read it all to the anxious crew of *Kingfisher*. She had, in fact, left out the most interesting parts—the sections about the temple and treasure, and the ways to find the hidden riches. The crew didn't need to know those details.

Mik remained unsure, in fact, if Lady Meinor believed in the prophecy. Possessing the parchment and finding the isles seemed goal enough for her. Perhaps gaining a treasure cache and a huge diamond seemed insignificant to her, at least compared with a trade route to one of the most wealthy lands on Krynn. To Mik, though, the treasure and jewel beckoned . . . the stuff of dreams.

Karista Meinor rolled up the prophecy scroll and returned it to its watertight case. Then she unfurled a map of the northern ocean, overlaid with a star chart.

"The meaning of the rhymes is clear," she said. "Following the course outline, steering by the constellations mentioned—Paladine, the Heavenly Palace, The Seven Cities, The Great Silver River—will lead to the Dragon Isles. Do any of you doubt this?"

"Not so long as you're paying us!" someone called from the back of the crowd assembled below the bridge.

Marlian crossed her slender arms over her chest. "I don't doubt it, Lady Meinor, but I don't understand this so-called prophecy, either."

The noblewoman-witch sighed and handed her map to Bok. The big bodyguard nodded deferentially as he took it and held it out before the crowd. Karista pointed at the route with a long fingernail as she spoke.

"The first stanza instructs the reader to sail north beyond known waters to find the isles," she explained. "The second says to follow the gaze of the constellation Palatine in midsummer to discover the 'divine' chart—the map laid out in the stars. The third and fourth indicate the isles lie beyond the constellation of the Heavenly Palace, and that you can find them by following the great Silver River in the sky toward the Seven Cities. This evening, the stars of the Seven Cities will be clearly visible in the northeastern sky. When we make the right conjunction, we will be less than two days sail from the isles themselves!"

The crew, even Marlian and Pamak, muttered appreciatively. Mik chuckled. Karista was a good saleswoman; he supposed the talent ran in her wealthy family.

He advanced to the rail beside Lady Meinor and said, "Everyone back to work. Now that you understand our goals, I trust we'll hear no more mutinous grumbling while we seek our fortunes."

"We're with you, captain!" old Poul called out. "Aye!" others added. Marlian and Pamak went back to their business with the rest.

Trip pushed close to study Karista's star chart, but Bok rolled it up before the kender could get a good look. Trip frowned fiercely; Bok frowned back, fiercer.

"Don't worry," Mik said to his small friend, "you'll have a chance to study it, soon enough." Then to Karista and Bok he added, "Bring the chart to the map room. I want to check our bearings before the sun sets. C'mon, Trip." He turned and went down the short stairway from the bridge to the quarter-deck. Trip went with him. Karista and Bok followed.

"I see no reason the kender should be included in this," Bok said, as they entered the map room below the bridge.

"No matter how he came aboard," Mik replied, "Trip is part of our crew now. I know him well and can vouch for him, but I'm sure he'll more than prove his worth to you before the voyage ends."

The big bodyguard frowned. "I'll have to keep a careful watch on my pockets," he said.

Trip's hazel eyes brightened. "Why? Is there something in them that I should know about?"

Bok reddened and looked as though he might strike the kender. "Shut your hole, you little—"

Mik stepped between them. "Karista," he said smoothly, "if your man can't control his temper, then perhaps he should go elsewhere."

Karista laid her long, tan fingers on Bok's arm. "Don't worry," she purred. "Nothing the little one 'borrows' can wander very far. Where could a kender hide aboard ship?"

Bok nodded and laid the star map on the table in the center of the open-walled room. Mik rolled it open and studied it. Trip crowded in near the captain's elbow and peered intently at the lines, colors, and notations. He considered himself a map expert,

"I see you've marked the passages from the Prophecy on the map," Trip said appreciatively. "But there were a lot more lines on that scroll than the ones you read to the crew. What about the rest of it?"

Bok glowered, and looked as though he might step in again, but a motion of Karista's shapely hand kept him in place. "The remaining stanzas are of no importance to finding the isles," she said calmly. "They deal with navigation within the archipelago to a specific destination. They are hard to fathom and seem of little import."

"I'm sure you're correct," Mik said, though that was the part of the prophecy that interested him most.

Karista Meinor laughed—a low, sensual sound. "I know, captain, that you believe the remaining stanzas lead to a precious treasure," she said. "No buried hoard, though, could match the wealth to be gained from opening the Dragon Isles to trade with the mainland. I've compensated you fairly, and I trust that you will be able to keep your mind focused on our mutual goal."

"Any ambitions that I might harbor on my own," Mik replied evenly, "are secondary to the goals of this voyage. My personal views will not interfere with how I run this ship."

Bok snorted skeptically and crossed his arms over his wide chest. He looked from Mik to Trip, and then frowned. Frowning, Trip thought, was what the big bodyguard did best.

Mik scowled back. "I know from which direction the wind blows, milady, and I've no desire to sail any other course."

Karista nodded. "Good. I'll leave you to your work then. Come, Bok." She turned, left the map room, and went to the hatch amidships. Bok followed. With a final suspicious glance from Bok, the aristocrat and the bodyguard went below deck to Karista's cabin.

Mik strolled to the edge of the room and watched their retreat. Then he turned and gazed toward the golden sun, already sinking low in the west.

"So we're getting close," Trip said, from near his elbow.

"Very close," Mik said, nodding. He went back to the map table, rolled up the star chart, and put it in its case. He then deposited the case in its slot below the table's surface, next to the other maps they anticipated using during the voyage. "I'll make our final course adjustment after the stars come out tonight. By tomorrow, we'll be well on our way to fulfilling the first part of the Prophecy."

"What about the rest of it, though?" Trip asked.

Mik arched one black eyebrow. "What about it?"

"Sounds kind of mysterious to me. I get the feeling that you're more interested in it than you let on." He grinned.

Mik laughed. "C'mon," he said. "I want to show you something." He walked through the door leading into his cabin at the back of the map room.

Trip closed the door behind them, and Mik knelt down to open his sea chest.

"If you're going to show me that nice piece of jewelry with the big black diamond in it," Trip said, "I've already seen it."

Anger flashed over Mik's tan face for a moment. But the feeling quickly passed and he smiled. "I shouldn't be surprised."

"No. You shouldn't," Trip replied. "I stumbled across it when I was looking around the other day."

"Stumbled across it in a locked box."

The kender, nodded. "I noticed that you had it wrapped in a copy of Karista's prophecy. What is it? Where did you find it?"

"Very little escapes you," Mik said.

"That's one of the reasons why I'm so useful to have around, I guess."

"I found the artifact a number of years ago, while diving the coral reefs north of Jotan." As Mik spoke, the memories came flooding back: the clear blue waters, fingers of colorful coral stretching toward the shimmering surface above, sunfish and spotted dominoes darting all around. And, amid the underwater glory, a strange wrecked galley—like none he'd ever seen before. The galley's lines were long and curved—its sides covered with scale-like clinking. Its bow was formed in the shape of a golden dragon.

The gold, though, was only paint on the wooden hull. The wreck yielded few treasures—mostly pottery, except for the looping artifact with the black diamond center. Mik had claimed it as his share for the voyage. The memory faded away.

Mik pulled the artifact out of the box within his sea chest. "I suspect it came from the Dragon Isles," he said to Trip. "I think it's part of a key to finding our way in."

"Hey, that Prophecy says something about keys, doesn't it?" Trip asked. He took the paper that lined the artifact's box and unfolded it. The writing on the vellum was a copy of the Prophecy Karista had read on deck earlier— including the parts she had omitted.

"Four keys, if I'm reading it right," Mik said, "and where to discover them."

"And what happens when we locate these four keys?" Trip asked.

A smile drew over Mikal Vardan's bearded face. "Then we find the treasure," he replied.

As the two old friends talked and looked over the artifact and the Prophecy, the sun sank toward the horizon. The waves of the Turbidus Ocean reached up, seeming to caress the golden orb. As the water touched the sun, the sea burst into brilliant, flaming color. The heavens turned crimson and the clouds pulled mantles of purple and orange around themselves against the coming night.

The first stars peeked out from under the sky's cerulean blanket, winking at *Kingfisher* passing far below.

Mik Vardan left his cabin, strode to the bridge, and took some bearings. Then he took the helmsman's place at the tiller and adjusted the ship's heading. Trip climbed atop the mast to the lookout post and gazed toward the silhouetted horizon.

"Adjusting our heading?" Karista asked, appearing unheralded beside Mik.

The captain nodded. "Tomorrow," he said, "or the day after at the latest, we should be sailing the course set by the Prophecy."

"May the lost gods be with us," Karista Meinor whispered.

"Or if they're not with us," Mik said, "I hope they'll at least stay out of the way."

* * * * *

Mikal Vardan did not sleep well that night. His dreams were filled with storm-tossed isles, drowned temples, and approaching typhoons. A blue-white diamond glittered in the darkness, like a beckoning star—but it seemed not to shed any light on the chaos surrounding him. Mik kept reaching for the gem, but it darted away—ever just beyond his fingertips.

He woke to find the hour before dawn bright and clear, the stars still beaming down, painting *Kingfisher* with their wan light. To the east, where the sky met the sea, a pale, greenish glow presaged the coming of the day. A cool salt breeze greeted the captain as he left his cabin. The scent of brine thrilled his nostrils, as the morning air danced over his flesh, raising goosebumps on his tanned skin.

Trip slept quietly in the rigging far above, his tiny form leaning against the topmost reach of the main mast. Mik shook his head fondly; it was pointless to try and stop the kender from sleeping aloft. Trip was as much at home clinging to ropes overhead as he was free-diving in the sea below. The kender would sooner roll off the spar and die of a bad dream than sleep on deck. Mik shook his head again.

He walked to the bridge and spoke with the night helmsman, checking that they hadn't deviated from the course he set. He took a brief tour of the caravel's small decks, making sure all was in order. Satisfied, he returned to his cabin and broke his fast—dining on bread, cheese, preserved spiced apples, and a bit of red wine.

Dawn crept over the ship as he ate. As he was finishing, a commotion broke out on deck; the sounds of the crew talking excitedly and feet stamping across the planking echoed through Mik's cabin.

Then the kender's clear voice rang out above the rest:

"Wreckage off the starboard bow!" Trip called. "I think there's a body, too! It looks like a woman!"

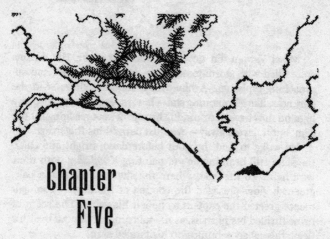

Chapter
Five

The Castaway

Most of *Kingfisher*'s sleepy crew had already gathered at the rail, as Mik pushed his way to the side of the ship.

"Where away!" he shouted up to Trip.

The kender shielded his eyes from the morning glare. "Fifteen degrees to starboard," he called down from the lookout perch.

Mik peered into the glittering dawn sea and spotted a tiny black silhouette bobbing over the waves.

"The kender has the eyes of an eagle," Bok said, looking in the same direction. "I see nothing."

"Adjust heading fifteen degrees to starboard," Mik called up to the helmsman.

"Aye, aye, captain!"

Karista Meinor pushed her way through the crowd to Mik's side. "I trust," she said, "that this is only a momentary diversion from our course."

"Naturally," Mik said, climbing up to the bridge. "But

the law of the sea requires rescue of shipwreck survivors."
He called up to Trip again. "You're sure there's someone
on that wreckage?"

"Positive, captain. Or I'm a monkey's cabin boy."

Mik glanced from Trip in the rigging to Karista, who
had followed Mik up to the bridge. She prowled the deck like
an anxious cat. *Kingfisher*'s captain knew the aristocrat
had little tolerance for the kender.

"Bok can come up," Trip called down, reading his mind,
"if he and Karista don't believe me."

Neither the aristocrat nor her bodyguard accepted
Trip's offer.

It took the ship just over an hour to reach the wreckage
Trip had spotted. The Northern Turbidus Ocean rolled
gently under *Kingfisher*'s keel as they sailed. The mild sea
showed no signs of the previous day's storm. The sun
stretched her fingers higher as they traveled, and soon lit the
whole sky with bright, golden light.

Mik knew the fair weather wouldn't last; at this time of
year, the Turbidus could change its character from seductive
to violent in an instant.

A cotillion of Turbidus dolphins arrived to watch *Kingfisher*'s passage. The aquatic mammals' sleek black and white
forms raced beside the ship or danced in front of the bow.
Trip climbed down from the rigging and leaned over the
gunwale to watch them. As they closed in on their goal,
though, the dolphins disappeared back into the deep.

Very little debris floated on the surface as they drew
near the wreckage. A single, wide swath of planking
bobbed on the ocean's green-gray surface. Strapped atop
the wreckage, lay the prostrate body of a slender, beautiful
woman. She was clothed only in soaked gossamer fabric and
delicate jewelry. Her long platinum hair lay arrayed around
her head like a sunburst, some of the delicate locks trailing
into the water. Her skin was as blue as the evening sky.
Whether alive or dead, none aboard *Kingfisher* could tell
from this distance.

"That's no wreckage," Mik said, eyeing the castaway's strange conveyance. "It's a raft."

"Not a very sturdy one either," Trip added. He squinted his hazel eyes and peered at the strange sight. The raft appeared to have been cobbled together quickly from stray bits of wood the ship's carpenter had lying around. Very little craftsmanship was evident in its plank and rope construction. The waterlogged deck was barely sufficient to keep its passenger above the surface. "And why do you suppose she's tied down?"

"To weather yesterday's storm, perhaps," Karista suggested.

"She couldn't have tied herself like that," Mik said.

"Maybe someone stranded her like that for good reason," Bok offered.

"Aye," agreed Pamak. "It's a bad omen. We should abandon her to her fate."

Mik frowned at them. "Lower the ship's boat and meet me at the raft," he called to the crew. He grabbed a full skin from near the water barrel and dived over the side.

"I'm coming, too," Trip said, bounding over the rail after his friend.

The captain and the kender swam quickly to the makeshift raft as *Kingfisher*'s crew unlashed the boat from amidships and lowered it over the side.

Mik and Trip reached the castaway quickly, and tread water at the raft's perimeter. "Scramble aboard and cut her ropes," Mik said. "This flotsam won't take my weight."

"Aye, captain," Trip replied. He pulled himself onto the small raft and began severing the woman's bonds with one of his pearl-handled daggers.

Mik swam around near her head, careful not to topple her into the deep as he skirted the perimeter of the rickety platform. The woman's eyes were closed tight and crusted over with dried salt. She didn't move at all or make any sound, and, at first, the captain thought they'd come too late.

As Mik watched, though, he saw that her chest rose in a slow, shallow rhythm, and a faint pulse throbbed in her smooth neck. "She's alive," he said. "Though not for much longer if we hadn't found her."

"Good thing I spotted her, then," Trip replied. He finished cutting the last of the victim's bonds and slipped back into the water.

Mik unstoppered the waterskin and poured a little over the blue-skinned woman's face, gently cleaning off the salty residue. She still didn't stir, so he dribbled a little onto her pale blue lips. Her tongue darted out and licked up the moisture and her eyes flickered behind her eyelids; she didn't wake, though.

Just then, the ship's boat pulled alongside.

"Lift her aboard," Mik said to Marlian, standing in the skiff's bow. "Gently."

"Aye, captain," Marlian replied.

Mik and Trip helped the crew carefully maneuver the blue woman off the raft and into the longboat. The captain and the kender then scrambled aboard, and they all quickly returned to *Kingfisher*.

Using some spare sail cloth as a sling, they hoisted the castaway up to *Kingfisher*'s deck and gently laid her down.

"She's blue!" Bok blurted.

"Well, she's a sea elf," Mik replied. "They're common enough in these waters—though seldom seen."

Karista Meinor frowned. "She's badly sunburned—almost purple," the noblewoman said. "I doubt she'll survive."

"I've some sunburn oils in my cabin that may help," Mik said. "If we can tend the burns and get some water into her, she may make it. Elves are hard to kill."

"Who could have left her like that?" Bok asked rhetorically. "She's so beautiful."

"Bah! You were right earlier, bodyguard," Pamak said. "A sea elf, shipwrecked? Tied to a raft? I repeat, she's a bad omen. We should throw her back to the fishes." A number of other sailors grumbled their agreement.

"Whoever did this to her, didn't want her with the fishes," Karista noted. "They wanted her to die stretched out like a skinned animal."

"We'll worry about how and why she came to be on the raft later," Mik said. "For now, take her to my cabin. I'll tend her burns. Trip, bring more fresh water."

"Aye, captain," the kender replied. Trip fetched several more waterskins while the crew gingerly carried the castaway into Mik's cabin below the bridge.

The captain set up a canvas pallet in the corner opposite his hammock and they laid the sea elf's unconscious body on it. Mik and Trip knelt down at her side. Karista, Bok, and a number of other crew members waited at the doorway.

"Do you have any magic that could help?" Mik asked Karista.

"I have some remedies to relieve fever," she replied. "I don't know how effective they'll be, though. I'll fetch the herbs I need from my cabin."

"Have the helmsman resume our previous course," Mik said to Bok.

The big bodyguard peeled his eyes away from the elf, nodded, and went to do as Mik asked.

"Clear the cabin," Mik said, indicating everyone else should leave. The fascinated crew members went back to their jobs as Mik and Trip tended to the castaway's injuries.

Mik gently massaged fragrant oils into the elf's blue skin. When she finally groaned slightly, Trip put the waterskin to her lips and made her drink. As she did, the kender eyed the glittering jewelry holding her scant costume together.

"No borrowing, Trip," Mik cautioned. "We wouldn't want her to forfeit her modesty."

The kender laughed, and reluctantly tore his eyes away from her jewelry.

Karista returned shortly with a silver brazier filled with burning herbs. She chanted and made passes with her hands over the injured woman—but none of them saw any obvious effect.

34

The aristocrat shook her head. "The magic does not work as reliably as it once did," she said. "I'm sorry."

Mik stood and stretched. "You did your best," he said. "We all have. There's nothing more we can do for her now. Undisturbed rest is probably her best chance at recovery. Besides, we have work to do. Saving this poor girl cost us valuable time. It'll take keen sailing to reach the proper coordinates by the time Paladine's constellation rises tonight."

"But shouldn't we change her sunburn salve?" Trip asked.

"Later," Mik replied. "This evening perhaps, before Paladine rises. We've a lot of ocean to cover before then. Let's get to it."

"Aye, captain," the kender replied.

* * * * *

The wind was against them for most of the day. Through clever sailing, though, Mik still managed to make up most of the time they'd lost.

As the sun settled behind the shoulders of the ocean, the wind shifted to the southwest, urging them on their way. Mik stood in the bow, watching the dappled red and orange reflections on the water creep into purple and indigo. He called back a final course correction to the helmsman, and then ate a brief supper with the crew on the deck amidships.

Karista and Bok took their meal below; they seldom deigned to eat with *Kingfisher*'s crew. Only as he washed the last of his bread down with a swig of rum did Mik notice that Trip was missing as well.

Mik found the kender, as expected, within the captain's cabin. Trip had opened Mik's sea chest once more, and taken out the golden artifact and the parchment with the transcribed verses of the prophecy. He sat perched on Mik's hammock, perusing the paper and turning the artifact over in his small hands.

"Honestly," Mik said, "I'm not sure why I bother to lock that chest."

"I'm not sure why you bother, either," Trip replied. "It's not a very good lock. Karista could probably open it if she had a mind to." He dropped out of the hammock and smiled.

"How's our patient?" Mik asked, gazing at the blue form of the castaway. Her skin looked very dark with the red light of sunset streaming through the cabin's small windows. Mik crossed to a hanging brass lamp in the center of the room and lit it.

"Better, I think," Trip replied. "She hasn't woken up or moved much, though. Should we oil her burns again?"

Mik nodded. "It's not much," he said, "but all we can do to help her survive."

Trip laid aside the Prophecy and the artifact, and both of them gently rubbed fragrant oil into the sea elf's blue skin. They worked silently for a while, pausing only to drip fresh water onto her pale lips. Then Trip asked, "When you look at the artifact . . . at that black diamond, do you . . . *see* anything."

Mik hesitated a moment. "Like what?"

The kender screwed up his face in perplexity. "I dunno. Like a bigger diamond surrounded by treasure, maybe."

Mik nodded and chuckled. "Never any secrets while you're around, Trip."

"Oh, I like secrets as much as the next fellow," Trip said, "just not when they're being kept from me. So . . . what do you see?"

"A storm-tossed ocean," Mik replied. "An island. A temple. Sometimes, a treasure." As he spoke, he continued massaging the sunburn oil into the elf's soft skin.

The woman's eyes flickered open. "Treasure?"

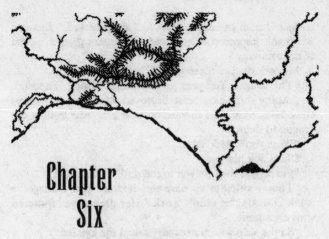

Chapter Six

The Course Is Set

"Y̶ou're alive!" Trip gasped. "You're awake!"

"Barely," the sea elf replied, her voice dry and cracking. "Where am I?"

"You're aboard *Kingfisher* in the Northern Turbidus Ocean," Mik replied. "I'm Captain Mikal Vardan, and this is my friend, Tripleknot Shellcracker."

"Hi!" the kender said. "My friends call me *Trip*."

The sea elf tried to speak again, but only a dry rattle came out.

"Here," Mik said, putting a skin of water to her pale, parched lips. She drank eagerly. "Who are you?" he asked. "Where do you come from?"

She smiled weakly. "My name is Ula," she said. "I come from . . . many places. Most recently, from a ship called *Golden Harvest*."

"Were you shipwrecked?" Trip asked. "How did you get tied to the raft?"

The elf woman laughed briefly, then a spasm shook her

37

and she began to cough. "Not . . . shipwrecked," she said when she stopped coughing. "My shipmates grew . . . tired of my company."

Mik's dark eyes narrowed. "Why?"

"The dragon Tempest prowls these waters," she said. " . . .Many ships have been destroyed. My . . . superstitious crewmates convinced themselves that I . . . was leading the dragon to them."

"Were you?" Mik asked.

Ula shook her head.

"But why'd they tie you to the raft?" Trip asked.

"They wanted to appease the dragon." She managed a weak chuckle. "It didn't work." Her green eyes fluttered shut once more.

"So the ship was destroyed?" asked the kender.

Ula didn't reply.

"We'll let you rest," Mik said. "Call if you need anything."

"All right," she said, her eyes still closed. "I still want to know . . . about that treasure . . . though." Her words trailed off and she drifted into sleep once more.

"What a rotten thing to do," Trip said, "tying someone to a raft to feed them to a dragon. Probably an interesting way to die, though. Just throwing her overboard wouldn't drown a sea elf. That must be why they tied her down."

"Yes," Mik said thoughtfully. "C'mon. She needs to rest." They left a waterskin by her bed and went out through the map room onto *Kingfisher*'s quarterdeck.

"Any change?" Karista asked when she saw them.

Mik nodded. "She woke, briefly."

"Did she say anything?"

"Not much," he said.

"You think she'll live?"

"It seems more likely now," he replied.

"Her former shipmates cast her overboard to appease a dragon!" Trip burbled.

All around them, the crew stopped working.

"Just superstitious nonsense," Mik said, shooting the kender an angry glance.

"How can you be sure?" Marlian asked warily.

A wry smile crept over Mik's face. "The girl's alive, isn't she?"

"She said her name is Ula," Trip ventured cautiously.

Mik nodded.

"The name means nothing to me," Karista said.

"I heard of a mercenary sailor named Ula once," Bok replied. "She was supposed to be very dangerous."

"If she's so dangerous, how did she end up tied to a raft?" Karista snapped. "We're wasting time. The blue siren isn't going anywhere—at least for the moment. We need to be about our business."

"Lady Meinor is right," Mik said in a loud voice, commanding the attention of all the crew. "The stars are rising. Soon, Paladine will show the way." He directed their attention to the constellations hovering above *Kingfisher*'s bow. "To your stations while I chart the stars and set our course."

The crew nodded and went back to their business, the possibility of the dragon—for the moment at least—forgotten.

Mik climbed to the bridge, followed by Trip, Karista, and Bok. He took sightings on Paladine and the Heavenly Palace, and set course on a line between the two.

Kingfisher's small crew scrambled across the deck, adjusting ropes and rigging as required. Mik took the tiller and, using the verses of the Prophecy as guide, set sail through the deepening night toward the Dragon Isles.

Karista and Bok soon retired to their cabin below. Mik and Trip, though, stayed on deck, tending the tiller and watching the stars.

Getting under way on the final part of the journey buoyed the crew's spirits. They sang as they worked—both to set the rhythm of their labors and to keep themselves awake through the long, cool night.

On a fair south wind we set to sail, blow winds blow
'Mid porpoise, manta, shark and whale, blow winds blow
Past Chaos' teeth we jigged around, blow winds blow
'Til treasure wreck at last we found, blow winds blow
  Hi-Ho!
Now haul the silver, gold and steel, blow winds blow
With arms to rope and backs to wheel, blow winds blow
Then home we sail with holds a-bulging, blow winds blow
To drink and brawl our hearts indulging, blow winds blow
  Hi-Ho!

Bok materialized to complain that the singing kept his mistress awake, though Mik and Trip suspected he was merely bellyaching on his own account. The captain declined to do anything about it, and chants persisted through the darkness, as the crew kept the rigging trim and the ship in top shape.

Several hours past midnight, Mik yawned and handed the tiller to old Poul. The wizened sailor took over gladly, and whistled an old seafarer tune as he held their course.

A fragment of verse from the sea shanty echoed through Mik's mind as he walked through the map room to his cabin.

Then down, down to the briny deep where sharks hold court
  and sailors sleep.

He yawned again as he opened the cabin door. What he found on the other side, shocked him back to wakefulness.

Ula, the sea elf, was awake and sitting up on her cot. In her slender blue fingers she held a folded piece of parchment and the artifact containing the black diamond.

Anger flared in Mikal Vardan's eyes. "Where did you get that?" he snapped.

Ula regarded him calmly with her green eyes. "I found it by my bedside," she said. "I recognized it as a very interesting piece—probably quite valuable. You really shouldn't leave such things lying about—especially when you have unexpected guests." She held the artifact and the parchment out to Mik.

He grabbed them, silently cursing himself. He and Trip had been so startled when the elf woke up, they'd forgotten to put the precious items back into Mik's sea chest. Mik inwardly cursed Trip for ferreting his possessions out in the first place. He locked the diamond key and the paper away once more—putting his enchanted fish necklace in the chest as well—then turned back to the elf and forced an easygoing smile.

"I didn't expect you up so soon," he said.

"I heal quickly," she replied.

"Very quickly."

"Do you have any food around? I'm famished."

Mik went to his sideboard, fetched some bread and cheese, and cut her some with the dagger from his waistband. "Is this all right?" he asked. "I'm not sure what sea elves usually eat."

"On land, we eat the same things you do, mostly."

He handed her a waterskin, which she set down on the cot beside her as she ate.

Mik watched her carefully, noting that her blue skin seemed to be healing. It was less burnt than before. She moved gracefully, even when eating, and her form and figure were among the most perfect he had ever seen. Elves were beautiful as a rule, but Ula was uncommonly lovely, even among elves.

She threw her head back, shook her long platinum-colored hair off her smooth shoulders, and took a long drink of water. As she put the skin down she sighed contentedly and said, "Maybe tomorrow, I'll be up for something a bit stronger."

Mik nodded, unable for a moment to find his tongue.

Ula laughed. "You look as though you need rest almost as much as I do."

"Yes," he said absently. "I'll need all my wits about me the next few days."

"Where are you headed?"

"A place that may not exist," he replied, "the Dragon Isles."

"The Dragon Isles? Oh, they exist, all right," she said.

He regarded her skeptically. "How can you be so sure?"

She yawned and lay down on her cot once more. "I lived there . . . once. A long time ago." She reached beside the cot and rescued her blanket from the floor.

"Perhaps you could help us find the place, then," Mik said. He crossed to his sea chest, pulled out a rolled silk tapestry, and rigged it to hang down the middle of the cabin, between her bed and his hammock.

"Perhaps I could," she said with a smile. "For a price. Everything has its price."

"You'd have to take that up with Milady Meinor," Mik said. "She's financing this expedition."

"I'd rather take it up with you," she replied sleepily. "In the morning."

"In the morning then," he said.

Mik blew out the hanging lamp and retired to his hammock, but he didn't sleep very well. His dreams were plagued by glittering diamonds, and the gemstones hanging at the sea elf's slender waist.

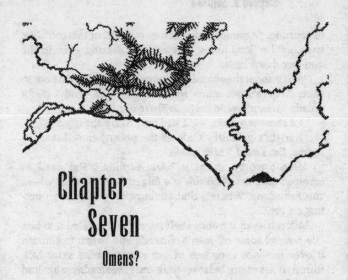

Chapter
Seven

Omens?

"Mik! Mik, wake up! It's nearly dawn."
The sea captain immediately recognized the kender's small voice buzzing in his ear, but felt reluctant to open his eyes.

"Tell your pup to keep it down," Ula called from the other side of the makeshift screen.

"I'm not a pup," Trip said, "though I've had people call me a minnow before—people I like, that is. You could call me that, if I decide I like you. I *did* have an *uncle* who got turned into a dog once, though. Great Uncle Figswallow . . ."

"The savage deep save us from kender in the morning!" Ula cried. A muffled sound from her side of the curtain indicated that she'd pulled the covers up over her head.

Mik laughed, rolled out of his hammock, and stretched. "Sleep in if you want," he called to Ula. "I'm sure you need the time to recover."

She sighed. "No, I'm fine," she said. "I'm sure I'll feel better after my morning swim." She rose and pulled back

43

the curtain. "Assuming my back recovers from this cot." She stretched her long limbs, looking very alluring, even in the dim, pre-dawn light.

"Sorry about the accommodations," Mik said, trying not to stare. "There's not much room in a caravel—and I doubt milady Meinor would deign to share her cabin."

"I'd share *my* cabin—*if* I had one." Trip shrugged.

"Karista's gallantry ends at the point her self-interest begins, I'm afraid," Mik added.

"Don't worry about it," Ula replied. "I'm used to cramped quarters. And this is a fair sight better than where you found me. Where's that sunburn oil you've been putting on me?"

Mik retrieved it from a shelf nearby and handed it to her. Ula poured some oil into her hands and began to smooth it over the vast expanses of her exposed blue skin. Mik found it hard to believe that only yesterday she had seemed near death.

"Are you going to swim home when you feel up to it?" Trip asked.

Ula laughed—a light, musical sound. "Home—when I had one—was a long way from here. Too far to swim." She smiled, and her eyes glinted predatorily. "You're headed in the right direction, generally, but you'll never get to the place in the isles where you're headed, without my help."

A cold chill ran down Mik's spine. "How do you know where we're going?" he asked.

"I read the Prophecy," she reminded him. "And I'm no fool, Mik Vardan, though I certainly met you through foolish circumstance."

"She knows about the Prophecy?" Trip asked, looking quizzically at Mik.

"Yes, she found the parchment and the artifact," Mik replied irritatedly. "We forgot to pack them away in the chest before she woke up."

Trip screwed up his small face. "Well, no harm done, I guess. Everyone on ship knows." His brows drew together in concern. "Maybe we shouldn't let her swim away, though. She might have friends nearby."

"The only 'friends' I have nearby tied me to that raft," Ula replied. "Besides, I'm not going anywhere until we've recovered that treasure."

"She knows about the treasure, too?" Trip asked.

Mik nodded grimly.

Trip ran his small fingers through his blond hair. "Oh, yeah. It was in the Prophecy."

"As I said," Ula interjected, "you'll never find the treasure without my assistance. You won't even find the Dragon Isles. I'm willing to help, though, for a price."

"And that price would be . . . ?" Mik asked.

"A share in the treasure—when we find it."

"What do you need more treasure for?" asked Trip, eyeing her bejeweled costume. "It looks to me like you're wearing plenty of treasure."

"These old things?" Ula replied, running her slender fingers over a few of the pieces. "Looks are deceiving. My people use such trinkets as money. Steel doesn't survive so well underwater."

A frown crept over Mik's bearded face. "Why didn't your former crewmates on the Golden Harvest steal your jewelry before they cast you adrift?"

"They were afraid to touch any of it," she said with a slight grin. "I told them the jewels were cursed."

"Cursed? Really?" the kender said, his hazel eyes lighting up.

"Deadly cursed," the beautiful elf said, straight-faced.

"Sleek," replied Trip, awe in his small voice.

"Why do we need you to find the Dragon Isles?" Mik said. "We have the Prophecy. We're on course. According to the parchment, we should reach our goal before the end of the day tomorrow."

She smiled again, finished oiling her long limbs, and set the bottle back on the shelf. "It's not so easy as you think."

"How would you know?"

"I grew up there. The Dragon Isles don't let just anyone in. You need to know the secret."

"What secret?"

"If she told us," said Trip helpfully, "then it wouldn't be a secret, would it?"

Mik scowled at him. "I'll discuss it with Karista," he said. Ula nodded.

"Now, I need to get on deck and check our course before the stars set."

"I'll go with you," she replied.

"Me, too," Trip added.

The morning air was crisp, with a stiff, salty breeze blowing from the south. The wind raised goosebumps on Mik's tanned skin, but seemed to have little effect on Ula. Living underwater, she must be used to the cold, Mik thought.

He reached reflexively for the enchanted fish necklace at his throat, then remembered he'd put it in his sea chest the previous evening. Wearing it too long became tiring and caused more of its jeweled scales to flake off. Mik knew the magic inside it wouldn't last forever. It was fading, like all the other enchantments in the world—and needed to be used sparingly. The lost gods willing, he'd have no need of the necklace today.

Mik took the tiller from the night helmsman, and adjusted their course to better follow the Great Silver River toward the Seven Cities constellation. Clouds were blowing in from the south, so he made some final calculations to help steer them through the day.

Ula hung a rope over the stern and climbed down into the water. Then she swam in the ship's wake, her lean form cutting gracefully through the dark water. Trip and the other crew members leaned on the rail, watching her in fascination. When she finally climbed out, the sailors on deck cheered.

Mik smiled and shook his head.

A brief squall that morning drenched the sailors' bodies, but did little to dampen their spirits. Warm late summer winds from the northwest soon dried out *Kingfisher*'s sails and her crew. The ship followed the course set by the stars, Mik using his calculations to guide them when the sun hid behind the cotton-like clouds.

He spoke to Karista about Ula's proposal, but the noblewoman wouldn't buy any of it. "Just another leech," Karista said. "We owe her nothing."

Ula, standing at the rail nearby, must surely have overheard—but she said nothing, only smiling her enigmatic smile. Mik tried not to think about her.

He also tried not to think about the huge diamond glittering amid a pile of treasure in the lost temple. The vision, though, kept tugging at his mind.

Ula retired to his cabin at midday—to escape the summer sun, which had broken through the clouds once more. She was still there when Mik came in for a lunchtime break.

"Well . . . ?" she asked, leaning forward on her cot.

"Karista isn't convinced you have any information we need," he replied. "And, even if she were, I doubt she'd be willing to give up a share of the trade concession she hopes to win."

"Trade concession?" Ula said. "I wasn't asking for a cut of the trade concession. I want a cut of the *treasure* you're looking for—the one mentioned in the Prophecy."

"Karista isn't interested in the treasure," Mik said. "I'm on my own in that regard."

"Not any more," she said with a sly smile.

"How can you be sure any treasure exists?" Mik asked, pouring them both a mug of rum. "Even *I'm* not sure it exists."

"I grew up in the isles," she replied. "I've heard rumors of such things before. And I saw that key-like artifact you have locked in your sea chest. Working together, I'm sure we can find riches beyond your imagining."

Kingfisher's captain raised his cup and drank. "I'm still not convinced I need another partner," he said stubbornly.

Ula shook her head and her platinum locks fell pleasingly around her smooth shoulders. "You'll never get there without my help."

"We'll see."

She raised her glass. "Indeed we will."

He left Ula in the cabin and went back to work. Karista Meinor and Bok kept mostly out of the way as the crew of *Kingfisher* kept the vessel on course. Occasionally, Mik spotted the aristocrat checking her copy of the Prophecy.

When the sea elf appeared back on deck in late afternoon, Mik avoided her. Ula took this in stride, and proceeded to mingle with the ship's crew—even lending a hand with the ongoing chores. Clearly, she knew her way around a boat, though her presence seemed to cause as much distraction as help.

Mik double-checked his headings and set the crew to taking depth readings, not wanting to come upon any reefs or submerged shoals unaware. He also kept a lookout aloft at all times.

Mostly this duty fell to Trip, as the kender actually enjoyed sitting atop the mast. Additionally, with Trip in the rigging, the rest of the crew didn't have to watch over their small possessions quite so diligently.

Trip scanned the horizon as much as he watched the seas ahead. He constantly reported interesting flocks of birds, or the distant spouts of whales, or the clowning of pods of black and white Turbidus dolphins.

At dusk, Trip spotted a storm system on the western horizon. Mik eyed the gale carefully until dark, and then watched its lightning flashes late into the evening. He knew the further north they sailed the more treacherous the weather would become. Few ventured into the depths of the Turbidus Ocean at summer's end, and fewer still returned to tell the tale. The chances of *Kingfisher* being swamped or wrecked if a typhoon hit them were high—and such storms moved faster than any ship could sail.

Mik considered adjusting their course, but a quick consultation with Meinor convinced him to keep the tiller steady. The sea remained clear of reefs through the night, and depth readings confirmed that they were sailing into ever deeper parts of the northern Turbidus Ocean.

Mik rose before dawn once more, and sneaked a quick glance at the black diamond while Ula slept. The sea elf had been up late the previous evening, chatting guardedly with the crew and—once—even approaching Karista Meinor.

Whatever Ula had said, though, Karista soon retreated with Bok to her cabin. The look of frustration on the sea elf's face told Mik she'd made no progress with the single-minded aristocrat. Mik had retired at that point as well, and not wakened when Ula returned to her berth.

She did not stir that morning as he locked the diamond artifact back in his sea chest once more.

The salt breeze had shifted during the night, and now blew in strong from the west—where the immense thunderstorm still clung to the horizon. The waves began to pile up upon themselves, growing larger until their peaks danced away in sprays of white mist.

Kingfisher ran before the wind all that day. Karista and Bok fussed around the deck, nervously awaiting the outcome. Ula walked from stem to stern—alternately peering toward their hidden destination, and the pursuing storm.

As dusk drew near, Trip began jumping up and down on the sparring so vigorously that Mik feared he might topple off the mast.

"I see them!" Trip called. "I see the Dragon Isles!"

Chapter Eight

Within Sight

All movement on deck ceased, and many sailors stood and peered over the forward rails. Karista, Bok, and Ula went to the bow as well.

Mik shouted up to Trip. "Where away?"

"Five degrees to port!"

"But that's not the course you've charted, captain," Karista called.

"We're on the course laid out by the stars," Mik replied, testily.

"Will you believe an ancient prophecy, or the eyes of your lookout?" Ula asked. Mik shot her an angry glance. and she chuckled.

"The elf is right, captain," Karista said. "If we can see the isles, we should steer straight for them."

"You're sure about the heading, Trip?"

"Positive, captain!"

"All right," Mik said. "I trust Trip's eyes more than I

do writing on an old piece of paper. I'll set our course by his sighting."

He brought the helm around, and soon those on deck saw the tips of blue-green islands jutting out of the pale mist on the horizon. The Dragon Isles glittered like gems amid a turquoise sea.

The crew laughed and congratulated themselves. Trip continued to jump up and down excitedly atop the mast. Karista even kissed Bok on the lips. Only Ula stood quietly against the stern rail. A knowing smile played across the sea elf's beautiful face. Her odd demeanor worried Mik.

Tales of vast wealth, nearly within their reach, ran through the ship like wildfire. Soon, every hand not otherwise occupied had assembled on deck for a glimpse.

"The isles are exactly the way I remember them," old Poul said. He wiped a tear from the corner of his eye with one wizened hand.

An occasional flash of brilliance high in the distant air caused the onlookers to gasp and point. Trip gave a whoop and nearly toppled out of the rigging.

"Dragons!" the crew whispered with a mixture of awe and fear.

"I thought the metallic dragons had left Krynn," Bok said a bit nervously.

"Only the *good* dragons left," Ula replied. "None of the dragons remaining in the isles are truly evil—but even metallic dragons have their share of rogues and renegades."

Mik folded his arms over his chest. "Whether 'good' or evil," he said, "I doubt that any of them have much regard for the affairs of men. We'll steer clear of all dragons if we can."

Karista leaned over the bow rail and grinned. "Look at them!" she beamed. "The isles are within our reach! Imagine the wonders when we get there. Imagine the *wealth!*"

All evening they sailed directly for the distant peaks. By nightfall they could make out the shapes of forests on the islands' rocky shores and trace the silhouettes of the towering mountains.

"We'll make landfall by morning!" Karista said.

Pamak finished pulling in *Kingfisher*'s depth cable, and frowned. He cast a puzzled look at Mik. "Shouldn't the ocean be getting more shallow as we approach the isles?" he asked.

"It should," Mik replied, "but maybe there's a steep drop-off on this side of the archipelago," Mik said.

"Aye," Pamak said. "That could be."

Secretly Mik doubted what he'd told the big deck hand. *Kingfisher*'s captain glanced at Ula, who was still leaning against the stern rail, smiling. Mik cursed silently and took the tiller once more.

All night, the storm brewing on the western horizon crept closer. It seemed of little import, though, since they were so close to shelter of land. Mik and his helmsmen kept *Kingfisher*'s course straight and true, though the darkness seemed to swallow the islands whole. Distinguishing the isles' shapes from clouds and shadows proved difficult in the gloom, and they saw no lights upon the distant shores.

* * * * *

"What's wrong?" Karista Meinor asked, as the sun rose the next morning. She pulled her silk dressing gown around her ample curves as she came up from her cabin. "Why haven't we made anchor?"

"We haven't made anchor because we haven't reached the islands yet," Mik replied. He sheltered his eyes from the morning glare and stared to the east. The sunrise obscured the isles' rocky forms, making them flicker and dance among the waves.

Trip, perched on the rail at the front of the bridge, crinkled his nose. "How can they be to *starboard?* We steered straight at them all night."

Meinor frowned. *"Well?"* she demanded of Mik.

"I steered true all night," Mik replied. "And the helmsman did the same on his watch. Maybe there's some kind of current or strange tide here that's pushing us off our mark."

Ula mounted the bridge and stood beside the captain. "Having trouble?" she asked coyly.

Mik frowned at her. "I'll re-set our course," he said to Karista. "We should still make landfall in early afternoon."

Karista glanced from the captain to Ula, and then to the isles. "Very well," she said. "Keep me appraised of the situation." She turned and went below.

"Mik . . ." Trip said from his forward perch.

"Yes, Trip?"

"The sky was red this morning. And that storm in the west is blowing in very fast. If we don't reach harbor by sunset . . ."

"I know," Mik said, "the sea elf will be the only comfortable person aboard."

Ula, leaning against the stern rail, laughed.

The captain and the kender both cast a wary glance aft. Storm clouds stretched long, dark fingers toward them and lightning licked the sky.

"We're close enough to the isles now," Mik replied. "The storm shouldn't be a problem. Get aloft and help keep us on course."

Trip nodded. "Aye."

By late afternoon, though, they'd drawn no nearer than they had the previous night.

Mik pounded his fist on the rail and cursed. "They never get any closer! How can that be? First they were north of us, then they were east, now they're north again."

Ula, perched on the stern rail, smiled but said nothing. She looked westward, toward the approaching storm. Distant echoes of thunder rolled across *Kingfisher*'s deck.

"The depth readings are the same as last night, captain," Pamak reported.

Karista Meinor, who had been watching from the bridge for the past two hours, scowled. "Perhaps, another tack is warranted, captain," she said. The aristocrat cast a glance toward the sea elf. "I did not believe her story the other night, but perhaps she does know the secret to reaching the isles."

"Don't trust her!" interjected Bok. "She's a sea-witch, that one."

"I *don't* trust her," Mik replied. "But it seems we *need* her. Ula . . . ?"

Ula lowered herself to the deck and walked to the tiller, her jewel-bedecked body shimmering in the waning light. "My price?" she asked.

"I won't give up my trade concession," Karista hissed.

"I'm not interested in that," Ula said. "You'll find it's harder to establish trade with the isles than you'd like. I want something more . . . substantial."

"A share in the treasure of the *Prophecy*," Mik said.

"Aye. A share equal to the highest share—which I'd warrant is the captain's."

"*If* there *is* a treasure," he added.

"I'll take that chance," she replied.

"I don't seem to have much choice. Okay. Done."

Ula smiled. "See? That wasn't so hard. Here's the secret: only a metallic dragon may enter the isles unbidden," she said. "Everyone else needs permission—or there is one other way."

Karista cursed. "Riddles!" she said.

The sea elf smiled. "You have an artifact . . . but *I* know how to use it."

"Well, don't be coy about it. Tell us." Mik's eyes narrowed.

Ula nodded. "Dragon Isles privateers use crystals—in many ways similar to your black diamond—to find their way back to the isles. I believe your artifact serves the same purpose."

"I'll fetch it from my cabin," Mik said, handing the tiller to Bok.

He went below and retrieved the golden artifact from his sea chest. As the black diamond brushed his hand, a vision of a temple filled with glittering diamonds flashed through his mind. He pushed aside the images and raced back to the bridge.

Karista's steely eyes focused on the golden looping key as Mik held the artifact out toward Ula. The wind lashed at his hair, and large drops of rain began to spatter the deck. An odd feeling made the hairs on the back of Mik's neck stand up.

"So, how do I use it?" he asked.

"Hold the diamond out before you," Ula said. "Turn until it glows. When it glows brightest, that's the true direction of the isles. Follow the glow."

Mik did as she said, turning slowly, starting with the heading they were following. The black diamond began to glow—dimly at first, but with increasing brightness as he revolved. Mik frowned.

"It's nearly fifteen degrees starboard of our present heading," he said.

"A Veil of deceptive magic surrounds the isles," Ula said. "It's like steering toward a mirage—when you get there, you find the mirage is gone. You can chase a mirage forever and never find it. The isles are the same way. Some mariners call the effect *The Maze*. Only the blessed or the very lucky can find their way through the enchantment without a key."

Karista's eyes glittered with reflected lightning. "Set the course! The storm is approaching!"

"I don't trust the sea-witch's magic," Bok grumbled. "There's something unnatural about it."

"It's either follow the magic," Mik noted, "or sail around in circles until the storm catches up with us."

Mik altered *Kingfisher*'s course, swinging the bow around until it matched where the light from the diamond key shone most brightly.

The air before them wavered, like heat above a rock on a blazing summer day. The captain felt suddenly hot. Looking around, he saw that the others were sweating as well—all save Ula, who looked as cool as ever. She stood with her arms folded across her chest, leaning calmly against the rail, the wind pulling at her long, platinum hair.

The crew working the decks below moved about agitatedly. The sailors grumbled, and some of them trembled.

Mik ordered a ration of rum for everyone, and that seemed to calm things down for a while.

Slowly, ever so slowly, the Dragon Isles crept closer.

Karista Meinor paced across the short expanse of *Kingfisher*'s bow, wringing her slender fingers together, and occasionally stopping to mop the sweat from her brow with a silk handkerchief.

Behind her stood Bok, perspiration running down his body from the tip of his shaved head to his bare feet. He kept a wary eye on both his mistress and the approaching islands.

Trip clung to the rigging near the top of the mast, refusing to come down even as the rainstorm broke in earnest. He kept his hazel eyes fixed on the distant islands, hoping to catch a glimpse of flying dragons or something even more wondrous.

The wind howled like demons, and many crew members wrapped scarves around their heads, or covered their ears with their hands—as much as they could—while they worked.

Thunder crashed and, before they knew it, a sailor had leaped overboard into the surging waves. He screamed an incoherent warning as he went, but there was no trace of him by the time a rescue crew reached the rail.

"Turn back!" Pamak said.

"We can't!" Mik replied. "Our only chance to survive the storm is to keep going!"

Thunderheads rolled up the sky behind *Kingfisher*, and lightning crashed into the ocean with frightening regularity. The seas mounted ever higher before the wind, and soon the water behind them looked like green-gray mountains. The storm's breath whipped the tops of the waves into froth; white mist danced high into the air.

"Come down, Trip!" Mik shouted up to the kender. "Before you're struck by lightning!"

"Aye, captain!" the kender called back. He swung around the mast and felt with his foot for the rigging. As he did, something in the breakers off the stern caught his attention. Trip put a hand over his eyes and peered into the storm.

"Crazy minnow!" Ula yelled up to him. "What are you waiting for?"

"I see something!"

"What?" asked Mik.

"Sharks! Sharks running before the storm! Hundreds, thousands of them!"

"He must mean porpoises," Karista called from the bow. "Sharks do *not* run before storms—not on the surface anyway."

"I mean *sharks!*" Trip called back, pointing. "Look for yourselves!"

The aristocrat and the captain peered in the direction the kender indicated. The wind whipped stinging spray into their eyes, and they had to blink away the brine to see.

The sea behind *Kingfisher* boiled angrily, and not just with wind and waves. Tall dorsal fins broke the whitecaps as schools of sharks swarmed forward: redtips, swordbeaks, manglers. Many leaped from the breakers, their toothy maws snapping at the salty air.

"What's happening?" Karista called from the bow.

Astern on the bridge, Mik shrugged and shook his head. "Maybe they're chasing something."

"Or perhaps something is chasing them," Ula suggested. Her green eyes went wide as she gazed at the foaming sea.

"What is it, girl?" Karista shouted.

"Can't you *feel* it?" Ula called back. She turned her head from side to side, as though seeking the cause of the feeling.

"I feel it," Mik replied. The sensation was like a large knot twisting within his stomach. He tightened his grip on the tiller; his brown eyes flashed, questing, across the whitecaps.

"I feel nothing!" Karista shouted, annoyed. "I . . ."

As she spoke, the waves behind them erupted, and the dragon burst from the deep.

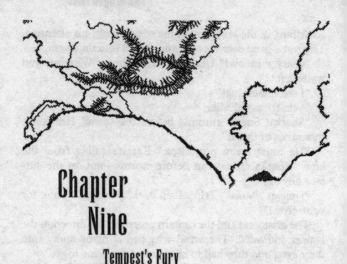

Chapter
Nine

Tempest's Fury

Tempest exploded from the breakers like a blue green mountain. Boiling steam erupted from her massive jaws; her yellow eyes shone with the fury of the storm.

Hatred of the Dragon Isles and all those who sailed to them burned in her black heart. She would make sure that if she could not reach the archipelago, no one would.

The sea cascaded away from Tempest in huge waves. The sudden torrent crashed against *Kingfisher*, threatening to tip it on its side. High on the mast, Trip clung desperately to the rigging. Sharks, razorfish, and Turbidus leeches as thick as a man's arm sped in a maelstrom circle around the tottering caravel.

The crew working *Kingfisher*'s deck toppled when the waves hit and screamed as the dragon-fear swept over them. Mik hung onto the tiller, but the backwash from the waves carried Ula toward the rail.

Mik stabbed his hand out, but Ula slipped away from him.

The sea elf slammed against the gunwale and regained her footing. A razorfish, carried high into the air by the swell, flashed past her face. Ula barely ducked aside in time. The fish flopped onto the deck, and she seized it in one slender hand. She dashed the fish's brains out against the hull and threw the body back into the raging surf.

At the front of the ship, Marlian, Karista, and Bok froze as the dragon rose before them. Marlian pushed them all to the deck as the breaker hit. All three of them got wrapped up in the anchor chain, which kept them from heaving over the side in the backwash.

Poul wasn't so lucky. The old man had been working amidships when the wave struck. The water seized his thin body and thrust him toward the bow. Marlian reached for him as he swept past, but her outstretched hand merely brushed his callused fingertips.

The tall sailor woman struggled out from under the tangled chains and lurched to her feet. Poul was hanging half over the rail, his feet dangling toward the raging water below. Marlian grabbed his right arm just as he went over.

"Help me!" she cried.

Bok lurched to his feet and toward the lanky woman sailor. Marlian's fingers dug into the old man's stringy flesh. Terror flashed across Poul's ancient face.

"I won't let go," Marlian said. "Hold on!"

A glimmer of hope lit within Poul's ancient eyes. The breakers clawed at his bare legs and feet as he tried to scramble aboard once more.

A huge mangler shark burst from the waves below the wizened mariner. The creature's blue-gray sides glistened with foam. Seaweed and huge Turbidus leeches hung from its flanks. Jagged triangular teeth jutted from its gaping mouth. Poul's legs disappeared into the fish's maw; the shark bit down on the sailor's midsection.

Poul gasped, and blood spurted from his mouth. Marlian screamed.

The shark lunged forward, clamping its jaws down over the

old man's head. A hideous crunching sound filled the air. The shark jerked its head to the side and dived back into the deep.

Marlian clung to the old man's arm, but Poul was no longer attached to it. The momentum of the shark's dive jerked her half-way over the rail. She flailed with her hands but found only rain, crashing water, and wind. Wide-eyed, she gazed into the deep. A dorsal fin cut through the water in front of her terrified face.

Strong hands grabbed Marlian's ankles. "Karista, help!" the big bodyguard cried. He clamped his thick fingers tight, but Marlian's legs were slippery with rain. Bok began to lose his grip.

Lady Meinor staggered forward, trying to keep her footing on the rocking deck. *Kingfisher* surged and she fell into the rail, almost going over herself.

Bok grabbed her and lost his hold on Marlian.

Marlian screamed as she disappeared into the brine. Razorfish swarmed in her wake and stained the ocean red with blood.

* * * * *

Trip clasped his fingers tight around the rope atop the masthead. He watched in fascination as the dragon dived past the ship on the starboard side. Several deckhands threw themselves off the ship in a frenzy of terror. What Trip felt was more of a thrill. He'd never seen a dragon before and was determined not to miss a moment of the experience, even if it killed him.

Lightning flashed through the sky, narrowly missing the mast. As quickly as he could, Trip scrambled down the rigging toward the deck.

Another dragon-spawned wave struck *Kingfisher*'s side. The boat pitched wildly, and Trip found himself hanging in the air, holding onto a rain-soaked rope by only his fingertips.

"Whee!" he squealed as his hands slipped free. The feeling of soaring unfettered through the air was one the kender knew he would treasure for the rest of his life—even if that life was about to end. Trip smiled at his friends on the madly bobbing ship below as the waves rushed up to meet him. "Will I hit the deck, or the water?" he wondered. "Will it hurt much?"

* * * * *

Karista grabbed Bok's shoulder and clung to him as he pulled her away from the rail.

"Lower the boat!" Karista cried, staggering toward the skiff, stowed amidships. "If we lower the boat, we could get away!"

"Away to where?" Bok replied, gazing frantically around the surging seas, trying to find the islands.

Dragon-fear held the crew firmly in its terrifying grip. Most of the hired hands dashed madly about the deck, or dived for cover through the hatch and into the hold. Following Karista's suggestion, several sailors began to unlash the ship's boat and push it toward the rail.

"Belay that, you fools!" Mik shouted from the bridge, but the crew wasn't listening. The captain cursed as the heaving seas threatened to yank the tiller from his hand. *Kingfisher* bobbed and swerved wildly, nearly heaving onto its side.

Ula staggered from the rail to help Mik. As she skidded across the teetering bridge, the sea elf looked up and saw a kender flying through the air toward her. She held out her arms, and Trip fell hard into them. The two of them thudded to the rain-soaked deck. "So kender fly now?" Ula asked.

"I wish!" Trip replied. The two of them struggled to their feet once more and lurched to the tiller.

"Hold onto this," Mik said, slapping the diamond artifact into Trip's small hand. "I don't want to lose it in this wash."

Trip nodded, and tucked the object into one of the many pouches on his lizard-skin vest.

"The dragon's submerged! I can't see it!" Bok cried. The big bodyguard looked around frantically.

"Maybe it's gone," said Pamak, trying to launch the boat.

"It could be anywhere!" replied a woman helping him. The two kept pushing the skiff toward the rail. A crowd of sailors had formed around them, but no one seemed to have a clear plan for accomplishing their task; the crowd hindered as much as helped the efforts to launch the smaller boat.

Meinor and Bok pushed up to the milling crowd. "Let us through!" the aristocrat bellowed. "I must get on that boat!"

"Turn the ship into the wind, or we'll be swamped!" Mik said to Ula as the two of them struggled with the tiller.

The sea elf nodded. Trip came to help them, wrapping his small arms around the steering board. A huge wave cascaded over the side of *Kingfisher*. The crew on deck were scattered like ninepins, and the ship's boat crashed through the rail and over the side. Bok went with it, but Karista got pinned against the gunwale, her foot caught in one of the scuppers meant to drain the deck.

A second wave crashed over the bridge. The impact jarred Trip's fingers loose from the tiller. The kender tumbled down the stairs, skidding helplessly toward the rail.

Karista reached out and Trip grabbed her hand.

"Thanks!" Trip gasped. They clung to each other and staggered away from the side, but *Kingfisher* lurched and threw them hard against the main mast. They grabbed a tangle of lines at the mast's base and barely avoided being sucked overboard in the backwash.

Thunder crashed and lighting splintered the ship's bowsprit. Karista and Trip staggered to their feet once more.

They all gazed out into the raging sea. Four lengths off the starboard side, the ship's boat floundered in the crashing waves. Bok and several other sailors had managed to pull themselves aboard the tiny vessel. They clung to the sides as the gale spun them about like a toy in an angry child's bathtub.

The skiff suddenly surged upward on a huge column of black water. The crew screamed as the water fell away and a lightning flash revealed the dragon beneath. Tempest held the tiny boat between her immense rows of teeth for a moment. Then her jaws snapped shut, and the boat flew into splinters.

The people manning the skiff disappeared into her gigantic maw—all but Bok, who had been flung out as the boat disintegrated. The bodyguard clung desperately to one of the huge Turbidus leeches hanging from the dragon's upper jaw. He screamed wildly as he tried to scrabble up the dragon's face to the imagined safety of her brow.

Tempest flicked her head, like a monstrous dog flipping a bone into the air. Bok lost his grip and flew up into the storm. Tempest caught him in her titanic fangs and crushed him into a bloody pulp. Sharks, razorfish, and Turbidus leeches swarmed forward to gobble up the crimson leavings.

Karista's eyes went wide with horror as the dragon surged toward *Kingfisher*. She screamed—a piercing, high-pitched wail from the center of her soul.

"Move!" Trip shouted, hauling on Karista's hand. "We have to move!" He tried to drag her toward the bridge, and finally her legs began to move. They scrambled frantically over the wet, slimy deck toward the aft stairway. On the bridge, Mik and Ula struggled with the tiller, trying in vain to bring the ship around.

The dragon's snout snapped the top off the main mast as Tempest crashed down on the bow of the ship. *Kingfisher* heaved forward, and Mik lost his grip on the tiller. He tumbled down the stairs onto the water-drenched quarterdeck, smashing into Trip. The kender lost his grip on Karista. She tried to grab them again, but they skidded out of her reach and crashed into the base of the shattered mast.

The captain and the kender barely had time to look up before an avalanche of rigging and tangled sails buried them.

* * * * *

The dragon whipped her head toward the bridge. Karista, soaked and shivering, clung to the stairs just below where Ula held fast to the tiller.

The sea elf shouted a defiant curse. She let go of the steering pole and seized a boathook from a rack near the rail. With all her strength, she threw the iron-tipped spear at the dragon.

The weapon's forward lance pierced the dragon's cheek, and the trailing hook caught in her lower eyelid. Tempest roared in pain and surprise. She reared back her head and belched scalding steam over the deck of the kingfisher.

Karista ducked as the boiling cloud thundered over her head. Ula screamed as the blistering steam hit her. She turned and dived over the side, disappearing into the swirling deep.

Tempest reared up, raising nearly all of her massive form out of the surging seas. Then she crashed back into the ocean, head first, smashing into *Kingfisher* as she came.

Kingfisher's spine broke in half as the dragon surged into the depths. In an instant the hold filled with water, smothering the cries of the crew still struggling below deck.

The center of the ship sank first, and with it the broken mast, the rigging, and the shroud-like sails that had smothered Mik and Trip.

Karista screamed until there was no air left in her lungs. She scrambled up the stairs to the bridge, knowing that doing so would only buy her a few more moments of life.

Thunder boomed in her ears. Sharks, Turbidus leeches, and razorfish swam through the heaving waves, picking through the bodies of *Kingfisher*'s crew. The wails of the dying mingled with the howl of the wind, the echoes of the thunder, and the deafening crash of the waves.

Wreckage from the ship dotted the ocean all around. Some pieces of *Kingfisher* were burning, though Karista couldn't imagine how they'd caught fire. The aristocrat scrambled to the aft end of the bridge, near the tiller, as waves greedily devoured the rest of the ship.

Terror threatened to overwhelm her mind, but her body remained determined to stay alive as long as possible. She had to try, had to fight! Then she remembered: Her magical seaweed! She always carried some in the pouch at her waistband.

Chewing on the seaweed allowed her to breath underwater—when the magic worked, which wasn't always. Underwater, perhaps she could avoid the dragon and the frenzied predators. She could hide beneath the waves until the danger had passed. It was a slender chance, but far better than she had on the surface.

The water to starboard began to bubble and roil, the waves crashing higher every moment.

The dragon!

The dragon was coming back!

Karista's hands fumbled across her waistband, trying to find the needed pouch. Her nails caught in the water-soaked crevices of the sash at her waist. Her fingers got knotted in the fabric.

Nearby, the long fins atop the dragon's head broke through the surf. Tempest's yellow eyes lit the waves, like huge lanterns lurking just below the chaotic surface of the sea.

Sweat poured from Karista's brow. Her body shook and shivered in the driving rain. The surging waves lapped over her feet as the last of *Kingfisher*'s deck submerged. She lurched forward, pulling her fingers free and grabbing onto the rail just in time. She stabbed her right hand toward her pouches, all the while clinging to the wreckage with her left.

She found the pouch and tore it open, thrusting her hand inside. Frantically, she pulled out the contents.

A sudden flash of lightning lit the crumpled-up handkerchief in her palm.

Not the magical seaweed, just a ratty handkerchief—like nothing Karista Meinor had ever owned.

The dragon rose from the raging deep.

The aristocrat gazed at the handkerchief, horror overwhelming her heart. Two whispered words escaped her lips.

"The kender!"

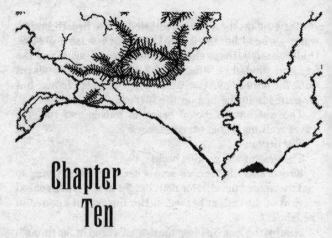

Chapter Ten

Perils of the Deep

Mik Vardan knew he was about to die. Wet ropes and canvas knotted themselves around his body, chaining him to the iron-shod mast of the doomed *Kingfisher*. He'd seen the rigging falling, but he and Trip couldn't get out of the way in time.

They'd struggled for a moment, then something big hit the ship and the water surged up around them. They were sinking now, and Mik was about to drown.

In his mind's eye, he saw his enchanted fish necklace. He saw himself in his cabin, putting the necklace in his sea chest, next to his copy of the Prophecy. The Prophecy had never mentioned *this*.

Mik pulled hard and ripped the canvas away from his face. In the glow from the lightning above, he saw *Kingfisher* sinking around him. The mast had splintered from the deck and sank by itself in the middle of the wreckage.

Through the gloomy water, at the edge of his vision, he could barely make out the shape of the captain's cabin and the bridge. His possible salvation—the fish necklace—lay within, but he would never reach it. The cabin was too far away, even if he weren't ensnared in the rigging.

He looked up and saw Trip, tangled in ropes and canvas, further up the mast, struggling to free himself.

Something slammed into the mast just above his head. He saw the tail fin of a shark slice away into the darkness. Struggling, he managed to pull his dagger from the sheath at his belt, then wondered if it was worth the effort.

Mikal Vardan could hold his breath a long time. He was an excellent diver—one of the best—and he'd gotten a good lungful of air before he went down, but he couldn't last forever. He didn't think he could hold his breath long enough to cut away all the canvas and rigging binding him. Pamak's last reading said the water was forty fathoms deep—a difficult dive for anyone, even a pearl diver, without magical aid. If he sank all the way to the bottom, he would likely never resurface anyway. Was it worth fighting sharks just to drown?

His boat was dead. His crew was dead. Perhaps he should die as well.

As the shark bore in again, Mik cast off his doubts and guilt. He would *not* die here, alone, fishfood for some predator. The ropes tangling the sailor gave him little freedom of movement, so he knew he'd have to time his strike just right.

The shark sliced effortlessly through the lightning-dappled water, its blunt head swaying from side to side as it homed in on its prey. The blue and gray mottling along its side marked it as a mangler shark—bane of shipwrecked sailors. Its jaws opened wide as it attacked.

Mik ducked to one side as the mangler came in, and stabbed up with his knife. The shark missed Mik's face by inches, its teeth ripping through the swirling canvas just beside his right cheek. The captain's blade hit home and opened a small gash in the mangler's belly.

The fish jerked aside, almost taking Mik's dagger with it. It turned slowly and came in again, trailing a streamer of dark blood. This time, it aimed for the sailor's gut. Mik knew he couldn't stop it; he braced himself to die.

Just before the shark struck, though, a dark shape flashed down on it from above. The two shadows struggled for a moment, the small shape rolling through the turbulent water with the much larger mangler. A cloud of blood sprayed into the brine and the mangler sank away into the depths. A flash of lightning from above revealed Mik's savior.

The sailor would have shouted for joy if he'd had the breath.

Trip's small form swam through the tangle of ropes and canvas and began to cut the bonds holding Mik to the sinking mast. Mik shook his head, knowing Trip couldn't have any more air than he did. He tried to motion the kender to surface, but Trip wouldn't have any of it.

Instead, the kender reached into a pocket and pulled out a small wad of damp weed. He thrust the mass toward Mik's face. "Take it," Trip burbled. "It's . . . magic seaweed."

Mik opened his mouth, and the kender popped the seaweed inside. Mik chewed.

For a moment, he thought that Trip had made a mistake. Pain like fire shot through the sailor's limbs, and his muscles spasmed. Multicolored lights flashed before his eyes, and it felt as though someone were sitting on his chest.

Then a familiar tingle began to build up in his toes. The sensation spread through his body until it reached his lungs and, finally, his skull. The sensation was similar to the one he felt when using his enchanted fish necklace. Mik took a deep breath of the brine and felt pleased when he did not die.

"Ugh! Tastes . . . terrible," he said, the words bubbling out of his mouth in garbled bunches. It wasn't the bell-clear words his enchanted necklace produced, but he didn't feel inclined to argue.

"I borrowed it from Karista," Trip replied.

"I hope . . . she won't . . . need it," Mik said.

Trip nodded. "Dunno how long . . . it works," Trip burbled. "Let's cut you free."

For long minutes the two friends hacked at the ropes and canvas as the mast binding Mik sank ever deeper into the darkness. Flashes of light from the surface above became more dim and distant, and the turbulence in the water around them grew less and less.

Several times, a razorfish with a Turbidus leech attached to its belly flashed by, but Mik and Trip were able to fend the predator off with their knives.

Just before the masthead settled to the silt forty fathoms down, Mik finally wriggled free. He took a long, deep breath of enchanted air and bubbled, "Thanks, Trip."

The kender merely nodded. The seaweed's magic allowed them not only to breathe but also to see—if imperfectly—in the twilit depths. It prevented the depths from crushing them and even kept the brine from stinging their eyes. Talking, though, remained tricky.

"Now . . . find my cabin," Mik blurted. Trip nodded.

It took a moment for the two of them to get their bearings in the ocean dimness. Soon, though, they spotted a likely looking silhouette.

Moving quickly, they bobbed over the ocean floor toward their destination.

Mik's cabin, and the bridge above it, had broken off from the rest of the ship when *Kingfisher* sank. The greater part of the two decks lay on the bottom, canted at a twenty-degree angle and shrouded in billows of settling mud.

The two divers swam cautiously to the wreck, keeping their eyes peeled for signs of the dragon, sharks, or other predators. They kicked past the remains of several bodies along their way—small bits of flesh difficult to recognize as human, never mind as former crewmates—and soon reached the wrecked cabin.

The door didn't give when Mik tried it, and it took them a few minutes to pull the wood off its bent hinges. The contents inside floated in a jumble, the shambles of Mik's life tossed everywhere. Some woven items—silks, clothing, blankets—hung eerily in the water, like strange and colorful jellyfish.

Uncovering the captain's sea chest took longer than either of them would have liked. Mik's trunk had settled to the bottom of the confused heap, but appeared otherwise undamaged.

The sailor quickly opened it and pulled out the box containing his enchanted necklace. The metal fish's bejeweled scales glimmered in the dim light inside the sunken cabin. Mik took the amulet from the box and hung it around his neck.

For a moment, he felt sick to his stomach, as the magic of the necklace tangled with the water-breathing spell from the seaweed. He spat the chaw of weed into his hand and immediately the pain passed. In a moment, the submarine world around him became brighter as the amulet's powerful enchantment sharpened his senses. His lungs filled with sweet, fresh air, and his limbs tingled with new vitality. Then a shiver ran through him, and he noticed that three more jeweled scales had flaked away.

Mik grimaced and handed the magical seaweed back to Trip. "Thanks," he said.

The kender frowned at the green-brown wad before popping it into one of the many pockets of his lizard-skin vest. "Dunno . . ." he said, "how good it is . . . used."

Mik knelt beside the sea chest and opened the box with his copy of the Prophecy. The box, though, was not watertight, and the parchment had already been ruined. A small cloud of blue-black ink puffed into the water as the paper floated out, like a pale bit of seaweed.

The two of them quickly sifted through the jumble and turned up Mik's sword. They took all the coins they found as well, knowing they'd need cash when they reached civilization again.

"You still have the black diamond?" Mik asked.

Trip nodded and patted one of the pockets of his lizard-skin vest. "Ula had . . . right idea about . . . money," he commented.

"The others . . . dead?"

Trip shrugged. "We were . . . lucky."

"Let's surface," the captain said. "If anyone's still alive . . ."

They swam back out the cabin door and took a moment to get their bearings. Light from the storm and the fire above had died away considerably. Darkness shrouded the sea, and even their magically assisted sight couldn't penetrate far.

A swift-moving shadow flitted past, just at the edge of their vision. As the captain and the kender turned to face it, something struck them both from behind.

A heavily weighted net encircled them, pinning their arms and making it difficult to move. Mik twisted against the ropes and yanked his specially weighted dagger free from its scabbard. He threw the knife at a shadowy figure nearby.

The underwater shiv sliced through the water and struck the object with a dull thud.

Deep laughter echoed through the darkness.

Mik reached for his cutlass, but the shadowed figure tugged on a line, tightening the net so he could barely move. Trip, though, had managed to pull both his daggers and was already working on cutting the sturdy mesh.

Another figure, swimming almost too swiftly to see in the darkness, yanked on another cord and toppled them off their feet. Trip's daggers fell from his hands and settled to the sea bed below.

The two figures circled quickly outside the netting, pulling the trap tight around the sailor and his diminutive companion. Try as they might, Mik and Trip could not break free. In moments they lay bound and helpless on the bottom of the sea.

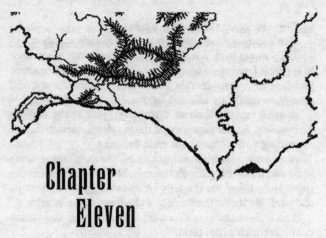

Chapter
Eleven

Scavengers

Mik struggled against the rope netting binding his arms and legs.

"We must reach the surface!" he said."

"Friends . . . may be . . . dying!" Trip burbled.

"Anyone on the surface is dead already," said a raspy female voice. The voice was far clearer than Trip's, or even Mik's magically assisted tones—as though it had been born to deep waters. "Sea dragons don't take prisoners, and Tempest is the worst of all," the voice continued.

"A bad break for sailors," added the deep voice they'd heard laughing before, "but very good for our business." This voice was just as clear as the first.

"Who are you?" Mik asked, peering into the shadowy deep. "What do you want?"

"Salvage," the raspy voice, which was attached to the slender, swift-moving form, replied. "Even half-drowned sailors have some value."

"We should go," the deeper voice said. "The dragon isn't

far off. We should return to Reeftown." A huge armored knight emerged from the shadows and began reeling in the net containing the captured mariners.

Mik and Trip glanced at each other in wonder.

"How . . . ?" Trip blurted.

"Yes," the raspy voice said, "we should hurry back. I want to see what our other salvage parties have brought to fatten my treasury. See to the prisoners, Shimmer."

Shimmer, the underwater knight, nodded and said, "Yes, Lakuda." As he drew closer to the captives, tightening the net as he came, his appearance became more defined. He was a tall man in shiny reddish armor decorated with fins, scales, and fishlike patterns. A spiky helmet completely covered his face.

The creature known as Lakuda swam forward with a few quick undulations of her lean body. Her black eyes peered at the prisoners in the weighted net. She was dressed in a combination of form-fitting black orca-leather and golden jewelry. Her face was thin and sharp-featured. She had tightly tied green hair and pointed ears. Even without her pale blue skin, Mik and Trip would have realized immediately that she was a sea elf.

Moving with the deadly grace of a razorfish, Lakuda regarded the prisoners with a cold, predatory smile. She poked a slender finger into Mik's shoulder; he struggled.

"This one seems strong enough," Lakuda said. "Tough, too, or he wouldn't have survived in such good shape. Perhaps he'll fetch something. The kender's next to worthless, though. We should leave him for the sharks."

"We've captured them," Shimmer said. "We have a duty to keep them alive—at least until we reach home."

Lakuda arched one eyebrow at him. "You'd do better if you abandoned such hopelessly idealistic notions, Shimmer," she said. "They're not profitable." She swooped down and retrieved Mik's knife and the kender's daggers from where they'd settled into the silt, and tucked them into a bag.

"We were traveling with an aristocrat from Jotan," Mik said. "Profit for her rescue would certainly be great." The tightness of the net made it difficult to speak, even with aid of the necklace's spell.

Lakuda gazed into Mik's brown eyes, trying to determine whether he was telling the truth. "Don't toy with me, sailor," she said sternly.

Shimmer turned his armored head toward the surface, two-hundred and forty feet above.

"If anyone's alive up there, they've either been taken by the dragon or by one of your other pods," he advised Lakuda.

"You can . . . see all that . . . from down here?" Trip burbled, awed. He peered up but saw nothing.

"We'll find out soon enough," Lakuda said. "Come, Shimmer." She put one of the lines securing the net over her shoulder and began to swim away.

Shimmer grunted and did the same.

"Is your shoulder acting up?" Lakuda asked.

"Not to worry about, Mistress," Shimmer replied.

"We could swim along with you . . . if you let us free," Mik suggested.

Lakuda laughed, a chilling sound rippling through the water. "And then you'd meekly follow us back to Reeftown to be ransomed."

"Where else would we go?" Mik asked.

"I've never seen . . . a sea-elf city," Trip bubbled, his eyes lighting up.

Lakuda ignored the kender. "You'd be fools to try to go anywhere," she said. "That doesn't mean you wouldn't *try,* though. You're already marked as fools to venture this far north. The continent is too far to swim, and no one enters the Dragon Isles—without permission."

"We make a living off fools like you," Shimmer added with a chuckle. "Business was good even before Tempest started patrolling these waters."

"I'm Captain Mikal Vardan," Mik said.

"Former captain, I'd say," Lakuda interjected.

Mik fought down a wave of anger and continued, ". . . and this is my ace diver, Tripleknot Shellcracker."

"Call me Trip," burbled the kender. "Can we . . . call you, uh . . . Lakuda and Shimmer?"

Both scavengers pointedly ignored him as they continued to drag the bound captives forward.

Shimmer glanced at his companion, his orangish eyes shining from beneath his bronze helmet. "Hauling them to Reeftown *would* be easier if they would cooperate."

Mik smiled. "Sure. Just cut us free, and . . ." He never finished his sentence.

As Shimmer turned toward the captives, he lifted the faceplate of his helmet ever so slightly. Beams of dazzling light shot out from the crack, filling the sea with multi-colored brilliance.

A wave of dizziness swept over the shipwrecked captives. Mik's senses reeled and he remembered no more.

* * * * *

When Mik woke again, he found himself bound by the waist to a long rope. Trip was tied behind him, like two caught fish on a line. Their hands had been tied as well, though their legs remained free for swimming. Lakuda darted in front of them, tugging on the rope; Shimmer brought up the rear. Mik's cutlass had been confiscated and, along with the daggers they'd lost earlier, put into a bag-like net hanging from Shimmer's right shoulder.

Whatever spell the Bronze Knight had used against them, the effects hadn't lasted long. Mik recognized the wreckage of *Kingfisher* around them as they swam forward.

Occasionally, Lakuda or Shimmer would break away and scoop up a piece of debris from the ocean floor. They'd examine the item and then either stuff it into one of the pouches hanging from their belts, or drop it back into the silt.

As they passed a large tangle of ropes and chains, Mik's heart fell. There, amid the wreckage lay the body of Pamak. Parts of his torso had been bitten away, and his bloated tongue lolled horribly out of his mouth. His eyes peered, unseeing,

Stephen D. Sullivan

into the endless deep. Already hagfish and other sea scavengers had begun to strip the flesh from his bones.

Shimmer paused a minute to yank the chain free from the tangle. Pamak's body danced horribly, like a puppet on a string.

Hatred for these heartless scavengers welled up within Mik's breast. He lunged forward, an incoherent scream on his lips.

The move yanked Shimmer off his feet and caused the knight to plunge into the silt. Lakuda darted back and swung the haft of her spear into the back of Mik's head.

The sea filled with bright points of light, and Mik's face smashed into the mud. A moment later, Shimmer's big hand jerked him up again. Mik blinked and tried to regain his senses.

Lakuda pointed her spear at the sailor's chest. "Try anything like that again," she said, "and I'll gladly run you through."

"He was part of my crew," Mik said.

Lakuda's black eyes narrowed. "Now he's just fish food."

They swam in silence for a long time after that. Lakuda snaked through the water in front of them; Shimmer plodded along behind, a large sack of loot on his armored back. The wreckage of *Kingfisher* soon disappeared into the indigo darkness.

Mik couldn't tell whether they were headed toward the isles or away. Their captors swam swiftly over the sparse patches of seaweed and coral. Clearly Lakuda and Shimmer knew the sea bed as well as Mik knew the stars at night.

The constant swimming soon fatigued the sailor and Trip. Lakuda and Shimmer pulled them along if they flagged, the ropes tugging uncomfortably at the captives' middles.

"Maybe I don't want to see a sea-elf city after all," Trip moaned.

"We're not scuttled yet," Mik said in a low voice.

Shimmer and Lakuda never seemed to tire, nor did they stop for food. Soon Mik found his eyes drifting shut, despite his discomfort.

Entirely without realizing it, he crossed into the land of dreams. There he sailed a fine, proud ship, larger and newer

76

than *Kingfisher*. Old friends, some long dead, others he'd left behind on this voyage, manned the ship. They dived for pearls and recovered sunken treasure. Trip clung to the rigging and prowled the deck, constantly getting underfoot. Mik smiled and breathed the clean salt air. The wind tugged at his hair and raised goose-bumps on his dark skin.

"Mik, look!" the kender burbled.

Mik blinked, and immediately the aches of captivity returned to his limbs. He felt the deep sea currents tugging at his hair and clothes, and he tasted the pristine magical air as it filled his lungs. "Trip?" he asked sleepily.

"The city! Look!"

Mik raised his weary head and gazed where Trip indicated.

Ahead of them, the ocean shimmered blue with flickering iridescent light. Within the glow, an amazing conglomeration of architecture rose from the ocean floor. Houses formed of coral, seaweed, and pieces of sunken ships dotted the submarine canyon. Each dwelling lay piled on top of the next, as the jumbled village reached toward the unseen surface far above.

Mountainous reefs surrounded the canyon in a horseshoe shaped wall, forming a natural bowl protecting the strange village. A tangled mesh of seaweed, like a living net, defended the front of the settlement. Sea elf guards swam patrol just outside of the netting.

Elves, fish, rays, and many aquatic creatures that Mik couldn't recognize darted in and out of Reeftown's gently swaying architecture. Tiny glowing life forms sped among the coral canyons like shooting stars flitting through the night sky. Cool blue and green lights leaked from windows cut into coral walls, or filtered between the cracks in the houses' odd construction. Some buildings looked like huge seaweed cocoons, while others were formed from the rotting cabins of submerged galleons.

"It's beautiful," murmured Trip.

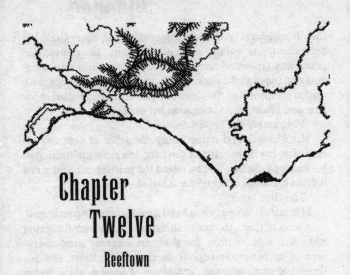

Chapter Twelve

Reeftown

Yes . . . beautiful," Mik replied. In his mind, though, a picture of the northern butterfly fish formed. It was a beautiful creature, arrayed in featherlike multi-colored scales. Each tip of its delicate-looking raiment, though, ended in a spine coated with deadly poison. That is how Reeftown looked to him.

They swam toward the titanic fronds of kelp circling the town's perimeter. The living barrier swayed gently in the current. Two Dargonesti sentries stood guard beside a coral gateway in a rocky wall at the foot of the weeds.

"Flimsy-looking . . . defense," Trip bubbled.

"Say that *after* the weeds have snapped your neck, crushed you, and left your body as fodder for the sharks," Shimmer replied.

"Test it, if you like," Lakuda added.

The kender might have tried it, if he hadn't been tethered to Mik. As it was, his wide hazel eyes scanned the fence's perimeter, hoping that someone else might give it a go.

As the four of them approached the coral gate, a lance-toting sentry in turtle-shell armor stepped up to meet them. He bowed low.

"Felicitous greetings at your return, Townboss Lakuda," he said.

"I trust your forage was successful," added an elf woman, wearing golden seashells and carrying a trident, who stood at the gate beside the turtle-shelled guard.

"Volrek . . . Tila," Lakuda replied, giving the man and woman a nod in acknowledgement.

The sentries stepped out of the way to let the Townboss of Reeftown pass.

"We've sent the other foragers straight to your villa, milady," Tila said. "It seems a fair haul."

"I'll be the judge of that," Lakuda said to the woman.

Tila bowed.

Mik and Trip exchanged a nervous glance.

Lakuda, Shimmer, and their captives passed through the gate into Reeftown. During the brief stop at the gate, Mik and Trip had recovered enough energy to swim along with their captors—which was better than being dragged.

Mik saw now that their previous observations about Reeftown were in error. Close up, the village looked less like a proud, undersea city and more like a refuse heap. The town was mainly composed of cast-offs and marine junk. The buildings seemed shabby and in ill repair. Scavenger eels circled through the streets, gobbling up pieces of rotten wood and decaying seaweed.

Despite the sorry state of most of the construction, the town pulsed with life. Sea elves bustled to and fro, swimming down the avenues, over and through the buildings.

Most of the inhabitants looked a bit ragged themselves. Certainly none had the proud grace and beauty of Ula, nor did they match the rakish vigor and confidence of Lakuda. None were as large or powerful-looking as Shimmer, either.

As they swam by, a number of the locals called out to them. Many shouted congratulations to Lakuda and Shimanloreth for another successful hunt. More than a few laughed at the captives and derided their situation.

"You won't get much for those, milady!" one elf called.

"Why not slit their wrists and leave them for the sharks?" added another. "Fish food is all they're good for!"

"Let them float back to the surface where they belong!" called a third. "We don't need their kind in Reeftown."

Lakuda merely chuckled in reply.

In short order they arrived before a huge structure leaning against the lofty coral escarpment at the far end of town. Boss Lakuda's undersea hall combined the best and worst of Reeftown architecture. In places the reef had been shaped into towers, which jutted out from the cliff face at odd angles, like the spines of a huge sea urchin. Corridors of woven seaweed connected some of the turrets. Others debouched into huge shells or the hulls of sunken ships.

The sides of Lakuda's reef glittered with luminescent undersea life. From a distance, it looked like a huge, glowing gem. Up close, though, it had the same decrepit, thrown-together appearance as the rest of Reeftown. Seaweed netting like that at the gate surrounded the hall, and armed guards swam patrol around the perimeter.

Lakuda led her captives to a big door at the head of a long coral corridor stretching from the manor out to the protective netting.

A muscular elf with a trident stood beside the door with another guard. The elf bowed, then he and his companion unlocked the big door and stepped aside.

Lakuda, Shimmer, and their captives swam through a long, iridescent, tube-shaped corridor into the interior of the hall. The entryway debouched into a huge grottolike room, with exits on many levels and no stairways. Four guards hovered by a huge golden double door near the top of the chamber. Servants bustled through the room, towing sacks and nets behind them as they swam from one corridor into the next.

Lakuda headed for the golden door, with Mik and the rest trailing behind. She bobbed her head to the lead sentry.

"Lady Lakuda," he said deferentially, bowing.

He rose and opened the door. They swam into a wide passageway with arching white ribs that supported a curving tube made of a pink, pearl-like substance. The corridor was short and emptied into a big room that appeared to be the interior of a massive conch shell.

Lakuda tossed the rope holding the captives to Shimmer and flicked across the room. She swam to a swath of golden netting on the far side and arranged herself comfortably within it. Several guards appeared from the seaweed curtains on either side of Lakuda's 'throne' as she settled in.

"That's better," she purred. "Home at last." The Townboss folded her skinny arms over her gold-encrusted chest and smiled. Her dark eyes strayed to a large seashell, brimming with treasure, hanging in the center of the room.

"A good haul today, milady," one of the guards said.

Lakuda nodded tersely. "Shimmer," she said, "combine our booty with the rest—per our custom. I'll divide it tomorrow, after all this outing's foragers have returned."

Shimmer nodded and emptied out the netting sacks he'd been carrying. "What about . . . them?" he asked, glancing at Mik and Trip.

"Take the prisoners to the holding chambers while we make a determination of their worth," she replied. "And make sure you relieve them of any valuables we haven't discovered yet."

"Yes, Townboss," Shimmer said with a slight nod.

He dragged Mik and Trip toward a curtained exit on the left side of the chamber and two guards escorted the group that way.

Shimmer pulled the seaweed curtain aside, then turned back to Lakuda. "I'll return shortly," he said.

"Of course," Lakuda replied with sly smile. "I look forward to it, Shimanloreth."

Shimmer turned away and swam with the prisoners and guards down a long coral tube that slanted at first into the reef, then turned upward once more. They passed through several side passages and soon came to a chamber that was only half filled with water.

Two more guards stood just below the water's surface, guarding the chamber beyond. They stepped aside to let Shimmer and the others through. The bronze knight led the captives up out of the water onto a shelf above the pool. A corridor stretched away from the pool into the darkness.

Shimmer unbound the captives while the guards pointed their spears at Mik and Trip. Trip hopped up and down, shaking his head, trying to get the water out of his ears.

"What happens now?" Mik asked.

"Now you wait," Shimmer replied uncomfortably.

"What kind of name is Shimanloreth?" the kender asked. "Solamnic? I've never heard of an undersea knight before. Does the salt water get inside your armor? Does it itch? How do you breathe? Is it a spell, or in the armor? Has the armor been giving you trouble since all the world's magic began to fade?"

"Hold your tongue, kender," Shimmer said. He held out one large, bronze-armored hand. "I'll take your breathing devices, please."

Reluctantly, Mik removed his fish necklace; Trip leaned forward and spat the remnants of his magical seaweed into Shimmer's palm. The bronze knight's orangish eyes narrowed behind his visor.

He handed the necklace and the wad of magical seaweed to one of the guards and said, "Follow me. There's a living chamber at the far end of the corridor. It's dry enough that you should be comfortable, and even has a view of the city. You'll be fed regularly—if not well—and you won't be mistreated. Trying to escape will just get you killed, so there's no point in attempting it."

"We wouldn't want to cut into your profits by dying," Mik said.

"Stay out of trouble and you may see your homes again one day," Shimmer replied stoically.

"Can we get a tour of the city?" Trip asked. "I'd really like a look around."

If Shimmer was amused, his bronze-helmeted face didn't show it. "You may see more of Reeftown than you want before your captivity is over, kender," he said. "Get moving, now."

With an insincere bow, Mik turned and walked away from the pool toward the inner chamber. Trip skipped along beside him, with Shimmer bringing up the rear. As they went, voices drifted to them up the coral hallway.

"It sounds like we have company," Mik said.

Trip's small face brightened. "Hey!" he said. "I recognize that voice!"

Mik smiled as he recognized it, too. With just a brief glance at his companion, he ran the last few steps into the chamber; Trip followed right behind.

Shimmer stopped dead at the entrance of the room, while his captives sprinted ahead.

Trip's childlike face broke into a huge grin as he saw his former shipmate, and shouted, "Ula!"

Chapter Thirteen

The Dragon's Rage

Mog crouched behind a screen of long weeds and peered at the amazing city of lights. He'd never seen anything like it before. His dragon-like senses drank in every sight and smell until he was nearly intoxicated with the novelty.

Still, even giddy, he was careful to keep out of sight of Reeftown's guards. Yes, the elfin patrols seemed weak and frail compared with his own might, but the dragonspawn knew that many feeble creatures might overcome a single more powerful one.

If Mog were to fail on his mission, he would face Tempest's wrath, and that was a fate worse than death. Mog felt the dragon in the back of his mind even now, calling to him, cajoling him, threatening him—just as she did all her servants. The tiny Turbidus leech on his back burned when she was angry, and sent thrills down his spine when she was pleased. Thus Mog's mood always mirrored that of his sea dragon mistress.

She had been angry for months now, frustrated with her inability to pierce the Veil protecting the Dragon Isles. She had destroyed dozens of ships in her fury, uncaring of their cargo or true destination. That some of them *may* have been headed to the isles had been enough reason to vent her fury.

The ships' contents satiated the hunger of Tempest's servants—sharks, razorfish, numerous and various-sized Turbidus leeches, and a small contingent of dragonspawn such as Mog. As the oldest, cleverest, and strongest of the spawn, Mog always got the juiciest shares of the prey. Even the sharks could not compete with him.

In that sense, the last months had been one long smorgasbord of carnage. The trail of destruction and chaos had been pleasurable. Those past pleasures, though, were balanced out by the fire of the sea dragon's rage now coursing through Mog's brain.

He could feel her prowling the deep at the furthest range of the Veil's magic. She had not been able to come close—but her servants had.

Trailing the shipwreck survivors was not easy; the magic of the isles confused the senses. Keeping the victims in close sight was a difficult task, since Tempest's spies had to remain hidden. Some Turbidus leeches were small, though, and communicated telepathically with their mistress. And the sharks and others she enslaved numbered many—enough, laid end to end, to stretch for leagues. Her servants formed a vast chain with Mog commanding them, following the battered mariners and their captors from the wreck of *Kingfisher* to Reeftown.

How could these fleshy, humanoid creatures penetrate the Veil when Tempest could not? It was Mog's duty to find out.

Scavengers swam near Mog's hiding place. They were only two—a Dargonesti man and woman—and they towed a largish seaweed sack of plunder between them. The size and the weight of the bag slowed them considerably.

Mog flashed from his hiding place and took the woman by surprise.

Before she even knew what had hit her, the dragonspawn snapped her neck, and her body sank to the sand below.

The man turned, a cry of warning on his lips, a spear in his hand. Mog clamped his jaws over the man's head, stifling the cry. The dragonspawn's rear talons opened up the man's belly, spilling the elf's guts into the dark ocean.

Mog drank the blood that leaked from the man's mouth until his victim stopped quivering, and the elf's blue limbs hung limply in the water.

Quickly, the dragonspawn dragged the corpses back into the weeds to feast.

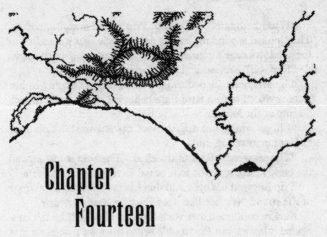

Chapter Fourteen

Allies & Adversaries

Mik smiled at the blue-skinned dargonesti. "It's good to see you, Ula," he said.

"And you, captain," she replied. Her skin looked slightly burnt, once more—a souvenir of her encounter with Tempest's steaming breath.

"Me too," Trip said.

Ula nodded indulgently, then the figure in the doorway caught her attention and her lithe body stiffened.

"Shimanloreth," she said, her voice almost a whisper. "I didn't expect to see you here."

"Nor I, you, Ula Drakenvaal," he replied, his voice cold and strangely formal.

"We thought you were dead," Trip continued, oblivious to the tension between the knight and the elf.

Ula took a long, deep breath. "I thought you were dead as well, minnow," she said. "Though I held out some hope, when I saw my cellmate."

"What cellmate?" Mik and Trip asked simultaneously. They looked around the room and spotted a figure standing in the shadows near a round window looking out over the city.

"Karista!" Mik said. "I can't believe you're alive!"

The aristocrat turned to face them, anger burning in her steely eyes. "I have a hard time believing it, too," she hissed, glaring at the kender.

"I hope you're not angry about the seaweed," Trip said, "I just borrowed it, and—"

"The seaweed!" Karista shrieked. "The ship is lost and all the crew killed, save the four of us! Everything is a disaster!"

Trip lowered his eyes and dug his toe into the coral floor of the room. "It's not like it's all *my* fault or anything."

Karista continued, her voice low and deadly. "I hadn't connected it before, but the trouble began *after* we picked up that ill-omened sea elf. What happened to the last ship you were on, Ula? Pamak and the other sailors *said* you were cursed!"

"Hah!" Ula said. "So *I* caused your ship to sink? It's that same kind of superstitious nonsense that got me tied to a raft and left to die in the first place. I caused *no* ships to sink. People—both human and elf—make their *own* luck."

"That's certainly true in *your* case," Shimmer added, speaking through clenched teeth.

Ula shot him an angry glance, then turned back to Karista. "Look to yourself, milady Meinor, if you don't like the way things turned out. What happened had nothing to do with *me*. I was just an innocent on *your* ruinous journey. What would I have to gain by wrecking your fine ship?" She ran one slender finger over her newly burnt skin. "A nice scalding from a dragon? A bludgeoning from Lakuda's scavengers? Being thrown in a cell owned by a woman who'd just as soon see my head on a pike?"

"How do we know you're not *in league* with these people?" Karista replied. "You seem to know them well enough."

"Yes," Mik said quietly. "You *do* seem to know them."

Ula turned back to Shimanloreth. "Let me out of here, Shim," she said angrily.

"You know I can't," the knight replied.

"I know you can do whatever you want to do," Ula said.

Shimanloreth shook his armored head. "No," he said. "Whatever we had together ended when you left Reeftown."

"Not by my choice alone," she replied. "Let me out. Unless, you'd like to see me dead by Lakuda's hand. Or," she added, nodding to her cellmates, "by one of my fellow prisoners."

"You have made your own fate," he said defiantly, "not I." Then he turned and walked out of the room.

"Lakuda will kill me!" Ula called after him. "You know that." She sat down on a chair made out of carved coral and cursed.

Karista Meinor crossed her arms over her chest and smiled in satisfaction. "You have a talent for making enemies, it seems, my ill-omened *friend*," she said.

"Don't flatter yourself that you're in the same league as Lakuda," Ula shot back.

"All right, you two," Mik said. "We're all in this together, and we need to work together if we're to have any chance of getting out."

"Why should I want to get out?" Karista asked. "My ransom will surely be paid. Escaping seems like a foolish risk."

"Hah! Let's hope there is no haggling over the price. Otherwise, Lakuda will cut your wrists and leave you for the sharks," Ula replied. "My likely end as well."

"Our mutual fate, I fear," Mik said soberly.

"Certainly not as interesting as being eaten by a dragon," Trip added forlornly.

"Were there any other survivors?" Mik asked the two women.

Both Ula and Karista shook their heads. "I doubt it," the aristocrat replied. "I didn't see any on the surface before . . . before the ship dragged me under. If Lakuda's people hadn't found me, I would have drowned." She glared at Trip again, who shrugged.

Mik sighed. "Little chance we'll be rescued or ransomed," he said. "So we'll just have to get out of this fix on our own."

He seated himself on one of the room's seashell-like chairs and rested his bearded chin on his hands. Trip plopped down beside him, and Ula pulled her chair in closer. Karista paced the room, running her long fingers over several potted plants that looked like stiff seaweed.

"What can you tell me about the guards?" Mik asked Ula.

"They're as good as Lakuda's rabble comes," she replied. "We wouldn't want to fight them without weapons—not in the water, anyway."

"And this Shimanloreth?"

"You don't want to tackle him," Ula said.

"I've never seen a knight underwater before," Trip said.

"And aren't likely to see one again," Ula replied.

Mik nodded grimly. "Maybe you can sway him to our side."

"I wouldn't count on it," Ula said.

Mik rose and walked to the room's sole window—round like a porthole and about the size of a ship's wheel—and peered out into the deep. The sun had long since set, but many small life forms, like undersea fireflies, twinkled in the darkness. In their flickering glow and the light from the town's windows, sea elves swam about their business.

"I will not participate in any plan to escape," Karista said stubbornly. "We are lucky to be alive. We've had enough trouble already—and this Lakuda woman seems nearly as ruthless as the dragon. Do whatever you like, but I will stay here."

"Suits me," said Mik. "Trip, I'm guessing Shimmer didn't search you well enough."

"No one ever does," the kender replied with a shrug, pulling another small piece of magical seaweed from an inside vest pocket. "I've got this, plus the wad you gave back to me."

Ula smiled. "Shimmer isn't very familiar with kender."

"Lucky him," muttered Karista.

"With three of us able to breathe underwater," Mik said, "perhaps we could take those guards by surprise."

* * * * *

Shimmer swam impatiently around Lakuda's audience chamber. Occasionally, he dipped down to the pile of loot waiting to be divided and ran his orange eyes over it. How much was it worth, this pile of treasure? Was it worth Ula Drakenvaal's life?

Lakuda's guards paid little attention to the bronze knight. They adjusted their grips on their tridents and pointedly looked the other way as Shimmer circled the big booty-filled shell tethered in the middle of the room. The guards knew his relationship to their mistress, and—even had they not—none would have dared to cross him anyway.

Several long minutes later, a circular side door to the chamber irised open, and Townboss Lakuda drifted in. Her green hair had been undone and trailed behind her like a long seaweed cape. In her left hand she held a stoppered flask of azure wine. In her right she carried the large shell of a half-eaten oyster. Her black eyes gleamed when she spotted Shimmer.

"Will you join me in a drink?"

"No," Shimanloreth replied.

"Rest beside me," Lakuda said, gliding into her golden throne and holding out one thin-fingered hand.

Shimmer didn't look at her but kept gazing at the treasure-filled shell. "I was wondering if my share of today's forage would cover the Drakenvaal's ransom," he said.

Lakuda's black eyes narrowed. "So," she said. "I knew you'd take an interest in her capture. You really shouldn't concern yourself, though. She lost all interest in you long ago."

"I know that."

"And still your feelings for her persist," Lakuda said sarcastically. "She's beneath you, you know."

"Some would say," Shimmer replied, his tone careful and measured, "that *you* are as well."

Lakuda laughed, her raspy voice echoing around the chamber. "A cut well placed! I won't hold it against you though—so long as you join me in a drink."

She dropped the empty oyster shell and unstoppered the wine. The shell drifted slowly down, but a servant appeared and scooped it up before it hit the chamber floor. The servant darted back out the door she'd entered through.

A small blue cloud formed above Lakuda's unstoppered flask. The mistress of Reeftown took a drink and then closed the top with her fingertip. "Well?" she asked.

Shimmer nodded slowly.

"I will drink with you," he said.

Without warning, the room shook. The water in the chamber quivered and Lakuda had to grab hold of her golden netting to steady herself. The guards looked around apprehensively, and even Shimmer adjusted his balance. Cloudy streamers of sand drifted down from the ceiling. A faint rumbling echoed through the room.

"What was that?" one of the guards asked nervously.

"Seaquake?" suggested another.

"Don't just float there, fools," Lakuda snarled. "Go find out."

* * * * *

Karista staggered, but Mik caught her before she fell. Ula jumped out of the way as a big piece of coral plummeted from the ceiling and smashed a driftwood table near one wall of the room. Trickles of sand drifted down from the ceiling.

"What was that?" Trip asked, rising and dusting himself off.

Mik walked to the window and peered out into the darkness. For a moment, he saw nothing. Then, swift shadows began to dart through the dim light surrounding the city. Giant razorfish, he realized, and sharks.

"Mik," Trip said, "I think we've sprung a leak." He held his small hand out under a trickle of water dripping from the ceiling.

The words barely registered on the sailor's mind. There, at the edge of the flickering city lights, he saw something that made his blood run cold.

Mik's mouth dropped open and he whispered, "The dragon!"

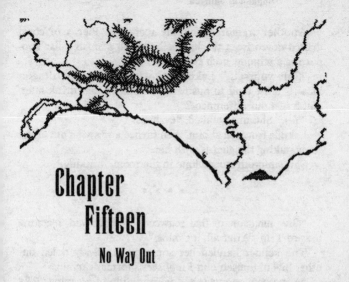

Chapter
Fifteen

No Way Out

A mixture of anger and fear flashed across Lakuda's gaunt face. "Tempest!" she gasped. Then her eyes narrowed. "It's that accursed Drakenvaal!" she hissed. "Isn't it?"

"Absurd," Shimmer countered.

"Well . . . she's been known to associate with dragons before!"

Shimmer said nothing, but his orangish eyes flared with anger.

Lakuda's angular face softened. "I meant no offense," she said. "Your choice of . . . friends is your own, of course."

Shimmer nodded slowly.

"Well?" Lakuda said, swimming to the exit of the throne room, "Are you coming?"

"I think," Shimmer said, "that I shall stay here and contemplate your words."

Lakuda's dark eyes narrowed and her lean jaw trembled. "This is no time to be petulant."

Another tremor shook the reef-villa. Pieces of coral drifted down from the hall ceiling, and a small pillar supporting a window arch crumbled.

"Suit yourself," Lakuda growled. "With the dragon loose, I must tend to business. We'll have that drink later, and forget our differences?"

"Yes," Shimmer replied. "Perhaps."

Lakuda frowned at him, then turned and swam out of the room, taking the guards with her.

Shimanloreth stood alone in the room, thinking.

* * * * *

"Give me some of that seaweed," Karista said, reaching toward Trip. "After all, it's mine."

The kender handed her some; he'd already doled out other bits to himself and *Kingfisher*'s former captain.

"A moment ago, you had no intention of escaping," Ula said slyly.

"A moment ago, we weren't in danger of drowning," Karista replied. She sloshed around in the rising waters of their prison chamber.

"We'd welcome any other aids you might have for the occasion," Mik said.

"I've nothing to weave spells with here," Karista replied. "It all went down with the ship. And, even if it hadn't, with the gods so long departed, my powers are next to nothing." She stuffed the magical seaweed into her cheek and glared at them.

"Maybe you'll assist us in overpowering the guards, then," Mik replied.

"If I must," she said.

Ula laughed.

The chamber shuddered again, and another leak sprang up.

Mik glanced out the window. Flashes like lightning in the darkness silhouetted a terrible battle between Reeftown's sea elves and Tempest's forces.

As Mik watched, a horrible visage appeared at the porthole. It was neither human nor elf. Blotchy scales covered its terrifying countenance. Its mouth was like a sucker ringed with sharp teeth. Its eyes glowed red. Small Turbidus leeches clung to its skin. The creature pressed its face against the glass of the porthole and leered at the captives inside.

Mik jumped back as the thing raised its clawed hand and pounded against the glass. Trip gasped and Karista squawked in surprise. The scaly fist smashed into the window, but the thick glass held firm.

"Time to go," Ula said.

"Agreed," said Mik.

All four captives splashed back down the passageway to where they'd first entered their prison. The corridor was partially submerged, but they found a dry ledge near the pool.

They all paused there, peering into the rising water.

"I can't see any of the guards," Mik said.

"They're probably just down the tunnel, out of sight," Ula replied.

"Any idea which way we should go if we get past them?" Mik asked.

"Follow me," Ula said. "I'll improvise."

The corridor shook, and another piece of coral fell from the arched ceiling. The water grew higher around them, nearly reaching the top of the small ledge they stood on.

"Let's go," Mik said. Ula dived into the water, and he jumped in right after her. Trip and Karista followed.

It took a moment for Mik's eyes to adjust to the gloomy waters. The magic of the seaweed wasn't as potent as that of his necklace. The air didn't smell so sweet, and he felt vaguely nauseous.

Ula streaked ahead as the guards turned to face them. Luckily, there were only two—the others having been called away to help fight the dragon. Ula ducked aside as the first man thrust his spear at her. The sea elf moved as swiftly as a barracuda and as gracefully as a dolphin. She clouted the guard on the back of the neck with the flat of her hand, and the sentry stumbled forward.

Mik grabbed the haft of the man's spear. He wrested the weapon from the sentry's grip and elbowed the man in the face. The guardsman went down.

The sailor swam forward as Ula struggled with the second guard. It was all Ula could do to avoid being skewered by his spear. As it was, the weapon's blade traced a long scratch up her side, cutting free a piece of her already scanty outfit.

Ula cursed and wrestled with the guard as Mik bore in. The guard ducked under the sailor's thrust, but Mik had expected that. He wheeled the spear in his hands and smashed the haft into the man's back.

The sentry grunted in pain. Ula clouted him on the jaw, and his head snapped back. The group quickly pulled the stunned guards up the corridor into the rapidly filling air pocket near the cell.

Trip and Karista confiscated the sentries' other weapons as Ula and Mik hefted their "borrowed" spears.

"Leave their daggers," Mik said.

"Aye, captain," Trip replied.

"Why leave them anything?" Karista asked.

"We've weapons enough," Mik replied. "I won't leave them defenseless in this chaos. They might need to protect themselves."

"Lead the way," Mik then said to Ula, and they all splashed back into the water once more.

They passed numerous corridors as they swam. Several times, they passed small breaches in the wall that gave them a glimpse of the fighting outside. Reeftowners swam everywhere, battling with evil fish under the dragon's command. Finally, they came to a branch in the tunnels where there seemed to be no good choice.

"This one will take us back into the palace," Ula said, "while I'm pretty sure this will take us outside—into the midst of the fighting."

"Doomed . . . either way!" burbled Karista.

"Not *either* way," said a deep voice.

From the inner corridor emerged the gleaming form of Shimanloreth. He looked even larger and more formidable in the confined space of the tunnel.

Mik and Ula lowered their spears at him, while Meinor and Trip drew their swords.

"We won't . . . go back," Mik said, the seaweed's enchantment distorting his voice.

"I'll fight you if I have to," said Ula.

Shimmer laughed, and the corridor shook. Fine sand floated down from the ceiling.

"You won't have to," he said. "Not today."

Mik and Ula lowered their weapons and breathed a sigh of relief.

"Not *ever*, I hope," Ula said.

"We'll see," Shimmer replied. "I was coming to free you, though you seem to have done the job yourselves. I brought your possessions. They would have been due me anyway, as my share of the forage."

"Our weapons?" asked Mik.

The bronze knight nodded. "Them as well." He handed two pearl-handled daggers to Trip and a dagger and cutlass to Mik.

Then he handed the enchanted fish necklace to Mik. The captain put it on, and immediately felt the nauseous tug of the different enchantments. He took the wad of seaweed out of his mouth and handed it to Trip, who stuffed it in a pocket.

"In case we need it later," Mik said to the kender.

Trip nodded his understanding.

The amulet's strong magic filled Mik's lungs and he felt better instantly. Another gemstone scale cracked and fell off the necklace.

"So many gems gone . . ." he thought. But, instead of voicing his concern, he said, "Which way?"

"Follow me," Shimmer replied.

* * * * *

As fighting swirled through the submerged streets of Reeftown, Tempest's dragonspawn lieutenant had taken on a special mission.

A convenient breach in a coral wall allowed Mog access to the inner corridors of Lakuda's undersea villa. A handful of razorfish, sharks, and Turbidus leeches—all under the power of the sea dragon—accompanied the dragonspawn as he swam through the murky corridors toward the chamber where he'd spotted the surface dwellers.

Mog's "troops" encountered little resistance during their journey; most of the sea elves were outside the walls of the town boss' home, battling Tempest's forces. Those few unfortunates Mog's troops met, they quickly slew and devoured.

The passageways of Lakuda's dwelling twisted and turned through the coral reef, so it took some time for Mog and his allies to find the correct wing of the villa. As they approached, a strange scent in the water caused Mog to pause.

The dragonspawn swam cautiously forward, sniffing and listening. Soon, he heard voices from the corridor ahead. He crept to the corner and peered around.

Ahead swam a small group of humanoids, including the surface-dwellers he'd spotted earlier—the ones Tempest was especially interested in. They numbered five, and were a motley crew: humans, kender, sea elf, armored knight.

Easy prey, Mog thought.

In his mind, he saw pictures of the dismemberment to come—his sharks biting the hapless victims in half, his razorfish stripping the flesh from the prey's bones, his leeches swirling in whirlpools of carnage.

He imagined himself cracking open the knight's bronze armor, breaking the man's bones, and sucking out the still warm marrow. The eyes of the victims would taste good as well—especially the succulent ones of the kender. Other soft, meaty portions of their prey he would savor as well—all the best parts, for was he not the commander of Tempest's legion?

Mog started forward. Then something brought him up short. He'd been so preoccupied with thoughts of the feast to come, that he hadn't noticed there was something strange about this rag-tag group. Something about the knight . . . perhaps.

Did his mistress share this feeling? Was this the reason she was so interested in these fleshy creatures? He tried to call to his mistress, but she was lost in the frenzy of battle. Images of blood and death clouded his mind. For a moment, Mog reveled in them.

When the red haze faded, the question remained. What was Tempest's interest in this group?

Mog did not know. Still, the strange scent lingered in the water. Uncharacteristically, Mog decided to fall back. There was something here that he must watch. Wait and watch.

No need to kill these creatures now. He and his minions could harvest them just as surely later.

Then, when the time was right, Mog would slay them all.

* * * * *

Mik, Ula, and the rest moved as quickly as they could through the tunnels beneath Lakuda's villa. Shimmer set the pace, swimming quickly and gracefully despite his cumbersome-looking armor.

The undersea hallways continued to shake as they went. Pieces of coral dislodged themselves from the ceiling, and some of the passages were clogged with great clouds of disturbed silt. Their voyage took them ever deeper into the bowels of the reef behind Lakuda's villa. Gradually, the hidden corridors began to slope upward.

"Ouch!" Trip stopped.

"What's wrong?" asked Mik.

"Something hot . . . in one pocket," the kender replied.

"What do you mean?" Mik asked.

Stephen D. Sullivan

Trip pointed to one of his vest pockets and mouthed the words, "The diamond."

"Give it to me," Mik said.

Trip nodded, fished the artifact out, and surreptitiously handed it to Mik while Ula, Karista, and Shimmer kept swimming.

Mik took the black diamond's setting. It didn't feel hot to him, merely somewhat warm. The sensation of holding it brought images of the lost treasure to his mind. He tucked the artifact securely within a hidden pocket in the waistband of his pants.

Swimming hard, they quickly caught up with Ula and Karista. The sea elf gave them a curious glance, and Mik said, "Nothing to worry about."

Suddenly, the coral tunnel shook more violently than it had before. The floor buckled, and huge cracks appeared along the length of the ceiling. Then, with a deep rumble, the passageway began to collapse.

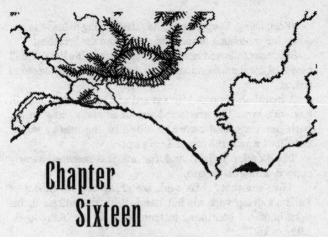

Chapter Sixteen

The Bronze Knight

Karista Meinor screamed and threw her arms up over her head. Small pieces of coral rained down from the ceiling and bounced off her, scraping her exposed skin. Tiny streamers of blood from her scratches clouded the water.

Mik pulled Trip out of the way of a large coral boulder as it crashed from the ceiling. The floor split into pieces under the rock's weight. Because they were all swimming, no one fell through the hole. However, as the floor caved in, it undermined the corridor's riblike wall supports.

The walls gave way and more of the roof collapsed. The holes opened the tunnel to the battle outside, and Tempest's minions streamed through.

A swarm of predatory fish quickly surrounded the beleaguered fugitives. Mik and the others drew their weapons and slashed at the attacking school. Great clouds of blood soon filled the corridors, attracting even more evil fish.

"Keep going! Keep going!" Ula called, trying to lead the rest down the crumbling tunnel and away from the breaches.

Shimmer followed her, watching the sea elf's back. Small pieces of coral crashed into his armor, but he didn't seem to notice.

A razorfish got past Mik's guard and tore a small gash in Karista's arm. The aristocrat screamed and swung wildly with her borrowed sword. Flailing in the murky water, she sliced across the top of Trip's knee.

The kender yelped, and the magical seaweed nearly popped out of his mouth.

"Give me that!" Mik said, snatching the sword out of Karista's grasp with his left hand. With the cutlass in his right hand, he continued to fend off a big Turbidus leech. "Stay calm!"

"But I'm bleeding!" Karista blurted.

"Not badly," Mik replied, the magic of his necklace projecting his voice clearly. "Stay calm. You okay, Trip?"

"Fine . . ." Trip gasped, nodding. He quickly rolled his pants leg into a makeshift bandage to cover the wound.

The delicious blood proved too much for Mog's fishy escorts. They left their master's side and swarmed ahead. Despite the bloodlust building within him, Mog remained hidden.

Ula cursed, then turned to fend off the new threat. She swam back quickly to the rear of the group, dodging a deadly hail of crumbling coral as she went. "Shimmer, this tunnel is going to collapse before we can get through it," she called. "Can you buy us some time?"

Shimanloreth nodded and, with two quick strokes, moved through the falling boulders to the back of the group. He picked up a huge section of bracing and threw it into the midst of their attackers. Many died, and many others fell back.

Shimmer drew his jagged-edged bronze sword and swung it in wide circles. More attacking fish died in droves, turning the water black with their blood.

Mog crept closer, staying carefully hidden from the humans and their allies.

The beleaguered fugitives retreated. The sharks and their kith swarmed toward them. The tunnel's final collapse, though, seemed imminent. Columns toppled like ninepins, and coral blocks big enough to crush the whole group crashed down from above.

"Keep swimming," Shimmer said grimly. "I can hold the rear."

Mik nodded and led the rest down the corridor. Ula, amazingly quick and agile, helped pull the slower Trip and Karista along. Even so, they barely kept ahead of the ever widening cracks in the walls.

"The tunnel burrows into the reef up ahead," Shimmer called, bringing up the rear. As he spoke, though, a huge slab broke off the ceiling directly above them.

Shimmer surged forward to meet the falling coral. He grew as he swam, his body expanding like an angry pufferfish. His armor twisted and changed. Huge spikes sprouted from his shoulders, and thick, scaly plates covered his arms and legs.

In moments, the knight filled nearly the whole corridor. He pressed his huge back against the ceiling to keep it from collapsing.

"Move!" he growled, his voice booming like thunder through the swirling currents.

Wide-eyed, Mik, Trip, and the rest darted into the safety of the coral hillside beyond, sparing only a few worried glances back for their savior.

Shimmer screamed in pain and, with one final surge, leaped from the collapsing passageway and into the tunnel beyond. He shrank to human size once more as he darted through the falling debris. Huge blocks crashed down on the pursuing fish, killing most of the evil throng. In moments, rubble blocked the corridor behind the fugitives.

Mik quickly slew the few snakelike Turbidus leeches

that had escaped the devastation. "Thanks, Shimmer," he said, panting and feeling bone-weary.

"Yes, thanks," Ula said. "We'd all be fish paste if it wasn't for you."

Shimmer nodded back. He brushed the silt from his armor and gingerly rubbed his left shoulder.

"That was the most amazing thing ever!" spouted Trip. He was out of breath and looked slightly blue.

"We should keep moving," Mik said. "That magical sea-weed can't last forever."

Karista, silt-covered, cut, and bruised, vigorously nodded her agreement.

With pursuit foiled, and the tunnel in no danger of further collapse, they moved quickly into the heart of the huge reef.

No one noticed the green, eel-like shape that wound its way out of the crevasses in the crumbled slabs blocking the corridor. The creature swam forward a short distance and then shuddered and resumed its true shape.

Mog peered into the semi-darkness after the fugitives. There were too many to fight—especially with this strange and powerful bronze knight among their number. He now understood his mistress' burning interest in the group. Taking care not to be seen, the dragonspawn swam down the tunnel after his prey.

* * * * *

The passageway wound deep into the reef before turning toward the surface once more. The fugitives passed numerous side corridors, always choosing the one that ascended most steeply. Small, bioluminescent creatures inhabiting nooks in the coral walls lit their course, giving the tunnels a pale green glow.

Shimmer, battered and weary looking, led the way. He glanced back now and again to make sure the rest were keeping up. They moved continuously, taking little time for rest. Though it seemed unlikely that either Lakuda's people or the dragon would be able to catch them, no one wanted to take any chances.

During one of their brief stops, Mik took the time to properly bandage Trip's leg wound. The kender didn't complain, but his friends noticed that he wasn't swimming with his usual verve. The captain treated Karista's cuts and scrapes as well.

All went well until they came to a three-way branch in the corridor. Shimmer closed his orangish eyes a moment and concentrated before declaring that he detected no preferable route among the three.

"Perhaps they *all* lead to the surface," Mik said hopefully.

"These corridors are part of the Maze," Shimmer replied, his deep voice clear, even through the water. "They're designed to confuse people and keep them from passing beyond the Veil. Chances are that two of these corridors lead to deadly traps."

Karista cursed and leaned against the corridor's rough coral wall. She looked pale and weary.

"Trip," Mik said, "Give Karista some of that extra seaweed I gave back to you."

"Yes," Karista said. "The magic is fading."

Trip nodded and took the small wad out of his pocket. He divided it and gave the larger portion to Lady Meinor.

Mik took a deep breath and leaned back. He felt tired, and slightly dizzy. A warm, almost burning sensation had sprung up in his gut. He slumped to his knees and felt something dig into his thigh.

He fished the diamond artifact out of his belt pocket and held it up. The golden loops felt very warm, and the black gem shone with a dim luminescence.

"A diamond key!" Shimmer said, his eyes shining with fascination. "Where did you get it?"

"Diving on an old wreck," Mik replied. "Ula said it would lead us to the isles. Could it still be working?"

"Yes!" Ula and Shimanloreth said at the same time.

"Hold it up before the passages, Mik," Ula said.

The captain nodded and got to his feet, holding the diamond in his outstretched hand. As he slowly approached each of the three corridors, the artifact sparked slightly toward the one on their left. Mik smiled.

Trip and Karista looked at each other in disbelief.

"The crystal is attuned to the barrier at the end of the maze," Ula explained.

"It's leading us toward the Dragon Isles," Mik added. "Just as it was aboard the ship."

"This way," Ula said, starting up the chosen corridor.

The passage sloped gradually upward and, soon, the way ahead grew brighter.

"Is that moonlight?" Trip asked.

"Not moonlight," Shimmer replied soberly. "The Veil."

"Once we're beyond the Veil," Ula said, "we'll be out of the sea dragon's reach. It'll be trickier for Lakuda to catch us as well."

"*If* you make it through," added Shimmer.

"We?" asked Trip. "Aren't you coming?"

"The Veil is designed to keep unwanted visitors out," Shimmer replied, ignoring his question. "If you are not born of this place, if you are not meant to be here, if you do not have the secret of passage, then you will go no further."

In Mik's mind, the image formed of an immense blue-white diamond waiting somewhere beyond the Veil. He couldn't believe that he'd come so far, only to fail. Somehow, they *would* pass the Veil.

As they swam cautiously over a rise in the tunnel, the barrier appeared before them. The Veil glittered like diamonds in the moonlight—a whirling phantasm of pale colors. The enchantment reached from the tunnel's floor to the ceiling. The magic seeped down through the reef into the earth below and high into the heavens above. The Veil permeated the isles, insulating it from the world outside.

Being so close to the barrier made the fugitives' skin tingle and the hair on the backs of their necks stand up.

Karista swayed woozily as though she might faint. Mik and Trip took her arms and guided her forward.

"Sleek!" Trip gasped.

Even Ula and Shimmer seemed affected as they drew near the enchantment. The sea elf blinked, the glow of the Veil reflecting off her green eyes. The bronze knight appeared to shrink slightly as he approached the barrier.

Mik rubbed his head, trying to remember where he was going or why he'd come to this place. He looked at Trip, wide-eyed and fascinated, then at Karista, more drowsy and confused-looking than either of them.

He felt a burning sensation in his palm and realized that he was still holding the artifact. Opening his fingers, he saw the black diamond glittering brightly within. Its radiance almost matched that of the Veil now.

The diamond's light grew in his mind. He felt his head clear. His resolve to go forward grew firm once more.

"The artifact!" he gasped. "It fights the barrier's effects!" He held the black diamond out before his friends' befuddled faces.

The light of the diamond gleamed in Trip and Karista's staring eyes. The blue-white light danced across their blank faces. The two light forms whirled around each other, finally merging to become pure white brilliance. The Veil's enchantment slipped from the faces of the kender and the aristocrat. They rubbed their heads as though awaking from a deep sleep.

"Beautiful," Karista said.

Trip looked puzzled. "Didn't see it from the ship," he said, then paused to gasp for breath.

"The Veil is only visible when you're very close," Ula replied. "And sometimes, not even then." Mik noticed she kept her eyes averted as she approached the glistening shield.

Shimmer held out one armored palm to the others. "Link hands," he said. "I may be able to lead you through."

Ula took his hand, and Trip took hers. Mik grasped the kender's palm, and Meinor laced her fingers around Mik's hand.

Shimanloreth stepped into the Veil. As he did, a jolt shot through the bodies of the entire group. As the magic surrounded him, the bronze knight flickered and changed—first large, then small, scaly, then spiky. For a moment, he barely looked human, then he appeared as a perfect, glittering knight. He passed through and vanished from the sight of the rest.

Ula followed quickly behind, fighting the barrier's distorting effects. She looked oddly fish-like, before vanishing as she passed through. Trip grew tall and thin, laurels decorating his hair—like a young god returned to Krynn. He pushed beyond the swirling lights and disappeared.

Mik felt the magic assaulting him as he entered. Unseen winds pulled at his hair, and fire burned in his breast. His skin tingled as though he had touched an electric ray. He wondered if his appearance had changed; wondered what he looked like to the others. The kender's strong grip kept pulling him through the barrier. Then something went wrong.

A jolt shot up Mik's arm and he stopped, frozen, in the middle of the Veil. The magic howled around him. Looking back, he saw Karista, wide-eyed and afraid. A huge ball of white fire engulfed their clasped hands.

Mik felt his trapped hand, hot and tingling, but it seemed a very long distance away. In his mind, he heard Karista screaming—though no sound escaped her lips. Her voice sounded shrill and inhuman.

Summoning all his strength, he pushed forward one final time, dragging Karista Meinor with him.

The barrier gave way. Karista surged through the magical eddy, crashing hard into Mik, and they both tumbled out of the Veil on the far side.

They floated there a moment, dazed and exhausted. Karista gasped for breath.

"What happened?" Shimanloreth snapped. "What did you do?"

Behind them, the Veil wavered and rippled, like the surface of a glassy pond into which a large stone has been dropped. In the center of the ripples, the magic seemed to have vanished altogether—though it was slowly reforming at the edges.

"I used the diamond to push my way through," Mik panted. He opened his fingers, revealing the dark form of the diamond artifact.

Shimmer glowered. "None of you were meant to be here," he said.

"We . . . *got through,*" Trip burbled cheerfully.

Mik took a deep breath of enchanted air and felt another scale fall from his necklace. "Trip's right . . ." he said. "The fact that we're here . . . means we're *meant* to be."

The bronze knight crossed his arms over his broad chest, and his eyes narrowed. "Perhaps."

"Lady Meinor is having trouble breathing," Ula said, a touch of concern in her voice.

"Me, too!" blurted Trip.

"The seaweed magic's fading," Mik said.

"The surface can't be far," Ula replied.

"Hurry!" Karista gasped.

They turned and swam quickly upward, Ula, Mik, and Shimmer helping Trip and Karista Meinor.

* * * * *

Mog's brain ached. He'd followed the fugitives through the tunnels for what seemed like hours. Several times, he became confused and almost lost sight of them before his keen nose set him straight again.

The water around him surged with unexpected currents. The sides of the passages wavered. Once he found himself turned completely around and realized his mistake only just in time to avoid losing his prey.

The problem grew steadily worse as he went. The tides roared in his ears, tiny glittering fish danced before his eyes, and his skin crawled with even more worms than usual. The Turbidus leech attached to his spine—his connection to Tempest—burned like a molten sword.

He almost turned back, but the thought of the sea dragon's wrath spurred him on. Ahead, he dimly saw the shapes of his quarry. They had stopped at some kind of glowing barrier. Mog tried to swim closer but found he couldn't. He bumped into one of the coral walls and clung there, dizzy and sick to his stomach.

A jolt shot through the water. Mog bit his tongue to keep from screaming. He looked up just as Karista Meinor passed through the Veil.

His mind suddenly cleared, and the dragonspawn swam cautiously forward as his prey disappeared into the distance. Ahead, the Veil wavered and rippled around a rapidly contracting hole in its enchantment.

Mog shot forward, swimming as quickly as he knew how. He thrust his scaly body toward the opening, but it shrank even as he did so.

His head slammed into the shimmering barrier. Fire shot down his spine, and his limbs twitched uncontrollably. His mouth felt as though it were full of sea urchins. Every scale on his body throbbed; his red eyes ached as though he'd rubbed them with sand.

He blinked back the pain and saw the Veil closing before him.

Summoning every iota of energy in his scaly flesh, he transformed into a sea snake and slithered through the hole just as it snapped shut.

Exhausted, he became Mog once more and settled into the sand at the bottom of the tunnel beyond the enchanted barrier.

His head felt clearer now, though his body ached as though a reef had fallen on top of him. The Turbidus leech burrowed into his mind howled with pain and indignation. It called to its dark mistress. Vaguely, like an echo in a typhoon, Mog heard Tempest respond.

For once, he ignored her and simply passed out.

* * * * *

Pure blue-white illumination flooded the tunnel ahead of them.

"Moonlight!" Trip bubbled. "For sure!"

The light rekindled the hopes of the weary fugitives, and they swam quickly toward it. An opening in the coral, distant and wavering, beckoned before them.

The tunnel leveled out and they walked up, out of the brine, onto a sandy-floored passageway.

Karista knelt at the water's edge and spat the seaweed from her mouth. She sputtered and gasped for breath. "At last!" she said. "Thank the lost gods we made it!"

Trip pulled the magical seaweed out of his mouth and stuffed it into one of the pockets of his snake skin vest. "Hope I won't need *that* again anytime soon," he said.

"C'mon," Mik said, leaning wearily against one wall of the tunnel. "It's not much farther." He glanced from his shipmates toward the sea elf and the knight.

Shimanloreth stood solidly on his bronze legs at the front of the group, waiting for the others to catch up. Ula leaned on her borrowed spear, taking a moment to catch her wind. Mik noticed that a circle of dolphins tattooed on her smooth, blue shoulder glittered slightly in the moonlight.

"Where do we go from here?" he silently wondered. An image of the huge blue-white diamond appeared in his mind, but he pushed it aside.

He and Trip helped Karista to her feet, and the three of them staggered after the sea dwellers and toward the light. It took them only a few moments to walk up, out of the tunnel and into the fresh air once more.

They emerged on a tiny coral atoll, its surface just tall enough to avoid submerging during high tide. They came out of the tunnel facing west, toward the way they'd come. Back, beyond the Veil, the ocean boiled with the sea dragon's fury. Stormclouds clashed overhead, and lightning flashed down into the breakers with frightening regularity. The crash of thunder and the roar of the winds seemed oddly distant—unreal—as though the storm were part of another world.

Somewhere below those waves, the people of Reeftown were still fighting and dying. Mik felt glad that he and his friends were no longer a part of that terrible struggle. He turned to the east, away from the storm, and his heart filled with wonder.

Overhead, the moon shone brightly amid a field of twinkling stars. A mantle of purple and deep blue draped the sky, fading to violet and pink near the eastern horizon. The sun had not risen yet, but already its glow painted the skyline with the colors of the coming day.

The ocean lay still and quiet, reflecting the moon and the stars in its mirror-like, azure surface.

Dotting the placid waters, like emeralds on an opal sea, lay the Dragon Isles.

PART II

THE DRAGON ISLES

Chapter
Seventeen

Beyond the Veil

Tempest's massive jaws snapped shut, splintering the coral tower into shards. She chewed twice, to stop the annoying thrashing of the building's defenders, then swallowed.

It had been a long time since the dragon had enjoyed herself so thoroughly. Around her, Reeftown lay in shambles. Blood stained the night sea black.

The sea elves fought back against the sharks, razorfish, Turbidus leeches, and Tempest's cadre of dragonspawn. But with the titanic dragon leading them, the Reeftowners stood little chance.

Tempest bit another elf in half, savoring the sweet blood as it rolled down her gullet. She butted her massive head against a bony woman trying to poke her with a spear. The woman sailed through the water and crashed into a crumbling coral wall. The wall collapsed, burying the spear carrier.

The dragon surged forward, shattering an old shipwreck that had been converted into a tavern. The patrons hiding inside scattered like minnows. Tempest gulped them down one by one.

Something tugged at the dragon's mind.

It took a few moments for her to recognize the familiar thoughts calling inside her brain.

The Veil! One of her minions had actually made it to the Veil's final barrier!

In an instant, Tempest ripped the vital knowledge from the informant's mind. Instantly, the path before her became clear.

Turning, she surged toward the distant reef, leaving her minions to fend for themselves.

The Veil shimmered ahead of her, penetrating reef and sea and sky. At its base stood a huge stone dragon, seemingly carved from the very bedrock. The statue's diamond eyes blazed with the power of ancient enchantment.

The sea dragon hissed her anger and dived forward. As she approached, the Veil's magic flickered, as though momentarily weakened.

Tempest flung herself against the barrier, summoning all her arcane might as she did so. The Veil shuddered, yielded slightly, then wrapped itself around the dragon's huge form.

Lightning flashed from both sea and sky. Tempest felt the Veil weaken, then spring back. She pushed forward, her titanic muscles burning with the effort. The barrier surged around her, turning the dragon's own force back against her. She flayed it with spells, but the magic ricocheted back against her iron scales. Tempest roared with fury and indignation.

The enchantment of the Veil swirled, twisting her mind and body. The evil fish who had accompanied her flailed about aimlessly, lost and confused. She tried to call them, but the Veil buzzed in her head, confusing her commands.

Through the whirlpool energies she saw the blazing eyes of the ancient statue. With a powerful slash of her flukes she propelled herself toward it. Energy from the diamond eyes leaped up, meeting the sea dragon head on.

Her mind reeled. She lashed out against it, smashing coral and stone with her talons and flukes. The sea bed shuddered with the assault. Currents swirled around her like a whirlpool. She summoned lightning, maelstroms, life-sucking darkness, and deadly rip-tides, and blasted them against the Veil's power.

Again she struck, again and again. Weariness drew over her mind, but still she turned and attacked. She battered her body against the magic until her scales bled. The world became a timeless, crimson haze.

Then the resistance ceased.

Tempest opened her yellow eyes, triumph filling her rotten heart. She looked for the hated isles and saw—

The reef, nearly a league away through dark, clouded waters. At its base a statue with glowing eyes, standing unmolested on the sea floor. And beyond the statue, her dragonish senses detected the Veil, still standing.

She had failed.

Once more, the ancient magic had tricked and confused her. Once more it had deceived her senses. The dragon howled her rage, belching a scalding torrent into the brine.

She devoured those of her minions unfortunate enough to be lurking nearby. The Turbidus leeches ringing Tempest's neck hissed with delight as they gobbled up the scraps.

By the time Tempest finally regained her composure, the morning sun was just peeking over the corner of the world.

"How?" the sea dragon wondered. "How do those small, weak creatures penetrate the barrier when I cannot?"

Very faintly, in the back of her mind, she heard Mog's answer: "A diamond," he said. "They used an enchanted diamond. They summoned its magic, and the barrier parted."

"Yes!" Revelation dawned in Tempest's mind.

"The black diamond would not be large enough for you, great mistress," Mog told her in his thoughts.

"No," Tempest agreed, "surely it is too small. There is one larger, though. The hated dragons placed an ancient diamond at the root of the Veil. It must be the key that opens all."

Pictures formed in her reptilian mind, a huge, glowing gem shining in the sky and a temple sunk beneath the waves.

More pictures came, elves and humans, and even a tasty kender, searching for the lost treasure. Tempest smiled.

"They will find the key to the ancient magic," she said to Mog. "And when they do, the Dragon Isles shall be mine."

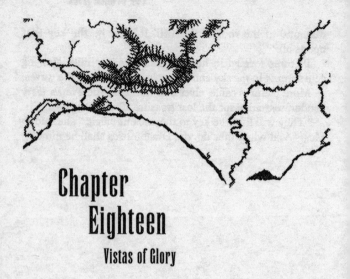

Chapter Eighteen

Vistas of Glory

S unrise lit the mountains of the Dragon Isles crimson and gold, making the snowy peaks glitter as though they were on fire. The archipelago dotted the glassy sea like exquisitely formed gems set down on an azure mirror.

Some isles lay so near that Mik could hear the whispers of the surf upon their shores. Others were so distant as to be only mirages on the far horizon. A few were tall and proud, thrusting towering mountains high into the air. Others crouched low in the water, like enormous basking sea turtles. A number of the isles looked big enough to hide large populations of people and even dragons. Some were so small that they could have disappeared entirely down a leviathan's gullet. Lush greenery tumbled down the sides of even the smallest keys.

Standing at the edge of this glory, it was hard to imagine a more perfect morning. No clouds besmirched the clear blue sky overhead. The sounds of the storm to the west had died away. A warm breeze wafted the earthy scent of the distant shores to the small band of fugitives.

"It's beautiful," Mik said, his voice low and welling with emotion.

Trip and Karista, too dazzled to say anything, nodded their agreement.

"So it seems," Shimmer murmured.

Ula leaned against her spear and gazed out over the quiet sea. "I wasn't sure I'd ever see this place again. I wasn't sure I *wanted* to."

"Imagine the wealth," Karista whispered. "Imagine the glory of opening a trade route to these isles."

Ula laughed. "Imagine being smashed on the reefs, or being devoured by dragons, or destroyed by the Veil in trying to bring an unwanted ship here," she said.

Karista scowled. "We passed the Veil ourselves. Surely there is a way for a fleet of ships to do it. You said yourselves that island privateers use crystals—like Mik Vardan's diamond—to sail back and forth through the Veil."

"With the blessing of the dragon overlords," Ula said.

"And such blessing is not easily won," added Shimmer. He rubbed his left shoulder absentmindedly.

Mik smiled. "On a morning this glorious," he said, "anything seems possible. Try to win your trade deal, Karista. I wish you well at it. Who's to say you can't? We all deserve a share of good luck after what we've been through." He stretched his arms wide to welcome the coming dawn and, in his mind, saw a glittering white diamond.

Shimanloreth stared out from behind his bronze helmet. His orange eyes looked grim. "I fear our trials are just beginning," he said. "Lakuda won't be pleased when she finds I've helped set you free. . . ."

"It would be just like that witch to send someone after us," Ula said. A grim smile cracked her pretty lips. "Not that they'd have much chance." She twirled her borrowed spear through the air, gauging the feel of the weapon on land.

"You think she'd waste her time?" Mik asked. "She said we weren't much of a catch."

"Lakuda is a proud woman," Shimmer replied. "Offended, she might do any number of foolish things."

"And Shimmer leaving is bound to offend her," Ula added, with a sly glance at the knight.

"Assuming," said Karista, "that Lakuda has lived through the dragon's attack."

"What's that?" Trip asked, pointing to something high in the sky.

At first, the creature looked like a distant bird circling above them. It grew larger as it descended—larger and larger still. The rising sun glinted off its beating wings and its armored back. It burned orange in the dawn, a creature of living fire.

"A dragon!" Ula said, making it sound like a curse.

"Sleek!" said Trip.

Awe and fear battled within Mik's heart, and his jaw went slack. True, the dragon was beautiful, but he found it hard to share the kender's enthusiasm.

Beside him, Karista gasped with terror.

"Brass, from the look of him," Shimmer commented. "He must patrol this area."

As he spoke, the dragon dived at them. The fugitives—all but Shimmer—instinctively ducked as the creature swooped low overhead. They felt the wind from its huge wings and heard the breath heave in its monstrous lungs. Its brass scales rattled like the armor of a battalion marching to war. Its talons, each as long as man's arm, shone like polished swords. The wyrm's green eyes blazed with fierce intelligence.

The dragon arced back into the sky, turning northwest toward one of the nearby islands. As it winged low over the isle and disappeared, Mik, Trip, Ula, and Karista rose once more; Shimmer gazed stoically after the departing beast.

"Did you see?" Trip said enthusiastically. "That was amazing!"

"We saw," Mik said, suppressing a shudder. He took a deep breath to regain his courage.

Shimmer rubbed the chin of his faceplate. "Kender have an odd sense of fun."

"Do you think one would give me a ride?" Trip asked, jumping up and down with glee.

"In its stomach, perhaps," Ula replied.

Mik looked at Shimmer. "You said it was patrolling. Patrolling for what?"

"Intruders. Outsiders," Shimmer replied. "People like you."

"And now that it's seen us," Karista asked nervously, "what will it do?"

"Consult its superiors," the bronze knight said. "Find out if it should kill you, capture you, or leave you be."

"We should," Ula said, "hide out under the nearest key until nightfall."

"The water's not an option," Mik said. "The magic of the seaweed is exhausted. Trip and Karista were lucky to make it out of the tunnels. We can't go back. There must be some other way off this reef."

"We could swim," Ula said.

"What about sharks?" Karista asked.

Ula turned to the bronze knight and said, "Shimmer, can you carry us to that atoll?" She pointed to a tiny island nearby.

Shimanloreth glanced from the beautiful sea elf to the others. He rubbed his left shoulder self-consciously. "Not all of you," he said. "Not all at once."

"How could he carry us across the water?" Trip asked.

Ula ignored him. "Then start with the aristocrat," she said. "I'll swim."

"I can swim, as well," Mik said. He ran his fingers over the surface of his fish necklace and was disturbed by the number of gemstones missing. He took a deep breath and put his doubts aside.

"Boy, that's something!" Trip blurted. "A moment ago, the sea was clear. Now there's a mist rolling in faster than any I've ever seen. The Dragon Isles are full of amazing things!"

Mik and the rest turned and saw a low bank of white fog scudding over the water toward them. It rounded the closest island and came with the speed of a gale-driven stormcloud, heading straight for the narrow reef.

Ula cursed. "Too late, now." She set her spear and gazed at the approaching cloud. "Brace yourselves. This could be bad."

Mik and the others—save Shimanloreth—drew their weapons. The bronze knight merely folded his arms and stood waiting.

As the fog drew closer, strange sounds echoed across the waves. First came a vague, rhythmic thrum—chanting or singing perhaps. A pulsing splashing sound followed, mingling with the thrum. Finally, a metallic creaking, like huge door hinges swinging back and forth, completed the weird chorus.

A bright yellowish shape took form in the center of the cloud. It was long and sinuous, raised up in the front like the head of a huge serpent.

"Another dragon!" piped Trip.

Shimmer put his armored hand over his eyes to block out the glare from the rising sun. "No," he said. "It's Lord and Lady Kell. You really might want to leave, Ula."

"I'd never give them the satisfaction," the beautiful sea elf replied. She tightened her grip on her spear.

"Back oars!" a woman's voice called over the chorus of strange noises.

The cloud of mist parted, and a huge dragon-headed trireme surged toward the reef. The ship was nearly twice as long as *Kingfisher*. Bright brass scales adorned its sides. Its three banks of oars moved in perfect unison, sculling the huge craft effortlessly through the water. Below the carved dragon head on its bow lay a wicked-looking brass ram.

The great ship turned gently and came to a stop thirty yards away from the coral reef. A muscular, auburn-haired woman sauntered from the deck to the ship's stern. Her stylish brass armor revealed nearly as much of her impressive anatomy as it covered. She leaned on the rail and regarded the castaways.

"Stand to and prepare to come aboard," the woman called. "We're taking you into the custody of the Order of Brass."

"We don't recognize your authority," Ula called back. "We're free people, and we'll do as we please. Perhaps if you ask nicely, we'll accept a ride. Which way are you headed?"

"I recognize *you,* Ula Landwalker," the woman said. "You're a well-known malcontent."

"Ula *Drakenvaal,*" the sea elf corrected. "My family never formally disowned me. I still maintain my rights as a citizen of the Isles, Misa Kell."

"The Order will determine that," Lady Kell replied.

A tall, similarly dressed, auburn-haired man joined Lady Kell at the rail. In his left hand, he held a long lance the color of pale orange coral. "We don't want to use force," he said, "but we will, if necessary. All intruders must be taken to Berann to judge their worthiness."

Shimmer stepped forward. "Will you judge me also, Benthor Kell?" he said, his deep voice echoing over the water.

Benthor and Misa Kell exchanged a wary glance.

"Forgive us, Shimanloreth," Lady Kell said, bowing slightly. "We did not recognize you at first. The report of our scout was . . . incomplete."

"Of course we don't presume to judge you," Lord Kell continued. "You are free to go your own way. However— by the rules of the Order of Brass—your companions must come with us."

"And if I refuse to let you take them?" Shimmer asked.

"Our escort, Tanalish, is not far off," Lady Kell replied. "She will help us enforce the law if need be."

"Surely that will not be necessary, Shimanloreth," Lord Kell added. "You know that these laws are vital for the safety of the Isles. You may come or go as you please. The rest, however, must accompany us."

As he said it, two dozen brass-armored warriors appeared at the gunwale. They stood with their swords at the ready, though none threatened Shimmer or the others directly.

Mik glanced at Trip and Karista. "It seems we have no choice," he whispered.

"They appear genteel enough," Karista said. "The elf and her friend may have been lying to us. We should go with this Order of Brass."

"My goals and yours," Mik replied, "are not entirely the same here. Nevertheless . . ."

He turned to lord and lady Kell and bowed slightly. "My companions and I," he said, indicating Trip and Karista, "will do as you request."

"No!" Ula hissed at him.

Shimmer put a gentle hand on her shoulder. "There is no other way," he whispered.

"We are shipwrecked travelers, of no threat to anyone," Mik continued, "and look forward to your hospitality."

"Our recent fortunes have been grave," Karista added. "We hope that meeting you may reverse our bad luck."

"Flattery will gain you nothing," Lord Kell replied. "The law sees through such shams. However, I welcome you aboard and will treat you fairly during our journey to Berann."

"Come alongside the reef!" Lady Kell called to her helmswoman. A drumchanter beside the tiller began to chant and the banks of oars dipped into the water once more. The galley executed a graceful turn and stopped only a few yards from the reef.

The warriors put a long boarding plank into the water and Mik, Trip, and Karista walked up it onto the deck of the brass boat.

"Well, Landwalker?" Lady Kell called. "Will you board as well, or shall we summon Tanalish?"

Ula glanced from Lady Kell to Shimmer, and then to Mik standing near the dragonship's rail. Fire burned in the sea elf's green eyes.

"We'll come aboard," Ula said.

She and Shimmer walked up the plank onto the galley's deck.

As Lady Kell escorted the prisoners to the bow and set guards around them—all save Shimanloreth. Lord Kell gave orders to the helm and oarsmen. A fine mist sprang up around them as the sleek dragonship cut through the water once more.

They sped quickly over the placid ocean, passing the small nearby keys and heading northwest toward a large wooded island crowned with snowcapped peaks.

"You should hide the artifact and the parchment with the Prophecy, or they may confiscate them," Ula hissed at Mik.

"I'll do what I can with the diamond," he said. "As to the Prophecy, it's already hidden in the best place of all."

"Where?" she asked.

In reply, he merely tapped his skull and smiled.

She nodded in return and whispered, "If you still want to try for that fortune, support me when I make my play."

"Have you figured a way out of here?" he asked.

"Maybe," she replied. "I can't fight the whole Order of Brass, but . . ."

Mik looked puzzled, but she said no more.

"Where are we going?" Trip asked their brass-armored captors. He hopped to the rail and leaned out over the gunwale so far that he nearly toppled into the drink.

"Berann," Lady Kell replied. "Home of the Order of Brass and our lord Thrakdar."

"A bag of wind," Shimmer grumbled. "Both him and his uncle Thracktil."

Misa Kell's eyes narrowed, but she did not react to what the bronze knight said. Instead, she turned to the others and said, "Turn over your weapons. We will return them to you after judgment."

"And if we're judged unworthy?" Mik asked, his hand resting on the pommel of his scimitar.

"Then they will be returned when you are cast adrift beyond the Veil," Lady Kell replied.

Ula rose from where she had been sitting, her spear clenched tightly in her fist. "I am no common prisoner," she said. "I will not give up my weapons."

"It is the law, Ula Landwalker," Lady Kell said.

"You apply your laws capriciously, Misa Kell," Ula replied. "They do not bind me. I am a Drakenvaal. I will not submit to you, or your order, or your laws. I am bound by the customs of *my* people—the Dargonesti. We roamed the seas when your people were but babes. Only the Dargonesti can deprive me of arms; only they can judge me. I demand that you take me to Darthalla."

Mik glanced at Ula, and saw cunning in her eyes. He nodded that he was with her.

"Those were the old ways, Landwalker," Lady Kell said. "Things are different since the gods of good and their dragon consorts left Krynn. Things have changed in the isles, and order must be maintained."

"Has honor changed as well, then?" Ula asked.

Misa Kell looked offended. "How could the laws of honor change?" she said haughtily.

A sly smile broke over Ula's beautiful face. "Then I demand honorable justice," she said.

"What do you mean?" Lady Kell asked.

"I demand trial by combat."

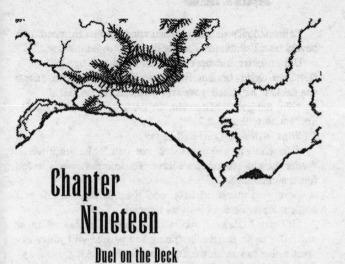

Chapter Nineteen

Duel on the Deck

Trip elbowed Mik. "What's she up to?" the kender asked.

"Trying to keep us out of prison," Mik replied, though he wished that he felt more sure of the sea elf's impromptu plan.

Lord Kell strode from the bridge to where Ula and the rest stood in the bow of the dragonship. In his left hand he held his long coral lance clutched tight. He took up a defensive posture beside his sister.

Misa Kell's gaze narrowed, and her brow furrowed with anger. She stared unblinking into the sea elf's green eyes.

"This is absurd," Benthor Kell said. "The law is clear, Ula Drakenvaal. You—and the rest—must accompany us to Berann."

"The Code of Honor is older than your order's laws," Ula said, never taking her eyes off Misa. "If you've abandoned it, say so."

Benthor Kell's rugged jaw tightened, and he frowned. "We would no more abandon honor than we would the law."

"Then I demand my rights," Ula said.

"Very well," Lord Kell replied, hefting his lance. "Clear the decks!" he called. "We will give this elf her trial."

"No, Benthor," Misa said. "It is *I* who was challenged—and I who will accept."

"But, sister—" Lord Kell began.

"Ula challenged your sister, not you," Mik improvised. "Only the challenged can accept. To do otherwise is to forfeit the challenge."

Lord Kell glared at Mik, and then at the sea elf. Mik smiled, knowing the lord was trapped.

"If I win," Ula said, "you will release the castaways to me and take us to Darthalla. There my people will judge our worthiness to stay in the Dragon Isles."

"And if you lose?" Mik whispered.

Ula winked at him. "Then we all go to Berann and stand before the Order." She turned to Lady Kell and in a louder voice said. "Do you accept the terms of the challenge?"

Karista Meinor looked from Ula to Lady Kell. She seemed to be weighing her options, but said nothing. Trip clapped gleefully in anticipation of the fight.

"I accept," Misa Kell replied through gritted teeth. "Clear the deck and we'll settle this." She loosened her brass-handled sword from its scabbard and tossed the sheath toward the stern deck.

The crew moved away from the center of the trireme's midship platform, leaving the women plenty of room to fight. Ula glanced at Mik. "Have Shimmer make sure they play fair," she said loudly.

Mikal Vardan nodded, as did bronze knight. Ula turned back to her opponent, spear at the ready.

With a snarl of rage, Misa charged forward. She swung at Ula's head, but the sea elf ducked out of the way.

Ula flipped her spear and clouted the brass-armored woman in the lower back. Misa staggered and barely ducked aside in time to avoid Ula's follow-up thrust. Lady Kell brought her sword up against the spear's haft and turned the weapon aside.

"You fight well," Misa snarled, "for someone dressed like a camp follower."

Ula laughed. "So do you."

Misa chopped at Ula's midsection, but the sea elf stepped back, her bare feet moving gracefully over the ship's smooth wooden deck. She pirouetted, spun her weapon, and clouted Lady Kell on the side of the head with the spear's butt. Misa reeled from the impact.

"She's fast!" Trip whispered, admiring Ula's grace.

"She's used to fighting in the pressure of the deep," Mik whispered back. "Above water, she's much quicker than any of us. Stronger, too, probably."

"Stronger than Lady Kell, I hope," Trip replied.

Misa Kell waved her sword before her as she staggered back. The brass weapon turned aside two of the sea elf's thrusts—more by luck than design. Ula stabbed at her again, and this time the blow got through, tracing a long cut down Misa's pale ribs.

"That scanty armor is just slowing you down," Ula noted. "You should design your next set for protection rather than show."

"Elf witch!" Misa snarled. "Stand still and fight!" She lunged forward suddenly and got her sword under Ula's guard. Ula turned Misa's blade aside, but they crashed together and the two of them fell to the deck in a heap.

Their arms and legs tangled as they wrestled across the deck, each trying to position her weapon for a telling blow. Misa smashed the pommel of her sword into Ula's hip. The sea elf grunted and clouted the brass lady on the chin with her fist.

Blood spurted from Misa's mouth. She tried to grab Ula's arm, but only ended up with a handful of jewelry from the sea elf's sparse clothing. A few tiny gems rolled across the planking and briefly settled onto the deck before finding their way into Trip's pockets.

Ula rammed her knee into Lady Kell's exposed gut. The air rushed out of Misa's lungs and Ula rolled out from under her. The Dargonesti quickly scrambled to her feet. Bloody-faced, Lady Kell did the same.

Panting, the two women regarded each other across the blood spattered deck.

"Slippery as a scavenger eel," Misa growled.

"And with twice the bite," Ula countered. "Submit. You're outmatched."

"Never!"

Ula lunged forward, stabbing at Lady Kell's midsection. Misa parried, but that was exactly what Ula wanted.

The sea elf allowed the shaft of her spear to skid up Misa's sword blade. Ula heaved hard, pushing the sword to the left, then thrust right.

She drove the spear point up, into the unprotected flesh just below Misa's shoulder guard. Lady Kell gasped. Her eyes grew wide, and her sword went limp in her hand. Ula gave her spear a final twist and thrust her opponent to the floor.

Lady Kell slumped to her knees. Ula pulled her spear out of her opponent's shoulder and stepped away. Misa gasped once and then collapsed on the deck, unconscious and bleeding.

Mik knelt down, tore off the sleeve of his shirt, and pressed it over Misa's wound. "Get a healer," he said, glancing up at Ula. The satisfied smile on her face sent a shiver down his spine.

"Get away from her, freebooter," Lord Kell said, pushing Mik out of the way. A woman dressed in white stepped forward and knelt beside her lord and lady. She began to minister to Misa Kell's wound.

"The wound is deep, my lord," the white-robed woman said. "It will take all my skill to stop the bleeding."

Fire blazed in Benthor Kell's gray eyes. "There was no need for you to wound her thus," he said, glaring at Ula.

"Ula gave her the chance to withdraw," Mik said.

"This was no game she and you entered into," Ula said, her green eyes flashing. "If you two weren't prepared to pay the price, you shouldn't have challenged my rights."

Lord Kell stood and drew his sword. Ula took a step back and aimed the bloody point of her spear at his chest. The two of them glowered at each other across the crimson stained deck.

"I should gut you where you stand," Lord Kell hissed through clenched teeth.

"Is this how you honor the laws of combat?" Ula asked. Shimmer took up a position behind her.

"It was a fair fight," Mik said, stepping between Kell and Ula.

Kell lowered his sword. "I will honor our word," he said tersely. "You and your friends have won the right to be judged by the Dargonesti." He turned toward the white-robed woman, "How is my sister?"

"Her injury is grave," the healer replied. "My power is not what it was before the gods departed. It will take a long time to heal."

"Take Lady Kell to her cabin and tend her there," Lord Kell said. He pointed to several brass-armored warriors and said, "Help the healer carry my sister."

The warriors nodded and assisted the healer in taking Misa Kell below deck. They moved slowly and deliberately so as not to aggravate the lady's wound. Lord Kell, his manner stern and formal, turned back to Ula.

"We sail for Darthalla," he said. "The others will go with you, all save the kender."

"Unacceptable," said Mik.

Ula shot him a stern glance.

Kell ignored the sailor and addressed Ula directly. "You know the laws concerning his kind. The code of your people is no different than ours. He must be taken to kendertown on the isle of Alarl."

"My people can take him to the city of Perch as easily as yours," Ula said.

"I think not," Kell replied. "Besides, we both know kender are slippery and hard to hold onto. Better he should stay with me—unless you'd care to dispute my claim . . . ?" He arched one auburn eyebrow and smiled wickedly.

Mik stepped forward, but Ula held him back. "Don't," she whispered.

"I'm not going to let him take Trip," Mik replied.

"You can't defeat him," Ula said. "We're both tired now. Kell would best either of us easily—which is exactly what he wants. Don't give in to him."

Mik glanced at Trip, then at Kell. The lord practically glowed with eagerness to fight. Mik felt the weariness within his own bones. He had barely slept in two days. Ula was right; Kell would win easily.

"We don't find the treasure without him," Mik whispered to Ula.

She nodded. "If you insist," she said. "We can pick him up later—after we've escaped Kell's clutches."

Ula turned back to Lord Kell and smiled. "As you say, Lord Kell, there's no point in fighting over a kender."

Trip jumped up and kicked Ula in the shin. "Hey!" he said. "I was rooting for you!"

Mik stepped forward and grabbed Trip by the shoulder as the kender reached for his daggers. "Belay that!" Mik whispered. "Hold your weapons! I'll explain later."

The captain reassured the kender with a look, and Trip stopped struggling.

Ula rubbed her leg and laughed. "He's given me better than the lady of the ship," she said with a wry smile. "You keep him, Kell. He's more trouble than he's worth."

Mik kept his hand firmly on Trip's shoulder. "I won't have you mistreating him," he said to Kell.

"Even kender are treated fairly by the Order of Brass," Kell replied haughtily.

"I'll take that on your honor," Mik said. "We've had a long and difficult journey. We're all tired and hungry. Any help you could give in that regard would be welcome."

Kell turned to a deck hand and said. "Bring them food and drink."

"I could use a clean bandage for my leg," Trip said. "Please."

"Have our healer tend the kender's leg when she has a spare moment," Kell added. "As to accommodations, you may sleep on the deck with the rest of the crew. We will, however, provide blankets." He nodded at the deck hand, who had stood awaiting the end of Kell's orders.

The hand nodded in reply and left to fetch provisions for Mik and the rest.

Lord Kell went to the ship's rear platform and gave their new heading to the helmsman. The ship's drum-chanter set the beat and began the rhythmic singing that Mik and his friends had first heard when Kell's galley emerged from the fog.

Kell took up his seat in the triarch's chair at the boat's stern. He made a tent of his fingers and glowered at Mik, Ula, and the rest.

The deck hand soon returned with five skins of water, a small flask of weak wine, some dried meat and bread, and a few light blankets. Shimmer declined to eat anything, though he drank some of the water.

Mik, Trip, Ula, and Karista ate as though they had not eaten for days. They savored each drop and morsel, and soon began feel themselves once more.

Solemnly, Mik offered a toast to their dead comrades. Even Ula joined in as they passed the wine and everyone told a brief story of Bok, Marlian, or some other lost crewmate.

Mik raised the wine flask again. "To the death of the dragon who caused all this!" he said.

Trip, Ula, and Karista murmured their assent and drank.

"I'll share that toast," Shimmer said. Mik handed him the skin and the bronze knight said, "To the end of Tempest and those who follow her!" He drank, then handed the flask back to Mik.

Morning slipped into afternoon under the steady rhythm of the oars. The crew tirelessly pulled the mighty trireme through the placid ocean. Mik and his friends spent much of their time leaning on the gunwales watching the scenery.

The sea around the Dragon Isles shone brilliant blue. The clear water allowed the travelers to peer into the depths below. Mik marveled at the varieties of colorful fish and strange sea plants. Turbidus dolphins and gray-striped porpoises, sleek "sea tigers," gamboled in the trireme's wake.

Small green atolls surrounded the larger islands, like schools of fish attending to monstrous turtles. The isles had a pristine quality, as if human beings had never actually lived here—though, occasionally, Mik saw small fishing boats plying the shorelines. Two kinds of waterfronts predominated: white sand, or forbidding rocks. Many game animals roamed the shores, but only a few people.

The clear morning sky gave way to puffy clouds, darkening toward a storm in the west. Blue and purple sea birds filled the air near the shores, diving for fish or hunting for prey along the beaches. Sometimes an albatross, a pelican, or some other sea-fishing bird would fly over the trireme.

Less frequently, they spotted the glint of sunshine off metallic wings high above the isles. Mostly the dragons were far away, and seemed to be tending their own business. Several times, though, a large brass dragon swooped near the galley.

"Tanalish," Shimmer said.

"Keeping an eye on us for Thrakdar and the Order," Ula added. She tightened her grip on her spear. "They're probably wondering why we're not headed for Berann."

"Let them wonder," Shimmer replied. His face remained hidden behind his bronze helmet, but they all got the impression he was smiling.

Mik leaned on the rail and sighed. "I wish that Poul were here to see this," he said. "He would have liked the dragons."

"Aye," Trip replied. Karista merely nodded.

Just before nightfall, the healer came and sterilized Trip's wound with alcohol. She put a few stitches in, then wound an new bandage around the kender's leg. She chanted a spell for quick healing, but no one seemed to believe this would do any good.

Lord Kell stayed away from the group. Mostly he kept to the triarch's chair, though he went below regularly to check on his sister. From the vague murmurings of the crew, Mik gathered that Misa wasn't doing very well. All of Kell's crew avoided Ula.

As the sun sank behind the clouds in the west, they passed into the vast channel between Berann and Jaentarth. Berann, the western isle, housed the headquarters of the Order of Brass. The galley's crew gazed at it longingly when they weren't working their shifts at the oars.

To the east lay Jaentarth, whose cloud-capped peaks were home to many silver dragons. Lush jungles tumbled down to the isle's rocky shores. As the trireme swung northeast, skirting Jaentarth's western cliffs, Ula stood in the bow and gazed east. A thin line of concern between her slender eyebrows marred her perfect face.

"I get the impression," Mik said quietly to Shimmer, "that she's *not* looking forward to going home."

The bronze knight didn't reply.

Night passed under a tapestry of stars. Mik and the others slept on the deck near the bow. The blankets given them were thin, but the night was warm. At dawn, the former captain found himself wedged between Ula and Karista. He gently extricated himself, rose, and went to the rail.

The morning wasn't so bright or clear as it had been the previous day. Thunder clouds still threatened in the west. However, by rowing through the night, the ship had stayed well ahead of the stormfront.

Mik admired the discipline of Kell's crew. They pulled at the oars tirelessly, working in shifts, never stopping. When not rowing or servicing the ship, the brass warriors frequently fished with lines or tridents.

135

Sometimes they even stripped off their armor and swam in the stern wash for a while—as Ula had done on *Kingfisher*, what now seemed so long ago. Kell's warriors always held a rope line when swimming, otherwise the trireme's relentless pace would have quickly left them behind.

Mist surrounded the galley during the early morning hours. Mik wondered if this was some kind of natural effect, peculiar to the area of the ocean and the boat's brass-coated construction, or if it was magic. Certainly the boat covered great distances in a very short time. Whether this was due to enchantment or to the dedication and training of the crew, *Kingfisher*'s former captain could not fathom.

Lord Kell treated his "guests" cordially that day, all save for Ula, whose gaze he avoided. Whispers among the galley's crew told the fugitives that Lady Kell's health remained in dire straits. Both Kell and the crew blamed Ula for this. "Unnecessarily brutal," the crew whispered, but only when they thought the sea elf wasn't listening. Mik suspected that the warriors applied different standards to "outsiders" than they did to the Order of Brass.

The dragon overflights continued during the second day. Most of the time the brass dragon watching them was Tanalish, Kell's dragon escort. Once, though, Shimmer identified their "guardian" as Thrakdar—sponsor of the Order.

"Probably wondering what's taking Kell so long," Mik commented.

"I'm sure he wants his pet warriors back," Ula said slyly. She glanced toward Kell, sitting in the triarch's chair.

A quick-moving squall blew through that night. It tossed the galley about and smashed lightning into the sea far too close to the brass-scaled ship. Lord Kell watched the storm carefully, and the crew on deck worked without their usual brass armor.

The soaking annoyed Mik and his friends. Shimmer and Ula appeared not to notice or, at least, not to care.

"I expect they're used to being drenched, living underwater," Trip said.

Mik, Trip, and Karista huddled close together for warmth under their thin blankets that night.

A spectacular golden sunrise quickly dried them the next morning. They rowed for several more hours, until Lord Kell finally had the crew back oars, bringing the trireme to a halt.

"This isn't Darthalla," Ula said, scanning the ocean to the east.

"Darthalla would take us too far off our course," Kell replied. "My sister is failing, and needs better attention than we can give her aboard ship. I will loan you a ship's boat, and you and your companions may continue on your own. Darthalla is not far, and you should be able to row there by day's end."

"That wasn't our agreement," Ula said.

"It will serve for honor's sake," Kell said. "My sister's welfare is of more concern to me, at this moment, than you are."

"Will you be going to Jaentarth, then?" Shimmer asked.

"Our course beyond this point is not your concern."

"Send Trip with us, then," Mik said. "We'll make sure that he gets to Alarl, if that's your custom."

Lord Kell gazed carefully at Mik's bearded face, then shook his head. "I do not think that will serve," he said. "I will take him to Perch on Alarl, as soon as my sister is tended to." He turned to Ula once more. "If you like, I will send rowers with you, to ferry you to Darthalla."

"The four of us can handle the oars," Ula said. "Just the boat and some provisions will be fine."

Benthor Kell nodded and motioned his men to make the skiff ready. They had the small boat provisioned and hanging over the side, ready to launch, in less than fifteen minutes. Trip stood at the rail, looking forlorn.

Mik kneeled down so he was face to face with his friend, and said in a low voice, "We'll pick you up as soon as we can."

Trip nodded and extended his hand for Mik to shake.

Mik pressed the diamond artifact into the kender's palm. "Keep it safe until we come get you," he said.

Trip's eyes lit up. "Thanks, Mik," he said. "I won't let you down."

Mik stood and clapped him on the shoulder. He slung his leg over the rail and climbed into the boat with Ula. Shimmer followed him. Karista stood at the rail, glancing nervously from the tiny boat to Lord Kell, then back again.

Jumping forward, she drew her borrowed sword and, with one mighty swing, hacked through the ropes supporting the skiff.

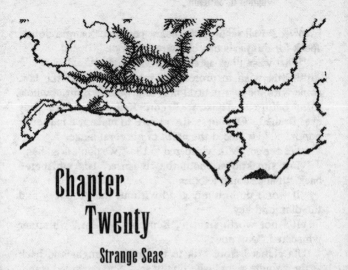

Chapter Twenty

Strange Seas

The boat tumbled over the side and into the ocean. It hit with a huge splash, and the companions had to grab the skiff's gunwales to avoid being spilled over the side.

Mik and Ula both cursed.

Kingfisher's former captain stared up at the rail and saw Karista Meinor gazing down on them.

"I'm sorry, captain," she said, "but this is where we part company."

"What in the names of the lost gods are you doing?" Mik asked angrily.

"You know that my goals differ from yours," Karista said. "Lord Kell's justice will serve my needs better to that end than the court of any sea elf."

Ula stood up in the bow of the skiff and addressed the master of the brass ship directly. "Lord Kell," she said. "I won the right to have this woman accompany me."

"That was when I believed you spoke on behalf of all

involved," Kell replied. "It seems, perhaps, that you do not speak for *this* particular shipwrecked soul."

"That wasn't our agreement," Ula said.

"If you wish to protest my interpretation of the law, come with me to a neutral port and we will put the whole thing before a magistrate," Lord Kell replied. His gray eyes flashed. "Of course, if you care to make it a matter of honor . . ." He raised the point of his coral lance.

"Let her go," Mik whispered to Ula. "We don't need her."

"But she knows about the treasure," Ula whispered back. "If she should tell him . . ."

"It won't do him any good without the Prophecy and the diamond key."

"It's not worth fighting Benthor Kell for," Shimmer whispered. "Not now."

Ula glanced from Mik to the bronze knight and back again. "You're right," she finally said. She remained standing as the skiff drifted away from the galley.

"Treat Lady Meinor well, Lord Kell, or I shall hear of it," she called back to the galley.

"I'm sure you will," Kell replied, a hint of sarcasm in his voice, "but have no concern on that account."

"And Trip, too," Mik added, as the kender waved at him. He tried to keep a straight face as a soldier's purse found its way into one of Trip's pockets.

"The kender will be treated with the respect he merits," Kell said stiffly.

Mik held the lord's eye and nodded slowly. "We'll meet again one day," he said.

"I look forward to it," Kell replied. "As I look forward to seeing Ula Landwalker again as well."

Ula spat into the ocean.

Kell laughed and turned to his helmsmen and his drum-chanter. "Set oars, course south by southwest." The crew of the galley responded immediately, and the trireme quickly pulled away from the skiff.

Trip stood at the rail, cheerfully waving goodbye.

Ula sat down in the skiff. "I need a rest."

Mik unshipped his oars and turned to Shimmer. "Well," he said, "where are we headed?"

Shimmer unshipped his oars. "Darthalla may not be the best place to start . . ."

"For a number of reasons," Ula put in. She leaned back against the skiff's small gunwale, dipped a hand into the water and dribbled some over her face, then closed her eyes. "Recite the parts of the Prophecy after reaching the isles."

"I assume we're sharing the treasure with your friend," Mik said, looking over at Shimmer.

"Equal shares," Ula said, "to all those participating in the recovery."

"Trip as well, then," Mik said.

Ula nodded slowly. "If you insist. But remind me of the Prophecy, sailor."

Mik shipped his oars, closed his eyes, and let the rhythm of the waves bring the verses of the Prophecy back to him. Soon, he began to speak:

"Blessed azure sea
Cloudcapped mountainsides
Verdant forests free
Forestalled from evil tides
Four keys beyond the gate
Veiled battlements deep lie
Bold wards to islands' fate
Span earth and sea and sky."

He recited more verses, ending with:

" 'Neath traversed azure wine
Converse with hoary fates
With tangled bones of vine
To root Green key awaits . . ."

Mik took a deep breath and opened his eyes once more. "I think the first two stanzas are just singing the praises of the isles," Mik said. "And the next refer to the power of the Veil."

"Amply demonstrated," said Shimmer.

"They also mention the treasure and the four keys needed to

find it," Mik continued. "Beyond that, though, I think you need to be a native or a scholar to make sense of it. I profess to be neither—but I'd hoped to solve it once we reached the isles."

"Lucky you fell in with some natives," Ula said. "I think you're right about the first four stanzas; island fish oil and building up the treasure. Kell, or his master, would be the 'lord of brazen keep.' The Order's base on Berann is the home of brass dragons."

"I think that's the key we already have," Mik said, "the black diamond artifact."

Ula nodded.

" 'Wisdom's highest throne' could be Aurialastican, on the Misty Isle," Shimmer said. "Golden dragons dwell there."

"And the 'hoary fates' stanza probably means Darthalla—the undersea home of . . . my people," Ula added.

"Is there more to the Prophecy?" Shimmer asked. "You mentioned four keys. The one you have, the Dargonesti one, and the one on the Misty Isle makes three. That leaves one missing."

"I think Captain Vardan is holding some secrets back," Ula said.

"Just until I know you better," Mik replied with a sly smile.

"Where to first, the sea kingdom or the island of the golden dragons? What about Jaentarth? Could we hire a ship there?" Gazing south, he could just make out the big island, hovering mirage-like on the horizon.

"Doubtful," Shimmer said. "They have no deep water port."

"Besides, we don't want to run into Kell again if we can avoid him," Ula said. "Chances are he's stopping there for medical supplies to help his sister."

"Aurialastican is almost straight north," Shimmer said. "But Darthalla is just a little way off course—and closer, too."

Ula sighed. "I'd rather put off my family reunion a bit longer, if you don't mind."

"What's a few more days of rowing between friends?" Mik said jovially. "North to Aurialastican it is."

They steered due north but soon discovered that though Lord Kell might have vanished from their sight, they had not vanished from his. Tanalish, Kell's brass dragon escort, kept an eye on them from high in the air.

Ula swore. "It wouldn't surprise me if Kell is plotting some revenge once he's spirited his sister to safety." She wiped the sweat from her smooth, blue forehead and slacked off her oars for a moment. The sun was just dipping behind the clouds blanketing the western horizon, and all the placid sea looked gray and gloomy.

Shimmer, sitting and resting in the skiff's stern, rubbed his left shoulder. "All we can do is keep rowing," he said.

"All right," Ula said, with an edge of weariness. She glanced back at Mik. "How's that black diamond artifact, sailor? Keeping it safe?"

"Actually, Trip's holding onto it for us," Mik said, pulling steadily on his oars.

"What?" she asked angrily.

"I gave it to him before we parted."

"Why in the deep blue seas did you do that?" Ula asked. "You know we need that key to claim the treasure."

Mik smiled. "That's exactly why I gave it to him."

Ula threw up her hands in frustration, and her oars almost slipped over the side.

Shimmer chuckled. "He knows you well, Ula, for such a short acquaintance."

Ula sighed. "You're right. I probably would have left the minnow behind. I'm fond of him, but taking a kender on a treasure-finding voyage is crazy."

"Actually, he's an expert treasure finder and a superb diver," Mik said. "I trust Trip with my life."

"Let's hope it doesn't come to that," Ula replied.

She and Shimmer switched places at the oars. "I'll spell you in an hour," she said to Mik.

Kingfisher's former captain nodded and kept rowing.

Night cast long, indigo fingers over the ocean. The wind picked up from the west, and small whitecaps lapped at the skiff's sides. The rowing became progressively more difficult. They switched rowers frequently, and took a cold supper during their breaks. Kell had not given them the choicest of provisions, but no one complained, given the circumstances.

"Another storm's coming," Shimmer said, gazing west.

"Maybe it will pass us by," said Ula.

"I doubt it," Mik replied. "Let's keep rowing. We can always abandon the skiff if the seas get too rough."

Ula smiled. "Most humans fear the deep," she said, "but not you."

"The sea's been my life for a long time," Mik said. "I'm comfortable above or below—with a little help." He patted the enchanted fish amulet at his neck.

The coming storm blotted out the stars, making the night black and chilly. Dismal fog swirled over the waves, dancing before the wind like wraiths anticipating a funeral.

Ula peered into the darkness. "Which way to Aurialastican, Shimmer?" she asked.

Shimmer turned his bronze-helmeted head from stem to stern. "We're headed in the right direction, more or less. We've a long way to go, though."

Ula cursed. "I'd turn back for Jaentarth if I didn't think we'd find Kell waiting for us."

"With peril ahead and astern," Mik said, "perhaps we should take the shortest route."

"The sailor makes sense," Shimmer said.

Ula frowned and sighed. "To me, too. Trying for Aurialastican was a mistake." Glancing at Mik, she added. "Pull with me, and we'll turn this boat around."

"Aye . . . captain," Mik replied.

Ula laughed and the two counter-rowed the oars a moment and turned the skiff around. Waves coming from the west rocked the boat precariously, making it difficult to stay on course. As they regained their bearings, a huge dark shape surged up out of the waves to stern. It flashed through the air overhead and disappeared into the swirling fog.

Ula cursed.

Black gloved hands suddenly appeared atop the skiff's gunwales, and with one sudden tug, the small boat went under.

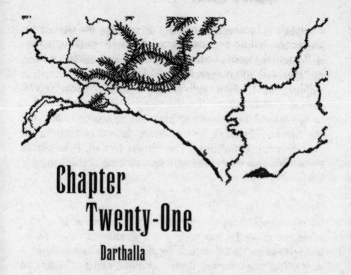

Chapter
Twenty-One

Darthalla

The fish amulet's ancient magic enveloped Mik as steely fingers pulled him down into the deep. He felt his stomach swirl and his eyes cloud over—sure indications that he'd worn the necklace too long. Abusing the power of artifacts like the necklace could be perilous—even deadly. Mik clenched his jaw tight and concentrated, trying to shake off his fears.

Shadowy shapes flashed through the water around him. He reached for his cutlass, but strong hands grabbed his wrist.

Something cold and rubbery wrapped itself around his lower body. He felt as though he were encased in a clinging blanket. A huge, bat-like form flashed by his face. Something struck him, and he felt a stinging, burning sensation in his cheek.

Only an arm's-length away, Ula and Shimmer were struggling against their attackers. A strange, warm sleepiness began to steal over the captain. He blinked and found it hard to keep his eyes open.

"They've drugged me," he realized. He discovered his hands were pinned to his side by the same rubbery blanket that encircled his legs. He glanced over his shoulder and saw the alien face of an enormous ray peering back at him. "I'm trapped," he thought, only slightly surprised not to be disturbed by that fact.

He heard Ula shout something, but he couldn't make out the words. Shimmer's bronze armor flashed brightly in the ever-deepening darkness. The knight turned, light blazed from under his visor, then Mik remembered nothing more.

* * * * *

Mik awoke, lying on a golden platform encased in a large, transparent bag. He was underwater, floating in a wide chamber with glass walls—which formed enormous windows—extending from curved floor to domed ceiling. Fist-sized glowing pearls lining the chamber provided the room with light. A huge pearl, as large as a man's skull, shimmered at the dome's apex. Mik's transparent cell was anchored near the chamber's sole exit.

Beyond the glass walls lay an amazing underwater city. This was no rag-tag settlement like Reeftown, but a beautifully realized whole. Buildings looped through the ocean outside the window, curving like graceful shells, some reaching toward the unseen surface far above. The architecture sprang from the huge reefs dominating the landscape, each structure seeming as though it had grown organically from the surrounding coral. Blue, green, and pale white lights streamed from the windows of the houses outside, dappling the water in shifting patterns.

All of the buildings appeared to be meticulously maintained. Some were clearly inspired by terrestrial architecture and seagoing ships, but most had a submarine beauty all their own. Great undersea gardens wound through the structures, providing the city's inhabitants with both privacy and beauty.

Blue-skinned Dargonesti swam around, between, and through the amazing structures. The sea elves' slender bodies darted in and out of the settlement's indigo shadows. Turbidus dolphins accompanied some of the fair folk, while other elves rode on the backs of huge manta rays. The rays drifted gracefully through the city's canyons like titanic bats.

Most of the elves Mik saw were dressed in a manner similar to Ula: Scant pieces of silky fabric held together by elaborate chains of jewelry. Some, however, wore armor of golden shells and pieces of turtle carapace. A few covered themselves in sinuous wraps of glowing seaweed. And some eschewed clothing altogether; only their long, sensuous hair obscured their considerable physical charms.

Mik was so entranced by the view outside the huge windows that, at first, he didn't notice the people floating near the far side of the room. Two shell-like thrones hung in the water at the chamber's opposite end. Perched in one of the chairs was a handsome warrior elf. Jewelrylike armor covered his muscular form, and a gem-studded diadem sat upon his forehead. The other chair sat empty.

The handsome elf regarded the two figures floating before him with grim majesty. One of the people Mik immediately recognized as Ula. The other was a tall, blond man in orangish armor. It took Mik a moment to realize that this second person was Shimanloreth, shorn of his helmet.

A female elf with flowing pearly hair hovered to the right of the enthroned man. This woman strongly resembled Ula, though she appeared older and somewhat fuller of figure.

On the throne's other side swam an elf in turtle-shell armor. Mik recognized him as the guard they'd met at the gates to Reeftown. He was Volrek, one of Lakuda's sentries.

Ula, the man on the throne, and all the others were engaged in an animated discussion. Shimmer, cool and distant, hovered off to one side, near Ula.

Mik turned and spied a sea-elf guard in golden half-armor treading water behind his baglike prison. "Where am I?" he asked. "Is this Darthalla?"

147

"It is, and you are ordered to remain silent," the female guard said. "Only Ula Drakenvaal and Shimanloreth have permission to speak before Lord Aquironian at this time." Her exquisite face looked stern, brooking no arguments.

"Your pardon," Mik said with a slight bow. He cautiously pressed his hand against the transparent wall of his prison. To his surprise, his fingers passed right through into the water beyond. He checked for his fish necklace and found it missing. He spotted it resting on a coral pillar behind the guard.

"Am I a prisoner?" he whispered to the guard.

"That is yet to be determined."

"Then return my necklace to me that I may silently observe this audience as a guest."

The guard looked skeptical.

"Do you have orders against it?" Mik asked.

"My orders were that you should cause no trouble."

"And I *shall* cause no trouble. I wish merely to observe as, I believe, is my due."

"Very well," the guard said. She fetched the necklace and handed it to Mik through the bubble.

Mik put it on and fought down the familiar wave of nausea. He steadied himself, stepped through the bubble, and took a deep breath. For a moment, he felt as though he were suffocating. At first the water pressed in around him and no air came to his lungs.

A moment later, though, another gem scale crumbled and the enchantment kicked in. He took a deep breath and swam—with as much decorum as he could muster— toward the group assembled near the throne. He took up a position hovering in the water just behind Shimmer, who barely acknowledged him. He noticed that the guard came with him and stationed herself on his flank.

"Ula Drakenvaal," Lord Aquironian was sayinng, "the guardsman Volrek has ridden here on the fastest draken ray at the behest of his lady Lakuda. He suggests that you may have had a hand in some trouble in Reeftown recently."

"The Landwalker led the dragon Tempest to our doorstep," Volrek said, shaking his fist so hard that his turtle-shell armor rattled. "She—and her companions—caused the massive destruction of Reeftown."

"That's absurd, milord," said Ula. "Why would I lead the dragon to Reeftown? I still have friends there."

"One, perhaps," Volrek said, "though I see *he* is at your side now—as we suspected. Milord, they are in this together."

"You have some proof of this?" the lord asked.

"All know the grudge the Landwalker bears against Reeftown and the lady Lakuda," Volrek said.

"Lakuda is a self-righteous, covetous bitch," Ula shot back.

Lord Aquironian, reclining in his shell-like throne, looked slightly amused. "A common trait among the scavengers of the outer reefs, it seems," he said.

Ula flushed.

"The dragon has never before penetrated so deeply into the Veil's enchantment," Volrek continued. "It does so shortly after *she* returns to Reeftown, and when it attacks she is nowhere to be found. I say that it clearly adds up against her."

"It was Lakuda's foragers who brought me back to the city," Ula replied. "Why don't you blame them? Or blame yourselves? I had no desire to return to Reeftown. And what would I gain from its destruction?"

"You are a well-known malcontent and rabble rouser. Is that not so, Lord Aquironian?"

Mik glanced at Shimmer but still the bronze knight remained impassive.

Before the lord could speak, the woman hovering near the throne swam forward. "Milord," she began, "while it is true that my sister is something of a rebel—a fact which has made her less than welcome many places, even in the house of our father—I find it difficult to believe that she would consort with this evil dragon."

"She's consorted with dragons before!" Volrek put in. "Perhaps . . ."

"Enough!" Aquironian cut him off. "You may be an envoy from our kin in Reeftown, Volrek, but there are still protocols to be observed. You interrupt me or members of my court at your peril."

The turtle-armored elf bowed low. "Your forgiveness, lord. We who live beyond the Veil are sometimes brash and ill-mannered. I intended no offense to you, or the lady Lyssara Drakenvaal."

Ula's sister, Lyssara, nodded in reply. She turned her gaze upon Ula and Shimmer and seemed slightly surprised to find Mik hovering next to them. "Though my sister has associated with some . . . disreputable types in the past," she said, her purple eyes straying to Mik, "she has no love for evil creatures, dragon or otherwise."

Ula, noticing Mik for the first time, gave him a discreet wink and motioned that he should keep silent.

"Perhaps your sister has changed since you last saw her," Lord Aquironian suggested.

"I do not doubt that she has," Lyssara replied. "And possibly not for the better. However, her Drakenvaal upbringing should not be entirely forgotten. No one of our line could intentionally harm either the Dragon Isles or the Dargonesti. She cannot possibly be causing the trouble with the dragon, nor the weakening of the Veil."

"You're right," Ula said. "I have nothing to do with this fish flop. But I don't need you sticking your big butt into this, Lyssara. This is between Lakuda's cronies and me."

Lyssara's purple eyes narrowed, but her voice remained calm. "Very well, little sister," she said, "since you shun my help, I leave you to your own devices." She slid back behind the throne and hovered there.

"What have you to say, Ula Landwalker?" Lord Aquironian asked.

"I demand to see my accuser," Ula said. "If Lakuda really believes all this sea-foam she's spouting about me, then she should stand before milord Aquironian herself. But instead, she sends this flunky to spread her baseless accusations."

"Milady Lakuda *cannot* stand before you, Lord Aquironian," Volrek interjected. "She was gravely injured in the fight with the dragon, and even now lies recovering from her wounds."

"Fish oil!" said Ula. "I'll gladly face Volrek, or anyone he cares to designate, in trial by combat to prove my innocence." She held her spear horizontally before her, in a traditional attitude of honorable challenge.

Volrek shifted uncomfortably where he was hovering.

"Ula doesn't have anything to do with the dragon," Mik ventured to say. "She could have been killed in the attack just as easily as anyone else."

The lord of the sea elves regarded the sailor with a mixture of surprise and disdain. "You have not been given leave to speak, surfacer," he said.

Mik bowed. "My apologies, lord."

"For what my word is worth, Lord Aquironian, I concur," Shimmer said calmly. "Ula is *not* in league with the dragon Tempest."

"He would say that," Volrek shouted. "They're in this *together.*"

Aquironian regarded Lakuda's messenger coldly. "Then you intend to challenge her word, Volrek? You will face Ula Landwalker in combat?"

Volrek shrank back. "It was not my lady's instruction to do so," he said.

"Then I will consider that you have withdrawn your complaint," Aquironian replied. "Ula Drakenvaal, also known as Landwalker, is free to go—though we suggest that she depart our city at her earliest convenience."

Ula bowed slightly, "I shall stay no longer than necessary, lord."

"What of this man?" Volrek said, indicating Mik. "He is the rightful hostage of Lakuda. Shimanloreth stole him from the detention chamber—along with several others."

"Shimmer came to our aid when the city was falling," Mik said.

"This man—and the other prisoners—may be set against my forage claims, if the Lady Lakuda so desires," Shimmer said.

Aquironian straightened up in his throne. "I've had enough of this squabbling," he said. "It's late, and my lady wife awaits. Since I see no way of determining whose lawful plunder this surfacer might be, I declare him—and any associated others who enter my realm—free from all bond and obligation. And since I see no evil in this man, he shall be treated as our guest."

He turned to the Dargonesti woman standing guard behind Mik. "Show him all due courtesy."

The elf in golden seashell armor bowed, "Aye, milord."

Mik bowed, too. "Thank you, most gracious lord of the sea elves."

"While you are in our city, you will obey our rules," the lord said to them. "If you do not, you will be dealt with accordingly."

"I understand," Mik said. "Thank you, milord."

"Lyssara," Aquironian said, "see that our surface-dwelling guest is given comfortable accommodations and that he understands the ways of our people. See to your sister and Shimanloreth as well." He rose from his throne and crossed the room with a few powerful kicks. "Now, if you'll forgive me . . ." Two guards opened the door at the back of the chamber, and Lord Aquironian exited.

Volrek glanced angrily from Ula to the doors and then followed the lord out.

Lyssara Drakenvaal swam forward once more. "I shall be delighted to do as my lord bids," she said, her smile lighting up the room. "I will show you to your chambers." She turned and led them all out of the room, through the same golden doors through which Aquironian had exited.

"Thanks for speaking up for me," Ula said to Mik. "It was a brave thing to do."

"You're welcome," Mik replied. Looking around the arching corridor, he said, "This city of yours is amazing."

"It's not my city any more," she said. "And Darthalla is about as shabby as Reeftown once you get past its gilt exterior."

Lyssara, swimming ahead, glanced at them over her shoulder. "Please try to keep up," she said. "We've some business to discuss before you retire."

Ula rolled her eyes. "I can't wait."

"Could we perhaps hold this discussion someplace *dry*?" Mik asked. "Our recent journeys have left me pretty worn out, and it would be nice to breathe without relying on enchantments for a while."

Ula's sister glanced at the sailor's jewel-scaled necklace. "As you wish," she said. "Follow me."

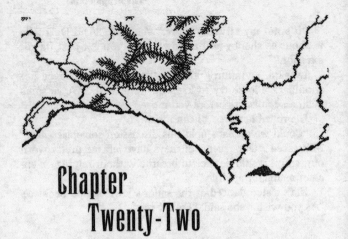

Chapter
Twenty-Two

A Kender's Visit to Jaentarth

Trip didn't mind being locked in a small room—to a kender, it seemed like quite a large room. He didn't even mind being tied up. The ropes weren't too itchy, and it gave him something to work on during the voyage. What he did mind was that the room had no window, and he really wanted to see where Lord Kell's galley was taking him. He hoped—if they were going to Jaentarth—that he might even see some pirates.

The brass warriors were more careful with knots than most humans. It look Trip the better part of two hours to work his way out, and then about ten minutes more to rig the ropes so that he could slip in and out without anyone knowing.

Occasionally, someone poked their head in and gave him some food. The food was never very well prepared, but Trip enjoyed it nonetheless. Hardtack, jerky, and water were better than some of the sea elf fare he'd had recently. He would have given a lot for a good tuna steak, though.

After fixing the ropes properly, he went to work on the cabin's door. This proved somewhat easier, since he had both his hands free, and because he had pieces of wire in his pockets, with which to pick the lock.

While digging out the hidden wire he was reminded of his other major annoyance: before throwing him in this small, windowless room, Kell's crew had searched him thoroughly—searched him like a gully dwarf, as his uncle might have said. He'd lost quite a few interesting trinkets in the process: some sharks' teeth, a tiny sand dollar, a bit of string that his cousin had given him, and a polished brass button that he'd taken from a prison guard in Khur. *That* was an interesting adventure!

Sadly, they'd also discovered and confiscated the remnants of his magical seaweed, his lucky kender treasure finder—a real blow, that!—and (he sighed just to think of it) the black diamond artifact. He hadn't hidden the artifact very well, assuming that Kell's people wouldn't be so rude as to search him, once Mik and the others had left. In fact, before they grabbed him, ransacked his things, tied him up, and thrust him into this dark closet, he had actually been looking forward to his forced voyage to Perch, on the island of Alarl.

Kell's crew hadn't bothered to expropriate the worthless-seeming tiny wires that served Trip as lockpicks, though. As he sprang the rusty lock on the door of the cabin, and stepped out, many of the crew were asleep. Still, the galley was a crowded place, and the kender had to use all his considerable stealth to creep along without being seen. Voices from the ship's stern attracted Trip's attention. He sneaked past several rows of sleeping oarsmen to get there, but the challenge of doing so only made him more eager to hear what was going on.

Two spartan cabins occupied the rear of the ship, one, Trip assumed, for Lord Kell, and one for Lady Kell. The crack beneath the door of one was dark; the voices came from the other.

"Anything we find at Jaentarth will only be a stop-gap at best," said a woman's voice that Trip recognized as the ship's healer. "The people of Jaentarth are the descendants of pirates and shipwrecked mariners. They've no true medicine. We'll still have to journey to Berann to save your sister's life."

Trip's heart soared at the mention of Jaentarth. He'd be meeting some pirates, after all!

"Are you suggesting we skip Jaentarth altogether?" Lord Kell asked.

Trip's heart fell slightly.

"No," the healer replied. "I need certain supplies to stabilize her. Even a Jaentarth cow-town should have what I require."

"Then tomorrow we'll stop just long enough to obtain what my sister needs, before setting course for Berann," Kell said.

"Milord Kell," interrupted a third voice which Trip was slightly surprised to recognize as Karista Meinor, "why not ask your dragon friend to take your lady sister back to Berann? Surely Tanalish can fly more swiftly than we can row."

Trip scratched his tawny head. It seemed that Meinor and Lord Kell had become quite friendly during the short time the kender had been tied up.

"In Misa's condition," the healer replied, "I would not recommend it. Perhaps if I can stabilize her at Jaentarth."

"Do whatever you can," Kell said.

"Of course, milord," the healer replied.

The cabin door opened, and Trip had to press himself back into the shadows against the bulkhead to avoid being seen. The healer exited Lord Kell's chamber and went into the room next door. In the brief moment before the healer closed the door, Trip saw that it was indeed Lady Kell's room.

Karista Meinor shut the door to Lord Kell's cabin once more, and Trip returned to his listening post.

"I pray that this anchorage may bring your sister much-needed relief from her wound," Karista said. "And I look forward to returning to your keep on the isle of Berann. Perhaps then we may seal the trade deal between your order and my people in Jotan. I trust the treasure I've offered as a token of good faith is adequate?"

That comment puzzled Trip. He didn't think Karista had salvaged any treasure to bribe someone with.

"Quite adequate—*if* it exists," Lord Kell replied. "We shall discover whether it does, in due time. For now, I am pleased that the first key has been returned to the Order. When it was stolen long ago, and the pirates lost at sea, Lord Thrakdar had little hope it would ever be seen again."

They were talking about Mik's artifact! The black diamond—which they'd stolen from Trip's pocket!

"Milord," Karista said, her voice sweet and soft, "I have fulfilled my part of our agreement: I help deliver the treasure to your order; you secure for me a reliable trade route to the isles."

"Yes, that is our agreement," Kell said firmly. "And I will honor it. Now, however, is not the time to consider such things. Misa's health must come first."

"Of course, milord," Karista purred. "Shall we drink to our success, then?"

"Aye," Kell replied.

Trip's small head swam with ideas. Karista had claimed Mik's treasure! She was bribing Lord Kell into giving her a trade route to the Dragon Isles! It didn't sound like Karista or Kell had have any plans to share the big diamond and the rest of the loot with him, Mik, Ula, or anyone.

Trip determined then to get off the ship and warn his friend at the earliest chance. How he might find Mik remained elusive. Still, "Every journey begins with a single step," or in this case, "plunge," as the kender saying went.

Sneaking past a sleeping oarsman and peering out the tiny oar hole, the kender saw only the dark, gray sea rising gently before a westerly wind. No sign, yet, of their destination. The thought of going to an island populated by castaways and pirates thrilled the kender. He doubted he'd have much time to look around and make friends, though—not if he was going to warn Mik.

Cautiously, Tripleknot Shellcracker crept back to his closet and put on his ropes. He'd make his move when they anchored at Jaentarth.

* * * * *

Trip woke with a start. The creaking of the ship had changed, and he no longer heard the rhythmic splash of the oars. An unexpected plate of cold food and a tiny skin of water lay at his feet, and he cursed himself for not being more wary. Footsteps on the decks above told him that it would be tricky now to slip out of his small prison.

Yet there was nothing else for it.

He shucked his ropes and quickly picked the lock once more. Peering out the door, he found himself in luck; nearly all of the deck's oarsmen seemed to be working somewhere else—probably on the main platform. Trip slipped out the door and made his way cautiously between the benches.

New sounds of splashing drew his attention to one of the oar holes. Swimming—the crew was swimming beside the ship. This might have been a break, had the galley been tethered to a dock—which is what the kender expected.

But when he peered out, he noticed that the trireme lay anchored quite far offshore. In the distance he saw Lord Kell's skiff approaching the mainland. The town they were headed for was *not* the romantic pirate village Trip had imagined. Rather, it was a ramshackle collection of rundown buildings clinging to the steep sides of the Jaentarth shore. Huge boulders littered the rocky shoreline near the town, and tall cliffs sprang up on either side of the tiny landing area. The black maws of a dozen tidal caves scarred the cliff face.

Trip saw now why his captors hadn't expected much from Jaentarth. Even to a kender it was slightly disappointing. It would have to do, however. He doubted it would be any easier to escape from Berann.

Ducking around the benches, he made his way to Lord Kell's cabin. A quick search turned up his confiscated items, including his lucky treasure finder and his daggers. Trip smiled and hung the thong attached to the shiny, pointed rock around his neck. He hadn't remembered to wear the treasure finder since stowing away on *Kingfisher*, but a bit of good luck now couldn't hurt.

He tucked the pearl-handled daggers' sheaths into the top of his boots and then packed away the rest of his small treasures. His hazel eyes strayed covetously toward the coral lance hanging over Benthor Kell's bunk, but he decided there was no way to take it with him at the moment. Rummaging around further, it didn't take him long to turn up the black diamond artifact.

Remembering that he had already once failed his promise to keep the ancient key safe, he removed it from the hidden compartment in Kell's sea chest and tucked the golden trinket even more deeply into his vest pocket.

Now to find his friends.

Going on deck to slip overboard seemed out of the question. Fortunately, Lord Kell's cabin had a good-sized porthole on the starboard wall. Unfortunately, the small window looked directly toward the ship's landward side—where the crew was swimming.

Trip guessed that Lady Kell's room would have a similar porthole in the ship's opposite hull. Moving quietly, the kender crept from Lord Kell's cabin and put his small ear to Misa Kell's door. No voices came from within.

As he opened the door, though, a quiet gasp came from inside. Trip froze. When no further cry went up, he decided to dare a peek.

Peering into the darkened cabin, he saw Misa Kell lying on a simple palette near the stern. She was alone. Sweat dripped from her brow, and—despite the freshness of the dressing on her wound—the room smelled of blood and old bandages.

Trip crinkled his nose and crept silently across the floorboards. Misa Kell groaned and her gray eyes flicked open. Trip froze again; he couldn't tell whether she was actually seeing him, or whether she was lost in some fever dream.

She reached weakly toward the kender; Trip backed across the room toward the curtained porthole.

"The light," she murmured. "I want to see . . . the light . . . before I die. Please."

Trip nodded and smiled. "I'll be happy to," he said. "I was going to leave that way anyway. I hope you don't mind."

Misa's eyes fluttered shut and she groaned again.

Trip pulled back the curtain and hoisted himself up to the lip of the portal. He checked outside to make sure there were no swimmers below. There weren't. Before scrambling through, he turned to Misa and said, "Goodbye. I hope you feel better."

Lady Kell didn't reply, and Trip couldn't be sure if she even heard him. With one final wriggle, he slipped through the port hole and dived into the water below.

Coming up for air, he checked the galley's deck, to make sure no one had seen him. The lookout was gazing past him, out to sea; the bulk of the ship hid the kender from the man's view.

Cautiously, Trip swam around to the bow. He knew that there might not be anyone watching that direction—while the helmsman would surely be stationed near the stern.

He paddled cautiously toward the ram, then noticed that some of the crewmen were clinging there, taking a break from their swim. Trip pressed himself against the hull and thought hard.

The kender knew he couldn't hold his breath long enough to swim all the way to shore. He also knew that he'd probably be spotted as soon as he surfaced. However, he had few other options. He checked the pockets of his lizard-skin vest and pulled out the last bit of magical seaweed. He stuck it in his cheek and chewed vigorously.

Nothing happened.

Either the magic had worn out or there wasn't enough left to make the spell work. Either way, it was no use to Trip, so he spat it out. Drat! He'd have to do this the hard way.

Taking a deep breath, he dived under the keel of the ship and headed for shore. He watched Kell's warriors swimming in the clear surf above him. They would certainly see him if they glanced down, but Trip hoped they wouldn't do that. He also hoped that anyone on deck looking might mistake him for part of the crowd in the water. He prayed that his leg wound wouldn't open up again and attract sharks.

He swam as fast and as far as he could, holding his breath until spots danced before his eyes. Then, with a final surge, he broke the surface about fifty yards from the boat. A quick breath and he went back down again, swimming for all he was worth.

The spots came more quickly this time, and he barely made it back to the surface. He sputtered and coughed as he stuck his head out of the gentle waves. For a few long moments, he gasped for breath. As he did, he heard a cry of alarm from the trireme. They'd spotted him.

He dived back under again. When he resurfaced, the shouting grew louder. Something splashed in the water nearby, and Trip realized they were shooting at him. He ducked back below the waves just as a brass-tipped arrow sailed over his head.

Again to the surface—nearly out of arrowshot this time. Trip's lungs burned, and his head felt dizzy and full of cotton. An arrow splashed into the water beside him, barely missing his shoulder. He swam on the surface for a while, trying to clear his skull. Another arrow whizzed past. Gazing ahead, he saw Jaentarth's rocky shores—still much too far away.

Once more under the waves. Good thing he was the best swimmer in a family of champion swimmers, if he did say so himself. He saw the rugged shoreline rising up under him now. The clear water made it easy to pick out the jagged rocks and coral lining the bottom.

On the surface again, breathing more easily now, well beyond the range of the ship's bowman. Before him, though, another problem. The trireme had alerted the landing party. He saw Lord Kell, Karista, the healer, and a number of brass-armored guards standing on the hillside. They were pointing his way and shouting.

The shore was close now. With every surge, the breakers carried him forward. "Don't get smashed on the rocks," Trip told himself.

The waves pushed him toward the boulders. Trip twisted his body to avoid being crushed and grabbed with his fingers. He caught a nook on one of the crags and held on. In the lull before the next wave, he scrambled up out of the surf.

He lay on the rocks for a moment, panting, every part of his body burning with exertion. Blood pounded in his ears, mixing with the crashing of the waves. Then, another noise rose above the sounds of blood and water—yelling.

Raising his tawny head, Trip saw the landing party coming for him. Every muscle aching, he thrust himself off the boulder and down the rocky beach. The beach's stones bruised his feet through his soft-bottomed boots. He ignored the pain and kept running. Good thing he was a champion runner too, from a family as good as running as it was at swimming.

The shoreline stretched before him, a hundred yards of rocks and coral. Beyond them, the surf again, and a sheer cliff face a hundred feet high. Trip liked to climb, but rock climbing wasn't his specialty; no, he was a swimmer and a runner and, if it came to climbing, he was far more at home in a ship's rigging.

"If I try to climb the cliffs, they'll shoot me like a duck in a barrel," he thought.

The sea caves in the cliff face presented a better option. He was willing to bet that he might be able to lose his pursuers there. And what other choice did he have?

Trip ran for the caves as fast as he could. He splashed into the surf and took them in turn, peering into each one he passed. He turned down the first two—obviously too shallow—and the third because he heard the sounds of water echoing back out.

The fourth looked more promising. It angled up, out of the water, and disappeared into semi-darkness. Trip might have explored further, but the sounds of pursuit made up his mind.

Not daring to look back, he ducked into the cave and ran up the slope. The light grew very dim as the tunnel leveled off, and he found himself squinting.

He hoped that his pursuers might not have spotted which cave he went into. That hope proved short-lived, though, as shouts from the cave entrance told him that Kell and the others were nearly on top of him.

Groping with his hands, he moved down the tunnel as quickly as he dared. The walls around him were wet and slippery. He dashed forward, and then stopped.

It was a dead end.

He'd picked a dead end.

The kender wondered briefly what they'd do when they caught him. Being locked in the cabin again wouldn't be so bad. On the other hand, maybe they'd decide that he was more trouble than he was worth. Maybe they'd decide not to take him to kendertown, and just get rid of him.

A half dozen interesting ways they might kill him ran through Trip's mind.

Then he noticed something he hadn't before. His eyes had finally adjusted to the darkness. There was something odd about the far end of the blocked tunnel—some source of vague, greenish light.

Racing the last few yards, his heart pounding in his throat, Trip gazed at the tunnel floor. He hadn't noticed the passage descending again, but it must have, because there, on the floor at the end of the tunnel, was a hole filled with sea water.

The opening was about four feet around, plenty big enough for the kender to jump into. The vague green luminescence was reflecting up out of the small pool. Trip looked in and couldn't see the bottom. Perhaps it was a way out.

The sounds of voices close behind him made up his mind.

Tripleknot Shellcracker took a deep breath and dived in headfirst.

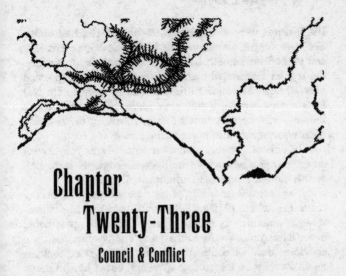

Chapter
Twenty-Three
Council & Conflict

T he large moray eel swimming surrepti-
tously through the coral canyons of
Darthalla was not an eel at all. It darted from shadow to
shadow, peering into windows, following its sensitive nose.
The scents of the elven city confused it, but strong purpose
burned in its mind: destroy the Veil, pursue those who have
pierced it, discover their secrets, find the keys.

The voice of Tempest hissed softly in the eel's mind; her
visage, huge and wrathful, danced before its eyes. The eel
who was Mog watched, and waited, and lurked unseen.

* * * * *

Mik swam beside Ula and Shimmer as they trailed
Lyssara Drakenvaal through the maze-like passages of the
palace in Darthalla.

Now that Mik had a chance to look more closely at him,
he could see that Shimanloreth was exceedingly handsome.

His features were strong and well-formed. His hair shone like spun copper, complimenting his orangish eyes. His skin was tanned and smooth. There was an elvish cast to his face: the regular features, the arched brows, the slightly pointed ears—though Mik didn't think he was actually an elf. Not for the first time the sailor wondered about the bronze knight—who he was, how he came to live in the sea, and what was the secret of his amazing armor.

Ula's sister, Lyssara, talked incessantly as they swam down the gently curving hallway. Her words were eloquent, though Ula seemed unimpressed.

"It's not just your family," Lyssara was saying. "This concerns the whole of Darthalla—and even the Isles themselves. Something is wrong with the Veil. Tempest could never have gotten so close otherwise. The weather has been erratic as well. Of course storms don't affect our people as much as they do the surface dwellers, but it *has* hindered shipping—which affects everything else."

"The departed gods forbid that Dargonesti should be self-sufficient," Ula said sarcastically.

Lyssara frowned. "None of us is alone in this world, Ula," she said, "no matter how much we might *like* to be. Ah, here are your chambers. I trust you'll find them adequate for your brief stay." She led them all up a short slope, and through a moon pool into a dry foyer.

"I'm sure it will be fine," Mik said.

Lyssara smiled at him, though Mik didn't think she liked him at all. "I'll leave you alone to get settled then," she said. "It's late, and I'm sure you're tired. We'll talk again during breakfast."

"Or perhaps we could enjoy our breakfast in silence," Ula said, imitating her sister's false smile.

Lyssara grinned back. "See you in the morning." She dove into the moon pool and swam swiftly away. Two guards emerged from the water and stationed themselves near the door to the chamber.

"We won't be needing you," Shimanloreth said.

The guards looked at each other, then bowed to Shimmer, and retreated back into the water and disappeared around a bend in the passage.

"They're probably lurking right around that corner," Ula said.

"A respectful distance," Shimmer noted. A smile tugged at the corners of his mouth, and his brazen eyes flashed.

Their apartment had a main room with five smaller sleeping alcoves arranged symmetrically around the edges. The chamber was composed of shaped coral, worn smooth by the Dargonesti. A large crystal window set into one wall overlooked the city. Comfortable-looking shells set along the walls served as chairs and couches. Several large nets for stowing possessions hung from the ceiling. An opening in one wall led down a short tunnel to a grooming chamber with hot and cold running fresh water. Each bedchamber featured a web of silky seaweed to support the sleeper.

The three guests took a few moments to freshen up before settling into their netting.

"A nicer prison than last time," Mik noted. He removed his necklace and set it on the hammock beside him.

"I hope your minnow's faring well," Ula said, "since he's got the key to finding this treasure."

"Trip won't let us down," Mik said. "I just hope you're reading those clues right."

"We'll know soon enough if I'm not," Ula replied.

"That's small comfort."

"We must remember that Aurialastican and its secrets belong to dragons," Shimmer said. "The owners departed along with the gods—but the Dragonheights are still perilous."

"How hard can it be to wander through a vacant house?" Mik asked.

"Just because the owner is away, doesn't mean that the house is unguarded," Shimanloreth said. He yawned.

"We'll crack that egg in the morning," Ula said. "Or after we rescue your kender."

* * * * *

The next morning, Mik woke to find Ula and Lyssara in mid-argument once more. He slitted one brown eye open and gazed at the elf women; even squabbling, they were still amazingly beautiful.

"If the overlords find the Isles, they will destroy us all," Lyssara said.

"And that should matter to me because . . . ?" Ula replied.

Lyssara gazed at her sister in disbelief. "Ula Drakenvaal, how can you even think such a thing?"

"Are the Isles any more precious than the mainland?" Ula asked. "I didn't see our people rushing to help Ansalon when the overlords came."

"The dragons did what they could," Lyssara said. "It was all that *anyone* could do."

"All save the gods, who turned their backs on the world," Ula replied. "No wonder the world turns its back on the gods. If the metallic dragons weren't willing to defend this place, why should I?"

Lyssara glared at both Ula and Shimanloreth, who was lounging on a shell nearby. "Some dragons are willing to fight, as are some people—both human *and* elf."

"Like Benthor and Misa Kell?" Ula asked. "Pardon me if I don't like the company you keep, sister."

"Ula, these are *your* people, too. We are in danger—even you and your friends. If you don't believe me, if you won't believe your family, speak to the Sage. She will advise you of the truth."

"Who?" Mik asked, sitting up in his hammock and stretching. He fetched his enchanted necklace from the bedding and stuck it securely in his belt.

Lyssara looked surprised, as though she'd forgotten about the sailor. "The Sea Sage—an ancient oracle, tied to the spirit of our people. She counsels us in times of trouble or need."

"The Dargonesti turn to her rather than think on their own," Ula said sarcastically.

Lyssara ignored her sister's jab. "The sage says that every Dargonesti soul—even the least—will be needed in the dark times ahead."

Ula's rolled her green eyes at Mik. "The *least* meaning *me*, of course."

Lyssara paced agitatedly around the room. *"No,"* she said, "I'm saying that *all* are needed."

Mik pulled himself out of his sleeping web and stretched again. "This sage sounds pretty wise," he said, catching Ula's eye. "Perhaps she could help us with our current . . . problem."

"As a matter of fact," Ula replied, "I'd already planned to visit her on our way to Aurialastican."

Lyssara's long eyelashes fluttered, and a surprised smile danced across her lovely face. "You have? I'm so glad. Some distrust you, my sister, but I know your heart will not lead you astray. Shall I make the arrangements for you?"

"No," Ula said. "I'll handle this on my own."

"Very well," Lyssara replied. "May the tides lift you to glory." She bowed slightly and left the chamber.

" *'Neath traversed azure wine—Converse with hoary fates—With tangled bones of vine—To root Green key awaits,"* Mik recited. "You think the 'Green key' lies with this sage?"

"I'm almost certain of it."

"It's a dangerous path, Ula," Shimmer warned.

"All our paths are dangerous," Ula replied. "It's true the Sea Sage can be tricky, but I've dealt with her before." She paced in tight circles around the chamber, rubbing her chin with one slender hand. "I'll make the necessary preparations. Mik, you and Shimmer should hire some draken rays for our trip to Aurialastican."

"No, I want to go with you to visit this Sage," Mik said.

Ula arched one platinum eyebrows at him. "Outsiders are usually not permitted."

"Worried about protocol, Ula?" Mik asked, his brown eyes twinkling.

"All right," she said. "You can come, but we need steeds in any case."

"I'll hire them," said Shimmer.

"Good," Mik said. He looped his arm through Ula's elbow. "You and I can pick up some breakfast on the way. I'm starving."

* * * * *

Shimmer left to find suitable draken for their trip while Ula and Mik stopped for breakfast and went to gather provisions to visit the Sage. Shimmer gave them some money to cover expenses and Ula converted the change into small bits of jewelry, which she wove into her sparse clothing.

Mik marveled at the beauty of the Dargonesti city; it was even more spectacular in the daylight than it had been the previous night. The shell-like spires and reefs of Darthalla stretched almost to the surface above, and far into the indigo darkness below. The city teemed with elves swimming about their daily business: aristocrats and traders, hunters and fishers, kelp farmers, tuna herders, and undersea vintners. Shell-armored riders on the backs of huge draken rays glided through the streets, keeping the peace.

The elves themselves were something to behold, too—slender and graceful, with delicate features and sparkling eyes. Few were as lovely as Ula or her sister, but most put human beauties to shame. Mik avoided gawking as much as possible.

The magic of his necklace worked well during their sojourn, though he lost two more jeweled scales. He experienced none of the difficulties he had earlier, which left him hoping that the problems were merely a side effect of Karista's magic seaweed. In his heart, though, he knew the magic of the amulet—like all magic in Krynn—was gradually failing.

After completing their errands, Mik and Ula hooked up with Shimmer near the edge of town. The bronze knight helped Ula and Mik mount their leathery indigo steeds, then swung into his own saddle.

"Follow me," Ula said, urging her draken ray forward.

Mik and Shimmer fell in behind, and they quickly faded into the hazy blue distance.

* * * * *

Mog could not hold fishy shapes forever. Lurking in the shadows of Darthalla taxed his ability, strength, and willpower nearly to its limits. He had used other disguises besides the eel: fish, octopus, and—once—even sea elf. This last had strained him mightily; his scales twitched at the thought of it.

Still, the dragonspawn's ruses had worked. Amid his enemies, he remained undiscovered. Several times he had been forced to take refuge in hidden places to resume his own form and rest for a while.

Doing so had hindered his mission to track Mik and the others—but always he had regained their scents. During the night, he had even taken time to feed. He'd hidden the elf's bones beneath a boulder, in the deepest trenches of the city. Likely, no one would ever find the remains of the dragonspawn's latest victim.

Hiding in the wide seaweed beds beyond the city proved an easier task. Mog's scales blended in amid the tall kelp near the Sea Sage's lair. The ocean floor fell away here, into a deep, weed-filled sinkhole. Mog's quarry tethered their draken rays in the kelp nearby. Then the blue elf woman and the sailor went down into the hole, while the bronze warrior waited near the top.

Mog wondered which one of them had the black diamond key. He considered slaying them one by one to find out, but a voice in the back of his brain whispered "No!" Wait and watch.

Mog shrank back into the weeds. His time had not yet come.

* * * * *

Mik and Ula wound their way down into the wide pit that formed the lair of the Sea Sage. The kelp around them swayed sensuously, like thousands of dancing snakes. It made the hair stand up on the back of Mik's neck; Ula showed no signs of feeling anything similar.

Mik pushed himself to keep up with the Dargonesti. She moved with the grace of a dolphin and the speed of a razor-fish. The weeds didn't seem to touch her; Mik had to work hard to avoid becoming hopelessly entangled.

They pressed ever deeper, and the azure light above faded gradually to indigo. As the light lessened, the weeds thinned out, until they saw the sandy ocean bed rising up before them. It was as though they were at the bottom of a very deep bowl, surrounded by seaweed. On one side of the clearing, a green reef rose from the silt. A cave, slightly taller than a man, opened up in the reef's face. The grotto was not very deep, and mossy emerald weeds lined its floor.

In the middle of the circle of sand at the clearing's center lay a small coral pedestal. It was shaped like a tiny column and carved with runes that Mik could not read.

"This is it," Ula said. "Remember, *you* are not supposed to be here. Say *nothing.*"

Mik nodded.

Ula opened the small sack she'd brought down with her. She pulled out five sand dollars and a large golden starfish. Tiny pearls decorated the starfish's arms and there was a circular depression, slightly larger than the tip of a man's thumb, in the center. Ula took a large bluish pearl from the pouch and placed it in the depression.

Immediately, the sea around them began to bubble and swirl. A ghostly wailing sound emanated from the cave and built quickly to a deafening roar. Mik covered his ears with his hands and squinted, trying to see through the roiling waters.

A shape moved at the cave mouth, just at the edge of his vision. The thing was huge, much larger than the wizened crone Mik had been expecting—taller and broader than even a minotaur.

Quickly, the bubbles faded and the water calmed to uncanny stillness.

Beyond the coral pillar, in front of the cave, stood the Sea Sage. She was twelve feet tall and made entirely out of seaweed. Her green eyes blazed brightly in the indigo darkness. She spoke with a voice like ancient ship timbers breaking.

"Who dares disturb my rest?"

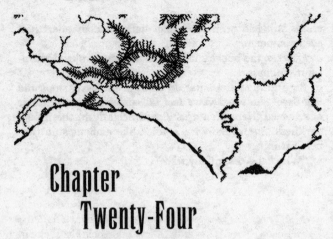

Chapter Twenty-Four

The Pirates' Lair

The water was chillier than Trip had expected, and he almost gasped out his air as he sank under the dark brine. In a moment, though, he regained his composure. Just before he was about to take a breath he remembered—and he was proud of this considering the fix he was in—that he didn't have any magical seaweed.

Green and indigo shadows surrounded the kender. He reached out with his hand to make sure they were as insubstantial as they seemed, and felt slightly disappointed when they were. Then he remembered the real threat—the men who were coming to catch him.

He gazed up at the surface, but saw only a vague, gray oval. No searchers yet—but he knew they couldn't be far behind. Turning, he dived down deeper. The strange green luminescence didn't make it much easier to see, and the kender had to grope his way through the semi-darkness.

The hole wasn't as deep as he'd thought. He found the rocky bottom only three fathoms down. For a moment, he feared he was trapped. Then he noticed that the passage split in three directions. Neither the green light nor the current gave any indication which would be the best way to go.

For a moment, he thought about turning back. But a quick glance upward showed that his pursuers had found his escape hole. Trip couldn't be sure if they saw him in the gloom, but he didn't intend to make things any easier for them.

Though he was an expert diver (part of his swimming talent), he doubted that he could hold his breath longer than they'd care to hang around the hole. He could think of only one thing to do.

Trip pulled the thong of his lucky treasure finder from around his neck. He knew it was a long chance, but the amulet had worked for him in the past. He held the rock out before him in the dim light, and moved it around in front of the three diverging tunnels.

Astoundingly, the small pointed rock began to spin in front of the right hand passage. He took a moment—but only a moment as he was fast running out of air—to check his findings. Then he kicked hard into the right hand tunnel.

He swam holding the treasure finder in front of him. The gloom seemed to go on forever as Trip swam. He was already tired from being chased to the caves. Soon his lungs burned and once more spots danced before his eyes.

Just as he feared he'd drown in the darkness, the green light grew stronger. The passage opened up before him and the ceiling fell away. Dizzy, the kender groped his way to the surface. He thrust his head out of the water and gasped for air.

He leaned against the lip of the opening for a few moments, panting to catch his breath. Then a vague rattling sound caught his ear. Trip looked up and nearly fell back into the water.

The green light suffusing the cave came from glowing lichens on the wet rock walls. A hissing breeze blew from some unseen source, making a sound like a snake ready to strike. The room was filled with human bones. Some lay scattered across the floor. Others dangled—like hideous marionettes—in mildewed netting. The breeze tugged on the bones, making the eerie rattling that Trip had first heard. The gruesome sight, though, wasn't what nearly caused the kender to lose his grip.

Trip broke into a huge grin. A vast store of pirate loot lined the tiny cavern: rusting weapons, tattered clothing, rotting draperies, some furniture, and several upturned chests of coins. The chests' contents lay spilled across the cave's stone floor.

"No wonder the treasure finder spotted this place," Trip said, his small voice filled with awe.

He pulled himself up out of the hole and took a good look around. While, to a kender, the cave seemed a veritable archive of interesting things, Trip's long years as a treasure diver made him realize that few of the items held any real value.

The steel coins—which must have formed the majority of treasure in the chests—were now little more than piles of rust. Some gold and silver pieces lay scattered among the detritus, though. Trip scooped up a few scant handfuls of these and stuffed them into the pockets of his lizard skin vest.

The bones, he assumed, came from pirates or their victims. All seemed to have met grisly ends; some still had rusting weapons protruding from their skulls and ribcages. Trip figured that everyone who knew about this place must have died in the massacre, or surely someone would have come for the treasure long ago—rather than leaving it here to rot.

The furniture and clothing had fared little better than the steel pieces. It saddened Trip's heart to see what must have once been wonderful things treated so badly. "Sea worms would have been kinder," he muttered.

He turned up a few small pearls amid the rubbish, but only costume gems and jewelry. A nice piece of gold embellished with cut rhinestones he stuck in a pocket. "For Ula," he told himself.

Then something in the corner of the room gave him a start. At first, he thought it was a person. Then he realized that it was actually an old, hooded cloak, propped on top of a chest and leaning against the cavern wall. The cloak looked bulky and solid—like a tarpaulin—and it shimmered in the dim light.

Moving closer, Trip saw that it was covered with tiny greenish scales. The cloak's surface rustled in the faint breeze, and the scales glistened.

Trip's mouth dropped open in appreciation and awe. "I wonder what kind of lizard it came from?" he asked himself. His face brightened as he gazed at the seaweed-like fringe around the cloak's edges. "Maybe it's from a sea serpent!" It didn't resemble the skin of the monster that had attacked him a few days ago, but it did remind him of a sea serpent he'd seen once on a previous voyage with Mik. His heart beat faster at the prospect.

Throwing caution to the wind, the kender skipped forward and grabbed the cloak by the hem. As he did, a creaking sound came from within the fabric. The kender looked up, and saw a skeletal face bearing down on him as the cloak lumbered forward.

Trip yelped and drew the daggers from his boots. He slashed with the small blades as the thing in the cloak lurched toward him. He stepped back, swinging again and again, trying to remember how far it was to the passage opening, hoping he could make it that far.

Then it fell on him. The kender went down, his legs and arms flailing. He felt his knives cut into something hard. Cold fingernails slashed his face. The cloak's darkness enveloped him. The thing's smothering presence bore him to the ground. Its foul odor clogged his nostrils.

He stabbed at it, again and again and again as its dead weight pressed down on him. Something clattered and the kender felt teeth scrape against his cheek. He tried to roll away, but the cloak wouldn't let him out. He was trapped—pinned in a heavy, dank robe of darkness, trapped with an undead creature that wanted his life.

Unable to think of anything else to do, he kicked hard, aiming at the creature's groin. His soft boot met only the yielding serpent cloak. The cloak flapped up in the back and the sickly green light of the cave beamed in.

Trip found himself staring eye to eye with a skeletal face. He smashed his forehead against the bridge of the things nose, then reeled back as sparks flew inside his head. "By all the gods, let go of me!" he shouted.

He tried to roll to the other side, away from the undead face. This time, the cloak gave way and he tumbled out into the light of the pirates' lair. He scrambled to his feet and backed against the wall, holding his pearl-handled daggers before him.

The cloaked thing lay between Trip and the underwater passage—his only means of escape. It crouched in a heap on the damp cavern floor, waiting for him to try and pass. Panting, Trip held his ground.

The thing didn't move.

Trip held his breath. The thing still didn't move. A small breeze wafted through the cave, and the scales of the serpent-skin cloak glistened in the wan light.

"Well? Come on!" Trip called to the undead creature.

Still the thing in the cloak did not move.

Slowly, a realization came to the kender. Mustering his curiosity, he strode over to the cloak and gave it a hard kick.

"Maybe your family should have called you 'Timberhead' rather than Shellcracker," Trip said to himself. "Because sometimes you're as dense as a pylon."

He grabbed one edge of the serpent-skin cloak and gave it a good yank, like the kender magician he'd once seen pull a tablecloth out from under a dinner service. The cloak flew into his hands while the thing inside it clattered to the floor—which, come to think of it, was pretty much the same result the magician had obtained.

Bones. Nothing but old bones with a curved knife sticking out of the ribs. The man must have died sitting in the corner of the cave with his cloak on. He'd been moldering there quietly until Trip yanked on the cloak—at which point the corpse tumbled on top of the startled kender.

"Timberhead," Trip said to himself. "Fighting a pile of old bones." He laughed, but the laughter echoed eerily in the small cave, so he stopped.

He held up the cloak and gave it a good looking over. "You're lucky you didn't cut it to ribbons, fighting imaginary spooks," he said aloud. Then he smiled.

The sea serpent cloak was quite beautiful, in a shabby sort of way—and in amazingly good condition for something that had been sitting in a dank cave for who-knew-how-long.

Trip threw it around his shoulders and immediately felt both warmer and not so wet. "You *must* be sea serpent skin," he said, "because regular lizard isn't so warm." Pleased with his find, he returned to poking around the pirates' lair.

Sadly, Trip had turned up all there was to see before his desperate fight with the dead pirate. After topping off a few pockets with the remaining coins, he looked for another way out. "They can't have brought all this loot through the hole in the floor," he reasoned.

He found a passageway hidden behind a rotting tapestry and decided to give it a go. The tunnel wound steadily upward, and Trip soon smelled the fresh scent of sea air once more. The glowing lichens quickly died away, but light from the outside leaked down the passage, enabling him to see.

He soon came to a cleverly concealed opening in the cliff face, about forty feet above the surging tide. The entryway was cut into the rock such that, from either direction, it appeared to be only a small crack in the surrounding stone. While enough to fool a human's—or perhaps even a dragon's—eye, the trick clearly had little effect on the bats whose droppings littered the cave entrance.

Trip crinkled up his nose and tried not to get his boots too messy as he peered out into the daylight beyond. Even with the cloak's hood pulled down nearly over his eyes, the light seemed unbearably bright.

"If you wait until nightfall," he thought, "you may have an easier time avoiding Kell and his men. On the other hand, if you do that, you'll have *no idea* of where you're going. Best to climb down now, have a look around, and then try to catch a boat to Darthalla."

He pulled the cloak's hood back from his head to have a better look at the cliff face; the light immediately seemed less blinding and the air felt less oppressive.

Being extra cautious, Trip slowly climbed down the cliff face to the waterline. By the time he got there, the tide had receded somewhat, leaving a thin, rocky beach along the bottom of the bluff. Taking his bearings from the afternoon sun, he quickly figured out in which direction the town lay.

He felt concerned about running into Kell again, but as the cliffs only grew steeper to the west, he had little choice. "It's either back to town or twice the climb you just made," he though.

His mind made up, he hiked down the rocky shore back the way he'd originally come. He hadn't gone far, though, when the sound of voices drifted to his ears.

"Must be around here somewhere," said a man.

"Check up the shore again," said a voice Trip recognized as belonging to Lord Kell.

"A lot of work for one kender," said the first voice.

"I'm inclined to agree, milord," said a voice belonging to Karista Meinor. "Why chase the kender when your sister is ailing?"

"Aye," Kell replied. "I did vow to take him to Alarl, though."

Trip smiled. They hadn't realized that he'd reclaimed the black diamond artifact yet. Good! If they left, it would be easier for him to get off Jaentarth.

Just as he decided to slink away and hide somewhere until they'd gone, though, the first voice shouted, "There he is!"

Trip cursed himself. He'd been so lost in thought—a very un-kender thing to do—that his enemies had sneaked up on him. He turned, but saw no easy escape down the western beach.

Kell and the others ran toward him, brandishing weapons. Trip's only alternative was a rocky, fingerlike quay stretching out into the ocean. He dashed down the quay with no clear plan in his mind. Kell and the others ran close behind.

"Perhaps I can find another underwater cave," Trip hoped. "Maybe one of those passageways I didn't take leads out here." Glancing back the way he'd come, it seemed a reasonable prospect.

An arrow whizzed by his head and shattered on the rocks in front of him. Another arrow clattered nearby. That made up his mind.

Not waiting to reach the end of the quay, he dived into the crashing waves.

* * * * *

Lord Kell and Lady Meinor watched in frustration as the kender disappeared beneath the pounding surf. They raced to where they'd last seen Trip, and stood there watching for long minutes.

"How long can he stay under?" Kell asked.

Karista shrugged. "They said he's a practiced diver. I wouldn't rule out five minutes or more."

"We'll wait," Kell said, and turning to his men added, "Keep watch up and down the beach. I don't know how he eluded us last time, but we don't want him slipping ashore unnoticed."

They waited. Five minutes. Ten. Fifteen. Twenty.

"Could he have drowned?" Kell finally asked when they'd seen no sign of Trip for a half hour.

"I don't know," Karista said with a shrug. "Probably he didn't intend to drown himself, but got caught in some undertow."

Kell nodded. "Aye, perhaps. We've wasted enough time, in any case. Our healer must have what my sister requires by now. We sail for Berann."

"And then the treasure?" Karista asked hopefully.

"If it exists, we'll find it," Kell replied, " . . .For the glory of the Order. Then you'll have your trade concession."

Karista Meinor smiled and her steel-blue eyes flashed at him. "Aye, milord."

* * * * *

Trip had spent many years diving, and once he had even beaten a pearl diver to the bottom of a six fathom bay.

Never before had he dived as he did when he leaped off the quay. The water surged around him; rocks, reefs, and seaweed flew past as though they had been shot out of a catapult. The water changed from clear, to hazy blue, to indigo in what seemed an instant.

Disoriented and nearly out of breath, he shot back up to the surface. He breached like a dolphin, shooting high into the afternoon air before crashing back down into the waves.

He sputtered and flailed for a moment before coming to rest, gently bobbing on the surface. Looking behind him, Trip saw Jaentarth and Lord Kell's ship—nearly a half league away.

Trip laughed and shook his fist in their direction, knowing they couldn't see him, but half-wishing they could.

Gazing at the distant island, he realized that this really *was* a sea serpent skin cloak—a magical one at that. That explained why the sunlight seemed so bright and the air oppressive when he had the hood on; the cloak was accustomed to the darkness of the deep sea.

That thought triggered another one. He pulled the cloak's hood up over his head once more and—carefully—dived under water. As he did, he felt a familiar tingling in his mouth, nose, and chest.

Cautiously, he took a breath.

Trip found himself greatly relieved not to be drowning. He breathed the water as naturally as if he had been born to it.

"Sleek!" he said aloud—and was happy to hear the words come out clear and undistorted.

Being careful not to go deep enough to lose his way, Trip swam underwater away from the island. To his delight, he found himself whizzing through the brine at speeds that would have made a razorfish envious.

He crashed out of the water and soared high into the air like a leaping manta ray. He cavorted with dolphins and porpoises, ran circles around sea turtles, and played "tag the fin" against a school of redtip sharks; fortunately, none of the sharks tagged him back.

As the sun touched the thunderheads clogging the western horizon, more practical matters seeped into Trip's mind—such as how he could find his friends.

Swimming to Darthalla seemed out of the question; he didn't know the way. Asking directions would be difficult, as there wasn't anyone around to ask, and he didn't know whom to trust, either.

He finally decided that his best course was to follow a ship into port and, once there, ask for directions. With the coins he'd found, perhaps he could even hire a ship to take him to Darthalla.

Being hungry, the kender grabbed some raw fish for dinner—a snap using the cloak—and thought the plan over while he ate.

No better ideas came to him, so he set out to find a likely boat to hitch up with. Spotting a white sail on the horizon, he dived under the surface once more. Trip reached the white-sailed galleon well before dark and—unknown to the captain or crew—hitched a ride.

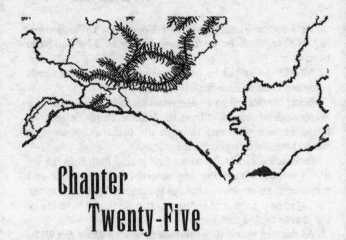

Chapter Twenty-Five

The Wrath of the Sea

A gentle current tugged at the sage's seaweed body, making the undersea titan sway slowly from side to side. Her monstrous form seemed to flow out of the coral grotto. Her leafy feet stood rooted to the sand at the cave's entrance. The creature's green eyes blazed in the deep blue shadows.

"Wayward Ula Drakenvaal," the Sea Sage intoned, "we foresaw that you might deign to visit us."

Ula bowed low and laid her spear in the sand before the weedy giant. "Great Sage . . ." she began.

"Insult us not with your false piety!" the sage snapped. Her seaweed form writhed threateningly, like a thousand angry snakes. "We see your mind, Landwalker. Your ambition—left unchecked—will bring ruin to all."

"I come because I have seen the Prophecy," Ula continued, trying to appear unperturbed. "I seek the green key."

"Care you nothing for your kith and kin?" the sage hissed. "Care you nothing for the Dragon Isles? Weak the

Veil is already. The fortune you seek lies at the corner-stone. Would you sunder all the Dargonesti have wrought?" The giant swayed back and forth like an angry cobra.

"So the treasure *does* exist," Ula said, her green eyes flashing. "Where can I find the green key? Do you have it?"

"Care you nothing for *our* people?" the sage bellowed, rattling her fronds.

Ula's eyes narrowed. *"Our* people cast me out and shunned me."

"All Dargonesti and the sea are one," the sage replied. "There is but one ocean—every drop of water touches every other."

"Which is one reason I walk on land," Ula said.

The sage's voice grew louder, like the rushing of a water-fall. "The ruin of one can bring the ruin of all. Will you be that one, Ula Drakenvaal?"

"I've no desire to be," Ula said. "I just want the treasure. The Prophecy says you hold the green key."

The sage roared her displeasure. "The key you speak of is dross! If the Veil falls, the sea dragon will be but the van-guard of evil. The Dragon Isles will succumb to the power of the overlords. I see fire, death, destruction, the boiling of the seas! I see the end of Darthalla and the Dargonesti."

Mik put his hand on Ula's shoulder. "This isn't helping," he whispered. "Try to calm her down and ask again. Tell her we're not going to destroy the isles."

The Sea Sage turned her blazing eyes upon the sailor, as if noticing him for the first time.

"Defiler!" the oracle shrieked. "You will bring ruin upon us all!"

Suddenly, the creature changed. She straightened and grew taller. Her leafy fronds wound more tightly around each other, forming into knotted muscles. Huge chitenous thorns sprouted from the tips of her fingers, and foot-long fangs sprang from her jaws. The sage's eyes blazed red, and the water around her swirled angrily.

She swung one huge hand at Ula and Mik. They ducked aside—barely in time.

The monstrous sea hag lumbered forward, tearing her roots from the sand. Her eyes were burning coals in the semi-darkness of the deep, and her weedy body writhed like a thousand serpents. A bright green spark flashed within the cave and billows of sand whirled up around the hag's footsteps. Powerful currents surged around her, hissing and gurgling with her fury. "Death to the unbelievers!"

Mik instinctively drew his sword and swung at the creature; the sword bit, but did no damage to the leafy form. The thing swatted him aside with the back of its hand. The sailor flew through the water and smashed into the sea-bed, kicking up a huge cloud of silt.

Ula ducked under the monster's follow-up blow. She darted forward and scooped up her spear off the sand.

The sea hag lowered one huge leafy foot at the elf, intending to crush her. Ula rolled aside, but not quite quick enough. Her long, platinum hair caught under the monster's clawed toes. Ula's head snapped back and she yelped in pain.

She swung her spear at the sacred column and batted the pearl-encrusted starfish off the top. The golden offering sailed through the water and skidded to a halt in the sand nearby. As it settled, the hag wobbled and her weedy muscles unraveled slightly.

Ula yanked her hair out from beneath the giant foot and turned to swim away. Before she could escape, though, the hag, with a roar like a typhoon, grabbed the sea elf by her ankle. Ula tried to kick free, but the monster held her in a grip like iron.

"The pearl!" Ula screamed. "Destroy the pearl!"

Mik blinked the dust from his eyes and rose from the sea floor. He lunged for the golden starfish and scooped it off the sand just as the hag threw Ula at him.

The sea elf hit the sailor full in the chest. Their bodies tangled together, and they both tumbled down into the muck.

The weedy hag lumbered forward, hissing and crackling as she came. "Death to the defilers!"

Mik dug the golden starfish out from under Ula's shapely leg and smashed the pommel of his scimitar down onto the central gem. The pearl erupted into a shower of blue sparks and the golden icon shattered into a hundred pieces.

Instantly, strong currents swirled around them, building into an maelstrom of angry water. The whirlpool tugged mercilessly at the leafy form of the sea hag. She began to unravel, like a great tangled skein being undone by an invisible weaver. The hag's huge body pulled tight, her form becoming thinner every moment. Knotted muscles, woody bones, and thorny fingers attenuated into loose strands of seaweed once more. The currents tugged at the thing's hair, quickly unraveling her whole face. The fire in her eyes became a dim spark, quickly extinguished by the dark waters. The rest of the body followed, swept up like stacked hay caught in a cyclone.

"Landwalker, you . . . shall destroy . . . us all!" the creature wailed as it dissipated. A few seconds later, only the empty cave and the gently swaying beds of seaweed remained.

Ula sighed with relief. She untangled herself from Mik and hovered in the water just above the sailor.

Mik picked himself up again. "That went well," he said.

Ula frowned. "And she didn't tell us where to find the key," she said.

"I think I know," Mik replied. *"To root Green key awaits."* He walked into the small cave and began to dig amid the weeds where the sage had first taken shape. Ula swam in beside him and dug as well.

Sifting through the sand, their questing hands discovered a hard, metallic object. Together, they wrestled it out of the muck and weeds and lifted it into the dim light.

The green key shimmered in the semi-darkness. Its looping golden whorls were similar to those of the black diamond key. The setting was rounder than the first key, and—like its companion—asymmetrical. At the center of the golden jewelry, rested a flawless emerald.

"Clever figuring out the 'root' was the root of the sage," Ula said.

"A bit of brainpower, a bit of luck," Mik replied. "I saw a reflection flash off something in the cave when the creature uprooted herself."

Ula puffed out her cheeks and blew off the fine sediment covering the artifact.

"I'll keep this one," she said, weaving the key into the elaborate web of jewelry holding her clothing together.

"Will she re-form, do you think?" Mik asked, as they exited the cave and dusted themselves off.

"We'll be to Aurialastican by the time she does," Ula said.

Mik rubbed his beard. "Do you believe what she said, about the isles being in peril?"

Ula shrugged and her platinum hair fell across her shoulders in a very alluring way. "Sages don't know everything," she said. "We're only two little people in a very big ocean. I don't buy all that fish oil about one person making a difference. Do you?"

"I suppose not. To Aurialastican, then?"

"And the next key."

Mik and Ula swam up out of the pit to where Shimmer stood waiting. Mounting their draken ray steeds, they set course for Aurialastican, the capital of the Dragon Isles.

Neither of them noticed the shark with eerie red eyes that followed them.

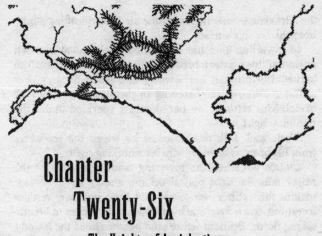

Chapter Twenty-Six

The Heights of Aurialastican

Shimmer led Mik and Ula up through the clear waters toward the sunlit surface above. All morning, the sea bottom had been rising steadily, a sure sign that they were nearing land once more.

They'd traveled on the surface the previous night—each tethered to their constantly moving steeds by leathery seaweed harnesses. They took watches in turns, though Shimanloreth watched longer than his friends. Ula had disquieting dreams, but nothing else disturbed them during the night. They ate a light breakfast and spurred their hired draken rays toward the dragon capital at Aurialastican—traveling below the water again when the sun came up, lest Lord Kell's spies should be watching.

The rays—huge batlike creatures with indigo bodies and pale, dappled bellies—moved quickly through the crystalline waters, gaining speed as the rising sun warmed their powerful winged forms. Now, at the height of noon, they burst from the water and into the open air once more.

The drakens soared high into the air before settling gently onto the ocean's surface.

Mik Vardan tied his enchanted necklace to his belt again and took a deep breath of the clean summer air. Ula looked stunning in her jewelry and scant drapery; her sculpted blue figure glistening in the sunshine. The ring of dolphins tattooed on her shoulder sparkled under the noonday light.

Their goal, Mik discovered as he wiped the sea water from his brow, was an equally breathtaking sight.

Clouds wreathed the towering mountain peaks of the Misty Isle. Sunlight played off the snowy upper slopes, making them glitter orange and gold. Long swaths of verdant forest ran down from the high slopes to the edges of breathtaking fjords. Brilliant white sand beaches lined the islands' shores. These natural wonders, though, paled next to the glory of the city itself.

Aurialastican dominated the entrance of a wide bay at the mouth of a vast fjord. Mist filled the defile's far reaches, making them appear unreal and ghostly. Aurialastican seemed the only solid thing in an ethereal landscape.

The city was larger than anything Mik had ever seen in Khur; as large, seemingly, as great Palanthas itself. Its buildings shone in the afternoon sun: white as marble, polished as silver, burning like bronze, glittering with glass and crystal. The metals beloved by the great dragons formed the city's decor. Gold, though, predominated.

The yellow metal glowed warmly amid the city's rooftops, towers, and minarets. Golden banners lined the city's broad avenues, waving in the breeze. Even the leaves of the trees lining the city street glistened with golden color. It was easy to see why Aurialastican was considered a myth in many parts of the world. It was also easy to see why it was called the "City of Gold."

But though the buildings lining the shoreline were impressive, the architecture on the ridge beyond them was even more astonishing. Huge monuments—as much sculpture as edifice—dominated the plateau: gigantic trees, mountains, ships, dragons, rings, pyramids, columns, as well as many abstract shapes. Some were made of brightly shining metal; others had been carved from stone or coral; still others seemed to have been shaped from the living rock itself.

The single unifying theme of these monuments was their titanic size. Every one dwarfed the largest building in the city below. Clearly none were fashioned by human hands; they had been shaped and erected by dragons.

Mik's jaw hung open in wonder. "Is that . . . the Dragon-heights?"

"Yes," Shimanloreth replied. "Repository of dragon wealth and glory."

Ula laughed. "It takes your breath away the first time you see it."

Mik found his eyes drawn to one of the bright pyramids on the ridge. Reflections of the sun on its surface, though, made it impossible to see clearly. "One step closer," he thought, and in his mind the image of the huge diamond became clear once more.

They steered their draken rays through the shallows and into the port of Aurialastican. Many tall ships lined the docks: galleys, caravels, galleons, longboats, fishing vessels, and several shell-like ships that could only have come from the undersea kingdoms of the Dargonesti. Proud sails, emblazoned with all manner of fantastic creatures—especially dragons—fluttered in the warm breeze. Brightly-colored banners flew from the tops of mastheads. The air was alive with the creaking of timbers and the shouts of mariners. The strong scent of wood and ship oils drifted across the warm breeze.

Mik gazed at the flotilla as they drew close to the docks. "Some of these ships have gemstones at their helms," he said. "Are they used to navigate the Veil?"

"Possibly, yes," Shimmer replied. "Though they might be for other purposes as well."

"Where do the gems that pierce the Veil come from?" Mik asked.

"From the dragon Oligarchs, to reward the worthy," Shimmer replied.

"Others of us have to *earn* our boons," Ula said. She stepped off the back of her draken onto the well-maintained dock and extended a hand up to Mik.

He hopped up onto the ancient timbers beside her. "Let's hope we can find the next key amid those monuments," he said, glancing at the Dragonheights once again.

"Let's hope," Shimmer added, "that we shall be allowed to look." He joined the others on the dock, then let go the reigns of his draken ray and whispered something to it. The lead ray dipped its head, as though nodding yes, then all three steeds disappeared back the way they had come. "They'll find their way home," the bronze knight said.

The three companions walked down the wharf toward the bustling city.

People of all kinds crowded the harbor's wharves: elves, dwarves, humans, minotaurs, and even a kender or two—though these last were always being chased by someone. Occasionally, a metallic dragon would flash by overhead. They saw brass, copper, bronze, but never a silver or a gold. Most of the citizens were so used to the sight that they never even glanced up.

The treasure seekers passed bars, inns, and eateries, all with smells that made Mik's stomach rumble. He convinced the others to stop at an open-air tavern for a bite. It was a small place with a green tabard over the door that read "Hender's House," and a number of tall, round wooden tables set up out front. A tall scraggly-haired man in a white apron bustled back and forth between the tables taking orders and serving meals. Mik ordered yellow bread and spiced stew; Ula and Shimmer had the same. In short order, the air was filled with the aroma of sage and boiled meat.

"What did you mean, earlier," Mik asked Shimanloreth,

"when you said you hoped we'd 'be allowed to look'?" The captain took a bite of the stew and savored its taste.

"Dragons guard their secrets jealously," Shimmer replied. "Few are permitted to climb the Dragonheights—though I believe they will let me do so."

Ula laughed. "I'd like to see them stop you," she said.

Shimmer fixed his orangish eyes on the sea elf. "I would not," he said simply. "You two should find a ship to hire while I search for the third key."

"I'm in this all the way to the Dragonheights," Mik said. "I haven't come this far to turn back—or to stay in town and search for boats while you do the hard work."

"He's earned the right, you know," Ula said. "Besides, I'm not sure the sailor trusts you quite yet, Shimmer." She grinned at the knight and winked at Mik.

Shimanloreth nodded slowly. "Very well," he said.

"Well," Ula sighed, standing and stretching, "I guess that leaves it to me to find a ship for our treasure hunt. I'll probably have to buy a captain as well. No offense, Mik."

"None taken."

Ula extended her hand to Shimmer, and he placed a pouch of coins in it. She took a moment to judge the weight and frowned playfully. "This will do for a start," she said. "See to the bill, will you?" She pushed her stall stool away from the table and turned to go.

"Ula, wait," Mik said.

"Hmm?"

"Let me hold on to the green key," he said. "It may help in locating the other one we're looking for."

"I suppose it might at that." She took a moment to undo it from her web of jewelry and placed the emerald artifact into the sailor's hand.

"Thanks," he said, tucking into his belt pocket.

"Take good care of it."

Mik nodded, and she disappeared into the crowd.

"I've known her a long time," Shimmer said when she'd gone, "yet I still do not understand her."

"She's not so hard to figure out," Mik replied.

Shimmer paid the outdoor tavern's bill and they left. It didn't take them long to push through the city's crowded streets onto the long avenue leading up to the Dragonheights.

Mik craned his neck upward, trying to take in the amazing structures towering over them. Halfway up the steep road they almost seemed no nearer at all. Turning a corner Mik came into view of a distant pyramid. Atop it rested a glittering crystal globe. The gem sprayed shimmering beams of blue light into the afternoon air.

Mik stopped and stared at it. The crystal grew larger in his mind and became the great blue-white diamond. The diamond blazed like the sun, and the sky flashed with lighting. The world sank away and he soared high in the sky, gazing down on the Dragon Isles. All around, storm clouds loomed.

"What's wrong?" asked a distant voice, sounding vaguely like thunder.

Mik blinked, and the bronze-helmeted face of Shimmer came into focus before him.

"Are you all right?" the knight asked.

"I'm fine," Mik said. "Let's keep going. I just had an idea, that's all."

"An idea about what?" Shimmer asked.

"That pyramid," Mik said, pointing. "I think it may be connected to our goal, somehow."

"That pyramid is one of the great libraries."

"Wisdom's highest throne," Mik said quietly.

"Part of the Prophecy, eh?" Shimmer replied. "Well, it's possible."

"Let's go," Mik said.

The bronze knight nodded, and they walked up the slope once more.

Long minutes later, they crested the hill and gazed across the plateau of the Dragonheights. Before them stretched the colossal plaza of the monuments. To Mik it seemed like an immense graveyard: nothing moved, no breeze disturbed the air, no smells wafted to his nose, nothing broke the eerie silence. The monuments—marble shapes, metal creatures, crystal plants, and glistening abstracts in every imaginable combination—towered over Mik and Shimmer, but seemed distant and unreal at the same time. It was as though the treasure hunters gazed at an immense still-life painting rather than a real place.

"Where are the people?" Mik asked. "Why isn't anything moving?"

"It's the magic," Shimanloreth replied. "Look there."

Mik looked and saw a aristocrat in fancy dress, frozen in mid step. Nearer by, a hooded woman had just topped the cliff face. She, too, hung rooted to the spot: unmoving, unbreathing.

"Are they . . . dead?" Mik asked.

"No," Shimmer replied. "But the dragons don't want them here. The enchantment has frozen them in time. A nasty surprise for that thief," he said, indicating the hooded woman.

"Let's hope the enchantment doesn't catch us as well," Mik said.

"It may. There's only one way to find out." The bronze knight stepped boldly into the plaza.

As he did, blue sparks blazed around his armored form. He paused, as though pushing against an unseen barrier. Then he lurched forward again very slowly, as though he were walking underwater. He motioned Mik to follow, but if he spoke, the sailor could not hear him.

Mik placed his foot upon the mosaic at the plaza's edge.

The sailor's skin caught fire, and his senses whirled. He staggered forward, as though he were walking through molasses. Every step became harder. He felt as if he were at the nadir of a long dive, the ocean pressing in on every part of his body. So much pressure.

His limbs began to tingle as though asleep. He blinked. It took forever for his eyelids to descend, and even longer for them to rise again.

Instinctively, Mik reached toward his belt pocket, where the emerald artifact lay.

Very slowly, his fingers crept forward.

Close.

So close.

Contact.

Fire burned through his body again. The magical blaze fought against the pressure—nearly tearing him apart.

The next moment, it ended.

Mik doubled over, sweating profusely, his guts in a knot.

"Are you all right?" Shimmer's deep voice asked.

"Fine," Mik gasped, struggling to his feet.

"For a moment, I didn't think you were going to make it," Shimmer said. "Your willpower must be very strong."

"I guess," Mik said, fighting down a wave of nausea. "Where's the library?"

"Not far, as dragons measure it."

"How about as sailors measure it?"

"A fair walk."

Mik bowed slightly, and swept his right arm forward. "After you."

The knight and the sailor walked toward the distant pyramid. They'd hardly gone a dozen steps, though, when a huge copper dragon dropped out of the sky and barred their way.

He opened his enormous maw and hissed, "Halt, trespassers!"

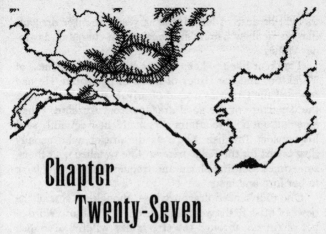

Chapter
Twenty-Seven
Plans & Schemes & Spies

Benthor Kell strode down the streets of Thrakton as if he owned the place— which, in one sense, he did. Thrakton, a tidy and well-ordered city, was the largest town on the island of Berann. Most of its buildings had been newly built or renovated. The style of architecture throughout was simple, utilitarian, and uncluttered. The fortress of the order reflected this Spartan style. Its cyclopean walls loomed over the streets, looking both protective and intimidating at the same time. The city's location at the head of the isle's only deep water harbor, at the mouth of Berann's main river, made it an ideal head-quarters for the Order of Brass.

Benthor and Misa Kell ran the Order, and therefore the town as well. Everyone was aware, though, that all humans lived on the island only with the sufferance of Berann's dragons.

Thracktil the Fierce, a huge, ancient brass dragon, was true lord of the island. He seldom appeared in public, though, because of his advancing years. Younger dragons, like his nephew Thrakdar, remained in charge of day-to-day affairs.

Thrakdar liked to keep a close claw on the business of Thrakton, and the Order of Brass in particular. He had founded the Order as a kind of private police force, after the departure of the good dragons from Ansalon. When he could not tend to affairs personally, he frequently sent his consort Tanalish. She was the dragon who usually flew escort for the Kells' trireme. She watched over them, sometimes scouting ahead and frequently reporting back to her lord and mate.

One didn't need dragon wings, though, to spread the news of Misa Kell's wounding through Thrakton. Word of her plight ran through the streets like wildfire. Tanalish had alerted the Order to expect casualties, but none of them guessed that the wounded would be their own beloved lady.

The Order mobilized quickly, bringing all their considerable healing skills to bear on the wounded woman. Soon concern in the ranks gave way to anger. Though Misa had been wounded in a lawful duel, many brass warriors spoke openly of hunting down and slaying the perpetrator of this terrible deed.

Benthor Kell threatened to severely punish anyone who broke ranks and carried out such a vendetta. Publicly he claimed that such feuds were bad for discipline, which was an essential element of the Order. Privately, he himself hoped to pay back Ula Drakenvaal.

His sister's grave condition added to Kell's sour mood as he walked the narrow streets of Thrakton. He strode away from the Order's fortress and toward the pier where his brass-sided trireme lay anchored. Benthor clutched his coral lance tightly in his fist, nodded curtly to those who greeted him, and growled quick orders to those under his command.

Karista Meinor walked with him, hurrying to keep pace. The aristocrat had acquired new, fashionable clothes during her short stay in town. Now she was in serious danger of dragging her hems through the muddy street. Because of her tenuous position in Kell's favor, she didn't ask the lord to slow down.

"Capturing this treasure will not make up for my sister's wounding," Kell said.

Karista smiled at him pleasantly. "I did not offer the treasure as a remedy, milord—merely as a token of my good faith in our future ventures. Surely you do not want Ula and her friends to gain these riches."

"Of course not," Kell shot back. "But my operatives have lost track of the Landwalker and her friends."

"A minor inconvenience that I'm certain you can surmount," Karista said.

Kell nodded. "My associates in Darthalla have sent reports that the trio has left the city—and they have not been seen since."

"We know the elf and her friends are clever," Karista said, "but we also know they are looking for the treasure. They cannot remain hidden forever."

"Perhaps," Kell replied. "Though that sea witch may have resources unknown to us." He clenched his brass-mailed fist tight. "If only the cursed kender had not stolen the first key! My people have scoured the seas around Jaentarth, but found no sign of it—or the kender's body."

"The kender will seek his friends, and they will seek him," Karista said. "I'm sure you can use your . . . influence to locate them." The aristocrat glanced from Lord Kell to the clouds high overhead.

Kell took the suggestion. "Yes," he said, glancing toward the mountainous lair of his dragon allies. Atop the distant peaks, the mysterious brass pyramids glistened in the afternoon sun.

"Thrakdar's people can turn them up," Kell said. "Above the waves or below, these rogues can't hide from the Order of Brass. We'll set course for their last known location and await word from my operatives. Our communications move with the speed of dragon wings. These sorry treasure hunters won't elude us for long."

Kell and Karista stopped on the pier alongside the lord's brass-scaled galley. His crew extended the gangplank and Lord Kell boarded the trireme with Karista Meinor at his side.

Chapter
Twenty-Eight

Paths of Knowledge

The copper dragon was huge, larger than the brass they'd seen flying over Lord Kell's galley. The sun glinted orange off his rough hide and glistened from the peaks of his horns and the spikes along his spine. Flexible metal scales covered his belly, and thick armored plating adorned its back. His blue eyes burned with terrible intelligence. Clearly, the Dragonheights were built by and for such creatures. The dragon hovered effortlessly before them, his great wings buffeting the plateau's still air.

Mik's knees went weak, and he had to fight to remain standing. Sweat beaded on his forehead, and the artifact tucked into his waistband felt suddenly hot. He found it difficult to breathe.

"How did you pass the barrier?" the dragon boomed. He extended his claws, and his tongue flicked out of his huge maw as if to taste the people standing before him.

"W-we seek wisdom's highest throne," Mik said. His

throat had gone dry and his words sounded faint and distant even as he spoke them.

"Kopernus . . . Is that you?" Shimmer asked. If the knight felt any of the same dragonfear, it didn't show through his bronze armor.

The copper dragon's eyes narrowed and he looked squarely at the bronze knight, but said nothing.

"It's me, Shimanloreth."

"Shimanloreth?" the hovering dragon replied. The creature scowled. "This is a trick. It could be *anyone* under that helmet." He peered at the knight as though he might stare through the bronze carapace.

Shimmer sighed and reached up as though to brush back his hair. As his metal-gloved hands touched armor, his helmet slid back like a window blind and folded itself into the collar of the knight's breastplate.

The copper dragon's frightening visage brightened. "It *is* you," he said. "You're smaller than I remember, but I'm glad you've come to visit me. Where have you been lately?"

"Exiled."

"Exiled?" The dragon frowned. "Who would exile you?"

"I exiled myself. I didn't like the company I was keeping."

The copper dragon nodded. "I sometimes felt that way— before the other dragons left. Most are gone, you know."

"I heard."

Mik screwed up his courage and spoke. "If so many others are gone, why are *you* still here?"

Kopernus puffed out his chest. "Someone has to guard the Dragonheights," he said. "So I took it on as my duty. Those haughty brasses wanted it, but I wouldn't let them." He rose into the air and circled the plaza twice, the sun glinting off his orange wings, before settling down again. "Now, the enchantment keeps all the rest out. Only *I* have the honor of protecting the monuments."

"Very impressive," said Shimmer.

Kopernus bowed his head at the compliment.

"We're seeking knowledge of a key," Mik said, feeling almost himself once more. "I'm sure a dragon of your immense . . . power must have some wisdom to share with your old friend Shimmer and me."

Kopernus glowered. "I'm a guardian, not a librarian handing out knowledge. My duty is to protect this place."

"And a fine job you're doing," Mik said. "Would you like to escort us to that pyramid over there?" He pointed toward their destination. "Make sure that we don't run into any trouble?"

"It would be my honor," Kopernus replied. "I'll scout ahead and clear the way."

He turned, flipping head over tail—barely missing tall monuments on each side—and streaked off through a towering bronze tree with jade leaves.

"I can see why few people venture up here," Mik said.

Shimmer nodded. "Kopernus can be deadly when provoked."

They moved as quickly as they could through the strange city: running over mosaics the size of city blocks, fording rivers frozen in time, and dodging around the titanic monuments.

"Like a graveyard for the gods," Mik thought.

The sailor's legs were nearly ready to quit when Shimmer finally pulled up before a huge, white marble pyramid. Kopernus hovered near a door in the side of the huge edifice.

"No scoundrels in sight," the copper dragon said.

"Thank you for your help," replied Mik.

The copper puffed out his chest again. "Please keep your visit brief, and let me know if you spot any rogues."

"We will," Mik said.

"Come visit again soon, Shimanloreth."

"When I can," Shimmer replied.

With a single flap of his huge wings, Kopernus shot into the sky. Moments later, the copper dragon disappeared entirely.

Mikal Vardan let out a long, relieved breath.

The doors of the pyramid stood recessed into the side of the immense structure. Each was five times as wide and tall as a human door. They were made of the same polished marble as the library's mountain-like exterior and had no doorhandles.

Shimmer stuck his fingertips into the broad crack between them and pulled with all his might. With a groan like distant thunder, the doors opened—just a crack.

Mik and the knight pushed through the opening and into a long, dimly lit hallway filled with hundred-foot columns.

Mik began to hike down the hallway; Shimmer followed behind, rubbing his left shoulder.

"This place looks even larger inside than it did outside," Mik commented.

"The gold and silver dragons who built it were powerful sorcerers," Shimmer replied. "The laws of time and space do not always apply to them."

Mik nodded, remembering the people frozen motionless in the plaza.

They passed through the end of the long corridor and into a huge, domed chamber. Hundreds of shelves, each as tall as a man, lined the walls. The shelves were filled to overflowing with books and scrolls, also of titanic size. Golden filigree, gems, and strange runes decorated the spines of the volumes. Some were bound in leather, other in armored hide or scaly skin, and still others in parchment alone.

"If the key were hidden in this room, it would take a lifetime to find it," Mik said.

"More than a lifetime—unless you're a dragon." Shimmer replied.

"Fortunately, I don't think it's here," Mik said, a smile cracking his bearded face. "I think we have to go *up* in the pyramid—to the *highest throne.*"

"A fair assumption." Shimanloreth shouldered aside a huge oak door on the far side of the chamber and discovered a staircase beyond. They went through and climbed the long stairway.

The chamber at the top of the stairs was built on a more human scale. The stacks were huge, but they had normal sized—if elaborate and beautiful—books, and long ladders for reaching the top shelves. Skylights dominated the vaulted ceiling, providing the room with plenty of natural lighting—though Mik didn't recall seeing any windows on the outside of the pyramid.

Going ever upward, they climbed a balcony on the far side of the room and opened a normal-sized oak door set into one wall.

The staircase beyond stretched high overhead into darkness. Hundreds of identical, brass-handled doors debouched onto the stairway. As Mik and Shimmer climbed, they opened a few of the doors they passed and discovered strange and wondrous things beyond. One doorway overlooked an endless twilit sea. They nearly fell through another into a black, star-dappled sky with no solid ground in sight. Musty, cobweb-covered scrolls filled one room beyond the stairs. Another was stacked floor to ceiling with polished obsidian orbs.

The climb to the top of the stairs was tortuously long, and they stopped several times to catch their breath.

"How long have we been here?" Mik asked.

"A moment? A day? A lifetime?" Shimmer replied. "Who can tell?"

At the top of the stairs they found a final golden door.

The portal resisted their attempts to open it until Mik held up the emerald key. Then the latch gave easily.

Mik shrugged at Shimmer. They walked through the door, down a short corridor, and into a huge spherical chamber. The whole of *Kingfisher*—masts and all—could easily have fit inside the room. Stunning mosaics entirely covered the vast, curving walls. The floor depicted the ocean, wide and blue and teaming with life. The walls—if the globular space could be said to have walls—were covered with scenes of the Dragon Isles: islands, beaches, forests, mountains, ships, and flying dragons. Overhead, an indigo sky sported countless shimmering stars set in the constellations of Krynn.

At the very center of the room, a huge golden chair with crimson padding hung motionless in the air. A strange, flickering golden aura surrounded the seat. A fist-sized multifaceted crystal had been set into the apex of the chair's back.

"Wisdom's highest throne, I presume," Mik said. He crossed the ocean mosaic and stood in the center of the room under the hovering chair. "Give me a hand up, would you?"

Shimmer nodded and came to help.

The golden throne hung nearly a dozen feet above the ocean mosaic. Mik had to stand on Shimmer's shoulders, and—even then—his fingers barely brushed the chair's dragonlike legs.

"Hold steady," Mik called down to the knight. "I'm going to jump for it." With that, he launched himself into the air and caught hold of one of the throne's legs.

As he touched it, first his hands, then his whole body began to tingle. The glow suffusing the chair increased, and the air crackled with magical energy.

Goosebumps rose on Mik's arms as he climbed, hand over hand, up to the blood-red seat. His dark hair stood on end and wavered as though tugged by an unfelt wind.

"Are you all right?" Shimmer called up.

"Fine," Mik replied, pulling himself into the seat at last. He took a long, deep breath and settled in.

"This is a foolish thing you're doing!"

"Who risks most, gains most," Mik replied, his body quivering so much that his teeth chattered. "I-I seek the key."

As he spoke, the chair began to spin. Faster and faster it went, until the room around it blurred and Mik felt himself pressed back, into the padded seat.

Golden lightning crackled all around. His hair shot straight out, and his skin felt as though it were being rubbed with sandpaper.

Then the world went away.

* * * * *

The cloaked figured hurtled into Ula, toppling the sea elf over backward. The thing smelled of sweat, brine, and rotten fish.

Ula cursed and rolled to one side, trying to kick the attacker off, but the cloak got tangled in her jewelry.

She cursed again and pushed hard. This time, the thing burst free, taking some of her jewelry and a bit of her modesty with it. Angrily, she thrust her spear at the flabby, baglike thing squirming on the street.

"Hey!" the creature cried.

"Drag me to the Abyss!" Ula said, not sure whether to laugh or weep. "What are *you* doing here?"

Tripleknot Shellcracker got up and dusted himself off. "Well, that's a fine hello," he said, frowning at Ula. "Do you always try to run your friends through?"

"Only when I don't know they're my friends," she replied, picking up her jewelry and putting her clothing back together. "You're lucky I didn't kill you."

"I suppose I am," the kender replied. "But it's really great to see you anyway." He stepped forward to embrace her, but she backed away.

"What *is* that smell?" she asked, crinkling her pretty nose.

"Smell?" Trip said.

The sea elf groaned. "It's the cloak. It smells like fish left in the sun for a week."

Trip lifted the ragged hem of the cloak and sniffed it. "Does it?" he said. "I hadn't really noticed. This is genuine sea serpent, you know." He lowered his voice and added, "It's *very* magical."

Ula huffed skeptically. "So, how did you get here, minnow?"

"Let's discuss it over lunch," Trip replied. "I'm starved. I'll even pay. I picked up a few coins on my way here."

By the end of the meal, Ula had wheedled out most of the story of how Trip obtained his cloak and how he got to Aurialastican.

"I've been trying," Trip finished, "to find someone to take me to Darthalla. It isn't a popular destination, though, and finding someone has been trickier than I thought it would be."

"I doubt many kender charter ships," Ula said. "So you escaped from Berann, Lord Kell, and the Order of Brass, made your way here by hitching a ride on a passing ship, and even arranged to hire a boat? I must admit, I'm impressed."

Trip beamed at her. "Thanks, Ula. Or should I call you 'Landwalker?' "

Ula fingered the pommel of a gem-studded knife hanging from the intricate golden chain at her waist. "Only my enemies call me 'Landwalker.' "

"Ula it is, then," Trip replied.

"About this ship you've hired . . ." she said.

"Well," Trip said, "perhaps *hired* isn't quite the right word. It was going to drop some supplies at Darthalla, they agreed to take me along—for an exorbitant fee, I might add. The captain might not have taken me at all. But he changed his mind when I mentioned Mik's name. I guess he's an old friend of Mik's or something."

"Really?" Ula asked.

"A burly, red-headed guy," Trip replied. "Said his name was Jerick. Funny thing is, Mik once told me he was dead."

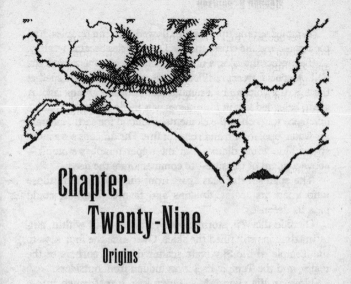

Chapter Twenty-Nine

Origins

aught in the center of the whirlpool, Mik spun faster and faster. The walls of the library had disappeared completely. A roaring sound, like storm-driven surf, filled his ears.

He felt himself surrounded by water, and then thrust into the open air. Waves crashed all around and thunderheads collided overhead. The squall moved away quickly, as though pushed from the sky by a titanic invisible hand.

Sunlight streamed over the aquamarine ocean, reflecting from the whitecaps and filling the air with dazzling color. Mik soared over the waves as the Dragon Isles rose majestically from the sea.

He saw it all: the glorious history, the glory of the isles. He saw the thousand metallic dragons, swarming over the islands, changing the shape and nature of the land. He saw the first people arrive and, with the help of the dragons, settlements became towns, and towns became cities.

Temples sprang up, treasure flowed into the temples, and the towns, and the cities, and the Dragon Isles became wealthy.

To protect the isles, a mighty enchantment was raised: the Veil. A special treasure-filled temple was built for the spell at the top of a volcano in a remote corner of the archipelago. A great, bejeweled key in four pieces was made to seal the pact—one piece for each of the elements: diamond for earth, emerald for water, opal for air, and ruby for fire. The dragons set a monstrous blue-white diamond at the upper temple's summit—above a hoard of treasure—to commemorate the deed.

The spell set the isles apart from the world—only those who knew its secret, dragons and favored mortals, could pass its defenses.

Outside the Veil, storm clouds gathered—but within, glittering dragons still filled the skies. Over time the four keys to the Temple of the Sky were scattered to the corners of the realm, and the Temple itself was hidden from outsiders.

Now, in his vision, Mik saw a key, transformed into a shining, golden gem, approach him before the floating chair, hovering in front of him and regarding Mik like a baleful yellow eye.

"I seek the third key," Mik said, fighting hard to hold his voice steady.

The gemstone flashed and sparkled, and within it Mik saw an image of the third piece of ancient jewelry: the opal key. It looked similar to the other two: twisting, asymmetrical golden lines, with the blue stone set in the center. Its shape, though, was not quite the same as that of either the diamond or the emerald key.

"Seek the key within," a voice in his head intoned.

A burning sensation welled up within Mik's breast. An image flashed within his mind. A satisfied feeling spread out from the center of his body toward the end of his limbs. Mik fought down the sensation and concentrated instead on the gem.

He reached out, and his fingers passed through the golden orb's surface. Fire sprang up around his arms; his hair burst into flame. The image in his mind spurred him on—the glittering shape of a huge blue-white diamond. He reached farther, farther, and at last touched the key.

Mik seized the gold and opal artifact in his fingers, just as the skin sloughed off his arm. He held it tight, even as his flesh turned to ash, revealing the white bone beneath.

The next instant, the gem grew very heavy. It pulled him from the chair and he plunged through the sky toward a volcanic island far below.

In his head he heard the voices of his friends and former shipmates, begging him to save himself—begging him to let go. Trip, old Poul, Marlian, Pamak, Ula, and many others— some alive, others dead—all beseeched him to give up the deadly artifact.

Mik refused. He clung tight, even as he plunged into the fires of the volcano and his bones turned to charcoal.

"I will not give up!" he thought.

Then suddenly he found himself sitting back in the golden chair.

The yellow gemstone eye hovered before him, staring into his soul. "Beware!" said the voice in his head. "The path you walk is perilous! Know yourself and you will know the consequences of your actions."

The world spun again. Lightning flashed through Mik's body. He struggled to breathe.

The mosaic floor of the viewing room rushed up to meet him. He smashed his head against the tiles and lights flashed inside his skull.

Instantly, Shimmer appeared at his side and helped him to sit.

"Are you all right?" the knight asked. "What happened? Did you learn anything? Did you *see* anything?"

Mik blinked, trying to fight down the aches in his muscles and the fire in his head. The opal artifact in his hand shone brightly. He took a deep breath, but things didn't become much clearer. "How long was I up there?"

"Only a few moments. What did you see?"

"I saw the isles," Mik gasped, his voice dry. "I saw them form from the sea. I saw the dragons claim the isles as their own. I saw the creation of the Veil."

Shimmer nodded grimly.

"A temple was at the center of it—a temple filled with diamonds."

"Our destination," Shimmer said, offering him a skin of water.

Mik drank. "Yes. I have some idea where it is, now." He stood and stretched, a faint smile parting his lips. ". . . Which I will share at the appropriate time."

Shimmer nodded. "I'm sure that Ula will be glad to hear it." He gave Mik a hand up.

"Let's find her," the sailor said.

Shimmer nodded again, and they left, winding back down the way they'd come. When they reached the city, they had little trouble locating Ula and Trip, who had never quite made it to the ship the kender was bragging about. Ula had, however, extricated their diminutive companion from a close call with the local authorities.

Mik was both surprised and glad to see Trip in Aurialastican. The kender and the sea elf were happy to discover that Mik had obtained the opal key.

"Three down, one to go," Trip said, beaming.

"Aye," Mik said. "Now let's find that ship."

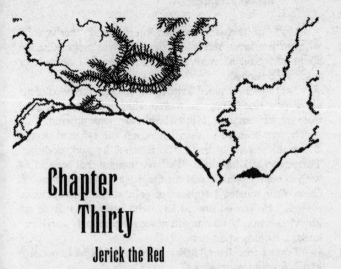

Chapter Thirty

Jerick the Red

Jerick the Red prowled the deck of his galleon like an angry wolf, barking orders to his crew. His men swung supplies onto the quarterdeck with heavy ropes and pulleys, then secured the reserves below. His ship, *Red Wake*, seemed in fine shape, with newer sails and rigging, a fresh coat of red and blue paint on the trim, and the barnacles recently scraped from its hull. From the way Red ordered his crew about, though, you'd have thought the ship was on the verge of disaster.

"It's a wonder," Mik called up to him from the dock, "that you can get anyone to sign aboard, with you prowling around like a mother cat."

Jerick turned, an angry retort on his bearded lips. Then he recognized Mik and broke into a broad smile. "Mik Vardan! While I live and breathe," he said. "I didn't expect to see you here."

"Nor did I," Mik replied. "I thought you were dead."

"That's quite a story, me lad," Jerick said. "Perhaps I'll tell it to you later. You know, someone was just asking me about you. Said he wanted to go find you in Darthalla or some such rubbish."

"That was me!" piped Trip, throwing back the hood of his sea serpent cloak. Ula, who was standing next to him, winced from the sudden odor. Mik and Shimmer kept upwind.

The red-bearded captain leaned on the rail and peered down at the four of them. "So it was," he said, nodding. Turning to Mik he added, "I'd have thought that consorting with kender would be bad for the salvage business—no offense, little master. I approve of your shapely companion, though." He bowed toward Ula, who nodded curtly in acknowledgment. "And one can never have enough warriors," he said, looking at Shimmer.

"Trip's a fine diver," Mik replied. "And he has a positive knack for finding treasure."

"I should say so," Jerick said. "He paid me with a very strange assortment of coin." He frowned. "I suppose you'll be wanting your money back now, master kender."

"Oh, no," Trip said buoyantly. "We want to hire you for an even bigger job."

Jerick raised his bushy eyebrows. "Well, in that case, you'd best come aboard."

They walked up the gangplank, and Jerick showed them into his cabin—a roomy chamber in the stern, just off the quarterdeck. His cabin boy brought them all rum, and they settled in around the table in the center of the room. Shimmer stood by the door.

"Excuse the mess," Jerick said, indicating the room's general state of untidiness, "but it's the maid's day off." He grinned, showing off a large golden tooth right in front.

"You have a maid?" Trip said. "Sleek. You should get a maid, Mik. Next time you have a ship, I mean."

"So," Jerick said, "you're between ships, are you?"

Mik's jaw tightened. "Aye. At the moment."

"A dragon sank our last ship," Trip added.

"Did it, now?" Jerick said. "Not one of 'ours,' I hope."

"No," Trip said. "It was a big old sea dragon named Tempest. Scuttled us outside the Veil, but Shimmer found us and took us in. He and Ula are old friends."

"That's the gist of the story, anyway," Mik said.

"Most outsiders arrive here in a similar manner," Jerick said. "Only a few are good enough—or lucky enough—to find the way on their own."

"Which were you?" Ula asked, arching one platinum eyebrow.

Jerick smiled at her. "Neither. I was a pirate—as Mik here could tell you—plying my trade in the waters beyond the Veil. Well, as it happened, I shared a common enemy with one of the lords of the isles. Sinking the blighter damaged my ship severely, but put me in good with the dragon. That earned me a spot as one of the isles' privateers. Been waylaying scoundrels for lord and realm ever since. Haven't been beyond the Veil lately, though. That sea dragon is a menace to shipping."

"As we found out," Mik said.

"Aye," Jerick replied. "I hope you didn't lose much that was dear to you."

"Only shipmates," Mik replied.

"Aye. I know how that is," Jerick said. He raised his mug. "Here's to 'em—and to the death of that dragon!"

They all raised their mugs in salute and drank, even Shimmer.

Jerick leaned back in his chair. "So," he said, "what kind of job is it you're needing me for?"

"We're going to find a temple full of treasure," Trip blurted. "If we can figure out where it is."

"I think Mik should do the talking from now on," Ula said, staring dangerously into Trip's hazel eyes. "Understand?"

Trip nodded.

"Fiery, isn't she?" Jerick said, winking at Trip. Ula frowned, but the red-bearded captain only laughed. "Of course, I *like* 'em that way." Turning back to Mik, he asked, "How much of what the kender said is true?"

"The general outline of it," Mik replied. "We've come a long way on prophecy and prayer, and recovered three out of the four keys we need to reach our goal."

"The last one came from the Dragonheights!" Trip put in.

Jerick's eyes widened. "You came back from the Dragonheights? How? There's a spell on the heights that won't be lifted 'til the good dragons return—if it's *ever* lifted at all. Those that venture atop the cliffs don't usually come back."

"Shimanloreth and I didn't have too much trouble," Mik averred.

"Shim . . ." Jerick began. His blue eyes widened. "I've heard of him. Then your pretty friend must be Ula Landwalker. I didn't make the connection before. Doubly pleased to make your acquaintance, miss. We 'black dolphins' need to swim together, you know. Glad to meet you, too, sir." He bobbed his head deferentially at Shimmer. "So, how long will you be needing me boat for?"

"A week or two," Mik said. "Perhaps less if the haul is not so good as we believe."

The red-bearded captain raised his bushy eyebrows. "Is that so? One or two days I might have done for friendship's sake, but shirking my 'patrols' for a week or two . . ." He shook his head. "That'll cost more than a fair bucket of steel."

"We have money," Trip put in, emptying his pockets on the table.

Jerick eyed the assortment of coins, rocks, strips of leather thong, buttons, and other oddments. He looked at Mik. "I might have missed it, Mik, old boy, but I didn't see a coin pouch on you when you came in."

Mik shook his head. "We're cash poor at the moment, unless . . ." He looked hopefully at Shimmer.

The bronze knight shook his head. "My reserves are nearly depleted as well."

"I'm afraid we're pretty tapped out," Mik said.

The privateer captain nodded knowingly. "Aye. You've already admitted that your ship's been lost," he said. "As I see it, there's no way you can pay the bill you'd run up on this venture—not if this lovely stripped off every bit of jewelry right down to her blue skin. I agreed to take one kender to Darthalla—an expensive idea in itself—not *three* people on a fishing expedition."

"Four," Trip corrected.

Jerick patted the kender's tawny head. "In any case, Mik, my old friend, I don't think you can afford me or my ship." He leaned back in his chair.

For a moment, only the creak of the Red Wake as it gently swayed in the water broke the room's silence.

Ula stood. "Come on. We'll look elsewhere."

"Now hold on there, missy," Jerick said. "I said you couldn't *afford* me. I didn't say I wouldn't do it."

"So what is it you want?" Mik asked.

The red-bearded man smiled. "A slice of the action, of course."

Ula frowned. "How big a slice?"

"I'd say six shares out of ten—in *my* favor, naturally."

Mikal Vardan threw back his head and laughed. "Without our expedition," he said, "you have no slice at all. We're supplying the goal, the location, and the recovery team. We can put four people—expert treasure finders—into the deep if need be. How many can you dive?" Without waiting for an answer, he continued. "I suspected as much. I think that *one* share in ten would be a reasonable fee."

"But I bear the majority of the risks as well as most of the costs," Jerick countered. "The ship is mine, the crew is mine. If we run into trouble, I'm far more likely to suffer losses. *Five* shares in ten would seem a reasonable cut."

Ula and Trip shrugged at each other and kept out of the dickering. Shimmer remained silent.

"We both know that it's experts that get shares on a voyage," Mik said. "The harpooner gets a better cut than the deck hand. That only makes sense. You have one expert, yourself, and perhaps two more—assuming your mates are any good. The rest are mostly ballast. I think two and a half shares out of ten is a good deal."

"Ha!" Jerick said. "Maybe if you've been raised in Khur, far from the sea! I'm tired of haggling, lad, so here's my final offer. Six shares out of ten, but you and your friends get the six."

"And you'll refund Trip's money?" Mik said.

Jerick frowned. "That seems a bit unreasonable. You'll pay your share of equipment costs?"

"Done," said Mik.

The two reached over the table and shook hands.

The privateer captain stood and stretched. "I think that calls for another drink," he said, whistling for the cabin boy once more. He went to his sea chest, cleared away the junk on top of it, and fetched out the fee that Trip had paid him.

He handed the purse to the kender and said to all of them, "I'll let you know how much the expenses are."

Mik nodded. "When do we leave?"

Jerick smiled. "We sail with the morning tide."

PART III
THE LOST TEMPLE

Chapter
Thirty-One
The Chase

Trip leaned on *Red Wake*'s rail and gazed out over the clear blue sea. To the south, the wooded hills of Alarl rose from the gently surging waves. Trip imagined the thriving settlement of kender on the other side of the pastoral isle. He pictured meeting old friends, some of whom he hadn't seen for years. Of course, there was no evidence that any kender he knew lived there. Nevertheless, he couldn't help sighing wistfully.

"Anything the matter, Trip?" Mik asked.

"Just wishing I could go to Perch *and* find the treasure," Trip said.

"I'm sure you'll have a chance to visit the island some day," Mik said, "after we find the diamond." He closed his eyes and rubbed his temples and saw the blue-white gem once more.

Shimmer, working on the deck nearby, looked up. "Anything wrong?" the bronze knight asked.

"Just a headache," Mik replied. "Nothing to worry about."

"Fast flee the isle of thieves, if I remember right," Ula said, appearing from behind him.

"Fast *quit* the isle of thieves, actually," Mik corrected her. *"Past furthest spits of sand, As soul, not mind, believes, Forsake at last the land.* And here, we quit the main archipelago and sail into the outer reaches."

"To the island of the temple and the treasure?" Ula asked.

"Hopefully," Mik replied.

"Do you trust Red not to double-cross us?" Ula asked.

"I trust him as much as I trust any former pirate who's an old friend. I should check with him on our progress, I suppose."

"I'll go with you," Ula said. Then, with a devilish smile, she added, "Your friend seems easy prey for my charms."

"What man isn't?" replied Mik. "Trip, Shimmer . . . coming?"

The bronze knight shook his head.

"I'm having too much fun sightseeing," Trip replied.

The sailor and the sea elf turned and headed for the bridge.

Shimmer went forward and stood in the bow. The sea breeze tugging at his brazen hair made him look like a young god returning to his kingdom. His eyes, though, remained cool and distant.

Trip joined the knight, and leaned over the rail to snatch at the tiny rainbows in the spray kicked up by the ship's passing.

* * * * *

Mog clung to *Red Wake*'s keel, his muscles aching from the tedium of the journey. Occasionally, he transformed into a shark and prowled the nearby seas for food. The effort of catching the ship again, though, almost wasn't worth it.

Mog might have given up this tedious chore were it not for the presence of Tempest in the back of his mind. The tiny Turbidus leech attached to his spine wriggled at the thought of its dark mistress. Mog felt a tingling in his body and knew that the sea dragon sensed his thoughts as well. He muttered obeisance to her obscene majesty and turned his thoughts back to his task.

Tempest had other spies inside the Veil, handfuls of minion fish who had broken through the rupture when she assaulted the barrier, as well as others. Mog, though, remained her most faithful, reliable servant. None of the rest, not even the ravenous sharks, shared the dark mistress' soul.

Bridle as he might upon occasion, Tempest had created the spawn with her own scales and blood. She imbued him with the power to change his shape. She gave him free rein to murder and feast as he chose, so long as he obeyed her.

If he failed her, though, she would destroy him utterly.

Mog clambered from the keel to the side of the ship, lurking just below the waterline. His steely claws bit deep into the wood, securing him against the rushing water.

Peering up out of the churning sea, he saw the kender leaning over the side.

"How simple," Mog thought, "to snatch the little pest and drag him under." Images of the kender's warm blood running down his throat flashed through his reptilian mind.

Then he mastered himself once more. His job was to watch, and wait for the proper moment to strike. Wait for the orders from his mistress. Tempest burned in the back of his mind like a hot coal.

Mog waited, confident his time drew near.

* * * * *

A day later, Jerick paced the bridge, his big boots making a clomping sound like the drums of distant giants. "I don't mind telling you," he said to Mik and Ula. "I'm beginning to think this is a fool's venture. If I turn back now, I might be able to recover me costs from what little cash you have on you." He glanced at the jewelry entwined around Ula's slender body.

"Turn back for what?" Mik asked. "Another day searching for wandering pirates? Or were you thinking of sailing beyond the Veil? Better booty out there, I hear."

The red-bearded privateer scowled at his old friend. "With that dragon lurking about? Not likely."

"Perhaps you should petition the Order of Brass to take care of Tempest," Ula suggested.

"I've no love for *them*, either," Jerick growled. "You think I haven't seen their patrols overflying us, high up in the sky? They're looking for something. I *hope* it's not you lot they're looking for." He clomped around the deck again.

"We've sailed according to the Prophecy," Mik said, reassuringly. *"Where light anew is born, To battle divine hound, Before the second morn, Know the last torch is found.* We've sailed east past the main archipelago, as it says, and sighted the War Hound constellation."

"So, we've got to find this *torch*, whatever that is, within two days," Jerick said.

"The torch is an isolated isle near the edge of the Veil, Ula thinks—the Isle of Fire," Mik replied.

"Ula thinks, you think!" Jerick fumed. "The trouble is *I* haven't been doing enough thinking. If I had, I'd never have taken this errand with you misfits. If we find that isle, and this supposed temple, how do I even know there's treasure there?"

"When the keys were split," Mik said, "the high temple vanished from the eyes of mortals. No one has seen it since the founding of the Veil. The fourth key will open it to us. *From fire, wind, sea and earth, At land beyond the end, Of passage keys give birth, To treasure now ascend*—The keys are the elements, and using them will lead us to the treasure."

"Which you're sure is a monster diamond amid a pile of treasure."

"Aye."

"Which you've seen in visions."

"Aye. Many times, both with the keys, and in Aurialastican. Trip saw it once as well."

"And the visions of a kender are supposed to make me feel better?"

"I've seen it, too," Ula said. "Just once, after I wove the second key into my jewelry. I'm *sure* it exists."

"And I'm half sure you're all mad," Jerick said. "Following some absurd rhyme, doled out to me a piece at a time by a shipwrecked mariner . . . I must be mad, too!"

He went to the blue-painted rail and leaned on it, gazing back past Alarl toward Misty Isle—now a tiny blur in the distance. Mik walked up beside the captain and clapped him on the shoulder. "If you turn back now, old friend," the sailor said jovially, "you'll never know if I'm right."

"Aye," Jerick replied. "I suppose I won't. Though I'm not sure that would be a bad thing. Show me those keys again."

Mik fished into his waistband and whistled for Trip. The kender slid down from the mast top. "Give me the black key, would you?"

Trip nodded, dug it out of his vest pocket, and handed it to Mik. He and Ula chuckled as Trip scrambled up the mast once more. The sea elf carefully extricated the blue key from her costume and handed it to the sailor.

"Aye," Jerick said, gazing at the collection in Mik's hands. "They're impressive all right. Old, too. Maybe there is something in all your talk."

"You know," Mik said, "It hadn't occurred to me before, but . . ." He deftly wove the three artifact pieces together into a larger whole. Diamond, opal, and emerald became part of a larger, key-like shape. The conjoined artifact began to glow with a faint blue-white aura.

"Still, one piece missing," Ula said, her green eyes flashing.

With a sigh, Mik went to disassemble the artifact, but the pieces would not come free.

"Is it stuck?" Ula asked.

"More than stuck," Mik replied. "I can't even find the places where the joints were."

"So which one of us keeps it?" Ula asked. Her green eyes darted from Mik to Jerick.

"I've just the place in my sea chest," Jerick said.

"I'm sure you have," Mik replied. "But the place I have in mind is just as secure . . . and vastly more visible."

* * * * *

The drumchanter set a brutal beat, but Lord Kell's oarsmen didn't complain. Kell himself paced the main deck, staring out to sea, as if he could will their quarry to appear. Karista Meinor stayed close by his side. Stormclouds trailed in the boat's wake, threatening to blot out what remained of a glorious afternoon.

Kell stopped near the bow and peered ahead, his mood mirroring the darkening weather.

"They can't be too far over the horizon," Kell said, as much to himself as to the aristocrat.

"Is that what your dragon allies tell you?" Karista asked.

"Aye."

"And you're sure you can trust them?"

Kell looked slightly offended. "Of course."

"The reason I ask," Karista said deferentially, "is that there may be quite a bit of wealth involved, and the propensity of dragons for treasure is well known. If one of them should find the hoard before we do . . . can we be sure they would use it for the glory of the Order?"

Kell smiled sympathetically at her and put his arm around her smooth shoulders. "If Lord Thrakdar desired this treasure, he wouldn't need *us* to get it. Indeed, I would give it to him gladly, if he asked. That he allows me to pursue this bounty for the glory of the Order is a great honor. To be aided by his consort Tanalish is an honor nearly as great. When you have been in the isles longer, you will understand these things."

Karista smiled up at him, her steely eyes flashing. "I'm sure I will, milord. I look forward to the . . . mutual edification our trade pact will bring."

The lord of the dragon ship gazed into her eyes; she did

not turn away. "Aye," he said quietly. "We have much to learn, you and I."

"My lord!" a brass-armored warrior called, pointing to the sky. "A dragon comes!"

Kell and Meinor looked up. Far over head, a bright yellow dot, like a shooting star, moved through the darkening sky. It arced lazily toward the ship, angling in from the east, to catch the onrushing wind.

Lower it streaked, resolving itself into the form of a huge brass dragon. The rays of sunlight leaking through the stormfront danced on her wings in a dazzling display. She dove straight for the trireme, not breaking speed at all.

Karista edged closer to Kell and put her hand on the crook of his arm. "Don't worry," the lord said. "It's just Tanalish."

"I fear, milord, that all dragons look alike to me."

"Another thing you will learn," Kell replied. "If she were a hostile, we'd be dead already." He and Karista moved to one side of the bridge as the dragon swooped toward them.

As Tanalish came in, she stretched and became thinner. Her wings trailed out behind her, becoming long, gossamer silks. Her face grew shorter and rounder. Her body twisted and took a womanly shape.

Flitting under the furled sails, she landed on the deck only three strides away from Benthor Kell. As her bare foot touched down, she was no longer a dragon, but a beautiful young woman.

Her eyes were bright green, like new-born leaves in spring. Her wavy golden hair hung down over her smooth, dark shoulders. Her body was that of a sensual young goddess, and she moved with the fluid grace of a dancer. A shimmering, gossamer gown clung to her perfect form. The dress glittered like brass in the sunshine.

Karista tightened her grip on Kell's arm, and her breathing became shallow; the ship's crew instinctively fell to their knees.

"Milady Tanalish," Kell said, bowing. "What news?" Lady Meinor bowed as well.

"*Red Wake* is near, Benthor Kell," the dragon in human form said. "I have seen the people you seek—the sea elf, the kender, and the human—wandering her decks." Her green eyes flashed. "Shimanloreth is with them, too, and this I do *not* like."

"He's a pale shadow of his former self," Kell replied. "The wound the overlords gave him grieves him still. I'm sure you can handle him should it become necessary."

The dragon nodded. "As you wish, Benthor Kell. The storm will break before we reach them, though."

"This cursed weather," Kell said. "We've had more of it lately than I've seen in my whole lifetime."

Tanalish frowned. "The Veil is weakened," she said. "Storms seep in from outside. It is a concern."

"Let the dragon lords worry about such things," Kell said. "You and I—and lord Thrakdar—must strengthen the Order, lest the encroaching chaos catch us unprepared." He paced to the bow and gazed toward the onrushing storm. Karista trailed behind.

"We must have these people, Tanalish," he said. "Or, at least, the keys they've stolen. Our mission depends on it." He turned back to the dragon and gazed into her bright green eyes. "See to it."

"Your will is mine as my lord's, Benthor Kell," Tanalish said, bowing slightly. The dragon-woman leaped over the side of the trireme, transforming as she fell.

Tanalish stretched out her arms, like a cliff diver aiming for the surf. Her glittering yellow gown lengthened, the sparkling metallic flecks on its surface changing to hard brass scales. The dress' billowing pleats became the leathery membranes between the bones of her wings. Tanalish brushed low over the waves, the armor of her huge belly sending a spray of mist into the sky.

With two quick beats of her titanic wings, the brass dragon soared high into the air once more. She executed a series of tight spirals and disappeared into the advancing clouds.

Lord Kell smiled.

* * * * *

"Damn this storm!" Jerick the Red bellowed. "Secure the hatches and trim the sails. Watch your feet, there! We won't be stopping to fish anyone out of the drink!"

Torrents of rain spattered *Red Wake*. Wind ripped across her sails and surging waves tossed the galleon up and down. The ship rocked precariously, but her seasoned crew was well used to squalls.

Mik slogged over the waterlogged deck to Trip and Ula, standing near the bow. The joined key shone faintly at the sea-elf's belly, making the other pieces of jewelry in her web-like attire glitter. Trip clung fast to the gunwale, enjoying the feel of the wind and rain on his small face.

"We should all get below," Mik said. "Red doesn't need our help on deck. We'll only get in the way."

"And miss this great show?" Trip asked, disappointed.

Mik ignored him and spoke directly to Ula. "I'd hate to have that bauble washed overboard with you."

"That would defeat the purpose of my wearing it," she said, a twinkle in her eye.

"Perhaps we should trust each other," he said. "At least a little."

She smiled; even in the rain she looked lovely. "Perhaps a little."

Shimmer appeared beside them.

"What's keeping you?" the bronze knight asked. He kept his helmet closed against the rain. "We should get below and let the captain's men do their jobs."

Ula smiled again and leaned against the rail. She looked nearly as comfortable in the downpour as she did underwater. "The minnow and I are in no hurry. We like the storm. You and Mik go below if you like."

Mik glanced from her face to the incomplete key at her belly. "We'll wait," he said.

"Light off the stern! Light off the stern!" the ship's lookout cried.

Jerick cursed. "Where away?"

"Ten degrees to starboard," came the reply.

"What kind of ship?" Mik called.

The lookout peered into the storm. "Sea's too high to be certain. Yellowish galley, I think. Closing fast."

Jerick cursed again. "Let's hope that's not Lord Kell."

"It's Kell, all right," Ula replied. "Only a fool or a fanatic would follow us into this storm."

Mik took Ula by the arm. "Now would be a good time to go below, I think," he shouted over the storm. Ula nodded, as did Trip and Shimmer.

The four of them had taken only a step toward the hatch, though, when the ship heaved and pitched them all to the deck.

Ula swore and untangled herself from Mik. The two of them rose unsteadily to their feet. Shimmer got up more slowly, leaning against the gunwale and clutching his left shoulder. Trip, still sitting, pointed and cried, "Look!"

They turned as a large brass dragon streaked out of the clouds. The dragon dove straight for the deck of *Red Wake*. Jerick's crew shouted futile cries of warning. Mik grabbed his sword, and Ula stooped to retrieve her spear from where it had fallen. Shimmer grunted and heaved himself to his feet.

In an instant, the dragon shrank smaller, darting between the galleon's masts like a huge metallic bird. Terrified sailors leaped out of the way as she passed; several fell to the deck with bone-cracking impacts.

The dragon extended her claws.

Mik brought up his sword and slashed at her, too late. The creature crashed past the sailor, toppling him to the planking before he could make a second cut. Trip stabbed at the dragon with his daggers, but the wyrm's armor turned the tiny weapons aside. A slap from a brass-scaled wing cast Shimmer over the rail of the ship. The bronze knight splashed into the dark, heaving waters below.

The dragon seized Ula in her hind talons and yanked the startled elf off the deck before Ula could even raise her spear. The impact knocked the weapon from the Dargonesti's hand, and it clattered to the deck of *Red Wake*. Growing to full size again, Tanalish dragged her captive into the torrential sky.

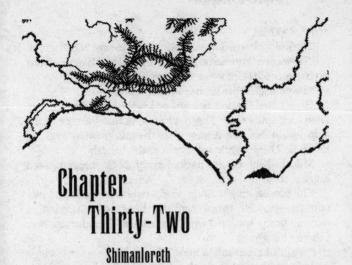

Chapter Thirty-Two

Shimanloreth

Ula!" Trip cried, peering up at the rapidly disappearing sea elf.

"Knight overboard!" Jerick called. "We can still reach him if he hasn't been swept away!"

Mik staggered to his feet. He glanced from Ula to the place where Shimmer had fallen over the side. The sea elf was too far away to help. "C'mon, Trip!" he said, shouting to be heard above the storm.

The two of them skidded up next to Jerick at the rail, where Shimanloreth had gone over. Luckily, the bronze knight had seized a frayed rope dangling over the side. He dangled in the waves, grunting with every impact as the surf battered him against the hull.

Mik, Trip, and Jerick grabbed the rope and pulled, but the three of them made little progress.

"He's heavier than he looks," Mik said.

"Where's Ula?" Shimmer called. "Is she safe?"

"The dragon took her!" Trip called back before Mik

could stop him.

The knight howled in anguish. "I have to save her!" he said.

"How can you save her?" Mik said. "Worry about saving yourself! Climb up the rope, blast you!"

"Stand back!" the bronze knight snarled.

He reached up and the tips of his bronze-gloved fingers grew long spiky nails. Digging his claws into the side of the ship, he climbed relentlessly up to the rail, growing larger as he came. The gunwale splintered under his grip.

Mik and the others backed away as Shimmer heaved himself aboard.

The bronze knight stood nearly twelve feet tall, and was still growing. He threw back his head and screamed as curving horns sprouted from his helmet. Thunder crashed, echoing his agony.

"What's happening to him?" Trip cried.

Shimmer's back bulged inhumanly, his huge muscles rippling and changing beneath his armor. Bronze spikes sprouted from his shoulders, at his elbows, and along his back. His metal-shod feet split into long, sharp talons.

He grew even larger. His body stretched and became more monstrous with each passing moment. The spikes at his shoulders shot outward and split into segments, like hideous, skeletal hands. Inhuman webbing knitted itself between the long, thin fingers.

His jaws thrust forward and his orange eyes bulged out of the eyeslits in his faceplate. He screamed, and the pointed snout of his face ruptured open. Shimmering light escaped from his mouth along with his terrible, tortured wail.

Striations ran along the length of his body as his armor cracked. Between the fissures, his bronze skin bulged in scaly, ragged lumps.

The ship seemed in danger of capsizing under his massive weight. *Red Wake*'s gunwale tottered toward the crashing waves. With a parting glance at Mik, Shimanloreth threw himself over the side once more.

Mik, Trip, and Jerick raced to the splintered rail and gazed over the stormy sea. They did not find their friend in the whitecaps below. His transformation complete, Shimanloreth was rising awkwardly into the sky as a large bronze dragon.

"I was wondering if he might do that," Jerick said.

"You knew?" Mik asked, incredulous. "You knew he was a dragon and you didn't mention it?"

Jerick shrugged. "Everyone in the isles knows the tragic story of Shimanloreth."

"What's wrong with his wing?" Trip asked, gazing in awe at the transformed knight. Shimmer's left shoulder and wing looked scarred, deformed.

"The dragon overlords crippled him," Jerick replied. "He can't fly very well—from what I hear. I think his injuries hurt less when he's in human form."

"Which is the only way we've seen him," Mik said thoughtfully.

"But couldn't the good dragons heal him or something?" Trip asked.

"If you want to ask them why they didn't, be my guest" Jerick said, "assuming you can find them."

"The other dragon is larger," Mik said. "Can he beat her?"

"Shimanloreth's toughness is legendary," Jerick replied, "but Tanalish is one mean dragon."

"Do you have a bow you could lend me?" Mik asked, trying to gauge the distance through the storm.

"They're out of range, mate," Jerick said. "There's nothing we can do but watch."

* * * * *

Shimmer rose quickly through the blinding storm toward Tanalish. Lightning flashed all around them, and thunder shook the heavens. The wind swirled and gusted, smashing the driving rain into the metallic bodies of the dragons and the form of the struggling sea elf.

Ula twisted in Tanalish's iron-thewed claw, but she couldn't even reach her dagger to fight back. The gemstone key pressed sharply into her belly, but her web of jewelry held it in place. Lances of pain shot up her spine as the dragon squeezed her. "Let go of me!" she yelled.

If Tanalish heard the elf, she made no reply. Rather, the brass dragon wheeled to face the oncoming menace. She opened her mouth and belched a burning, sulfurous blood-red cloud. The cloud sparked and sizzled, billowing large despite the wind. The toxic vapors fanned out across Shimmer's flight path.

"A warning, Shimanloreth," Tanalish hissed. "Keep back. This doesn't concern you."

"Ula concerns me," Shimmer rumbled. "She's my friend. You have no right to take her."

"She's a thief, an enemy of the Order of Brass and a threat to the isles," Tanalish replied.

"Fish oil!" Shimmer boomed. "Give her back or you'll regret it."

A smile creased the brass dragon's scaly lips. "You're no match for me, Shimanloreth. Your wing is crippled, almost useless. Fly back to the ship and lick your wounds."

Shimmer didn't reply. Instead, he lunged forward, extending his jaws toward Tanalish's long neck. The move surprised the brass, and she barely jerked her head aside in time.

Shimanloreth's fangs raked across her throat, and his powerful hind talons seized the leg holding Ula.

"Let go or I'll drop her," Tanalish hissed. She snapped at Shimmer's face, but he ducked out of the way.

"You don't dare," Shimmer said. "Kell wouldn't allow it."

Tanalish tucked her wings and sent them into a frenzied spiral. She coiled her tail around Shimmer's and continued to bite at his face. Shimmer fought back, fending off her fore-claws with his own and counterattacking with his horns.

Red, oily sweat began to bubble up on his bronze carapace. He panted with the effort, his breath sounding like huge bellows.

Tanalish laughed and brought one armored knee up into her opponent's belly. She jerked away, disentangling the two of them. Ula's guts jumped as the brass dragon lurched upward again.

Momentarily falling, Shimmer lashed up with his head. One of the long spikes behind his horns slashed across Tanalish's cheek, close to her eye. The brass dragon screamed.

"Son of a fetid egg!" she howled. "You'll pay for that."

Turning, she lunged straight at Shimmer's eyes. The bronze dragon ducked aside, but it wasn't his face Tanalish aimed for. Throwing her jaws wide, the brass dragon sank her long fangs into Shimmer's left shoulder, right where it joined his crippled wing.

* * * * *

"Look at them go!" Trip said, using one hand to shield his eyes from the wind and rain. The battling dragons looked like metallic birds high up in the storm. "I wish they were closer, so we could see better."

"So do I," Mik added, hefting Ula's fallen spear.

"Thank the gods they're not," Jerick the Red growled. "We've enough trouble as it is." He was rallying his men to secure the sails before the storm ripped them to tatters.

Mik ducked out of the way of a loose line whipping over the deck. "Ship to starboard!" he cried, pointing. "Ship to starboard!"

Over the top of a huge swell surged Lord Kell's trireme, its brass ram aimed straight at *Red Wake*'s hull.

Chapter
Thirty-Three
Collision Course

Shimmer howled and tried to pull away, but Tanalish shook her head and sank her teeth further into his shoulder. They writhed together amid the storm, thunder crashing all around.

Ula felt as though she would be shaken to pieces in the lady dragon's claw. Closing her mind to the crushing pain in her guts and spine, she wormed her left hand toward the hilt of the dagger at her waist. Her fingertips brushed the pommel, and hope sprang anew in her heart. Slowly, she wrapped her fingers around it and pulled the knife from its sheath.

Shimanloreth bellowed in pain as bits of flesh and blood splattered out of his wounded shoulder and wing. He smashed the side of his head against Tanalish's face. They were falling now, her wings barely holding them aloft. She didn't seem to care if they crashed into the raging sea far below.

He snapped at her eyes. The brass dragon blinked and loosened her grip momentarily. Shimmer rammed Tanalish with his nose, and her jaws ripped free from his shoulder. She spat out his flesh and turned to attack once more.

Shimmer opened his mouth and flashing white energy leaped from his maw into Tanalish's startled face. The lady dragon screamed, writhing in pain. Her talons flailed wildly as every muscle in her huge body spasmed.

Tanalish's claw jerked open. Before Ula could grab hold or lash out with her dagger, she fell, plummeting toward the storm-tossed ocean far below.

* * * * *

"Hard to port!" Mik yelled. "Hard to port!"

"Do it!" Jerick bellowed at his startled helmsman.

The mate spun the wheel frantically with all his might.

The brass-armored trireme lunged toward them over the heaving waves. A flash of lightning revealed Lord Kell standing by the triarch's chair in the stern, his gray eyes gleaming in triumph.

Red Wake responded slowly, fighting against the pull of waves and wind. She veered left, her gunwale nearly dipping into the water as the raging surf threatened to roll her over.

Another flash of lightning. The trireme drove in on them, its brass-headed ram aimed for the galley's starboard flank. A huge wave surged over *Red Wake*'s side, dashing seamen to the rail; many barely avoided being swept overboard.

Mik and Trip kept their feet amid the chaos. The sailor grabbed a boat hook and tossed it to Jerick, then retrieved two more for himself and Trip. "If the angle is shallow enough," he shouted, "we can turn them away!"

"Man the boat hooks!" Jerick cried. "Prepare to repel attack!" But only a few crewmen reached the rail with boathooks in their hands. Mik and the rest braced themselves as the trireme swept forward.

The rhythm of Lord Kell's drumchanter rose above the voice of the storm. The trireme's triple banks of oars cut through the crashing waves. Standing in the stern, Kell shouted orders to his helmsmen.

Red Wake kept turning ever so slowly, the waves surging against her sides. She swung nearly parallel to the trireme's course, presenting a difficult target for Kell's brass ram.

"It's going to miss us!" Trip cried.

"Not without our help it won't!" Mik said. "Ready on the boathooks! Heave!"

They stabbed the long poles over the side and pushed with all their might. The iron heads of the hooks lanced into the trireme's sides, each minutely altering the enemy ship's course. The impact nearly knocked Mik and the others from their feet.

They held on and watched triumphantly as the brass warship swung alongside. The crew of *Red Wake* cheered, but Jerick barked, "It's not over yet!"

The trireme shipped oars to avoid having them sheared off in the collision. The two ships groaned as their hulls met, side to side.

"Now!" Lord Kell called.

A company of brass-armored warriors threw grappling ropes onto *Red Wake*, catching her rail and tangling her rigging. The brass mariners hauled on the lines, lashing the ships into close contact.

Mik hefted his boathook like a spear and took careful aim. As the brass galley settled alongside, he heaved the weapon toward Lord Kell. Kell didn't see the makeshift spear coming; it flew straight toward his unarmored neck.

In the next moment, though, a huge wave rocked the two ships. The boathook sailed past Kell's left ear and stuck in the triarch's seat behind him.

The lord of the Order of Brass whirled toward Mik, murder flashing in his eyes. His deep voice thundered over the raging storm. "Take them!" he called to his warriors. "But leave Vardan for me!"

In response, three dozen brass-armored seamen swarmed across the ropes binding the two ships together.

Jerick's crew responded quickly, drawing their weapons and snatching up belaying pins, boathooks, and anything else that might serve to fend off the invaders.

But just as the two forces were about to meet, Jerick called, "Hold! Lay down your weapons!"

"What?" Mik and Trip asked simultaneously.

"Lay down your weapons!" Jerick repeated. "We surrender."

* * * * *

Cold, swirling winds buffeted Ula as she fell. The wicked rain lashed against her body. Above her, Tanalish writhed in agony, the she-dragon's brass-armored head charred and blistered.

The joined key at Ula's waist blazed brightly. An image of a huge diamond formed in her mind—but she pushed it aside. *Red Wake* looked so tiny below. And was that another boat alongside it?

"What a stupid way to die," she thought. "Dozens of enemies howling for my blood, and I'm going to be killed in a fall."

Though she knew hitting the water would undoubtedly kill her, she twisted her body and arced into a diving position. She ignored the aches of her flesh, the screaming of the wind, and the lashing of the rain, and focused on the surface of the sea far below.

"Key to a fortune at my waist, and I'll never get to see it," she thought.

A dark-winged shadow flitted overhead.

Suddenly, she stopped falling.

Shimmer screamed in agony as he swept Ula into his arms. The wind turned the spray of blood from his mangled shoulder into a clinging red mist. As he gazed at the sea elf, his face and form became slightly more human.

Ula smiled at him. "I knew you wouldn't let me down," she said.

"I'm not sure . . . I can save us," he gasped.

"At least you tried."

Something hard smashed into them, and the world went black.

* * * * *

"How can we surrender?" Mik asked angrily.

"Use your head, lad," Jerick replied. "We're outnumbered and out-armed. A storm is no place to be fighting. We'll need all our strength and wits just to pull through this."

"What makes you think they'll let us live?" Mik asked.

One of the brass warriors near him charged. The sailor spun and clouted him on the back of the head with the pommel of his scimitar. The man crashed to the deck with a soggy thud.

"Call off your dogs, Kell," Mik barked. "I won't be so kind to the next one."

"Hold!" Lord Kell cried. "Hold!"

"Any of my crew who fights," Jerick bellowed, "will be answerin' to me!"

The crews of the two ships cautiously backed away from each other, leaving Kell, Jerick, Mik, and Trip standing alone in the middle of *Red Wake*'s quarterdeck.

Mik and Trip glanced at each other, neither willing to put down his weapons just yet.

Jerick threw his arms wide. "What is this, Lord Kell?" he said. "We've no need to fight. I've no quarrel with either you or the Order of Brass. If you'd asked us to heave to, we would have. Gladly."

"I doubt some of your passengers would comply so willingly," Kell said.

"I gave your man no more than he deserved," Mik replied. "Have you taken up piracy now, Lord Kell, or are you still out to avenge some imagined slight to your honor?"

"Look out!" Trip cried, pushing Mik aside. As the sailor and the kender fell, a huge shape crashed onto the deck beside them.

The crew gasped as part of the battered and bloody form moved. It was a half-dragon, half-human creature, slightly larger than a minotaur, and covered with bronze armor.

"Shimmer!" Mik said.

Shimanloreth rose slowly to his knees as Mik and Trip knelt by the prostrate form of Ula, lying on the deck beside him. The sea elf was covered with blood, though how much of it was her own Mik could not tell. The bejeweled key at her waist glowed faintly.

"Take them!" Lord Kell barked, pointing at the group. "Alive, if you can, but take them!"

"Stop!" Jerick said. "We have no quarrel!"

"Stay out of this," Kell replied. "Do as I say! Now!"

Kell's brass warriors surged forward. As they did, Shimmer opened his half-human mouth. A huge cloud of greenish black gas belched forth. Shapes writhed within the roiling cloud—hideous shapes culled from the nightmares of each warrior.

The seamen stopped and retreated. Some dropped their weapons and fled back to their own ship. Others cowered in the corners of *Red Wake*'s deck—keeping as far away from the bronze dragon as possible.

"Must I do everything myself?" Kell asked, striding forward. He lowered the tip of his coral lance.

Mik rose to meet him, standing between the lord and his wounded comrades.

"Ula! Are you all right?" Trip whispered frantically. "Wake up! We're in a real jam here!"

"She's alive," Mik said to Trip, though his gaze remained fixed on the brass lord. "Though not for much longer if Kell here has his way."

Just then, Karista Meinor clambered aboard the Red Wake. "The key, milord," she said. "Vardan, the kender, and the elf aren't important. We came for the key. Remember?"

A thundering scream rent the air. All eyes turned skyward as Tanalish, burnt and bloody, swooped down toward the ship. Her body melted and changed, adopting both human and dragon characteristics until she resembled a hideous, bat-winged harpy.

"Let me destroy them, Benthor Kell!" she bellowed as she approached. "The sea elf and her hound are no match for me!" The dragon dove through the rigging toward Shimmer and Ula.

Mik stooped down and ripped the bejeweled key from Ula's waist. Before anyone could react, he rose and sprinted to the rail.

"Stop her!" he commanded Lord Kell, dangling the artifact over the crashing waves. "Call your dragon off, or you'll never see the key again!"

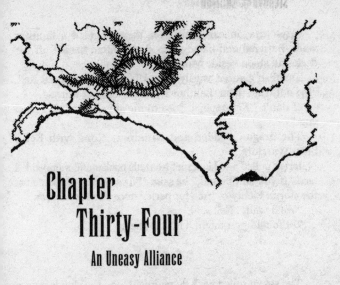

Chapter
Thirty-Four

An Uneasy Alliance

"M ilord!" Karista gasped, eyeing the artifact nervously.

"I mean it," Mik said, as Tanalish swooped closer. "I'll drop it and neither you nor your dragon pals will ever see it again."

"Hold, Tanalish!" Kell cried. "Don't kill them."

The harpy-like dragon backed her wings and hovered overhead. "They are worms, Benthor Kell," she said. "They deserve death. If he drops the trinket, I will find it again."

"Call her off," Mik repeated. "Then maybe we can talk."

Benthor Kell glared at Mik, then Ula. "Very well," he said, not taking his eyes off the sea elf. "Leave them, Tanalish."

The dragon's green eyes flashed, but she said, "As the will of my lord, so is your own, Benthor Kell." She landed on the deck and resumed her human form—though the damage from her battle with Shimmer had scarred her perfect face and figure.

"Send your warriors back to your ship, first," Mik said.

"Your dragon can look after them," added a familiar voice. Battered and bloody, Ula slowly lifted herself off the deck and stood beside Mik.

Tanalish glanced warily from Ula and Mik to Lord Kell. "Do not trust them, Benthor Kell," the dragon warned.

"I don't," Kell replied. "See to the ship. I'll call if I need you."

The dragon nodded and withdrew, along with Kell's brass warriors.

Jerick pulled a red kerchief from his pocket and mopped his face. "If you don't mind," he said, "I'll secure my ship against the storm. Plenty of time for parley once this blows over."

"We'll wait," Kell said.

"I thought you might," Mik replied.

* * * * *

The storm rolled back by midnight, and the clouds parted just enough for the silver moon to peek through. Sporadic rain still dappled the waves, but the winds died down and the surf ebbed considerably.

The crews of both ships worked diligently to return their vessels to fighting trim, and soon repaired most of the major problems. Tanalish kept watch on the bridge of the brass galley, while Lord Kell and the others met in Jerick's cabin aboard *Red Wake*.

Ula's wounds were superficial; the bronze dragon's injuries were grave, but *Red Wake*'s excellent healer patched him back together with bandages and herbs. By midnight, Shimmer felt well enough to join the parley.

The two factions stared at each other from opposite sides of the room, while Jerick sat in the middle, trying to arbitrate. The bronze knight leaned against a wall, his visor closed, his orange eyes grim. Mik, Ula, and Trip stood near him, unwilling to relax in the presence of their enemies.

"My old friends," Karista said. "I'm so sad that we've reached this impasse. As I see it, you need our protection and aid as much as we need the jeweled key. If we are to ally, each ship should gain equal shares."

"Before we parted," Mik said, "you told me you had no interest in the treasure."

Karista shrugged. "Situations change. You know that, Mik. The treasure is the dowry I need to win a trade concession. I know the Prophecy as well as you. I hired the expedition that brought us here. It's only right that I should share in the proceeds."

"Fish oil!" Mik said. "The chance for the treasure was the price I agreed to when you hired me."

"That, and the retirement of your previous debts," Karista said. "That was, of course, before you sank my ship."

"*I* sank your ship!"

"We'll get nowhere hashing over old accounts." Jerick said, interrupting this argument, not for the first time. "The point is, why fight over this loot if there's enough to share?"

"Perhaps you can find this treasure without us," Kell replied, "and perhaps we can claim it without you. However, you're fools if you think we'll just row away and leave you to it. We can stay at sea much longer than you can; Tanalish is our supply line. We'll wait you out if we have to."

"You forget," Mik said, "we still have the key."

"Now, now," Jerick said. "No need to get hostile again. It seems fair to me that we should divide the treasure between our ships. The question remaining is, how to make the division?"

"I'll take nothing less than half," Kell said.

"Nor will I," Karista added.

"So, we give you half, or you dog us until we quit?" Mik said.

Kell nodded.

"Since the Order patrols these waters and keeps them safe," Jerick said, "a half share seems fairly reasonable."

"But no more brawling or back-stabbing," Mik said. "Everyone gives up their grudges and works together. Otherwise we'll refuse. I won't have the Order plotting against us while we search, or after we've found the loot. I'll throw the key into the ocean before I allow that. We split anything we recover in half, then everyone walks away with no hard feelings."

"Agreed," Karista said, smiling.

"And the brass dragon goes," Ula added.

"Preposterous," Kell replied.

Mik shook his head. "Ula's right. Either Tanalish goes away, or the deal is off. She's too big an advantage for your side. I won't have you playing her against us when things get rough."

"What about *your* dragon then?" Karista asked pointedly.

"Shimmer is part of our crew—and he's wounded besides," Mik said.

"The dragon goes," Ula insisted.

Karista smiled sweetly at Kell. The brass-armored lord nodded slowly.

"Good," Mik said. "And keep your other spies at a distance, too. This deal is between our ship and yours—not between us and the Order of Brass."

"Very well," Kell said flatly. "I suppose you'll want to sail in the lead."

"Of course," Mik replied. "Do you think we'd give *you* the key?"

"No more than I'd care to let you out of my sight," Kell said.

"But you and the Lady Meinor can be our guests for the duration of the voyage, Lord Kell," Jerick said. "I assume you have a mate capable of piloting your ship?"

Kell exchanged a glance with Karista, and nodded.

"Shall we start, then?" Karista asked, fiddling absentmindedly with the braid on the sash at her waist.

"A grand idea," Jerick replied. "First, though, a drink to seal the bargain."

He tapped a cask of ale, and they drank a round—though only Jerick seemed to enjoy it.

* * * * *

Lord Kell did dismiss Tanalish. The lady dragon seemed none too pleased about the arrangement, but she bowed curtly and did as she was told. Only after she'd disappeared into the high clouds did Mik and the others breathe a sigh of relief.

"I think it's time to reveal the rest of the Prophecy," Mik said. He, Ula, Trip, Shimmer, Jerick, Kell, and Karista stood gathered on *Red Wake*'s bridge, under the wan light of the beclouded stars. "Will you do the honors, Lady Meinor?"

"Certainly," she said. She rolled up her silk sleeves, took a deep breath, and began to recite:
"Where light anew is born
To battle divine hound
Before the second morn
Know the last torch is found
The final hallowed key
Illumes the deepest night
At lord of fire and sea
Seek pillars' sacred might
From fire, wind, sea and earth
At land beyond the end
Of passage keys give birth
To treasure now ascend
The heart beats at the source
Of bastions unveiled
Portends the final course
And stands alone unfailed."
She finished with a smile, showing her straight white teeth.

"We've sighted the War Hound constellation," Mik said.

"And now we sail to the Isle of Fire," Kell said impatiently. "Yes, yes, we know that."

"The storm has slowed us, but we should reach the isle soon," Mik said. "When we get there, the fourth key is our objective. I believe that it lies beneath the waves, in 'deepest night.' Trip and I are experienced divers; Ula and Shimmer are used to working beneath the waves as well."

"How will we find the key, though?" Karista persisted.

Mik smiled roguishly. "I need to save some surprises for later, don't I?"

Mik, Jerick, and Kell took sightings on the War Hound once more, and both ships set sail for the Isle of Fire.

* * * * *

By morning it was pouring again. Jerick eyed the western horizon, worrying that the storm might build to gale force once more. Mik and Ula wondered if the burgeoning clouds hid the Order's dragonish spies.

The rain didn't dampen Trip's spirits—though it did increase the stench of his sea serpent cloak. Everyone except his friends avoided him, but Trip was having too much fun to notice. He frequently consulted his treasure finder. The only time it spun, though, was when it came too close to Ula, who had reattached the jeweled key to her clothing, or Jerick's money purse.

Lord Kell kept careful watch on the crew of the *Red Wake* and on his own galley, trailing close behind them.

Karista Meinor stayed close to Lord Kell, speaking to him in hushed tones and frequently looping her arm around his. Mik thought that even without the treasure, she had a pretty fair chance of landing her trade deal.

Ula kept watch on Kell and his ship, and scanned the storm-tossed skies for signs of Tanalish or other dragons. The sea elf seemed edgy and full of energy. "I hate waiting," she told Mik. "I'd rather fight my way to a treasure than hang around a ship."

Mik nodded. "You may soon get your wish."

For a day and a half they traveled east. They'd passed beyond all sight of land now, though they were still within the protective influence of the Veil.

"Look at the storm," Jerick said, pointing east to a towering bank of thunderheads. "That's where the Veil ends."

Mik squinted into the black clouds. "I see the island," he

said. "It's almost the same color as the clouds." He pointed, and Jerick followed with his eyes.

"Aye," he said, a faint smile cracking his red beard. "Can't say I like the look of the place."

"You'll like the look of its treasure, though," Mik replied.

"Aye."

By mid-afternoon they'd drawn close to the island's rocky shores. The Isle of Fire was a volcanic peak jutting nearly straight up out of the surging sea. Its almost sheer sides were black, craggy, and unforgiving. Only at the very bottom did a few sparse copses of vegetation cling to its meager shore. The eastern side of the mountain had fallen away, leaving a large **V**-shaped gully in the side of the escarpment. A faint red glow emanated from within the crack, making the island look as though it peered toward the sunrise with an eerie red eye. Within the volcano, the immense fires that had helped forge the the Veil still burned bright.

"Where is this supposed lost temple?" Kell asked skeptically.

"It's hidden," Mik replied. "It's been hidden for centuries."

"If it wasn't," Ula said, "someone would have taken the treasure long ago."

"The water is very deep here," Jerick said. "More than fifty fathoms. Are you sure diving is the right way to proceed?"

"The final hallowed key, Illumes the deepest night, At lord of fire and sea, Seek pillars' sacred might," said Karista.

"The Prophecy, and the visions I've had, make me think we're looking for a temple under the sea," Mik said.

"Sacred pillars in the deep," Trip added smartly.

Jerick rubbed one callused hand across his balding red pate. "Well, it's your necks," he said. "I'll set anchor and keep an eye on things." He shouted for his men to do so, and both his and Kell's ship anchored well clear of the island's dangerous shores.

"I'll summon my divers," Kell said. He moved to the rail and whistled a signal to his brass-armored ship. A dozen warriors appeared in shell-like helmets and diving gear.

"Oh, no," Mik said. "You're not going to outnumber us down there. Pick just three other divers besides yourself, Lord Kell."

Kell gazed into Mik's brown eyes; Mik didn't blink.

"Very well," Kell said slowly. "Will you be coming, milady?"

Karista Meinor nodded. "If you will loan me a helmet," she said. "I've not been able to replenish my supply of magical seaweed."

"And it tasted terrible anyway," Trip put in.

"Are you up for it, Shim?" Ula asked.

The bronze knight stood and slowly stretched. He'd removed his bandages, but his shoulder didn't seem quite healed.

Mik worried about the dragon-man's usefulness in a fight, but said only, "Everyone, prepare yourselves. We'll meet at the rail in twenty minutes."

Kell nodded and signaled for a longboat to ferry his equipment and two divers over to *Red Wake*.

Mik put on his enchanted fish necklace. He hadn't worn it since they'd left Aurialastican. His fingers traced the empty pockmarks where there had once been jeweled scales. The magic felt weak and tentative. He hoped it would be enough to complete at least one final task.

"You're sure this cloak of yours works, Trip?" he asked.

"Better than your feeble old necklace," the kender replied, pulling the serpent skin tight around his small body. "I'll swim circles around the rest of you."

Kell, Karista, and two brass-garbed warriors joined them at the rail. They all wore uncomfortable-looking brass helmets in the shape of sea huge seashells with clear quartz faceplates. The strange helmets complimented the design of the warriors' sparse brass armor. Karista just wore the helmet and a brief swimming outfit, but looked uncomfortable, nonetheless.

"Very nice," Ula said. "Can you actually hear or speak in those things?"

The Dragon Isles

"Well enough," Kell replied, his voice sounding metallic and distant. "Thrakdar himself helped forge them; their magic is strong. Do not worry on our account."

Mik nodded. "Then down, down to the briny deep, where sharks hold court and sailors sleep," he said, reciting an old diver's saying.

He was the first to step to the rail and plunge over the side.

Chapter
Thirty-Five

Into the Deep

M og watched as a large contingent of surface creatures dropped down into his domain.

First came the young ship captain, followed by the kender, then the sea elf, a bronze knight and a brass one. Then these were followed by a helmeted woman and two more brass-garbed swimmers.

The dragonspawn hid himself behind the keel of the galleon, lest they detect his presence. A tingling in his spine told him that other agents of Tempest lurked nearby. Soon, he would have need of them. Soon they would wrest the treasure from these pale, fleshy creatures and open the Veil for their mistress.

Then Glorious Tempest would invade the Dragon Isles, and Mog and his kin would feast on the flesh of humans and elves.

As the divers moved away from the ship and sank into the deep, Mog left his hiding place and followed—cautious to remain out of sight.

* * * * *

Mik led the treasure hunters into the depths. The sea water quickly faded from clear as glass, to blue, indigo, and then black. Mik and Trip's magic-assisted eyes adjusted quickly to the gloom. The water-born senses of Ula and Shimmer needed no such aid.

Nor did the fish living in the dark waters. Many sported huge eyes to navigate and find their prey. Others had grown their own lights, for purposes of mating or communication. The black waters twinkled with their presence—a starry sky within the ocean deep. A barrelmouth shark swept past; it looked fierce, with jaws wide enough to swallow a man, but Mik knew it was harmless. Barrelmouths had no teeth and fed only on tiny shrimp.

Without warning, light burst around them. Mik blinked and whirled, his scimitar in his hand. It was only Kell and his warriors, though. Small gems set atop their brass helmets shone with bright white light.

"Put those bloody things out!" Ula hissed. "Do you want everything down here to know we're coming?"

"Dim them," Mik added. "There isn't anything to see here anyway. What we want is on the bottom—*the deepest night*—and that's still a long way down."

Kell ordered his warriors to turn off their lights and did the same himself. They left Karista's light on but dimmed it to a dull red glow. The aristocrat sweated uncomfortably within her metal helmet, even though the artifact's powerful magic protected her from the cold and pressure of the deep.

Several times, the brass warriors spun to face something flashing through the water, only to discover it was merely Trip in his sea serpent cloak. The kender swam rings around the rest of them, like a playful dolphin.

"I'll admit," Ula whispered to Mik, "that cloak is impressive."

They snaked down ever farther into the deep. The

blackness closed in around them as the luminous sea life grew progressively less numerous.

"Is anyone else cold?" Karista asked, her teeth chattering. "I feel strangely cold."

One of Kell's warriors took a moment to adjust the position of a dial which controlled the spell on the aristocrat's helmet. "Thank you," Karista said. "That's much better."

* * * * *

Mog knew his time had almost come. The small Turbidus leech attached to his spine wriggled and burned as the dragonspawn sent out his telepathic call.

The message summoned Tempest's other minions lurking inside the Veil. They came swiftly—sharks, razorfish, and other evil fish—all trailing the tiny Turbidus leeches with which Tempest poisoned and controlled their minds. Mog felt them connected to him as he was connected to her.

When the mistress came, she would release thousands of her beloved Turbidus leeches. They would swarm the tepid waters of the Dragon Isles and make the denizens of the islands their own. Legions of creatures would join her black-hearted troops: humans, elves, minotaurs. Some had fallen already; soon all would be hers.

Mog reveled in the presence of his allies. He pictured them swarming through the seas, following him to battle. He imagined the blood of their enemies staining the seas red. He relished the hot, salty taste of his victims' vital fluids.

He longed for this pleasure. Perhaps it was *not* too soon to sample it. Slowly he drew closer to his prey, looking for a straggler—a weakling who could slake his thirst. Acid saliva ran across his fangs and made his black tongue tingle.

He chose a victim and waited for the moment to pounce.

* * * * *

"I see the bottom!" Trip called back to the others. He swung low over the seabed before arcing back up to his friends. "There's a huge canyon—but I don't see any sign of a temple."

"Perhaps the temple is within the canyon," Kell suggested.

Trip held his kender treasure finder out before him. He moved it back and forth over the course they might take. As it passed the canyon, the necklace began to spin wildly.

"Something's down there, all right," Trip said.

"Are we going to trust that dubious magical device?" Karista Meinor asked.

"I see no other course," Kell replied.

Trip beamed. "I'll scout ahead."

"Stay out of trouble," Mik said.

The kender nodded and sped down into the canyon.

"You and your people go first, Vardan," Kell said. "We'll turn up our lights and follow behind so as not to obscure your vision."

Mik nodded, and he and Ula darted ahead with Shimmer just behind. The bronze knight swam more slowly and less gracefully than he had before his wounding by Tanalish. Kell came next with Karista at his side. The two brass warriors brought up the rear.

The walls of the undersea canyon sprang up around them—towering cliffs disappearing into the indigo waters both above and below. Fissures pockmarked the sides of the defile. Some of these bubbled with hot water and brackish clouds that looked like black smoke.

Strange undersea creatures swam past them as they ventured into the deep canyon: white, eyeless shrimp as big as a man's hand; long, luminous eels whose guts they could see inside the fishes' transparent bodies; hideous sharp-toothed fish that seemed all head and eyes and no body; a slender octopus that flashed with the colors of the rainbow, and tiny clouds of orange-white krill. A redtip shark dipped down from above, but darted away when Kell's people turned their lights on it.

Trip reported back at regular intervals, though his findings consisted mainly of, "More canyon. I'm sure we're going the right way, though."

Gradually, the canyon ceiling began to close over them. Black, jagged coral sprang from the pockmarked walls and knitted together like huge knotted brambles. Long, pale seaweed intertwined with it, forming an impassible wall of spikes and tangled netting.

Karista glanced around nervously. "Much farther and we shall find ourselves trapped."

"We can always return the way we came," Mik replied.

As they swam cautiously forward, the bottom of the canyon loomed into view. It, too, was covered with the strange thorny coral and pale weeds. As the canyon closed in around them, they felt as though they were swimming down the gullet of some thorny aquatic beast.

They passed huge, carved columns, each as large as Kell's galley, lying broken among the weeds and spikes. They also saw the skeletons of ancient ships poking out amid the wreckage.

Ahead, the living tunnel opened up into the vast, dark sea once more. Beyond the opening loomed a pale shape of towering pillars, curving walls, and domes.

"The undersea Temple!" Mik crowed.

They swam ahead heedlessly as the canyon walls closed in around them. Soon, the divers were passing through a narrow tunnel of pale weeds and sharp black coral.

Something blocked their way. It was ethereal, cloudlike, and huge. The pallid form obscured the shapes of the temple behind it, while not blotting out the architecture entirely.

"A jellyfish?" Trip asked.

Ula shook her head. "It's not one creature," she said, focusing her keen elven eyes on the thing. "It's *many.*"

"Crabs!" Shimanloreth said.

Tiny albino crustaceans swarmed over them, pinching and biting. The creatures were only the size of a child's ear, but had oversized serrated pincers on their eight limbs, and wicked beaklike mouths. The four eyes atop the stalks on their thorny heads glowed with an eerie green light. The movement of the school made an unnerving clattering sound, like knives running across old bones. The crabs paddled swiftly with their oarlike legs, surrounding the divers like a school of piranha. They wheeled their way under clothes and between cracks in armor. The treasure hunters swatted at them, but there were just too many.

"Fall back!" Kell cried. "Split up! They can't follow us all."

"No!" Mik countered. "Stay together! Work together!" He and Ula swam back to back, protecting each other. Shimmer went with them, but the cloud of crabs forced him apart from the others.

Kell and his warriors quickly vanished back into the darkness, their cries of frustration and pain drifting through the deep.

Trip had disappeared entirely.

* * * * *

Mog's chosen target struggled amid the tiny, swarming creatures and the tangled weeds.

With sharklike speed, the dragonspawn shot forward, claws extended. His talons bit through flesh, filling the water with tasty blood. He grabbed his prey and dragged the squirming, bleeding victim into the weeds to feast.

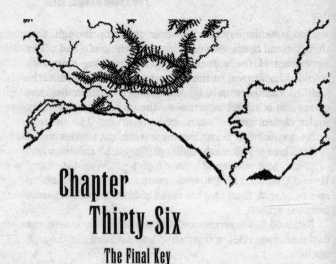

Chapter Thirty-Six

The Final Key

Mik and Ula whirled in a frenzy, fighting back-to-back, swinging their weapons and waving their hands, trying to ward off the thousands of miniscule predators. The tiny crustaceans kept coming.

"I've heard of the death of a thousand cuts," Mik said, "but I didn't think it was administered by crabs."

"Where's Shimmer?" Ula asked. "We need Shimmer!"

Mik looked around, but the entangling weeds and the swarm of crabs obscured his vision. "I don't see him," he said. "Let's fight our way to the temple. The tunnel opens up ahead."

"Right! Ouch!"

"A crab get you?"

"No. I stabbed my leg on this gods-forsaken coral."

They swam toward the glow from the temple, struggling to avoid the weeds and the razor-sharp coral. Against the swarming, nipping crabs, they made slow progress.

Just as they seemed about to break through, the water around them went dark. A swirling black cloud surrounded them. Horrible shapes lurked in the cloud—things Mik had only glimpsed in the darkest corners of his mind: swarming scavenger eels; black horsemen riding across the desert with scimitars raised high; the mangled, decaying body of old Poul.

Mik tried to swim away, but the nightmares surrounded him. Something grabbed his wrist in the dark. A voice boomed, "Mik!"

He tried to pull away, but the thing's webbed fingers gripped him like iron. He slashed down with his sword, trying to cut the arm off. "Hey! Watch it!" the voice thundered.

A blue fist flashed out of the darkness and clouted him on the jaw.

Stars flashed before his eyes, and then both the horrible visions and the black cloud vanished. Ula Drakenvaal held Mik's wrist tightly in her blue fingers.

"It was Shimmer," she said, shaking him lightly. "He drove the crabs away." She pointed to an ethereal white cloud of crustaceans receding into the distance.

Mik nodded, remembering what Shimmer had done to Lord Kell's crew on the deck of *Red Wake*. Now he knew what it felt like to be on the receiving end. Shimmer hovered nearby, rubbing his left shoulder.

"Where are the others?" Mik asked.

Shimmer peered into the darkness up the canyon. "They're coming," he said. "All but the kender."

A cold hand gripped Mik's heart. "Trip!" he called. "Where are you?"

"Here I am!" the kender's happy voice replied. He zipped back into view from beyond the weedy tunnel. "I tried to get the crabs to follow me, but it didn't work. Sorry."

"No apologies necessary," Mik said.

Kell and his warriors returned. Karista Meinor looked very frightened, and her diving briefs hung in tatters, but she didn't seem much the worse for wear. The brass lord brushed pieces of crab from his armor. Kell's two warriors trailed behind, tending to their armor and numerous small cuts. The woman looked badly shaken, and the man was very pale.

"Everyone accounted for?" Mik asked.

Kell nodded.

"Good. Let's get moving before the crabs come back." Mik turned and swam toward the temple; the others followed.

The thorny coral passageway opened up, and the weeds fell away on each side. Before them, the Temple, in all its drowned glory, rose from the abyssal canyon.

Billowing towers of white steam, ghostly sentinels, surrounded the sunken edifice. Columns of marble and crystal jutted up like broken teeth from the silty sea bottom. Piled on top of them lay the domes of the temple, splendid even in their decay.

Eerie, black-bodied fish with glowing eyes populated the submerged building. Funereal processions of shroudlike jellyfish and squid wound through the columns, slowly chasing one another through the bubbling water.

It was hot. Mick felt the heat even through the enchantment that protected him from the cold pressure of the deep. People did not belong here. Rather, the temple was a stygian landscape reserved for the lost, the cursed, and the drowned. The huge domes and columns looked like titanic cracked eggshells crouching atop piles of bleached bones. These strange tombstones stood in silent procession amid a landscape of pale weeds and broken flagstones. Only the farthest reaches of the temple, at the edge of sight, seemed to retain any cohesion. All the rest looked ravaged, as though by an ancient, undersea war.

Mik looked around the group, to see if anyone else shared his apprehension. Only one of Kell's brass warriors, standing near the back, fidgeted nervously. The other stood in rapt attention, gazing at the wonders of the ancient structure.

"It's beautiful," said Trip.

"And deadly," Mik added.

"Aye," said Ula.

"Why build it so deep?" Lord Kell asked.

"Dragons are people of the sea as well as sky," Shimmer replied.

"It may have sunk more since the building as well," Mik added. "It's certainly suffered over the years."

"It's *still* beautiful," said Trip.

They all stood there for a long moment, drinking in the glory of the submerged temple.

Karista finally broke the silence. "Where do we look for the key?" she asked.

"It's somewhere in the temple," Mik said. "Probably the innermost precincts nearest the mountain. The Temple of the Sky was atop the volcano."

"To treasure now ascend," quoted Karista.

They took their bearings and swam toward the undersea slopes of the ancient volcano. Far overhead, they saw the shadows of the thorny coral, arching over the temple and forming a cave-like dome.

"I think I see it," Trip called, flashing ahead of them. "But it's a bit of a wreck."

At the base of the mountain, the temple's blue domes lay smashed and broken like titanic cracked eggshells amid the sturdy columns. The treasure hunters swam swiftly toward the shattered dome at the top of the temple complex. Trip circled the remains of the dome twice before the others arrived.

They hovered a moment outside. Then—taking a deep breath—Mik swam forward through the cracked dome and into the chamber beyond. Ula and the others followed.

Rubble filled the room's interior. Broken shards of the dome, sand, and pieces of coral littered the floor, nearly filling the room.

"Ouch!" said Ula.

"What?" Mik asked. "More coral?"

"No," she said. "This accursed thing just got hot." She unlaced the bejeweled key from the golden chains at her waist and held it in her hand. It glowed brightly.

"The final key must be close," Mik said. "Maybe under the rubble."

"You're right," Trip said. "Look at my treasure finder!" The trinket was spinning so fast that it churned the water into a froth.

The others settled on the temple floor and began to dig frantically.

"You," Kell said, pointing to the rearmost guard, "stand watch. Warn us if anything approaches."

The guard, looking pale and vaguely unsettled behind his brass helmet, nodded and swam back out of the opening. He took up a position near the top of the dome, swimming in slow circles and scanning the surrounding ocean.

Silt quickly clouded the waters of the chamber as the treasure hunters pushed aside the detritus of centuries.

"I've found it!" Mik cried, breaking caked mud off some hidden object.

The others gathered 'round as Mik brushed away the last bits of debris.

In his palm lay an intricate golden lacework, similar to the artifacts in Ula's hand. In its center rested a large, glowing ruby.

"This is it!" Mik said. "The final key!"

Chapter Thirty-Seven

The Silver Stairway

Everyone in the room stood silently for a moment, and all eyes fixed upon the glittering ruby.

"You do the honors," Ula said quietly, handing her portions of the key to Mik.

Willing his hands not to tremble, Mik joined the final segment of the key to the first three. As he did, the temple shuddered and the key shone with a blue-white brilliance as intense as sunlight on a summer day.

Mik squeezed his eyes shut against the blinding glare and, when he opened them again, the light had died away. As his vision cleared, on the far side of the room he saw a set of massive silver doors that had not been there before. The portals were carved with the likenesses of sea creatures, people, and dragons. They had no doorhandles; only a single large keyhole marred the sculptures on their surface.

"The doors to the Temple of the Sky," he said. The others nodded, too stunned to say anything—even Trip.

Stephen D. Sullivan

Finally, Karista Meinor broke the silence. "Open them," she said, rubbing her long fingers together in anticipation.

Mik swam across the room and inserted the key into the doors' immense lock. As he turned it, all of reality seemed to tremble. The room shook, and he felt lightning coursing up his arms and into his brain. In his mind, he saw an enormous blue-white diamond hovering in the air before him. Lights flashed inside his eyes, and thunder roared in his ears.

Slowly and without a sound, the giant metal doors parted.

At first, all any of them saw beyond the doors was the ruined temple and the craggy mountainside beyond. Then, like ice melting from a windowpane, the rocks faded away, revealing a long silver staircase.

The stair was wide enough for dragons, but its smooth treads were spaced on a more human scale. The risers supporting it were carved in the same elaborate manner as the silver doors. The stairway stretched up, out of the ocean deep to the fiery cleft in the volcano rim above. At the top of the stair, its white pillars looking as new as if it had been made yesterday, lay the Temple of the Sky.

"Wonders upon wonders," gasped Mik.

The stairway was immensely long, but there were terraces or plazas along the way—each one surrounded by pillars, forming a kind of miniature open temple.

"Up we go," Mik said. He tucked the key in his belt and swam through the silver doors and up to the stairway.

"Don't forget your man outside," Ula said to Kell, before following the sailor. Trip darted ahead of her and reached the stairway at the same time as Mik. As the kender headed for the stairs, though, he dived facedown onto the treads. "Ouch!" he cried.

Mik swam to help him, and nearly tumbled down himself. He landed on all fours, and then stood before helping Trip up.

"There's an enchantment on the stairway," Mik called to the rest. "Trying to swim over it is like fighting your way up

264

a waterfall." He took a few tentative steps up the stairway. "It seems easy enough to walk, though."

"One does not *swim* up a temple stairway," Shimmer noted.

Mik and Trip began walking upward toward the first plaza. Ula and Shimmer followed, then the female guard, then Karista and Kell. Finally, the pale guard who had been stationed outside the temple brought up the rear. He walked tentatively, glancing from side to side, peering into the deep as he came.

They reached the first terrace, and Mik bobbed quickly across. "The spell doesn't affect the plazas," he said. "We can swim normally here."

The group took a moment to relax and admire the decrepit splendor of the sunken temple below. Kell's male guard took the lead as they ascended the stairs once more, while the female brass warrior brought up the rear.

They passed beyond the thorny ceiling overarching the submerged temple and trench just before they reached the next plaza. The waters around them became less dark, and the sea life grew more numerous. Spotted dominoes swam overhead, beyond the reach of the stair's enchantment.

"Watch out for predators," Kell told his warriors. The brass-armored man and woman nodded their understanding.

As they reached the third platform, the surface of the sea became visible above them. A supernatural clarity surrounded the stairs themselves—and the path to the volcano's rim appeared as lucid as gazing across the ocean on a cloud-free day.

In the area surrounding the stair, though, local conditions prevailed. The storm brewing in the sky above churned up the water, making it translucent and opaque. Thunderheads gathered over the mountain, though a tiny circle of blue sky shone through above the distant temple.

Kell's lead guard forged ahead while the others rested. Hiking up the steps was as tedious as it would have been on land—and the stairway was far longer than the climb to the Dragonheights.

Mik leaned against a pillar and caught his breath. The next plaza was above the waves, and the weather there looked none too pleasant. Ula swam lazy circles around the perimeter of the area, stretching her long limbs. Trip kept pace beside her, using the ancient power of his sea serpent cloak.

Kell and Karista Meinor stood close together, between Mik and the ascending stairway. Shimmer sat on a coral bench opposite, rubbing his wounded shoulder. Kell's brass-armored woman warrior stood atop the descending steps, watching the way they'd come.

"Let's keep moving," Mik said. "We don't have much daylight left." He headed for the stairs once more, and the others followed.

A shape flashed past ahead of them, beyond the plaza's massive columns. Mik turned and saw the tail fin of a mangler shark angle up, over the stairway. He wondered, briefly, why Kell's advance guard hadn't warned them about the predator.

The next instant, the brass guard shot down the stairway like a man surfing a powerful wave. Sharks and razorfish, each with a small Turbidus leech attached to its spine, followed him. The guard streaked across the terrace, his brass spear pointed at Lord Kell's back. Kell's other guard stepped in front of her master, and the traitor thrust his spear into the female warrior's gut.

The woman gasped, and her weapon fell from her hand onto the coral flagstones below. The guard cursed in a guttural voice and yanked out his spear. The woman warrior hung limply in the water, dead.

Lord Kell spun, a cry on his lips. His outrage echoed through the brine as everyone in the plaza drew their weapons. The evil fish swarmed down the stairs and attacked.

Kell stood between Mik and the traitor, but a mangler shark buffeted the lord aside. It was all Kell could do to avoid being bitten in half. The renegade guard flashed by his master, headed straight toward Mik.

Mik cursed himself for not noticing the guard's odd demeanor earlier. He brought up his sword to defend himself. The traitor batted Mik's weapon aside and, on the backswing, deftly knocked the Key to the Temple of the Sky from Mik's belt.

The artifact spun through the water and landed near the renegade's feet. The traitor stabbed at Mik, and the sailor dived back. The guard stooped to retrieve the fallen key.

Mik lunged forward and slashed at the man's exposed spear-arm. The scimitar found its target, and the guard's flesh ripped off in a long pale ribbon, revealing the scales beneath.

Shocked at the sight, Mik hesitated, and the imposter's counterattack nearly impaled him. Fortunately, Ula dove in and shoved the sailor out of the way. She thrust her spear up into the brass warrior's crystal faceplate. The helmet, and the warrior's dead face beneath, ripped off—revealing the horrifying reptilian visage of Mog.

The dragonspawn inside the dead warrior's skin batted aside the shaft of Ula's spear and stabbed at her midsection. Ula parried the blow and aimed a counter thrust. Before she could deliver it, though, Mik put his shoulder into Ula's gut and drove them both across the plaza onto the coral flagstones.

A torpedolike redtip shark flashed harmlessly over their heads. The fish had been aiming for Ula's exposed back. "Thanks," she said. Mik nodded.

Mog's fishy minions circled the plaza, keeping the rest of the treasure hunters busy. Karista put her back against a pillar while Kell stood in front of her, warding off attacks. The brass lord swung his coral lance in short arcs, slashing the flanks of the sharks and razorfish pressing in around them.

Trip played a deadly game of tag with the evil fish. His sea serpent cloak gave him more speed and maneuverability, but the enchanted plaza gave him little room to move. He bobbed and twisted, shooting between the enemy, and striking them with his twin daggers.

The predators' teeth had little effect against Shimmer's bronze armor. Mog had counted on this, though, and directed the bulk of his forces to attack the bronze knight. Enthralled fish surrounded the human-shaped dragon like a whirlwind, battering him from all directions. Shimmer swung his saw-toothed sword at them, killing many, but more fish swarmed in from the sides to replace the dead.

Mog seized the glowing key. He shrieked as the energy of the artifact ripped through him, blowing the remnants of his hideous disguise into streamers of crimson flesh.

Writhing in agony, he swam to the edge of the silver stairs and began to shamble up its wide treads.

"Give it back!" Karista shrieked. She dodged out from behind Shimmer and flung a thin-bladed dagger at the dragonspawn.

The knife pierced Mog's left hand. He howled, staggered backward, and lost his balance on the edge of the staircase. The key dropped from his hand and tumbled down the stairs.

"Trip! Grab it!" Mik called, as he gutted another dragon-enthralled shark.

The kender dodged through the temple pillars and caught the ancient key on the fly. The gems in the artifact sparked, but it did not burn him. He gazed at it in rapt attention.

"Look out, you fool!" Kell shouted.

Trip ducked just in time to avoid the jaws of a speeding razorfish.

The enraged and bleeding Mog lunged down into the plaza and commanded his fishy allies to destroy the kender. The sharks and razorfish swarmed in on Trip, trying to surround him.

But the sea serpent cloak gave Trip greater speed and maneuverability. He raced away from his pursuers, darting in and out of the terrace's pillars. Mik, Ula, Shimmer, and Kell tried to cover Trip's position, but their enemies crowded between them, making it impossible for anyone to help the kender.

"Up the stairs!" Mik said. "The next plaza is above water. The fish can't touch us there." He and the others formed a tight group at the stairway's base, using the pillars on each side to protect their flanks. Karista retrieved her fallen dagger, stained black with Mog's sticky blood, but kept well back of the fray.

"Fight your way to us!" Mik called to Trip.

"Duck your head, little one!" Shimmer shouted.

The visor of the bronze knight's helmet opened and his scintillating dragon breath blasted across the briny deep. Dragon-enthralled fish withered and died where Shimanloreth's power struck them, cutting a path through the swirling predators. Exhausted, the bronze knight collapsed to one knee, nearly toppling off the edge of the plaza.

Trip darted through the opening toward his friends, but Mog rose up before him. The dragonspawn grabbed the kender's cloak. His talonlike fingers raked toward Trip's eyes. Trip struggled frantically in Mog's grip.

Mik and Ula shot through the gap in their enemies and drove straight for Mog.

Ula thrust her spear under the dragonspawn's arm, but the point got caught in the armor of the dead guard that Mog had been impersonating. Mik cut at the creature's head, but Mog ducked out of the way. He whirled in a tight circle, yanking Ula and her spear with him.

The sea elf smashed into Mik and the kender just as her spear yanked free from Mog's stolen armor. The three of them tumbled back, limbs flailing, as a group of razorfish flashed past. The fishes' sharp teeth missed the treasure hunters by mere inches.

The key flew from Trip's hand and landed near the steps ascending from the plaza. Lord Kell snatched it up before anyone else could reach it. "Up the stairs!" he called, and he, Karista, and Shimmer began to climb.

"Give me the key, Kell," Shimmer said. They'd gone a dozen steps, and the spell over the stairs was keeping the evil fish from following. The bronze knight looked pained and exhausted, but his orange eyes blazed. The bottom of his visor raised slightly, showing the scintillating energies within.

The brass lord gritted his teeth and handed Shimmer the artifact. "We're all in this together," he said, barely meaning it.

In a flash, Karista smashed the pommel of her dagger across Kell's helmet. He reeled, dropping his coral lance, and tumbled down the stairs into the plaza where Mik, Ula, and Trip were still fighting for their lives. Karista picked up Kell's fallen weapon.

"Why did you . . . ?" Shimmer began. But he never finished his sentence.

Karista thrust the weapon between Shimanloreth's ribs. The coral lance's magic pierced the dragon's bronze armor and drove deep into his side. Shimmer's humanlike eyes went wide, and he dropped the bejeweled key. "Why . . . ?" he gasped.

The aristocrat gave the spear a final twist and pushed Shimmer off the side of the stairway. He disappeared into the dark waters below, Kell's lance still protruding from his side.

Karista smiled, and spoke in a voice as much Tempest's as her own.

"The key is mine!"

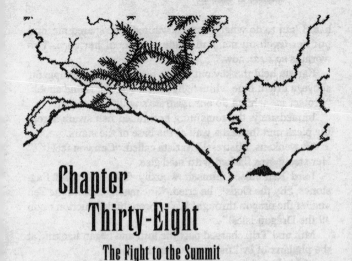

Chapter Thirty-Eight

The Fight to the Summit

Mik and Trip stood frozen in disbelief as Karista pushed Shimmer's bleeding body off the stairway.

"No!" Ula shrieked. She broke off fighting and leaped off the platform into the darkness after her wounded companion.

Karista picked up the ancient key.

"No!" Mog wailed.

Fire burned in Karista's steely eyes. "You haven't the strength necessary to open the Veil," she said. "So Tempest has chosen a more suitable vessel."

She clutched the key to her breast and began climbing the stairs once more.

"Lady Meinor! What are you doing?" Trip cried.

The aristocrat paused and turned toward her former companions. Her pretty face cold and distant. "What I *must*! She would have killed me if I hadn't become her thrall. I didn't want to die there, in the middle of the ocean, like Bok

had. I *had* to do what Tempest wanted. She spared me, and
put her leech on me, and made me one of her own. The
world is so *clear* now."

Karista held the key out before her, and in the temple far
above, a bright blue-white light flared, and the island shook.
"Protect me while I do our mistress's will!" she called.

Immediately, the remaining enthralled fish swam across
the plaza and formed a wall at the base of the stairs.

"It weakens, Mistress!" Karista called. "Can you feel it?!"
Her steely eyes flashed with mad glee.

Lord Kell raised himself woozily from the coral flagstones. "By the Gods!" he cried. "She means to rend the Veil
and let the dragon through! We've brought destruction upon
all the Dragon Isles!"

Mik and Trip charged past the lord and began hacking at
the phalanx of evil fish protecting the stairs.

Mik's jaw tightened. "I've been a fool!" he hissed, cutting down a razorfish. "The treasure we sought—the great
diamond—it wasn't just part of the ceremony to create the
Veil. It's part of the *fabric* of the Veil. It's a cornerstone of
its defense!"

"The key is the key to the Veil?" Trip said.

"Yes," Mik replied. "It opens the magic of the diamond."

"What can we do?" Trip asked. He grabbed a Turbidus
leech as big as his arm and smashed it into a redtip shark.

"We have to stop Karista before she reaches the diamond," Mik said.

The water around them became a bloody cloud as Mik
and Trip fought their way toward the stairway separating
them from Tempest's thrall.

* * * * *

The sea dragon's mighty flukes propelled her toward the
wavering barrier. Her evil hordes swam with her: sharks,
razorfish, Turbidus leeches, and a half dozen dragonspawn—
all ready to die at their mistress' command.

Tempest threw herself against the Veil. It shuddered but did not break. Her mind remained clear, though; the barrier's vexing enchantment had failed. Tempest roared with laughter.

Now it was only a matter of time. Her thrall's power grew as she brought the key closer to the great enchanted diamond. As Karista's power—and through her, the power of Tempest—escalated, the Veil weakened. After the sea dragon passed through, she would then snatch the key and use the great diamond to destroy the Veil once and for all.

Again and again, Tempest crashed against the barrier as Karista bent the Veil's magic to her mistress' will. Finally, a tiny rift formed in the shield's magical surface. The sea dragon ripped it open.

With a hideous bellow of triumph, Tempest and her minions surged through the breach into the Dragon Isles.

* * * * *

"She's coming!" the aristocrat cried. "She's coming!" She held the key high overhead and rejoiced. Mog glanced from the glowing key toward the bright temple at the top of the stairs. The diamond within the temple flared as the key summoned its power. The sky opened up and lightning flashed.

Mik and Trip pushed forward through the cloud of blood, killing many of Karista's fishy bodyguards as they came. Lord Kell charged the rear of the frenzied mass, but he was far behind the sailor and the kender.

"Fight it, Karista! Fight the dragon!" Mik shouted.

"Milady," Kell called, "this is not you. You do not want to destroy the isles!" His voice sounded tinny and strained through the magic of his helmet.

"Of course it's what I want, fool!" Karista shrieked. "It's what Tempest wants, and I am her creature! The Veil will open to . . . to my ships, as well." She turned and began to climb once more. The wave-tossed surface loomed just twenty steps over her head.

"The isles will be destroyed!" Mik called. "There will *be* no trade!"

"Fight back!" Trip yelled.

Mik and Trip broke through the line of enthralled fish and ran up the stairs toward Karista. The fish remaining in the plaza tried to follow them, but the stairs' enchantment pushed them back down. A few left the plaza to try and circle down from above, though the ocean's surface left them little room to do so.

"Karista!" Mik called.

She turned and looked back.

Mik pulled his dagger and threw it at her.

Mog stepped between them and batted the blade aside. It settled on the stairway near the dragonspawn's feet.

Madness played across the aristocrat's face. She turned toward her former companions and extended the key.

"Flee or I shall kill you!" she cried.

The gems on the key blazed to life, and lightning flashed from the artifact toward Mik and Trip. They dodged aside, and the bolt cracked a coral pillar in the plaza behind them. The kender hurtled off the stairway and into the swirling waters beyond.

Mik picked himself off the stairs and kept climbing.

Mog charged down the stairway at Mik. The sailor ducked under Mog's spearthrust and grabbed the dragonspawn by the front of its stolen armor. The sailor fell backward, thrusting hard with his legs as he did.

Tempest's lieutenant sailed over Mik's head, down the stairs, and into the cracked pillar. The column broke into smaller pieces and toppled onto the startled dragonspawn, burying him beneath it.

Mik ran up the stairs and retrieved his dagger from where it had fallen. "Karista," he called, surging forward, "I don't want to hurt you, but you *must* stop."

"I can't!" she cried. The power of the key coursed around her, building for another strike. She pointed her hand toward Mik's heart, her fingers glowing with deadly energy.

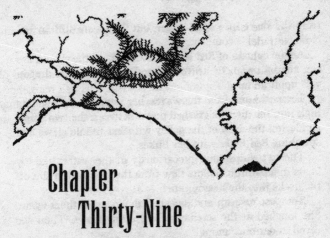

Chapter
Thirty-Nine

Sea, Storm, and Tempest

The storm that had been lingering above the ocean for days gathered into a typhoon and whipped the waves into titanic mountains of water. Jerick the Red barked frantic orders to his crew, trying to keep his galleon from floundering in the terrible weather. Exploring the strange stairway and temple that had suddenly appeared on the side of the volcano would have to wait.

Only a bow shot away from *Red Wake*, the crew of Kell's trireme struggled as well. The brass-covered gunwales of their ship were not as high above the water as *Red Wake*'s. Huge whitecaps washed over their decks, threatening to swamp the galley with every surge.

Jerick cursed himself for sailing so close to the Veil during typhoon season. The Isle of Fire had no harbor, no shelter from the storm. Its rocky shores were treacherous. They could easily rip the bottoms out of *Red Wake* and Kell's galley.

The red-bearded captain had ordered both ships away

from the shore into open water, but they were still far too close for Jerick's comfort.

As the captain of *Red Wake* worried about the shoals, the sea nearby began to heave and roil. Suddenly, the dragon was upon them.

Tempest burst from the waves, her immense bulk sailing high into the air. She crashed down between the two ships, sundering the deck of the galley with her titanic claws and smashing *Red Wake* with her flukes.

The two ships spun precariously in the water, like toy boats in a bathtub. Sailors flew from the rigging and slid off the decks into the heaving surf.

Tempest rose up and smashed down upon them again. She laughed at the screams of the dying crews. Then she dived under once more.

A huge breaker washed Jerick to the shattered rail of his galleon. *Red Wake* listed badly to starboard, taking on a frightening amount of water.

Just to port, Kell's brass-armored ship lay in splinters. Its keel had been broken, and each wave threatened to pull it to the bottom.

The cries of wounded sailors in the water and aboard the crippled vessels echoed above the wail of the wind. Sharks and razorfish swarmed in the dragon's wake, attacking anything that moved. The sailors in the water stood no chance of swimming to the Isle of Fire's rocky shore.

Jerick spat the brine and blood from his whiskers and called to his men. "Sing out if you're injured! Those who aren't, help the rest! Get our people out of the water! Throw some lines to the remains of that galley, too—maybe we can save some of them as well! Then bail for all you're worth and pray to the gods that the dragon doesn't return!"

* * * * *

It took Mog only a moment to recover his bearings. The huge pillar pinning him resisted his strength, so he changed himself into a scavenger eel and wriggled out from under it. As he did, Lord Kell somehow grabbed him by the tail.

Mog changed back to his draconian form just in time to ward off a blow from the brass lord's dagger. Kell stabbed at him again but, as he did, Mog lunged forward. The dragonspawn's forehead smashed hard into the human lord's gut.

Kell reeled back, and Mog clouted him across the helmet with a scaly fist. Benthor Kell grunted, and Mog kicked him hard in the belly.

The armored man fell back, head over heels, crashing into the stairs and rolling down them into the undersea darkness. Mog turned and loped up the steps to join Karista.

Kell thudded to a halt halfway down to the next landing. His head spun, and every muscle in his body ached. He groped his way to his feet and began to climb once more.

* * * * *

A tiny figure streaked down the stairs through the water and grabbed Karista around the waist, spoiling her aim. The deadly energies coruscating at her fingertips ripped wildly through the depths. The spell missed Mik and smashed into the stairway near the last plaza.

"Good work, Trip!" Mik called, realizing the kender had circled around from the upper part of the stairway.

Now Trip brought his small fist up and clouted Karista in the jaw. The aristocrat reeled back but did not let go of the pulsating key. She screamed in pain and frustration.

Mik surged ahead, slashing at her with his cutlass. Karista stepped back, out of the way, confusion clouding her steely eyes. "Keep at her!" Mik said. "If she can't concentrate, she can't summon a spell to kill us."

"I hope you're right," Trip replied.

Karista punched Trip on the chin, and the kender reeled and tumbled down the stairs. She pointed at Mik, energy blasting from her fingertips.

Mik dived out of the way and almost fell off the stairs. He grabbed hold of the edge of the steps and hung on as the surging waters outside the stairway's enchantment tried to rip him away into the sea.

Karista turned and staggered up the silver stairs, out of the raging surf, and into the open air. The stairway's preternatural calm fell away at the nexus of water and wind. The swirling waves tugged at Karista, like breakers crashing against the shore. She stumbled and nearly lost her grip on the key.

Trip helped Mik pull himself back onto the stairs, and they both ran after her. The waves buffeted them as they made the transition from sea to land. Mik gasped for air and noticed that a half-dozen gems had flaked off his enchanted necklace.

Trip's waterlogged cloak clung to his skin, and its long hem tangled under his feet. He fell to his knees, the waves lapping at his back. Mik struggled to keep going.

Karista reached the next plaza and turned toward the sailor, a mixture of murder and regret in her eyes. She raised the key to blast him again—but, depleted from her previous efforts, its energy glowed more faintly this time.

The sailor crested the platform and dove under her arms. White lightning blasted from Karista's hands, searing over Mik's head. He grabbed the aristocrat around her slender waist, and they fell hard onto the wet flagstones.

The lady Meinor gasped, and Mik felt something wriggling under one of his arms. "Tempest's leech!" he called to Trip. "It's at the base of her spine!"

"No!" Karista screamed. "You'll not have it!"

"I could use some help here, Trip," Mik said. He tumbled across the rain-drenched flagstones with her, tearing at the leech but getting no good purchase. Karista's blouse tore at the back, revealing the writhing, slimy parasite.

Trip struggled to this feet, but a wave broke over him and swept the kender underwater once more.

Mik clung desperately to Karista. Madness reigned in the aristocrat's steely eyes. She drew power from the key, increasing her strength. Mik tried to turn his sword on her, but she slapped it from his hand. The scimitar skidded across the landing and came to rest against a pillar.

Grappling together, Mik and Karista rolled across the water-drenched plaza. Mik's head cracked against a pillar near the stairs, and lights burst before his eyes.

Cackling gleefully, Karista raised the faintly glowing key high to smash it down upon Mik's unprotected skull.

Then Trip burst from the water below. His prodigious, dolphinlike leap carried him up the steps to the landing where the aristocrat sat astride the sailor. The kender's daggers flashed, and Karista lurched away from Mik, screaming.

She landed hard on her back, and the key to the Temple of the Sky skidded out of her hands. The Turbidus leech that had controlled her wriggled on the wet paving stones; Trip had sliced it in two. Both halves of the foul creature flopped around for a moment before finally lying still.

Trip had no time to rejoice in his victory. The kender's momentum carried him past his foe and into the pillars at the landing's edge. He slammed up against them, and the breath rushed out of his lungs.

Karista lay on the marble flagstones and moaned as though waking from a long nightmare.

Mik blinked the rain out of his eyes and tried to regain his bearings as the bejeweled key slid across the plaza toward the silver stairs. Just as it reached the edge, Mog leaped from below and seized it.

The dragonspawn's baleful eyes flashed across the stunned mariner and the groggy kender. Then—without even a glance at Karista—he crossed the plaza and loped up the final stairs leading to the temple.

Mik cursed and rose to his feet. A pounding, roaring sound filled his ears, but he couldn't tell if it was from the storm, the surf, or the blow to his head. He retrieved his scimitar and climbed after Mog just as Lord Kell staggered out of the surf behind him.

Kell spotted Karista, lying half-conscious on the flagstones, and knelt down beside her barely conscious form. "Why?" he asked.

"It was the leech," Trip explained, getting up slowly. The kender slogged across the plaza toward the stairs, his cloak dragging behind him like a huge, clumsy tail. "The dragon was controlling her."

As the kender plodded up the stairs to help Mik, Kell took Karista in his arms. The brass lord brushed her rain-soaked hair from her face and gazed into her eyes. She smiled weakly at him.

Mog mounted the final stair and reached the temple. The key in the dragonspawn's hand glowed brightly. Small bolts of lightning danced from it, encircling Mog's reptilian body and raising small puffs of smoke wherever they touched. Mog growled and hissed, but did not let go of the artifact. He turned to meet the sailor as Mik bounded up the last steps to the temple platform.

The Temple of the Sky was an elegant structure, beautiful even with driving rain bouncing off its marble surface. A circular colonnade surrounded a round hole in the temple's floor. In the center of the hole stood a carved pillar, scribed in an ancient language that Mik could neither read nor recognize. Glowing orange light shone up from beneath the pillar through the treasure piled high in the yard-wide pit surrounding the column's base. Diamonds, gold, silver and gems brimmed to the top of the hole—ancient offerings to the gods of Krynn.

The radiance seeping up through the treasure echoed the volcanic glow on the far side of the temple. The mountain's great crater yawned just beyond the edge of the structure: natural destruction waiting at the edge of civilized creation. Fiery red light shone up from the lava in the heart of the mountain.

Atop the pillar, amid the glowing treasure, rested the massive blue-white diamond Mik had seen in his visions. It was twice as large as a man's skull and cut to faceted perfection. It shone with blinding brightness as the key drew near.

Mog, key in hand, loped toward the diamond. Slender bolts of lightning danced from the key to the surface of the great gem. Mog grunted with each electrical flash.

Mik darted forward, his feet nearly skidding across the rain-slick marble, an angry scream on his lips. He aimed a deadly cut toward the back of the dragonspawn's neck.

Mog spun and brought up his brass spear, holding the weapon with one hand. He parried the scimitar, and the sword's blade slid down the shaft of the dragonspawn's spear.

Mik flicked his blade to the left, off the spear, and cut a long gash in Mog's right arm. The dragonspawn shrieked and swung his spear at the sailor's head. Mik ducked and thrust. The point of his sword struck the bejeweled key, knocking it from Mog's hand. The key scudded across the floor, stopping just short of the silver stairway.

Tempest's minion roared with anger. Seizing his brass spear with both hands, he charged at Mik. The sailor stepped nimbly aside, but his boot slipped on the temple's wet flagstones. He skidded across the chamber, nearly falling into the treasure-filled pit surrounding the great gem. His head dangled over the edge of the floor, and the light from the huge diamond dazzled his eyes. He felt the heat of the volcano on the back of his neck.

Mog stabbed at him, but Mik rolled aside just in time. He kicked the dragonspawn in the legs, and Mog toppled backward and slid toward the edge of the stairs. Trip had to dodge out of the way as he reached the top of the staircase, and the dragonspawn nearly bowled him over.

"The key, Trip!" Mik called. "Grab the key!"

The kender reached down and picked up the artifact while Mog struggled to right himself. Before Trip's small fingers could close around the key, though, Mog swung his bronze spear and swatted the kender's hand.

The key flew through the air and bounced down the stairs and into the landing below the temple. It tumbled across the rain-soaked plaza toward the final stairway leading to the raging surf.

Just as it neared the precipice, Benthor Kell stabbed out his hand and seized it. Battered and bloody, Karista Meinor rose to her feet beside the brass lord. Benthor Kell held the key tight, feeling the power throbbing within. Behind his bronze helmet, a smile of triumph broke over his handsome face.

As he and Karista gazed at the key, the ocean surged, and Tempest rose from the depths once more.

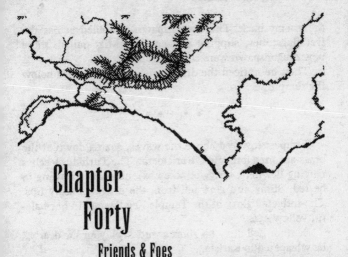

Chapter Forty

Friends & Foes

As the sea dragon broke the surface, her dragonspawn troops swarmed up the sides of the volcano and into the Temple of the Sky. Though not as clever or powerful as Mog, these six creatures still possessed sharp fangs and claws, as well as cunningly crafted weapons. In each of them burned their mistress' unquenchable thirst for blood.

Trip didn't spot the dragonspawn until they were almost upon him. With a startled cry, he hopped away from the temple's perimeter, keeping his daggers between himself and the new menace. The Trip didn't notice as Mog rose behind him and aimed his spear at the kender's back.

Mikal Vardan scrambled to his feet and raced to his friend's side. He turned aside Mog's thrust barely in time, then batted aside a sword-cut from a second dragonspawn that had meant to disembowel him.

Mik surged forward, slashing with his scimitar, driving

the enemy back. The dragonspawn scrabbled across the wet flagstones, slipping and cursing. Mik smiled; these new dragonspawn were clumsy on land.

Then he noticed the dragon rising from the sea below the temple.

* * * * *

Tempest towered above the waves, gazing down at the brass-armored lord and the aristocrat. The Turbidus leeches ringing her neck wriggled like obscene snakes waiting to be fed. Slime and gore fell from the dragon's scaly lips. The reflected glory of the Temple Key flashed in her baleful yellow eyes.

Benthor Kell drew his short sword. "Sell your life dearly," he whispered to Karista.

"I will," Lady Meinor replied.

The aristocrat pulled her dagger and plunged it into Kell's breast, just below his brief armor.

The brass lord spun, stunned horror on his face.

Karista pulled out the knife and pushed him away. As Kell toppled backward, she snatched the bejeweled key from the shocked lord's grasp.

Lord Kell tumbled down the stairs and came to rest at the edge of the surf. Waves washed over his prostrate form, staining the sea with his blood.

Karista Meinor held the key to the Temple of the Sky high above her head. Slowly, she climbed the steps toward the Temple above. The dragon kept her yellow eyes fixed upon the blood-spattered aristocrat.

"S-see, my mistress?" Karista cried. "Even without the leech, I *still* do your will."

* * * * *

Ula's tears mingled with the brine as she searched the dark waters for the body of her friend.

Was Shimmer dead?

If so, she would avenge him.

She spotted his body on a plaza below, nearly at the bottom of the silver stair. He lay unmoving, the coral lance still protruding from his side.

"Shimmer!" she cried, swimming down to him and kneeling on the coral flagstones.

His orange eyes flickered open. "It's a good thing," he gasped, "that Lady Meinor is no warrior."

"She's near enough to have killed you," Ula said, examining his wound. It was deep, possibly fatal.

"Pull out the lance," he said.

Ula shook her head. "It could do you more harm that good."

"You must," Shimmer replied. "It is powerful. Not a dragonlance, but perhaps enough . . . to wound a sea dragon." He shuddered and struggled for breath. "Tempest is here; I feel her presence. Karista called her. Tanalish and the other dragons are too far away. *You* must stop Tempest." He winced again, and his orange eyes dimmed. "Pull out the lance!" he gasped.

Ula gritted her teeth and took hold of the weapon's long shaft. "Ready?" she asked.

"Never . . . readier."

With a swift jerk, she pulled the lance from Shimanloreth's side.

Shimmer groaned and clamped his armored hands over the bleeding wound. His blood turned the water around them black.

"I'll get some seaweed to bind that," Ula said.

"No time," he replied. "Go!"

Ula nodded once, then turned and swam for the surface, not daring to look back lest she lose the will to leave her old friend behind.

The sea elf rose from the raging surf at the foot of the long staircase. She fought against being toppled by the crashing waves and sucked back into the deep by the undertow.

With a final desperate heave, she pulled herself onto the silver stairway.

The sea dragon towered out of the ocean nearby, poised like a serpent ready to strike. Ula hunched down, fearing that Tempest might see her. The monster's attention was fixed, though, on the stairs below the temple, where Karista Meinor held up the glowing key.

Ula noticed people fighting within the temple, though she could not identify the combatants through the rain and stormy darkness.

She spotted the bloody form of Lord Kell, lying prostrate on the stairs nearby. She knelt beside him, and was surprised when his eyes flickered open.

"Help me . . . !" he gasped, fumbling to remove his enchanted helmet.

Ula reached up and unfastened the brass and crystal headpiece from Kell's armor. He was pale—deathly so—and blood trickled from his lips.

"Thank . . . you," he murmured.

"Did Karista do this?" she asked.

Kell nodded. "The dragon controlled her at first, but— even after . . . her lust for wealth and *power* . . . her fear of death . . . was too great. Too late for me . . . I'm afraid," Kell gasped. "You must . . . protect the isles."

Ula nodded grimly. "Karista and the monster will pay for what they've done. I'll see to that."

He nodded at her weakly, but said nothing.

Ula stalked away from him up the stairs toward where Karista Meinor stood trying to supplicate the dragon. The sea elf kept to the shadows as best she could she could, to avoid attracting the dragon's attention.

A moment later, Benthor Kell rose and shambled after her.

* * * * *

Mik turned, slashing and darting, trying not to slip on the wet marble flagstones of the temple, trying to protect Trip's back. Seven against two was not good odds, even without the dragon waiting below.

He tried not to think about the fate of his friends. Kell and Shimmer were gone, Kell's guards dead, and the lost gods only knew where Ula was.

Anger festered within Mik's belly for all that this treasure quest had cost him. He parried a blow aimed at Trip's back and gutted the dragonspawn attacking his friend. Stinging rain washed the gore from the sailor's skin. The roaring thunder and the crashing surf echoed the blood pounding in his ears.

A slimy talon sneaked in under Mik's guard, shredded his sopping shirt, and traced a long gash across his ribs. Mik spun and sliced the offending claw from its owner's arm. The wounded dragonspawn screamed and tumbled off the temple courtyard, over the cliff-like face of the volcano and into the whitecaps.

Trip fought valiantly, but his sea serpent cloak slowed him out of the water. More than once, he barely avoided being skewered on a dragonspawn's spear.

"We have to get the key from Karista before the dragon does!" Mik yelled.

"Too late!" said Trip.

As he spoke, Tempest spewed a huge gout of boiling steam upon the aristocrat. Karista's skin blistered and peeled away from her flesh in long ribbons. Her eyeballs exploded, and she toppled to the ground, the meat sloughing from her bones. The temple key landed with a soft plop in the middle of the pool of bubbling ooze that had once been the most powerful merchant in Jotan.

Tempest laughed, her booming voice shaking the heavens. She began to dwindle and change, shrinking—as Shimmer and Tanalish had done—until she stood only a foot or two larger than a man.

Her skin was pale, greenish, and slightly scaly. Writhing Turbidus leeches and dark green seaweed dangled from her head—living hair, covering the decrepit curves of her body. Her yellow eyes blazed with hatred. She sprang from the raging sea and settled gently onto the steps below the temple.

Tempest reached down, and her clawlike hand seized the key to the Temple of the Sky.

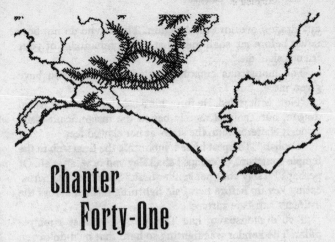

Chapter Forty-One

Tempest Triumphant

Slowly, the humanlike Tempest climbed the stairs toward the ancient temple. She moved with deliberate, measured steps, as though she were unused to walking on human legs. Magical energies from the glowing key danced around her. She laughed, and the island trembled.

"She needs to reach the diamond to destroy the Veil," Mik said urgently to Trip. "We have to keep her away from it." He parried the thrust of a dragonspawn and kicked the creature in its gut. The minion screamed as it soared over the edge of the temple courtyard and fell into the molten crater of the volcano.

"Clever man," the dragon hissed, her voice echoing up from the stairs below. "Perhaps, out of gratitude, I'll let you live long enough to see my triumph.

"Once I rip the Veil from the heavens, my minions will swarm the Dragon Isles. We will scour the oceans and pick clean the bones of our enemies. I will make myself equal to any dragon overlord on Ansalon. Those who do not bow down before me shall die—just as the remainder of your friends shall die."

The monstrous creature smiled. "All this, you have given me."

"No!" Mik yelled. He flung his dagger at the transformed dragon, but Tempest merely batted the insignificant blade aside. It clattered onto the stairs at her clawed feet.

"Foolish," Tempest hissed, mounting the final step to the temple courtyard. "Perhaps I shall slay you now, after all. Or perhaps I'll slay your pet kender first." She raised the coruscating key up before her. Pale lightning flashed across the artifact's intricate surface.

Two dragonspawn had Trip pinned against a temple pillar. The kender was fighting so hard that he didn't even see the dragon turning toward him.

Mik parried a blow from Mog, as a shadow moved on the stairs below Tempest.

Ula Drakenvaal strode up from the plaza below and hurled the coral lance at Tempest's exposed back.

Mog leaped away from Mik and shouted a warning. Tempest turned just in time to avoid a mortal blow. Yet the coral lance traced a long gash up the dragon's human-like arm. Tempest shrieked, her hand flexing open. The key fell from her grasp and tumbled off the mountain into the surf.

Ula cursed as the lance ricocheted off a pillar and clattered back down the stairs, landing too far away for her to retrieve it.

Tempest whirled to face the sea elf. A deadly spell formed on the transformed dragon's scaly lips.

Mik leaped with all his might—across the rain-slick courtyard and into Mog, knocking the dragonspawn onto its backside. Mog skidded over the wet surface into Tempest, cutting her legs out from under her.

The dragon's spell blazed into the sky as she toppled down the stairs. Tempest shrieked with rage and indignation. Mog rose, but Mik was on him before he could recover.

The sailor slashed down. His scimitar sliced across Mog's reptilian face, staining the wind with a misty spray of blood. Mog staggered back and stepped off the edge of the temple plaza. The dragonspawn tumbled down the mountainside, screaming. He hit the cliffs several times before being swallowed by the raging surf below.

Enraged, Tempest's human form rose and refocused her lethal spell toward Ula. Energy blasted from the dragon's clawed fingertips, but the sea elf dove off the stairway. Ula arced over the cliff face and sliced into the storm-tossed sea.

Tempest bellowed her fury, and the temple shook. "It seems I must slay you all before I can recover the key and destroy the Veil," she roared. In an instant she swelled to three times human size. Armored scales sprouted from her skin. Her neck became long and sinuous, her muzzle grew pointed like a crocodile's.

Growing larger by the second, the sea dragon lumbered up the stairs toward the temple, deadly steam pouring from her jaws.

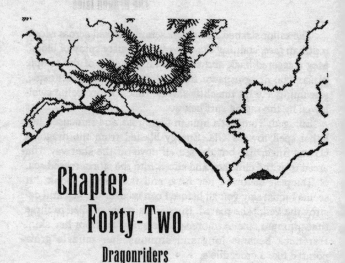

Chapter Forty-Two

Dragonriders

"Dive for it, Trip!" Mik yelled. He jumped with all his might as Tempest swiped her huge claw across the terrace. The claw smashed and scattered her remaining dragonspawn. Their bodies bounced lifelessly down the cliff face.

Mik and Trip barely avoided the deadly talon. They arced over the volcanic cliff face and sliced cleanly into the surging waters at the mountain's base.

The dragon's flipperlike hand smashed into the great diamond—the cornerstone of the Veil. Lightning flashed from the artifact, wracking the sea dragon's body. Tempest screamed as the scales of her forelimb caught fire. Howling in pain, she turned from the ruins and dove into the pounding surf to extinguish the flames.

* * * * *

One bleeding man met another on the landing below the

temple. Lord Kell looked up from where he sat, oozing blood, with his back against a pillar. The breath wheezed raggedly in his lungs; blood coated his lightly armored body. He smiled wanly as Shimmer lurched over the top of the stairs and into the plaza from below.

The orange eyes of the dragon-man met the gray eyes of the human lord. They nodded at each other. The rain washing over their bodies mingled their blood in pools on the marble flagstones.

"We have much to make amends for, you and I," Shimmer said.

Kell nodded and coughed up blood. He glanced up the stairway to where his coral lance had fallen. "Perhaps for one of us, at least," he said, "there is still time."

* * * * *

Trip leaped high into the air as the dragon surged after him. Tempest belched boiling steam at the kender, but he ducked back below the waves just in time. The dragon lunged after him.

Moments later, Mik and Ula surfaced together. "I found the key," she said, "and a couple of the dragonspawn's spears too. Do you want one?"

"No," Mik replied. "If I'm going to die, I'll die with my own scimitar in my hand."

Ula nodded. "Let's try not to die, though."

"You're more agile in the water than I am," Mik said. "Feel up to helping Trip keep the dragon off my back?"

She looked at him skeptically. "What are you planning?"

"I'm going for Kell's lance. If it can kill Shimmer, maybe it can kill Tempest as well."

"Shimmer's not dead," she replied. "At least, he wasn't when I pulled the lance from his side."

"Can he help us?"

She shook her head, sadness flashing across her green eyes. "I'll be surprised if he lives."

"It's up to us, then," Mik said. "Give me the key. We've seen its power. Maybe between it and the lance, we can kill this bitch."

"It's worth a try," Ula said. She undid the chain fastening the key to her waist and gave them both to Mik. "Good luck," she said, kissing him on the cheek.

"Stay alive," he replied.

Tempest surfaced a hundred yards away and scanned the waves for her enemies. Mik and Ula ducked under the surface as the dragon's baleful yellow gaze turned in their direction.

Trip's small form leaped from the breakers. Tempest lunged at the kender, her massive jaws snapping shut mere inches from the hem of his sea serpent cloak. The two of them dove out of sight again.

Mik swam as fast as he could toward the Isle of Fire. He surfaced only a few yards from the silver stairs. He felt bone-weary, and his muscles ached as he paddled the last strokes to the volcano's rocky face. Fighting against the pounding surf, he dragged himself out of the water and onto the silver stairway.

Instantly, his chest felt as though someone were sitting on it. Mik gasped for air, but none came. Something cold squeezed tight around his neck, choking him. He brought his hands to his throat and felt the pockmarked metal of his enchanted fish necklace.

He pulled the necklace off, and it crumbled in his hands—its magic finally exhausted. Mik drew a deep breath and forced his legs to carry him up the stairs to the plaza below the temple.

When he arrived, he spotted Shimmer and Lord Kell sitting to one side, their backs against a pillar. A huge pool of blood lay on the flagstones beneath them; both the bronze knight and the brass lord appeared dead.

Mik spotted Kell's coral lance on the far stairs, where it had fallen after striking Tempest. It lay close to the landing. Mik sprinted across slippery stones and seized the weapon in his aching hands, looking around for the sea dragon. Lightning flashed, casting the pounding sea into sharp relief, but Tempest was nowhere to be seen.

A cold chill gripped Mik's heart. Had the monster found and killed his friends?

Lightning flashed again and, in the plaza below, the bronze knight's eyes flickered open. "Vardan . . . !" Shimmer whispered.

Mik skidded down the steps and ran to the wounded dragon's side. "I thought you were dead."

"Not quite," Shimmer replied. "Not yet. Dragons are hard to kill. Apparently *you* are as well. Kell, though . . ." He pointed wanly toward the unmoving brass lord. "His spirit was strong, but his body . . ." He took a ragged breath. "Where's Ula?"

"Below the waves somewhere, trying to distract Tempest."

"Not dead, then."

"No. Not yet."

Slowly, the dragon in human form struggled to his feet. "We must help her, then."

"The best help we can give her is killing Tempest," Mik said. "Can you fly?"

Shimmer nodded grimly. "One last time, I think."

A hard smile cracked Mikal Vardan's bearded face. "Then let's take that sea dragon down." He pulled the key from his belt and fastened it around his neck with the chain from Ula's waist. The key glistened in the storm-clouded darkness.

Out to sea, Tempest surfaced once more, chasing the slender form of Ula Drakenvaal.

Shimmer groaned and stretched his arms out to each side. Fresh blood oozed from his wounds as his body grew and lengthened. Tangled, misshapen muscle piled up on his shoulders as his wings sprouted. His jaws became long and pointed, showing row upon row of sharp fangs.

The bronze dragon gritted his teeth and suppressed a scream. His entire, scaly body shook with pain. He swelled up to his full size—huge, but not nearly as huge as the sea dragon.

Tempest had her back to them as she focused every evil fiber of her being upon destroying Ula. She didn't notice the bronze dragon growing on the temple stairs, or the man with the lance standing at the dragon's side.

Shimanloreth gasped and extended his right forearm to Mik. The sailor scrambled up onto the dragon's back. He perched himself in front of the shoulders, just above Shimmer's deformed wing. Shimmer winced as Mik got a good grip on the bronze dragon's rain-slick back.

The sailor hefted the dead lord's coral lance. "Let's save our friends," he said.

"Yes," Shimmer hissed through gritted fangs.

Lightning crashed, and thunder shook the ancient island. Slowly, painfully, Shimmer took to the air.

* * * * *

Trip burst out of the water directly in front of the enraged sea dragon. He fastened his tiny hands on Tempest's mane of Turbidus leeches and yanked hard. The snakelike creatures squealed in pain. Their enormous mistress shook her head to free herself of the annoying kender.

She turned just enough that Ula avoided her deadly plunge. As the sea dragon passed by, surging into the deep, the Dargonesti drove one of her two spears into the monster's magic-scorched shoulder.

The spear pierced the dragon's blackened scales, and Tempest howled in pain. She plunged into the swirling darkness with the kender clinging to her mane and Ula hanging tightly onto the spear. The water around them swirled as Tempest twisted back on herself, snaking her reptilian head toward her shoulder.

The sea elf planted her feet against the dragon's scales and reeled back with the second spear—the bronze one Mog had once used.

As Tempest lunged toward them, Ula threw the bronze spear into the dragon's yellow eye.

Tempest roared and shot to the surface once more.

She breached, arcing high into the sky and shaking her head like a wounded dog.

Several of the Turbidus leeches clinging to her neck came loose, and Trip lost his grip along with them. He sailed into the air, only to have Tempest's flailing skull smash into him.

The kender cartwheeled end over end, hit the water hard, and disappeared below the raging surf.

Ula regained her footing on the dragon's scaly hide. She pulled on the shaft of her spear, then shoved it back in, putting all her weight behind the blow.

Tempest roared in pain, and dark blood gushed from the wound.

Ula stabbed her again. Tempest writhed through the waves, sending spray high into the rainswept air, trying to shake the elf from her back.

Tempest dove under again, but Ula clung tenaciously to the spear. She wedged her toes under the dragon's scales and hung on as the monster gyrated through the deep.

When the dragon broke surface, Ula yanked on the spear with one hand while clinging to the dragon with the other. Again she stabbed the spear into the wound. Again and again. Black blood spouted from the dragon's shoulder, covering the Dargonesti in gore.

Tempest howled with pain. She writhed and bucked, diving repeatedly into the heaving ocean, only to leap into the air once more.

Ula reeled back for one final deadly thrust.

The dragon snapped her neck to one side and, suddenly, Ula lost her grip. The elf soared into the sky then crashed to the storm-tossed ocean below.

* * * * *

Mik and the bronze dragon angled up toward the clouds, gaining height for one desperate attack. Shimmer turned into the heart of the storm.

Mik lowered the ancient coral lance, the key to the Temple of the Sky glowed brightly at his neck. "For lost friends!" he said.

Shimmer nodded and hissed, "For the Dragon Isles!"

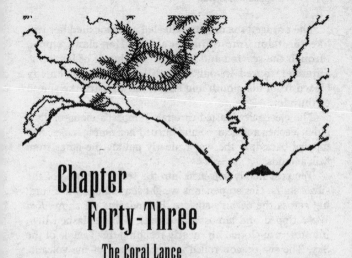

Chapter
Forty-Three
The Coral Lance

Lightning flashed as Mik and Shimmer dived out of the rain toward Tempest's exposed back. The sea dragon cast her gaze across the surface of the sea, seeking the bodies of her foes, or perhaps Mik himself.

In the pulsating light of the storm, she spotted Shimmer's shadow streaking across the surging waves toward her. Tempest turned just as the sailor and the bronze dragon closed in—but she couldn't avoid the allies' desperate charge.

Sparks shot into the rainswept air as Mik drove the coral lance deep into the sea dragon's throat, just below her long neck.

Tempest squealed in surprise and pain, then bellowed with rage.

Mik and the bronze dragon lunged forward again, driving the coral lance deeper into the wound. Mik twisted the lance, trying to hit some vital area; the key dangling at his neck glowed, adding its power to the magic of the lance.

The enraged sea dragon wheeled and smashed her fin-like foretalon into Shimmer's side. Her claws ripped through the scarred and battered membrane of his wing. Shimmer roared in pain. Scintillating magical energy blazed from his mouth and shook the air with the sound of thunder.

The electricity blasted through Tempest's mane of Turbidus leeches and scarred and burned her titanic scales. She toppled back into the water, nearly pulling the lance from Mik's hands.

Tempest's body smashed into the sea at the base of the silver stairs. Her stupendous weight sent a huge wave surging across the ocean's surface. Floundering off shore, *Red Wake* tipped and almost rolled over. Brine splashed high into the rain-clotted air, nearly reaching the Temple of the Sky. The sea dragon rolled across the base of the volcano, thrashing like a titanic beached fish.

Tempest's black blood dripped from Kell's lance, spattering Mik's face and arms. Hanging over his heart, the bejeweled key glowed brightly. He grabbed onto a bronze spike in front of him as Shimanloreth wobbled in the air.

Shimmer struggled to stay aloft. The wind whistled through the tears in his wing, and his wounds filled the air with a fine spray of blood. Mik clung precariously to the bronze dragon's scaly back. Bracing themselves for a final attack, they spiraled down toward their enemy on the mountainside below.

* * * * *

Ula thrust her head above water. Every bone in her body ached, and lights danced before her eyes. The entire world seemed distant and unreal—some nightmare reality unconnected to her.

Lighting crashed into the sea, and the waves heaved up like mountains. *Red Wake*, not so terribly far away, listed horribly, as though it might sink at any moment.

From the sky above, Shimmer fluttered down toward Tempest, who writhed upon the steep slopes of the Isle of Fire. The bronze dragon looked worse than Ula had ever seen him, but somehow he persevered. And was that Mik on Shimmer's back?

Yes, it was! The sailor held Kell's coral lance in his hands, poised to strike Tempest's black heart.

As Ula's friends drew near the sea dragon, though, Tempest turned toward them, steam leaking from between her hideous teeth.

"Look out!" Ula cried, though the crashing of the waves and the din of the storm smothered her warning.

* * * * *

Tempest threw her jaws wide and belched a cloud of boiling steam at the bronze dragon and his rider.

Shimmer thrust the remnants of his tattered wings wide, trying to shield Mik from Tempest's scalding blast. The bronze dragon's eyes and scales blistered, and the membranes covering his wings sizzled away, but his stratagem worked.

Mik gasped for breath, and his skin scorched, but he held on. "Shimmer!" he cried, but the bronze dragon could not hear him. Blindly, Shimanloreth fell toward the Isle of Fire.

Tempest snapped at them, but missed, as they passed her awful head.

Shimmer crashed heavily into the plaza below the Temple of the Sky.

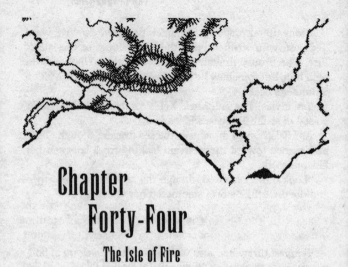

Chapter
Forty-Four
The Isle of Fire

The bronze dragon's weight shook the courtyard and smashed the marble flagstones into shards. The landing's decorative columns toppled like ninepins, but the silver stair persevered.

The bone-jarring impact of the landing threw Mik from Shimmer's back. The sailor twisted in the air and hit hard in the rubble near the base of the final stair. Thunder roared in Mik's ears; he fought to keep from blacking out.

Shimmer, slowly shrinking into a smaller, half-human form, lay broken and bleeding amid the remnants of the plaza. He breathed in ragged, shallow gasps, but otherwise did not move. Rain cascaded down around them, pelting Mik's scorched skin like a thousand tiny needles.

The coral lance lay near the mariner's right hand, and he picked it up. Groggily, he got to his feet and peered toward the ocean below. What he saw froze his heart.

Half-blinded and maimed, but not nearly dead, the immense form of Tempest crawled up the silver stair toward them. In her remaining yellow eye burned all the fires of hatred within the evil dragon's soul.

"Thank you . . . for bringing me . . . my key . . . little man!" she hissed, her voice shaking the mountain.

She belched another gout of boiling steam, but Mik ducked back toward the upper stairway, and the angle of the plaza shielded him from the blast.

He turned and ran up the stairs toward the temple, his exhausted muscles burning with every step.

Tempest reached the shattered landing and glowered up at him. A long trail of her blood covered the stairs below, and her heaving breath shook the broken flagstones. With barely a sideways glance, she batted Shimmer's body off the plaza. The bronze knight sailed through the air, trailing streamers of blood, and crashed into the sea at the mountain's base.

Mik reached the Temple of the Sky. The ancient key burned on his chest, and the great diamond flared in its presence. The cornerstone of the Veil shown nearly as bright as the sun, chasing away the storm's dark shadows.

The sailor cursed himself. He was no magician, as Karista had once been. He didn't know how to turn the power of the gem or the key against the monster pursuing him. He had already used every trick he knew. Before him lurked the sea dragon, at his back, the fiery maw of the volcano. All his friends were dead, and he had no place left to turn.

The coral lance throbbed within his grasp and Mik fought to maintain his grip. His scorched, blood-stained hands looked ghostly pale—almost white in the blinding light from the glittering diamond. The key hanging at his chest burned almost as brightly. He could not bear to look at either of them.

A deadly smile drew slowly over Mik Vardan's battered and bloody face.

Roaring her pain and rage, Tempest lumbered up the steps and into the temple. She cast her undamaged baleful eye around the temple plaza, seeking her foe, but did not see him.

The great diamond burned at the center of the temple, bright as the sun. She could not look at it and turned away. As she did, Mikal Vardan stepped from behind the diamond and thrust the coral lance into her remaining eye.

Tempest shrieked and thrashed her head, yanking the lance from Mik's hand. The weapon shot out of her punctured eye and soared through the air into the surf far below. The weapon, though, had done its work.

Blinded, Tempest surged toward Mik, smashing the temple's columns as she came.

The sailor grabbed the keystone diamond and dove out of her way—not quite fast enough.

Tempest's body hit him hard, and he flew through the courtyard into a fallen column. Agony like lightning shot up his back, and the huge diamond slipped from his grasp.

The sea dragon barreled on, unaware in her agony that she had already struck her enemy. She thundered through the temple, howling in rage and pain. By the time her webbed foretalons hit the rim of the volcano, she had too much momentum to stop.

With a startled shriek, Tempest fell over the edge of the crater and into the volcano's fiery heart. In an instant, the lava consumed her.

Dazed and bleeding, Mik rose to his feet.

The island shuddered with the dragon's passing, and the volcano stirred to life.

Though the Temple of the Sky lay in ruins, miraculously, the rune-carved column at its center remained standing. Mik retrieved the great diamond—glowing only dimly now—and placed it back on its pedestal.

He took a long, deep breath, but it cleared his head only a little. The temple floor trembled again, and the red glow from the crater beyond increased.

Mik gazed down at the key hanging around his neck. Its bejeweled surface sparkled seductively, and a picture formed in his mind—a monstrous, glittering diamond, not nearly so precious now as the friends he had lost.

The treasures in the pit surrounding the pedestal glowed bright red—the color of blood. The diamonds and jewels whispered to him. In his mind's eye, Mikal Vardan saw himself surrounded by wealth, he saw the Veil fading into the mists of time, and he saw the Dragon Isles fall.

"No," Mik said softly.

He pulled the jeweled key from around his neck and cast it into the rising lava.

As the key's magic abated, the temple around him grew transparent, like a mirage that disappears when approached. Mik felt the flagstones under his feet quiver. He cursed himself for a fool and sprinted toward the stairs.

"Serves me right for not understanding more about magic," he said to no one in particular.

Mik leaped down the silver stairway, taking three or four steps at a time. As he neared the plaza below, though, the stairs seemed less like stone and more like clouds beneath his feet.

Knowing he had little time left before the silver stair disappeared altogether, he raced to the precipice and threw himself over the edge. He cleared the volcano's cliff-like face easily enough, but his mind was still groggy, and the ocean below seemed to be rushing up to greet him awfully fast.

Mik hit the surging waves like a sack of bricks; the ocean smashed the breath from his weary body.

He tumbled head over heels through the breakers and sank below the surface. Instinctively, he reached for his enchanted fish necklace, only then remembering it was gone.

The brine crushed in around him. He clawed frantically, seeking air but finding only more water. He couldn't tell which way was up or down.

Mik struggled, kicking as hard as he could. The world around him exploded into white light, then receded into placid gray.

He felt warm and comfortable. Why was he exerting himself?

How much simpler just to go to sleep.

Down, down to the briny deep, where sharks hold court and sailors sleep.

Mikal Vardan closed his eyes and sank serenely into the indigo darkness.

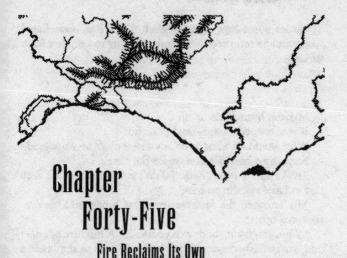

Chapter
Forty-Five

Fire Reclaims Its Own

The shock wave from the erupting volcano nearly cast Jerick the Red from the deck of *Red Wake*. He cursed and grabbed hold of the ship's wheel again, struggling to turn the helm into the waves.

The galleon responded like a crippled scow, nearly heaving over in the swells. Jerick got her bow around just as the big surge hit. *Red Wake* climbed up the wave and nearly leaped into the sky before crashing down to the sea once more.

Jerick's golden tooth rattled out of his head and flew into the ocean. He blinked once, twice, and when he opened his eyes again, the temple at the island's summit was gone.

Lava poured down the volcano's slopes and into the sea, sending up great gouts of white steam. The storm overhead died away quickly. Perhaps, with Tempest dead, the typhoon no longer had its strength.

"If I didn't know the gods had left Krynn, I'd swear it was a miracle," Jerick said, watching the rapidly calming sea.

He let out a long sigh of relief. Then *Red Wake* listed again, and he returned to the task of trying to keep her from sinking.

* * * * *

Mik felt himself rising up.

It was beautiful here—and peaceful.

Why would he want to be anywhere else? he wondered.

Something hard hit him across the cheek.

"Wake up!" a voice cried. "I didn't pull you out of the deep just to have you die on me!"

Mik coughed the seawater from his lungs, and his eyes flickered open.

"Were you trying to drown yourself?" A mixture of anger and worry flashed across Ula's beautiful face as she cradled him gently atop the swells.

Mik managed a weak smile. "I thought drowning preferable to being fried," he said.

"We'll still be boiled alive if we don't get out of here quick. That lava's heating up the sea awfully fast."

The two of them glanced back at the spot where the temple had once stood. Lava flowed through the cleft, down the mountainside, and into the breakers.

"It's almost as though the dragon and the temple never existed," Ula said quietly.

"If the dragon hadn't existed," Mik replied, coughing, "a lot more of our friends would be alive."

"Well, at least someone we know is still kicking," she said, pointing toward the floundering *Red Wake*.

The sea elf towed the battered sailor over the rapidly calming waves and, in short order, they reached the crippled ship.

Jerick pulled them aboard. "Ready to work?" he asked, smiling broadly. "We need some new hands." Then peering over the side, he said, "By the lost gods, what's *this* now?"

Mik and Ula turned and saw a shape moving just below the waves headed toward the ship. It was about the size of a redtip shark, but no telltale fin broke the surface. A moment later, Trip's smiling face poked up out of the surf.

"Did I miss anything?" he asked. "The dragon really knocked me silly. Where'd she go, by the way?"

"To the abyss, I hope," Mik replied.

"Great," Trip said. "I didn't like her anyway. Could you give me a hand? I don't think I can haul Shimmer up by myself. You wouldn't believe the trouble I had dragging him here."

Instantly, Ula jumped over the side and helped Trip push the bronze knight onto the galley's listing deck. She climbed back aboard and knelt at her friend's side.

Shimmer's left shoulder looked as though it had nearly been torn off, and he bled from more than a dozen wounds, but he was alive.

"Hey," Trip said, "did you see? The volcano blew up. How did that happen, by the way?"

Mik leaned back and closed his eyes. "When Tempest fell into the crater, the volcano erupted."

Shimmer's orange eyes flickered open.

"You're alive!" Ula said.

"Barely," he replied. "But I think . . . I will heal."

"I wish," Mik said, "that everyone who began this journey could say the same."

They all fell silent for a moment, remembering their lost friends and crewmates. Jerick's healer, sporting a nasty cut across her forehead, came to the bronze knight's side and began tending his injuries.

"Look!" said Trip, pointing toward the clouds.

A brass dragon arced high overhead, flying just below the receding storm. It circled the ship twice and then winged off to the west.

Mik shook his head and sighed. "*Now* the Order of Brass shows up," he said.

"Don't stop to help or anything, you accursed metal beastie!" Jerick called, shaking his fist at the far-off wyrm.

"I'm sure they'll send someone out to check on Kell's men," Ula said, "and the fate of their lord."

"He died . . . trying to save the isles," Shimmer gasped.

"So the temple is gone," Jerick said. "But what about the treasure? Did you ever find it?"

Mik looked at Ula, Trip, and the wounded dragon. "Oh yes," he said, "we found the treasure." The four survivors nodded wearily at each other.

Jerick frowned, his bushy red eyebrows nearly meeting over his hawkish nose. "So, where's my share? The key? The diamond?"

"Gone," Mik replied, "in the service of the isles."

"The service of the isles . . . !" Jerick sputtered. "Don't tell me you've gone *do-gooder* on me, Mik me boy. Next thing I know you'll be wantin' a job aboard *Red Wake*!"

Mikal Vardan laughed, and put his arm around his friend's shoulder. "This old scow?" the sailor asked jovially. "Not likely. Not while there's a fresh wind at my back and an open sea before me. Not while there's a coin of treasure left to be found somewhere in the Dragon Isles."

Tales that span the length and breadth of Krynn's history

The Golden Orb
Icewall Trilogy, Volume Two • Douglas Niles

The Arktos prosper in their fortress community, while the ogre king and queen seethe and plot revenge. Humans and highlanders must band together to defend against an onslaught that threatens mass destruction.

Sister of the Sword
The Barbarians, Volume Three • Paul B. Thompson & Tonya C. Cook

The village of the dragon is under siege. Riding hard to the rescue is the great nomad chief Karada. Can her warrior tribe overcome a raider horde, mighty ogres, and the curse of the green dragon?

Divine Hammer
The Kingpriest Trilogy, Volume Two • Chris Pierson

Twenty years have passed since Beldinas the Kingpriest took the throne, and his is a realm of unsurpassed glory. But evil threatens, so Beldinas must turn to a loyal lieutenant to extinguish the darkness of foul sorcery.

October 2002

The Dragon Isles
Crossroads Series • Stephen D. Sullivan

Legendary home of metallic dragons, the Dragon Isles attract seafaring adventurers determined to exploit the wealth of the archipelago, despite the evil sea dragon that blocks their success.

December 2002

Dig deep into the War of Souls

Can't get enough of the newest DRAG-ONLANCE® epic, the War of Souls? Delve into the details of the characters, events, and consequences of this sweeping battle.

The Lioness

The Age of Mortals • Nancy Varian Berberick

Learn the legend of the Lioness....

The Lioness is on a clandestine mission from the king of the Qualinesti elves. She must turn outlaw and knit a rebellion from disparate forest factions, aimed at keeping the occupying dark knights off their guard. But another mission arises for the mythical outlaw: she must defeat a mysterious knight-executioner whose sole job is terror.

Bertrem's Guide to the War of Souls, Volume II

Sequel to Bertrem's Guide to the War of Souls, Volume I

How far does the War of Souls reach? This collection of correspondence, reports, and essays, compiled by Bertrem the Ascetic, vividly reveals the impact of the War of Souls on everyday occurrences across the land of Ansalon.

November 2002

The Summer of Chaos is over, but the trouble is just beginning.

This is where the new era of DRAGONLANCE® began, heralding a new age and new heroes— The Dragons of a New Age trilogy, by Jean Rabe. These all-new editions of this pivotal trilogy feature handsome new cover art by award-winning artist Matt Stawicki.

The Dawning of a New Age
Volume One
Magic has vanished. Evil dragons conquer the land. Despair threatens to overwhelm Ansalon. Now is the time for heroes.

The Day of the Tempest
Volume Two
As the dragon overlords bicker among themselves, a band of heroes stumble upon a new form of magic: the power of the heart.

The Eve of the Maelstrom
Volume Three
The most powerful of the dragon overlords is determined to ascend to godhood, and a single band of heroes must find a way to stop her.

November 2002

The Dhamon Saga
Jean Rabe

The sensational conclusion to the trilogy!

Redemption
Volume Three

Dhamon's dragon-scale curse forces him deep into evil territory,
where he must follow the orders of an unknown entity. Time
is running out for him and his motley companions—a mad
Solamnic Knight, a wingless draconian, and a treacherous ogre
mage. Is it too late for Dhamon to redeem his nefarious past?

Now available in paperback

Betrayal
Volume Two

Haunted by the past, Dhamon Grimwulf suffers daily torture
from the dragon scale attached to his leg. As he searches for a
cure, he must venture into a treacherous black dragon's swamp.
The swamp is filled with terrors bent on destroying him, but
the true danger to Dhamon is much closer than he thinks.